OSGOOD AS GONE

A Spectral Inspector Mystery

COOPER S. BECKETT

HORROR &
CARNAGE
PRESS

Cover Illustration by Anthony Diecidue

Interior Illustrations by Shane Hunt

Book Design by Cooper S. Beckett

1 2 3 4 5 6 7 8 9 10

Published Internationally by Horror & Carnage Press

ISBN: 978-1-946876-13-3

BISAC: Fiction / Horror / Mystery

Horror & Carnage Press - Chicago, Illinois

CooperSBeckett.com

Osgood as Gone

A Spectral Inspector Mystery

Cooper S. Beckett

HORROR &
CARNAGE
PRESS

For Giles
My buddy
He was a good boy

Missing him.

M

azarowskis idea. rest stop plees. drumbeats .find the hinterlands

Osgood squinted. "Please or pleas?" she asked her laptop. The beat-up ThinkPad with duct tape holding the front half together had nothing to add to the email. She clicked reply and asked, **Elaborate?** Sent.

Moments later a notification returned, the status bar listing **unknown address**. She pursed her lips and scrolled through the email's header, a collection of data that seemed to indicate a lot of things, though she understood few of them. The piece that did jump out was the obvious one. Where usually she'd find another email address, she saw a lonely @ sign. Odd, for sure. The code below that meant nothing to her, and she forwarded it to Zack with the subject line, **the fuck?** He'd at least be able to track it back to its source, if not to a real person behind the spoof.

She tipped her glass to her lips and poured back the last of the bourbon. The legs of liquid slowly ran down the bottom of the glass as she stared into it, yearning.

That's it, she thought. *Nothing more in the apartment.* How had she allowed her alcohol supply to dwindle to zilch? Oh, yes, money is required to procure alcohol. She set the glass down on the end table next to her bed, giving it one more forlorn look. If she wanted more now, there'd be no choice but to get dressed and go downstairs. Maybe she could pull off a robe. Her kimono looked fashionable.

She raised her thumb to her mouth, noticing, next to the hangnail she couldn't quit, that her midnight blue nail polish had scuffed off almost entirely. She shook her head, feeling a boozy sway but not the sweet relief of drunk. Barely even into tipsy now.

"Downstairs?" She answered her question with a shake of her head and stuck her right hand back in her mouth. She tapped out **rest stop plees** into the search bar with her left. The website helpfully made a suggestion that Osgood immediately rebuffed. "If I meant 'rest stop *please*' I would've typed that." She clicked the small text below its absurd suggestion to view results for her spelling. This time the engine was even less helpful. **rest stop ~~plees~~** produced links to articles about Illinois rest stop revitalization, locations, assistance, and not unexpectedly, hookup requests.

She felt her teeth finally grab at that bit of flesh that had annoyed her all evening with its exquisite pain. With purchase, she yanked. Her mother's voice in her mind reminded her, *Nice girls don't bite their nails, Pru. They get cuticle scissors and cut it.* She knew that Cynthia Osgood also wouldn't approve of the way she spat the cuticle and its trail of skin into the trash can next to her bed, which overflowed with crumpled paper, dirty tissues, a McDonald's fries container, a couple of condom wrappers, and the empty fifth of Kentucky bourbon. Osgood stared at her thumb, now sporting an angry elongated V of deep pink tender flesh.

She prodded it with the index finger of her other hand, mumbling, "Nice girls," to herself. Back to the search engine, this time copying and pasting the entire contents of the email. **mazarowskis idea. rest stop plees. drumbeats .find the hinterlands**

The search engine, perhaps shocked by her audacity, didn't even bother with **did you mean?** Instead, **0 results found.**

"Alright."

Osgood lifted her phone off the bed beside her and stared at it for a moment, trying to remember the app she was supposed to be using. One of those that randomly dropped vowels. Life would be far easier if Zack would just let her use regular text messaging to talk to him. Instead, he'd installed this frustrating separate app that she knew she should've put on her home screen.

"It has end-to-end encryption," he'd told her.

"Why do I need that?" she'd asked.

"Privacy."

"From who?"

"Whom," he'd said, and she'd stared at him for a silent minute before dropping the issue.

Finally, she found the app and tapped, **Anything?** into the field under his user account, a seemingly random string of letters and numbers. As Zack Nguyen was her only contact in the app, this abstraction hardly mattered.

Minutes passed. She glanced at the empty glass on the table.

A ping from Zack. **Gimme time, woman!**

Osgood threw her entire body into a sigh. Patience had never been in her wheelhouse. She debated chastising him for calling her "woman," but had no mood for a fruitless discussion that would likely teeter and fall apart when he inevitably asked how she would like to self-identify. One needed to be confident of that oneself, first, right?

She tossed the phone back atop the notepad beside her on her bed. The pad itself was lousy with doodles but held little in the way of actual content. She cracked her knuckles, hearing the voice of her mother in her mind scoffing again at that unladylike action, and returned to the search engine. **mazarowskis idea** went in.

The results dropped the "**s**" which she presumed was possessive with a forgotten apostrophe. While not a terribly common surname, **Mazarowski** yielded a diverse array of results, including meeting minutes from a nonprofit org, a law firm associate, a bridal design company, a linebacker at the University of North Dakota, a few news articles, and other minutiae.

"Nothing worthwhile." Osgood sighed once again, a dramatic flourish that would've made an impact if she didn't live alone.

She slid her cursor over the last portion of the email and dropped that into the waiting maw of the search engine. Below its **0 results** initial find, she saw **drumbeats .find the hinterlands** with a result. Lyrics from "The End of What's Real" by the band Rhapsody in the Shallows. The title pulled at the corner of her mind, like one of those moments you can't remember if you lived or dreamed.

She scrolled through the lyrics and there, bolded, midway through the third verse, was **Drumbeats in the Hinterlands.** She scanned the remaining lyrics, finding nothing about rest stops. The album's title, though – *Ramparts Over the Hinterlands* – suggested the reasoning for the word's appearance in the song.

She clicked for more information on the band. Four members, one dead, none named Mazarowski. She closed the tab and refreshed her email. She slapped her laptop shut, noticing the bottom jiggle. Going to need more duct tape. The *buzz* of her phone drew her attention.

She tapped the notification, hoping for news from Zack, but instead found Carla. **I don't want what was said today to be the last things said between us.**

then you shouldntve said them, thumbed back Osgood before tossing the phone onto the pillow next to her. *Well, that's the mature way to handle things, isn't it, Pru?* She scowled. At least she hadn't said more.

It buzzed again. She stared at it awhile, then picked it up. "If we have to have it out now, I suppose we—"

Email is obscured, said Zack in the encrypted app. There was another notification from Carla as well, but she ignored it.

"I know," said Osgood. **Can you go deeper?** She scowled after she sent the message, waiting for the twenty-six-year-old's glib reply.

Zack didn't take the bait. **I can, but it'd be pointless. The obscuring isn't particularly novel.**

Okay, asked Osgood. **Do you know where it came from?**

I do. Mother Russia.

Osgood frowned.

Emailer isn't from Russia, though, assured Zack. **So don't make me follow that train of thought all the way down. IP address is routed through Super Sekret VPN.**

Osgood didn't ask if that was actually the name of the service or if he was just enjoying the Russia connection a bit more than he ought.

The rabbit hole goes deeper, though. Probably a VPN stack.

Osgood shook her head, wondering if he told her stuff like that just so she'd ask him what it meant and make him feel smart. **Meaning?**

It's turtles all the way down.

She sighed. **Can you do a deep-web search on the content?**

... Zack's ellipses may as well have been an eye-roll.

The better search engines you're always talking to me about but won't tell me how to use.

I've asked you to come over *many* times to show you how these all work.

I know, she said, **but I don't have the patience for this stuff and you're *good* at it!**

Don't worry, said Zack. **I'm sure you'd need plenty explained to you even if you could use them.**

I'm sure, said Osgood, wondering if her sarcasm translated via text. **Until then, could you just look?**

Already doing it. Need anything else?

Distraction.

I could bring over a movie.

She snorted. **Different kind of distraction needed, Zack. And your gender alignment isn't ideal for that.**

Goodnight, Os.

Osgood smiled, but her heart wasn't in it. She tapped out her own **Goodnight** and dropped the phone into her lap. Her current outfit, boxers and a bra, wouldn't cut it to go down to Mary's. She considered layering her trench coat over, bare legs poking out, and was reminded of the illusory scourge of flashers her mother used to warn her about until young Pru had thrown back, "I'm curious what *it* looks like."

"*Prudence!*" her mother had shrieked, almost as though purposefully emphasizing exactly how inappropriate the name she'd bestowed was.

With a reluctant climb out of bed, feeling every ache in every muscle, Osgood added unseasonably-early snowflake pajama pants and a *Hedwig and the Angry Inch* t-shirt, grabbed her phone, keys, and wallet, pulled her battered maroon trench coat off the hook on the back of the door. She'd had it for the last twenty-five-ish years, ever since she'd decided she'd rather be Carmen Sandiego than the gumshoe on her trail. Or maybe she just wanted to fuck Carmen Sandiego. It certainly got attention from adult women of a certain age.

She left her apartment in search of misadventure.

2

"To death." Osgood stabbed her Milwaukee style old fashioned into the air, toasting toward no one in particular in the dining room of Mary's Diner and Bar, a staple in the Andersonville neighborhood of Chicago for longer than Osgood had been alive.

Even at this late hour, the place was hopping, and she could hear roars of applause from the side with the stage, where a drag burlesque version of *Twin Peaks* was happening tonight. Osgood didn't feel at home many places with her gawky body, her reluctance to appear feminine (something that always seemed to rile up guys), and her hair's ever-changing colors. But here at Mary's, here on the north side of Chicago, she could always be sure to find a mix of queers and straights playing nicely together.

That had even been part of her landlord's pitch years ago. "Queer-friendly, baby," had not been a phrase she expected to hear from the balding bearded Bulgarian. But she took the apartment above Mary's and fell in love with the refuge below, her place of safety where she could come and drink and not be terribly concerned about roving bands of toxic masculinity. There were still a few individuals, of course, but Osgood could spot them a mile away. Only one or two here tonight.

She smirked at a cluster of very young and likely incredibly straight women near the windows celebrating a bachelorette party – all feather boas, blinking LED rings, and dildo tiaras.

Beside her, her phone vibrated a call notification for the third time since she'd sat at the bar.

"Must not be important," said Terry, sandy-haired and thin as a rail, in a blue and white striped shirt that emphasized the slightness of his frame.

A chime. "Not important to me," Osgood said, barely giving the phone a glance.

Eight new voicemails.

"Eight?" asked Osgood incredulously. She turned to Terry. "Has this buzzed eight times?"

"I have a job, honey."

She waved in his face and sipped her old fashioned. "For someone who doesn't want to talk to me, you're sure spending an awful lot of time cleaning that spot on the bar."

"You keep spilling." He wiped up fresh droplets. "You appear to have a drinking problem, Osgood."

She scrunched her nose at him. "That's neither here nor there."

Another buzz from the phone. "Who are we ducking?"

"A breakup last week." She downed the last of her drink, reaching ice barely melted. "End of an era."

"A relationship is a tough thing."

"Relationship*sss*," said Osgood, putting a full snake into the word.

"Plural, huh?"

"Monogamy is for straight people," she said, setting her empty glass on the bar in front of her. "I'm gonna do this again."

He looked from the glass to her eyes, to the glass, to her eyes.

"I live upstairs," she said, as though it was the answer to every question he could possibly have tonight.

"I didn't say anything." He walked away to make her drink.

"Plural," she repeated to herself, looking over the crowd. Several people pinged the radar between her legs, mostly ladies, but she thought she could eat that boy over there by the window alive. His outfit suggested that he slid all the way down Kinsey's scale to gay. But that was okay, Osgood didn't think a romp with anyone would be on the menu tonight, regardless of their position on the gender spectrum. The old fashioneds were disappearing fast enough that she might be able to stagger back upstairs, thoroughly exhausted and drunk, into a vast dreamless sleep.

Now a text notification. Perhaps Yann and Carla had gotten the hint that she didn't want to talk. Their triad had seemed so perfect once upon a time, a relationship with her, with him, with them. Their third. The connection in the middle. And now: breakup. But if they'd never officially acknowledged togetherness to the world, could they even call it that? Never been social media official, after all. In the end, she was just their toy, their accessory, their— "Motherfucking unicorn," said Osgood under her breath. "I have the hair for it."

Another notification. She could see what they wanted. Pick up the phone and see. Would it be a **We need you** text? A **We can't live without you** text? A **You left your shit at our place now come and get it before we dump it** text? Could be any. Could be all, couldn't it? "Most likely passive aggressive bullshit," said Osgood and squeezed the power button until the phone returned to silence. She stared at the purple rectangle. Silent. Dead.

To death.

She put her back against the bar, elbows up, thrusting out, she realized. Emphasizing her tits in this shirt. Maybe she *was* trying to pick someone up. Or maybe things were just getting sloshy. Her elbow knocked into her phone and shoved it away to the floor.

Amidst the thinning crowd, the bachelorette party had turned on itself, with at least one face full of running mascara. The blonde with *Bride* embroidered on her black ballcap made out furiously with the redhead next to her. The text on that

9

cap was smaller, but even with Osgood's lack of focus, she could make out *Matron of Honor*. Hands drifted.

"Such honor." Osgood laughed. "What would your husband say?" She watched the exploration for a moment longer, wondering if it was sudden and random, or something long repressed.

The remainders of the group dispersed as Osgood sucked down another drink, leaving only the blonde and redhead, who moved to a booth in the corner to have what seemed to be an intense conversation.

"Would you take our picture?"

Someone thrust a phone into her hands and she nodded, holding it vaguely in the direction of a cluster of college students. "Say mac and cheese!"

"Mac and cheese!" the group enthusiastically returned.

Osgood tapped the circle on the screen several times, each accompanied by a fake digital shutter click.

"Yay!" the kids called.

"Thank you!" The girl took the phone and kissed Osgood's cheek, then returned to her seat.

Osgood nodded with a somewhat dismissive wave. She reached down to get her phone off the floor, managing to snag it after only three grabs. Nausea hit when she returned to vertical, and she flopped into a chair at an empty table between the bar and the kids.

An old fashioned appeared in front of her, held by fingers with crimson nails, and Osgood felt her face light up, a smile widening across it. She thought she might look like a cartoon character, with her curly purple hair and saucer eyes, pink hearts for irises.

Helen, the last waitress on duty, all legs and cleavage in the retro-fabulous teal diner uniform of Mary's, sat across from her. "Terry said you live on the block."

Osgood nodded and pointed at the ceiling. "I live on top of you." She sipped at the drink.

"He also said you're good people, which is why I brought this to you."

She nodded again.

"But this is your last call."

Osgood closed her eyes and nodded a brusque final time. Helen didn't know that she had *planned* on this drink being the last anyway. When she reopened her eyes, Helen had moved on to the kids' table. Osgood stared into the old fashioned, twirling ice around the glass with her finger. "Last call for the washed-up ghosthunter."

"Ghosthunter?" asked…someone…somewhere.

Osgood turned, but in the wrong direction, and saw only purple. The purple corner. The purple wall. She reached for her phone. Had to be here somewhere. She could hear the vibration. Carla and Yann calling again, prob'ly. Where the fuck was—

And blackout.

🜪 3 🜪

"**F**uck, Prudence," said Osgood, squinting at her phone. The squint was enough to dim the light blasting through her window, privacy curtains most egregiously opened, but too much to focus more. She closed her eyes for a moment, breathing through a throbbing headache, throbbing hard enough that, were there someone else in bed with her, they might be able to hear it.

Finally, she could focus on her phone.

had a fantastic time last nite! U had bacon so I made it. Had to get to class, but left a bunch for you on the stove! <3

The second text bubble included an additional less-than-three and the name, **Nora.**

A third bubble offered, **oh, and i washed the...stuff. Drying in the sink.**

Okay, Osgood thought, *time to stand up and figure out what kind of fuckery you got up to*

(at the crossroads)

in the blackout.

Ignoring the tangential thought, Osgood swung her legs off the bed and put her feet into a pile of fabric she assumed were last night's clothes. Her hand found the bedside table and her fingers were instantly wet. She took her hand back out of the fuzzy shape of a cup. Next to it, a slippery bottle. Next to that, thankfully, her glasses.

The world came into focus, and Osgood looked down, finding herself not unexpectedly naked. A pink-brown hickey stood out over her right nipple. She squinted at the dimly lit room beyond the shafts of light from between the curtains, trying hard to put a face to the name "Nora." Surely the woman had a face. Likely a body as well. A face and body to conjure whomever the hell she brought home last night. Whomever the hell she did…whatever the hell with.

Had to get to class.

"She was at a bar," reasoned Osgood. "Gotta be at least…" she frowned. "Nineteen."

Half her age plus seven was…nearly a decade above nineteen. *Fuckity fuck.*

Osgood rested her chin in her palm and her elbow on her knee. She closed her eyes and could see the pulsing colors of her headache, fractals keeping time with her heartbeat, the Winamp visualization of her misery. All attempts to move through the pulsing tunnel and remember Nora only led back to where all blackout memories led: the crossroads. Today, naked on her bed, it seemed the blinking amber beacon at its center mocked her.

She couldn't remember much else about last night's visit to the crossroads, only that it ended with the crush of metal on metal, the rending of flesh, with death. "Same as it ever was," said Osgood.

Her old fashioneds had nearly done their job, too, with the blackout almost scrubbing the crossroads from her mind. Instead, they'd just ripped out the entire person that preceded her dreams. One day she'd find the right ratio.

Thanks to a generous assist from her dresser, Osgood managed to stand and shuffled into a tattered blue dressing gown.

Such progress should be rewarded, she thought between throbs. But since she'd finished all the bourbon in the apartment, with what would she reward herself? All that made itself available to her was the gift of standing in place, eyes closed, fingers pressed against her temples. The darkness and the pressure from her fingers made mild improvements – any gains were most welcome.

"Last night," she reminded herself, eyes still closed.

Yes, last night. Last night had included grocery shopping and sushi and drinks with Albrecht. She'd been sober through all of that. Unless you wanted to count the sake with sushi, that is. Sober enough to drive her ancient academic adviser home and then head back here, anyway.

Mazarowskis idea. Rest stop plees. Drumbeats .find the hinterlands

Yes! The weirdo email and ensuing text conversation with Zack. And a text spat with Carla. And no more bourbon, so back out into the world. Probably Mary's downstairs for a nightcap or six. Then what? Had she stopped somewhere else before climbing back up to her apartment? Picked up some Andersonville rando named Nora?

Osgood opened her left eye and felt the ice pick of daylight jam straight through into what she was now sure was a headache factory, no longer a brain. She held her phone at arm's length so as not to allow its brilliant digital light to contribute. Even at the lowest brightness setting, a brand-new set of spikes jammed their way into her visual cortex. She thumbed her pin, then swiped from screen to screen. Not a single dating or hookup app on the phone. Still long-press-uninstalled.

With the Nora texts swiped away, she stared at a fresh and empty notification bar. A perfect start to a craptacular day.

Her nose twitched. The scent of promised bacon. As the prophecy had foretold. Just a room and change away. And all she had to do was stop standing here with one eye scrunched shut squinting at her phone and walk into the kitchen. Bacon was there, waiting for her, courtesy whomever the hell Nora was.

She nodded to herself and took several deep breaths, each time insisting that this would be the one to kick her into gear, out of the stasis in which she found herself, back to the world of the ambulatory. The repetition became so rote that Osgood startled herself when she actually moved in the direction of her hallway.

Thankfully, she hit the bathroom off the hall before arriving in the kitchen, or she would've made a puddle upon discovering Zack at her kitchen table, tablet in hand. "Morning."

"Jesus!" exclaimed Osgood, hastily tugging her dressing gown closed. She felt a flush cross her cheeks, then scolded herself for her embarrassment. She'd goddamned well walk around her goddamned apartment semi-nude all she goddamned wanted, and if people showed up unannounced, then they'd get the goddamned eye-full they deserved.

"Your doors were unlocked," said Zack, lifting a brick off the kitchen table, crumbs of dirt next to his plate of bacon. "And this was wedged keeping the street level one open."

Osgood snatched the brick away from him. "Sometimes that's necessary."

"And the apartment door."

"You're not my dad."

"No," said Zack, finally looking up from his tablet. "But I *am* the guy who has provided you with plenty of better-than-legal equipment and thus am also invested in your security. I mean, how hard is it to lock the door?"

A scowl on Osgood's lips. All she'd wanted was bacon. Bacon to quell the headache. Now here sat Zack, still wearing what looked like a tactical windbreaker to go with his judgment. His glasses sat atop his short black hair, as he couldn't read the tablet while wearing them. The reproach on his face looked every bit a man two or three times his age, so much so that she had to remind herself of the decade and a half she had on him.

"Nora probably—"

"Thought you'd want coffee and an update." He tapped the white plastic top of the green cup positioned across the table from him. "It'll go well with your bacon."

"Thank you," said Osgood. She folded her arms tightly across her chest, not quite ready to let the irritation go.

"Between your staggering, squinting, and the…impressive

collection in the sink, I guess you had quite a night."

"Yes," said Osgood. "So?"

"None of my business," said Zack.

"No," confirmed Osgood. "It isn't." After a moment she grabbed a plate and tossed some bacon on it from a foil-covered pie plate on the stove. "What'd you find?"

He looked up now and shook his head. "Tell you what. I'll meet you at Mary's in twen— let's say a half hour. That'll give you time to shower because you absolutely *reek* of sex."

Osgood frowned and sniffed the air. Yes, there, below the scent of the bacon...

Zack snapped his tablet case closed and flicked his glasses back down onto his nose. "Thirty minutes?" he asked. He shoved his chair back from the table, its feet screeching against the faux tile floor.

"Good morning, Zack," she said and kissed his cheek.

She'd not meant to snap at him. Of all the various men who'd come in and out of Osgood's life over the years, Zack had always been the most respectful of her boundaries and that their friendship didn't include "benefits."

"Vietnamese parents make sure you don't get anyone pregnant," he'd once told her. "And what's the safest form of sex?"

"Lesbi—"

"Abstinence," he'd replied. "Right."

"I'm buying downstairs," she told Zack.

"Oh, yes, you are," he replied, shoved an entire last strip of bacon into his mouth, and went to the apartment door. Before he left, he made a big production of showing her how to lock and unlock the knob lock and deadbolt.

"Shower," she said after he'd gone. "But I'm going to take my bacon 'to-go." She lifted the plate from the table, throwing a quick glance at the sink. The sheer volume of accessories in there indicated a wild and raucous time with whomever Nora was.

"My, my," said Osgood.

She nibbled her bacon as she headed down the hall to shower.

⚔ 4 ⚔

"**Y**ou look like shit," said Zack.

"Ah, but do I look like I care?" asked Osgood.

"No. Probably why you look like shit."

"Good fucking morning, Zack." She said, sitting across from him in a booth by the window in the purple-toned dining room of Mary's Diner and Bar. Outside, Clark Street bustled. "Thanks for breaking into my apartment. I sure hope you have something worth getting me up this earl—"

"It's nearly noon," said Zack. "Mary's is almost done serving brunch."

"Good, I want a cheeseburger." Osgood picked up the menu and perused their burger offerings. She held the menu between the two of them so he couldn't see her, so she couldn't watch him look at her. "I can feel your judgment," she told him through the menu.

"And what is it you feel I'm judging you for?"

She slapped the menu down on the purple Formica tabletop.

"Morning, Osgood."

Osgood turned her face to Inez, dark-haired and dark-skinned, overflowing her diner uniform most gloriously. "I'll have—"

"I brought this," said Inez, setting a glass in front of her, a

19

bloody Caesar overflowing with a skewer containing bacon, sausage, and a quarter of an Eggo waffle.

"That," said Osgood with a smile. "I'll have exactly that."

"Hair of the dog," said Zack, and Osgood threw him a look.

"Yes," said Inez. "Terry said you were...quite..."

"Drunk," said Osgood, taking a long sip of the Caesar before her. The burn of the spice, the burn of the vodka, such varied yet exquisite flavors. "This shouldn't be a surprise to him any longer." She shook her head and glanced at Zack, full of twenty-six-year-old baby-judgment. "Which reminds me. Do you know anyone named Nora?"

Inez shook her head.

"Someone named Nora came—"

"Oh," laughed Inez. "Is that her name."

"Aha."

"Yeah, Terry said you took some little girl home with you."

Osgood sighed. "And by little girl..."

"Of age, don't worry," said Inez. "Terry checked her ID himself."

"Well, that's good," said Osgood.

"Yes, Osgood," said Zack. "It's terrific that the girl you took home was old enough to not put you in legal jeopardy."

Osgood didn't care for the derisive grin on Zack's face.

"Thank you, Inez. I'll have the Buffy burger. Extra garlic."

"Absolutely."

"And he'll have something cheap," she said, extending one scuffed midnight blue nail toward her dining companion.

"He's already ordered appetizers and a meal."

"Of course."

Inez smiled, gave a nod, and walked back past the bar toward the kitchen, leaving the two of them nearly alone.

Osgood turned back toward Zack. "Okay, so, do me a favor, just add the judgment to the pile you've already got and give it to me later. Maybe wrap it up for Christmas. Right now, I'd like to—"

"Talk about Mazarowski, rest stops, and hinterlands?"

"Yes," said Osgood. "Let's start with who sent that email to me."

Zack shrugged.

"You're going to shrug that one off?"

"I really don't know. I've got some trace programs on it, but below the stacks of VPNs and the bouncing off of some unusual relay stations, it sorta looks like the email came from," he paused, a pause Osgood had suspicions was entirely for effect, "nowhere."

"Nowhere," Osgood repeated, flatly.

"Nowhere."

"Well, that seems needlessly eerie, for eerie's sake. You'll update me if—"

"When."

"—you get anything more."

"Yes. Now, onto…" Zack placed his tablet between them and called up a picture of a man well past his prime, overweight, grayed hair, cragged face. "Clinton Mazarowski."

"I didn't see him on my search."

"Of course not," said Zack, dismissing her by swiping the picture to a second, this one of a lime green Volkswagen bus with enough antennas on it to cover the roof.

"That's not getting through a car wash." Osgood sipped her drink and coughed the ghosts of smokes past from her lungs.

"Your search, I assume, was just for 'Mazarowski,' and there's plenty of Mazarowskis. My searches on the other hand, were Boolean, combining all of the content from that email, along with looking in the right places."

"And what are the right places?" Osgood couldn't keep her eyes unrolled any longer.

"Roll your eyes all you want, Os," said Zack, his tone serious. "If we want to assume that this is a message actually intended for you, and not Bizarro World spam, we have to treat it like that."

She stared at him, waiting. He stared back at her, his dark brown eyes unblinking. "Okay," she said after a while.

"If it's a message to you, to Prudence Osgood, the Spectral

Inspector, podcast host and blogger about the strange and unusual…" Zack twirled his hand in the air between them.

Osgood reluctantly picked up what Zack was putting down. "Then it stands to reason it would involve the strange and unusual in some way."

"Exactly." Now Zack's smile turned genuine, and his enthusiasm cranked up a notch.

"With that premise, we can dismiss things like the wedding planner, and the corporate suits, and the lawyers." He leaned forward across the table. "Unless someone is suing you that you haven't mentioned to me."

"Not suing, no," said Osgood.

"And that leads us to," Zack swiped back briefly to the old man. "Clinton Mazarowski. I think you'd like him, actually. Conspiracy theorist, paranormal kook…"

"Kook?"

"Well, he did believe that Lincoln's ghost was influencing policy in the Oval Office through late night conversations in, well, his bedroom."

Osgood laughed.

Zack swiped back to the image of the Volkswagen. "He was a pirate radio broadcaster, who drove this nightly around the country spouting his theories into the darkness. His broadcasts became popular enough that ham radio operators all over the country would rebroadcast it through relays. College campus radio stations, too. All over. Called *Across the Backroads*."

"Shit."

"You've heard it?"

"Yeah," said Osgood. "I found it when I was in junior high. Audrey and I used to—" She stopped. The memories of those sleepovers with Audrey. Those balmy summer nights in a tent in their backyards. The endless discussions of what dwelt in the world beyond their own. The first tentative fumblings toward sexuality. She cleared her throat. "I remember the host calling himself the Guardian."

"Oh, yes," agreed Zack. "Mazarowski did everything he could to conceal his identity after trouble with the FCC about his broadcasts. He spent the last decade of his life a wanted criminal. Though not a particularly pressing catch."

"Last decade," repeated Osgood.

"Yeah. Clinton Mazarowski died in 2008."

"Oh." Osgood sulked. "I assume he had a *lot* of ideas, too; so many that it might be difficult to narrow down without his help."

"Well, I thought that too, but most of the ideas were the Guardian's."

"Mazarowski."

"Yes, Mazarowski was the Guardian, but the Guardian wasn't necessarily Mazarowski."

"Zack."

"Yes."

"Pretty please, I'm hungover, I'm exhausted, just tell me what you've got."

Zack pouted. "I was giving you—"

"Color, yes, and I really do appreciate it."

"Wouldn't kill you to show it."

Osgood threw up her hands. "I'm buying you breakfast!"

"Lunch," corrected Zack.

"Zack!"

"Okay," said Zack, diving back into his notes. "So, before he died—"

"How long?"

"2006."

"Okay.

"Before he died, he wrote a report called 'The Rest Stop Papers' and sent it to law enforcement agencies all over the country."

"'Mazarowskis idea. Rest stop plees,'" said Osgood.

Zack nodded.

"That sounds exactly like what we need!"

"It does, doesn't it?" Zack gave another dramatic pause, this one so long Osgood considered leaning across the table and swatting at his head.

"Unfortunately, this is all that exists." He swiped again, this page showing a paragraph of text.

"'In my decades of study,'" read Osgood, "'and the sheer volume of horrors that I have come across, many can be explained away as man's hatred of man. But our own government hiding it. I cannot abide that. What I intend to lay out in the following pages, however, cannot be explained away so easily. This may be the single largest network of gateways ever encountered, as they've so hungrily taken in the most vulnerable, the young people of our world. Of the utmost importance is expediency, for if I'm right and these rest stops really do reveal the locations of… *See more.*' Reasonably lucid there."

"There's no more," said Zack. "That came from one of the Internet archives. The rest of the report is a ghost, and not the kind we're looking for. We don't know what agencies he sent it to, either, but I'm sure you can imagine that their interest was not piqued into believing that a 9/11 truther, chem-trail believer, and full throttle Kennedy conspiracy theorist with a warrant for his arrest for continued FCC violations had any worthwhile ideas about rest stops."

"No," agreed Osgood. "Probably not."

Zack slid his tablet into his messenger bag.

"That's it?"

His face fell. "I thought that was pretty good."

"Well…" Osgood took a deep breath. "Yes, you're right."

"In only a few hours I connected Mazarowski to his alter-ego the Guardian, something that as far as the searches I did last night showed, no one else has done before."

"Possible no one else cared."

"Thanks, Pru."

She scowled. "You're right, I'm sorry."

"Thank you."

"Anything on the drumbeats and the hinterlands?"

Zack shrugged. "Only that it's close to a lyric from a song by In the Shallows."

"Rhapsody in the Shallows?"

"They were just In the Shallows by that album. Dropped the Rhapsody at the end of the '80s. Too floofy, perhaps."

"Any connections between In the Shallows and Mazarowski?"

"None that I could find."

"And did In the Shallows write about rest stops?"

"Not in a single lyric."

"One Captain America and one Buffy Burger," said Inez, setting massive burgers before each of them.

"Thank you," said Zack.

"Your wings are coming."

"You can eat that burger and wings?" asked Osgood after Inez left.

"And mac and cheese fritters."

"Where do you store it?"

"Same place you store your liquor."

Osgood had to snicker. *"Touché."*

D one with class! how r u?

Osgood swiped away Nora's text unanswered and turned back to the spot where her car had been parked last night. There was no hydrant next to it. She looked up at the parking restrictions, despite having lived on this street for years, and saw only snow restrictions. As the leaves had not yet begun to fall, snow was likely the furthest thing from the weather's mind.

"You remember that you live upstairs, right?" Zack asked, emerging from the restaurant. He struggled to buckle the straps on his messenger bag.

"Thank you, Zack."

She glanced back down at her phone. The text from Nora seemed so optimistic. She took a deep breath, swiped open her text app, and replied to the number with the 224 area code. **Shitty. I think my car got towed.**

fuck, said Nora.

"Yes," Osgood agreed aloud. "Fuck."

"Do you need anything?" asked Zack, his own keys in hand.

She could ask for his help. He'd take her to get her car now, but that wouldn't change the fact that she'd need a couple hundred dollars, and the tow place vultures don't like credit. What if they made her pay her outstanding parking tickets, the ones that likely got her towed, as well? "No," said Osgood. "Thanks, I'm good."

"Okay," he replied. "Well, you live up there." He pointed with his keys at the second-level windows, bisected by a neon marquee advertising Mary's Diner and Bar.

"I know," said Osgood.

"You're good?"

"Yep," Osgood said. "Send me what you've got."

"Will do. And I'll keep digging," said Zack, before, with mild hesitance, turning and walking away.

She watched him head south on Clark Street and considered the moments in their conversation that she'd been challenging. It wasn't hard to find those moments. Osgood could often be challenging.

That's why you have so many friends, Pru.

Osgood took one more look at the spot where her car had been, then back at her phone.

do you need me to pick you up?

No, I'm good, said Osgood.

yes you are.

"Jeez." Osgood dropped the phone back into her coat pocket and, finding the street-level door still unlocked, climbed the stairs to her apartment.

After packing away the evidence of last night's debauchery from the sink, Osgood crossed the apartment to her office. She sat behind her desk, an oversized wooden monstrosity that was one of the few keepsakes she'd gotten when her grandfather passed.

Mounted to the top of it were a goose-neck stand and hanging microphone, an offense she still regretted. Black and pendulous, it mocked her apathy, her lack of direction, her lack of enthusiasm. She hadn't posted a new blog, essay, or podcast in... Weeks? Months? She couldn't remember the last time, or what it'd been about, only that Zack had insisted she create new content. Now the microphone suggested to her that she really ought to "do the thing." After all, here it hung, violating the antique desk. She swiveled it over and smacked her mouse to wake her computer. The first icon on the screen read Live Broadcast, and when she clicked, opened a chat room on the right, and an image of a microphone on the left.

Osgood took a deep breath, then another, then clicked the microphone.

In the days where this had been more fun, when she'd felt more like the Spectral Inspector she claimed to be, she'd envisioned flocks of spectral birds going forth from that click, bursting from her window overlooking Clark Street and heading toward the lake, spreading to the four winds, to wherever people listened to her pontifications. After such an extended hiatus, though, she found it hard to imagine even a single bird, a single notification.

But the microphone, and Zack, she supposed, were right. She should do something other than drink and fuck. Both noble pursuits, to be sure, but didn't tend to pay bills. At least not for her. For a moment, seeing her reflection in the black mirror of her monitor, she wondered what type of client she could gather, were she to change professions at this late date.

"Weird ones," she told herself and blew a purple curl out of her eyes.

She put back the fantasy and pulled the microphone closer to her mouth, her lips just barely touching the mesh of the pop filter. The intimacy of it always sent tingles through her. To be able to speak so quiet and candidly here and have people *out there* hear.

Time to begin again, she told herself. *To do that voodoo that I do so well.*

"Been a while, hasn't it?" she said into the microphone. On the screen, an equalizer bar bounced along with her voice. She raised an eyebrow, noticing a single listener had just shown up on the chat. "Your old Spectral Inspector has been dormant, hibernating, and for that, I apologize. Not by choice, really. Though one supposes mental health, physical health, and general malaise does figure in. Mostly I've been dormant because I've had nothing to say." Osgood laughed. "I know, right? I'm sure you Specterinos would have a hard time believing that. But I honestly had nothing of substance.

Nothing memorable. Nothing...mysterious. And with no mystery, what's there to investigate?

"Well, last night, thankfully, the barest inkling of a mystery dropped into my lap. I know, I know, 'Tell us about it, Janet!' While I usually wait until I can be sure that something is a bit more substantial before putting it out there, as that keeps us from—" A chortle from somewhere deep inside her brought her to a stop. "I just realized I was about to say chasing phantoms, but that's what we do, isn't it? How about keeping us from going on an old fashioned snipe hunt?

"But this lead last night tugged at me, pulling at some deep-down threads. Thrumming a bass-line that hasn't been thrummed in quite a while. I know, 'get to the fucking point, Osgood!' These three snippets of sentences came to me in an email last night: 'Mazarowskis idea. Rest stop plees. Drumbeats .find the Hinterlands.' And I will note that Hinterlands is capitalized, plees is spelled p-l-e-e-s and Mazarowskis doesn't have an apostrophe before the 's.' Zack says that the email came from nowhere..." She waved her hands dramatically at the microphone. "Oooh. Though I imagine that nowhere is far more likely to be an obfuscation technique that he has yet to crack than anything genuinely sinister or, spectral.

"That email led us to Clinton Mazarowski, who hosted *Across the Backroads* for years under the name the Guardian, of whom I imagine you've heard. I honestly thought he still hosted it, as there's a guy who calls himself the Guardian on there, whenever I stumble upon it. The *new* Guardian, though, is much harder to listen to. Who really wants to hear the paranormal guy talking about his Donald Trump-as-Jesus theories? Not this gal." Osgood leaned back into her plush leather chair, reaching up and pulling the microphone along with her.

"So, there's that, and a missing report he wrote, called 'The Rest Stop Papers,' back in 2006 that even the extensive internet archive can't find. Where does that leave us? Nowhere, at the moment, which is why I'm telling you. Zack and I will continue to tug at errant threads, but I do wonder if I'm forcing the mystery. Yearning for the investigation.

"It's hard not to feel like a lost fraud sometimes, Specterinos," she tells the void, noticing that the number of "listen live" members has climbed to six since she began. "Of course, fraud is in my blood. I'm sure some of you have heard this before, but please do indulge me as I've had almost no quality sleep, and Mary's bloody Caesar was *strong* this morning. My family, the Osgoods, were grifters way back. My great-grandfather and -mother. Called themselves the Psychic Osgoods. Clever, right?" Osgood rolled her eyes. "Lilian and Ernest, for two bits or whatever, would bring you into their parlor and call forth your deceased family members from the margins. They'd manifest as a shake of the table or a flicker of the lighting. Maybe even an ectoplasmic performance, if the Osgoods were feeling clever. They didn't believe a word of what they were saying or doing, of course. Their fraud was a cynical cash grab. They often made the argument that they were bringing peace to those who came to them for guidance. Because aren't imaginary glimpses beyond this life worth some cash if they bring real peace? Religions the world over would certainly agree with that, in private if not public. But these are the things that liars, cheats, and frauds say. These are the lies they tell themselves and each other, so they don't feel as though they're taking bread out of hands or shoes off feet. It's not snake oil, but it ain't much better either."

Osgood laughed mirthlessly and felt her throat catch. "I don't want to be a fraud," she said, looking beyond the microphone to the wall of the office, where a photo hung that had the power to tug her guts out. In the picture were two smiling faces. Young Prudence, not yet a college drop-out, curly hair flowing down her back in her natural chestnut color instead of the purples and blues and greens that it usually was these days. She even had a sundress on, for chrissakes.

"I was femme in those days," she said in a voice low enough to be a whisper. Next to her in the photograph, in a one-armed side-hug embrace, stood Audrey Frost, best friend since the days where those words meant something. Both of them beamed. Both of them loved each other. Not in that way – those experimentations had ceased, and Aud wound up tragically straight – but in the way that you can love another human being so much that you'd do anything for them. Anything to help them succeed.

Including lie for them. Lie *to* them.

"And ruin their lives," said Osgood. The microphone reentered her sight, seemingly from nowhere. "Sorry, I got lost in my own margins. I guess that happens more and more as you near forty. But all I want to do is help, and all I want to feel is that thrill of discovery. Is that too much to ask? Are there so few mysteries to uncover anymore? Even if the answers are mundane, are the mysteries and the journeys they take you on somehow…less?"

Her phone's vibration drew her attention. She flipped it over.

Any chance youd like to get lunch? i'm starving!

Osgood stared at the question, nibbling on her lower lip hard enough that she yelped in pain. **No, thank you.**

O alright. Ellipses, ellipses, ellipses, typing. **Maybe another time.**

Maybe.

You want to help people, Pru? Maybe don't pick up young women in a blackout, introduce them to your life, and then leave them stranded. Osgood nodded. But she couldn't unfuck this girl. And what would young Nora have to gain by hitching her wagon to Prudence Osgood? Someone who has her life ahead of her doesn't deserve to partner up with someone who'll likely be dead of liver failure before fifty.

But you know where it'll end, don't you?

Osgood nodded, though the voice had changed, not her mother in her head now, no, something that sounded like her, but darker. "It'll end where it always does," Osgood suggested. "At the crossroads, under the beacon." She sat for a moment, pondering her own existence, before looking back to the computer screen where her live listen numbers had topped two digits. She wondered why on earth they'd be listening to this self-indulgent nonsense, and considered asking that very thing, but knew that striking at your audience, whatever the reason, wasn't helpful, smart, or a good strategy for success.

About as smart as committing fraud on TV, right, Pru? There was her mother's voice again. She almost welcomed it over the alternative.

She knew what they, her live listeners, wanted, anyway.

"Then why do we keep searching, when it seems that there's so little to investigate? When it seems as though mystery has left our lives more and more as data is collated and democratized?" She took a deep breath. "Because answers are important, no matter how thin they may be. Because as much as Lilian and Ernest Osgood were liars and cheats, sullying their family, *my* family, and would've been run out of town by Houdini if he'd ever met them, they still realized what the yearning was, the desire. It's closure. When someone close to you dies, there's a hole in your world. They're just gone. The belief in a ghost or a spirit, one that could answer our questions, could tell us where they left that amazing trinket from our childhood, could tell us they love us still, is the desperate hope that this life isn't the one and only. That it's the prelude to something beyond. A chance for us all to be together again. Call it heaven, call it postscript. That conformational desire has been omnipresent since the dawn of our species when we first looked up at the stars and imagined them as people, gods…monsters.

"We're drawn to the mystery. Whether there is something else, something after – and I believe that there is. That makes it far more likely that there's some truth to centuries of paranormal stories. Sure, vampires may have just been people suffering from porphyria, their gums receding, so teeth appear as fangs. The Erlking snatching children may have been an attempt to deal with the horrors of childhood mortality or infanticide. Our urban legends of the last hundred years, from hook-handed men to alligators in our sewers, right through to Slenderman and creepypasta, are just more evidence of the desire, the desperation to believe in the otherworldly. We couch it in horror and danger because that's

33

easier somehow. But also, perhaps, because it's difficult to believe that there's just this and nothing. A now, and then. The cosmic light switch that turns off when we shuffle off this mortal coil.

"When you open that door of belief in the afterlife, in ghosts, in the paranormal, and go beyond the Christian dogma of heaven, or at least look deeper within that dogma, you'll find the implication of so much more. Because unless you believe in a literal stairway to heaven with a literal Saint Peter at the top who *literally* says, 'I've got your table ready, sir,' when you arrive, you must recognize that the afterlife, that ghosts and spirits and energy, are something altogether different. That it implies dimensionality, that it means space…between."

She's on fire! pinged a Specterino into the live chat-room. Osgood gave it a smile.

"And mysteries pull us along with them because they cluster, both because a town or community or society shares its myths, but also because I believe there are spaces in the world that are thin. Where the barrier, a membrane between this world and the next, between life and beyond, is thin. And that thin spot seems to attract interest on both sides, from spirits, entities in this world and that space. Scratching at the vellum between them. Is that the afterlife? Who knows? I've always called it the margins, a way station between this world and the next, that we move through before we move on. It exists between space, between time, between dimensions.

"Anyway. I know you haven't heard much from me recently. Mostly because with nothing to investigate, I can only talk about Cuba Road and Hunter Noyce and the Waverly Hotel so often before you all tune out. I guess, like Maddow, I'll say, watch this space. And if you've got anything, any information, about Clinton Mazarowski, *Across the Backroads*, 'The Rest Stop Papers,' or whatever Drumbeats find the Hinterlands means – and yes, *I know* it's close to a lyric from that band In the Shallows – please ping me.

"I'll update you when I know more, Specterinos. This is

Osgood, the Spectral Inspector, signing off." Osgood clicked stop and exported her file, throwing it into the folder that Zack had created for her to ease her micro-podcasting habit. He'd take it from there.

As she moved her mouse to close the live listener chat room, a direct message popped up. **I don't know if it'll help, but some of the older** *Across the Backroads* **episodes are online. A guy who recorded a lot of it has been digitizing his tapes and releasing them as a podcast. Might have something helpful?**

Osgood thanked Phantasmama1983 and closed the window. She picked up her phone and opened her podcast app. A search for *Across the Backroads* yielded a hit. On the top of the podcast's page was a disclaimer: **The unauthorized** *Across the Backroads* **archive digitization project. If you have old episodes and want to help in our effort, email us!**

Subscribing to the 'cast revealed that the project's progress seemed to have halted in the early '90s, with hundreds of entries from the '80s up until there. With a frown, Osgood copied and pasted the email address and fired off a missive asking about episodes from the mid-aughts.

Leaning back in her chair, her eyes returned to the photograph of those two happy girls, best friends, on the wall, yearning that one day may bring absolution, trust, forgiveness. She felt her eyelids grow heavy and the world swam away, returning her, as always, to the crossroads.

6

The mottled lens of the beacon fills Osgood's vision. Despite being a good ten or fifteen feet above her head, she sees it in front of her face. The beacon is enormous, its amber light clicking on, then off, then on, *ad infinitum*. She looks up at the enclosure above her, where the beacon actually is, not in front of her, after all. The click is far louder than it should be, as the amber lights cycle from the north-south position to the east-west position. *Cha-click cha-click cha-click cha-click.*

Caution. She hears the word in her voice but is not the one who says it. She thought it, though. Always thinks it. Caution. That's what the blinking amber light means. Especially here in the dark, at the lonely crossroads that should've long ago been upgraded to a real traffic light, or, fuck, even a stop sign. Don't they know that these blinking beacons do nothing to slow marauding teenagers bombing down the backroads of the world, windows open and music loud, carefree and careless because, of course, they'll live forever.

And you?

Osgood shakes her head, ignoring the strange loud questions both spoken and in her mind. She follows the cable extending off the northwest corner of the beacon enclosure, all the way to the crooked pole at the corner and then down.

Now she can see the intersection, as her eyes have gotten used to the darkness. Though, can one ever get used to *this* darkness? There's nothing beyond the poles, not yet anyway. Right now, there's just the vague circle created by the alternating amber lights above her.

Soft notes lilt on the wind, and she shudders. She closes her eyes. She knows this one. The tune is the same, isn't it? This dance. This is a dream, right? She's in the dream, not the reality. If it were the reality, of course, she wouldn't be standing here in the center, and the intersection wouldn't be empty. There'd be a semi-truck and a Buick Skylark that never stood a chance. This isn't then, she's confident. This isn't *then*. It's now. But what is now, anyway? Is she even really here? She looks down at her body. If this were *then,* she sure as fuck wouldn't be standing here with her tits and bush out. *Jesus Christ, why aren't I cold?* The melodic breeze has ceased, and the night air is calm. Its warmth feels the same temperature as her skin, as though there is no division between her body and the world.

Then the thought strikes her. *Is there even a world beyond the amber light?* Down the road a piece. Is this intersection all there is? No, that's foolish talk. Besides, she's been here before. For real. This intersection exists in the world. In Illinois. DeKalb County. She's been back to it since the accident, outside her dreams. Just to see. It seemed smaller more than a decade on. On from *then.*

"I've been here before," Osgood shouts into the dark. No echo returns. She lifts her face back to the beacons. Beyond it, the sky is inky black emptiness, absent of clouds and stars, as though her world has shrunk down to only this place, swallowed up into darkness by some great leviathan, or cruising through outer-outer-space in a bubble of black. She startles herself by barking out a laugh that sounds more like a rough cough. A wave of relief washes over her as the laugh is reflected and echoes back to her. There's movement in the air again, now sans melody. She hears the sounds of a highway somewhere over the horizon, low and hushed.

Headlights appear in the distance, and a shudder rocks

her body. She's unsure if it's a chill or reflexes? Is there danger? Should she have—

Caution.

She looks south, noting a lonely Amoco gas station. The station is dark, only a single fluorescent street lamp illuminates its lot and the two cars parked there. One is a deep blue Buick Skylark. She doesn't doubt for a moment that it's hers. *TARDIS blue,* she told people when she got it. Back then, her only concept of what the reference meant had to do with the guy in the scarf with the impressive amount of curly hair. The car itself was big and boxy, the way they used to make them. "When boats roamed the earth," she whispers to herself.

The Amoco's soda and snack machines hum, drawing her attention. There's something near them, hidden in shadows. It *clicks.* But she's not sure if the sound originated from the thing itself, or from something it has done in the dark. She can just make out its edge, illuminated from behind by the phosphorescent pink-orange glow of the street lamp. As she watches, it *clicks* again, a sound that reminds her of her grandfather's dentures clacking together. The thing becomes more evident, either because it is moving further into the light or she's gotten used to the dark. Whatever the reason, her chest burns with fear. Without question, even still mostly hidden, she knows it now. Something she saw once, a massive humanoid sculpture standing along the highway, belonging to a weirdo Minnesotan artists' colony. Audrey was with her then, and they both found the thing incredibly unsettling. Knowing what it is, being sure, just confuses her further because it can't be here. The humanoid creature with the gaping screaming mouth. The figure that made no earthly sense amid the other beautiful art projects that populated the compound. It makes more sense here, of course, human-sized, in the dark at the crossroads. A monster from the depths of time.

Osgood looks from the shadow of the thing in the dark to the Skylark in the Amoco parking lot, *her* once-and-now-deceased Skylark, back out to the oncoming headlights, closing the distance.

"That time on the road when I saw the Lord." Osgood wonders what she means by that. A part of her, a growing part, knows that it's just something she said last time and the time before. Because she's just running this nightmare on a loop, isn't she? Probably will until the end, until she's back here for good. Back here, because she knows that it'll end at the crossroads.

"Doesn't it always?" asks a voice behind her. Its voice. Not in her head this time, but here, with her. She knows, though, as the déjà vu begins to collapse on itself and she remembers as she turns, that it isn't her. Never was her. Even knowing doesn't prepare her, as she stares into the horrid empty eyes of the screaming thing from the artists' colony. From Minnesota. Hundreds of miles away from here. Rear-lit by the now massive headlights. She staggers back, away from its

(why the long face?)

gaping maw. The paint of the screaming thing is chipped in places, revealing something moving beneath that she doesn't have time to see. She falls to the ground, directly below the beacon. The screaming thing begins to expand, growing up past the beacon to its size on the art colony. Ten feet, fifteen, twenty... Taller and taller. Sounds of wind, from the horrible beast's yawning mouth, blow harder and harder, the melody returning, gaining speed and volume. The wind goes from gale to tempest to—

This is the end. Beautiful friend.

Air brakes blast, car brakes screech, and a semi-truck meets the side of a 1982 Buick Skylark, as it had years ago and nearly every night since. Meeting and crushing below the beacon, with Osgood between them. She has enough time to look right and see her own terrified face in the Skylark, decades younger, and left to see the mustachioed head of the trucker pop off like a cork and tumble down into the wheel well of the semi.

Then there's just darkness, and shaking, and—

⚔ 7 ⚔

Hands on her. The screaming thing grabbing at her.

"Jesus, Os!"

"Fuck!" Osgood exclaimed and bolted forward, launching herself out of the leather chair onto unsteady legs. She fell to her knees beyond the edge of her desk, the room aglow with amber light. Instinctively she covered her head, crouching the way they once did during nuclear bomb drills in the early days of the '80s, when her generation got its own apocalypse and learned about existential dread. The Skylark and semi hadn't come. The vehicle sounds were cars driving up and down Clark Street outside, and the amber light in the room was just the red/pink of Mary's neon marquee outside her window.

A hand on her shoulder. She smacked it away, shoving the figure backward. "Whoa!"

Click!

The room flooded with light and the dark figure resolved into Zack in his windbreaker. "Os. You okay?" He held both hands in front of him, seeming to simultaneously reach for her with concern and stand ready to hold her off if she launched herself at him again.

She could feel her chest aching from the throbbing of her

heart. She nodded, slowly, trying to breathe, taking in one stuttering gasp, letting out another. "I haven't..." Another breath, she held up her hand, asking for a minute.

"I know," he said. She could see he did in his face. He might decry her drinking, and most of the decisions she made while she did so, but he knew why she did it.

She slapped her hand on the corner of the desk to pull herself up and found her arms useless. Crouching on the ground, she pitied herself, a thirty-nine-year-old wretch, single and useless, with muscles that decided at random to remind her that they'd been damaged in that accident so long ago, the collision that never left her, the crash at the crossroads. Chronic back pain that no specialist could figure out beyond, "It has to do with that accident, likely."

Ya fucking think?

"I shouldn't have..." she began but could think of so many ways to finish that sentence. Fallen asleep in that chair. Fallen asleep sober. Allowed herself to run out of alcohol in the apartment. Not kept her fucking Oxy tincture nearby.

"Pain?" asked Zack.

Osgood nodded, and even this drew the lightning along the spinal column, directly into the back of her skull.

"What do you need?"

"So many things."

He crouched before her. "Well, what can I get you right now?" His face was so open, yearning to help. Not at all the exasperated face that had welcomed her to her kitchen this morning. Not a trace of judgment that she must have, again, left the doors unlocked so he could come right in. She'd offered him a key multiple times, but he'd wanted to maintain a respectful distance. As respectful as one who wanders in if the door is open can be. But is she just conflating her pain and anger?

That's not like you, Pru, is it?

She shoved herself backward, because sitting would be better, but didn't calculate the drop and her ass hit the hardwood floor. That completed the network of pain. From cranium to coccyx, from brain to asshole, Osgood felt broken.

"Gather the lord's horses and men?" She said it with a laugh but felt no mirth.

"*King's* horses?" asked Zack.

Theatrically she added, "Bid them ride across the Hinterlands to put me back together again."

Zack stared at her.

She shook her head. "In the medicine cabinet. The brown bottle. You know the one. Top shelf."

He stood and made a quick beeline for the door.

"And Zack?" she called after him.

He looked over his shoulder.

"I swear to god if you pass any judgment for the rest of that medicine cabinet, I won't speak to you for a month."

He lingered, his face...hurt? Then he left the room. Had she hurt his feelings?

It'd been so long since this extreme level of pain had crushed her, but also so long since she'd spent any time of note, anything more than hazy muddlings, at the crossroads. The pain was always there, but sometimes it felt like noise. Sure, her energy was lower than most, and sometimes she just ran out of spoons, but she'd done well. For a long while.

The crossroads were always there too. That place where she'd died. She'd lived after all, of course, but that didn't mask the fact that she'd died, crushed beneath a semi, in a Buick Skylark at the crossroads.

"Never go to bed sober, kiddo," she told the empty room.

Pru, the junkie.

She waved away her mother's voice. Osgood hadn't listened when she'd lived with her, why listen now? Her mother had taken up this residence, this space in her cerebral cortex. Judging and talking endlessly. Of course, Cynthia Osgood still lived in Rolling Meadows, a forty-five-minute jaunt on a good day into the white bread suburbs. The white bread suburbs that, even today, didn't quite know what to do with all six feet of strange that was Prudence Osgood. A spindle of a woman, leaning as far into androgyny as one could with tits as big as hers that made binders exceedingly painful. Her continually changing carousel of hair colors fit here, in Andersonville – once the lesbian haven of Chicago, now a bouillabaisse of hipsters, queers, and old Swedes.

Here she belonged. Not there.

She had left her parents behind, but her mother had never gone, had she? She'd just dug herself deeper into Osgood's subconscious mind after Cynthia and Basil had decided they didn't want a queer boyish-girl for a daughter, especially not one who seemed to rotate between infatuation with boys and girls on a weekly, sometimes daily, basis, and had no respect for fundamental ideals like monogamy.

A jolt of pain shot through her pelvis and down her left leg, making sure to set her ovaries throbbing as it went. *Jesus, fuck,* she thought. What she wouldn't do right now for a bottle of—

"Got it." Zack reappeared, holding the small brown bottle with the O in silver sharpie on it. Her liquid relaxation, the sweet relief. Not all of it, no, never all of it. She also still had that other *thing* to contend with at the crossroads, but, just now, the liquid Oxy would do.

"Thank you," she said, reaching out for the bottle. A *gimme* gesture. A *please* gesture.

She squeezed the dropper, far fuller than she needed, but under that OD level because she'd purposely bought a dropper that couldn't possibly hold enough to do that. After all, who knew what she'd do when she went into the blackout.

"Aren't you supposed to mix that with—"

Zack swam away, and the room receded as the relief took hold. Her entire office seemed to take a few steps back, as though she sat in the audience, looking into a set. Then even that grew pleasantly hazy. *But we mustn't sleep*, she reminded herself. Not now. Because the screaming thing had found the crossroads, and if she went back now, it might still be right there, its mouth enormous, devoid of teeth or definition. No uvula, no tonsils. Just a maw of the blackest black. Jaws of nightmare.

"Keep me awake," she told Zack, who'd taken her seat at

the desk on the set. Then she shoved herself against a file cabinet across from him, brought her knees up to her chest and waited for the Oxy, like Calgon, to take her away.

8

When the haze of the Oxy had mellowed, and her pain had drifted to the dull ache that filled much of her waking life, Osgood and Zack sat in her living room to plot the next steps. Just now, those next steps seemed to be the two of them, staring, waiting for the other to present a great idea.

Zack's face was a portrait of concern, his youthful features sagging. Wispy stubble barely touched his cheeks. Worry made him look like his father, a man she'd met only once, who spoke broken English interspersed with Vietnamese. Mr. Nguyen's face, too, had been youthful but exhausted. She'd been able to tell within moments that the man wasn't fond of his son hanging out with her, and perhaps wasn't even sure why, but she did him the favor of not coming around.

Sitting across from Zack, Osgood ran her fingers through her curls until they snagged, then gripped with her fist and tugged. She must look a right horrorshow. The supplemental pain, the deep pleasure of hair pulling, distracted from the ache, and she felt herself waken more.

"Do you want...to talk...about the dr—"

"No," said Osgood.

He'd asked before, and he would ask again, she was sure. But right now, she wanted to be taken out of herself, led away from the vivid and visceral feelings of being crunched between those vehicles and the image of the screaming thing. Their appearances in her head were as real as though they'd happened, just now, and had not yet begun to fade like an old photograph, foggy and reddened.

"I did a micro-cast," she told him.

"I heard it," said Zack. "I wasn't certain that sharing so soon would—"

"We need a kickstart. Something beyond the vagaries that feel urban legend-y."

Zack nodded and looked out the windows. From this room, next to the office, you could see the full extent of the Mary's Diner neon sign, its electric glory running between the two front windows of the small living room nook.

"There's a podcast version of *Across the Backroads*," offered Osgood. "It's as good a place as any to continue the investigation."

"Wow," said Zack. "For a show so anti-technology, I'm surprised they'd do a podcast." He looked down. "Also surprised I didn't find it."

She moved past his self-deprecation, having learned years ago not to engage with it. "Whomever the Guardian is now isn't the one doing the digitization. It's a community archive project. Unfortunately, the collective has only reached the early '90s. But—" Osgood remembered her email in a flash and dashed to the office. As she searched her desktop for the phone, under folders, behind Coke cans, on the floor, she regretted the dash, the throb returning to her aches.

"What's going on?" asked Zack from the next room.

"Got it!" Osgood held her phone above her head, then lowered her arm at the sharp pain. For a moment she wondered if this was to be her new baseline, even with the Oxy. *Or is it just because I slept weird? Because I was tense from the dream? Is this the New Normal?*

That phrase had scared her since the beginning. She'd relearned to walk, and the doctors were optimistic, but the others in physical therapy had told her the unvarnished truth, that sometimes you can't put Humpty Dumpty back together again, or at least back together correctly. As her insurance funded stint in therapy ran out, they'd sadly looked on at her and said that the best thing to do sometimes was to accept the New Normal. That she just may be one of the Unlucky Ones who had difficulty getting around, moving, even occasionally feeding herself, for the rest of her life. Thank whatever gods that Audrey had been there because Osgood's parents had been shits, even then.

She thumbed in her passcode and saw a reply email.

Re: Digitization Episodes

The aughts actually have one of the largest collections, as that's when people first started rebroadcasting digitally. Are you looking for something specific?

She returned to the living room, tapping out her response as she walked. Without looking up, she asked, "What was the date on that 'Rest Stop Papers' essay?"

Zack stared at her for a moment, perhaps still confused by her sudden bolting from the room. But he seemed to get over that and snapped to it, yanking his tablet out of his bag and inhumanly quickly typing a seemingly endless series of numbers as his passcode. When it opened, he swiped a few times, then scrolled. "September 7, 2006."

She tapped out, **Maybe a week on either side of September 7, 2006.** She moved her thumb toward send, then paused, adding, **Have you ever heard him mention the Rest Stop Papers?** and sent it off.

"Correspondence with the guy leading the digitization," she told Zack, and he nodded.

"I found a couple of references to something that could be connected. There was some scuttlebutt on the urban legends forums and Snopes in the first half of the 2000s that rest stops were somehow collecting missing people."

Osgood narrowed her eyes.

Zack shrugged. "The user presenting the theory was rather crackpotty, but the responses said that some rest stops seem to have a shocking number of those missing kids posters."

She remembered seeing those, when her family would take road trips, back when her parents still were proud of their daughter. Next to the big state map with a "You are here!" arrow, and the various photos of nearby attractions, she'd always had a morbid fascination for the crudely xeroxed pictures above stats and "last seen" dates. She wondered if the kids were ever found, and if they were, did someone come to take down the flyer? Or was it like a band paste-up? When tonight's show finished, just paste up tomorrow's.

"An amusing guy seemed to think that the rest stops that were on Ley Lines—"

"Audrey used to talk about those."

Zack paused at the name, eyes on hers.

"But I don't remember what they are," she told him.

"It's an old theory that there are, uh, mystical connections between important sites. Like Stonehenge, etcetera. And where those lines cross, the world tends to be more active with…'energy?'"

"Yes," said Osgood, feeling a bit of defensiveness at Zack's implied air quotes. "Don't you believe in paranormal hot spots?"

"I don't believe in the symbology of ancient sites. And, they claim you can use these lines to predict earthquakes and the like. They've been right enough times to be statistically less valuable than flipping a coin."

Osgood nodded.

"They're the Nostradamus of cartography," he said, finally. "Do *you* think there's validity there?"

"I think there are hot spots, yes. I don't know that they're connected to anything. But there are areas where the fabric of our world is thin. Like window paning when you're baking bread."

"You bake bread?"

"I'm a Renaissance Woman," she said, throwing him a dismissive wave. "Like when walls between apartments are thin, sometimes in spots you can put your heads to the wall and actually have a conversation. And the more you rub at a thin spot, the thinner it gets."

Zack seemed uncertain. "Do you want me to pull up the Ley Lines theories?"

"No," said Osgood. "I think Ley Lines can be a last resort. Our best bet right now is chasing down more about this report."

A ping caused her to glance at her phone. *A reply already?* Sure enough, an email back with the subject line, **Re: Re: Digitized Episodes.**

"That was quick," said Zack.

She nodded and read the email aloud to Zack.

The Rest Stop Papers were an ongoing puzzle for us all to solve. It was during the period I started listening. He used to list new rest stops at the end of the week as people sent them to him. I never was quite sure why. It'd been going on for a while when I first heard it. I'm not sure when it started, though.

I liked the rest stop lists because they felt eerie, like lists of dead cities in a post-apocalyptic world. And why else would you listen to a paranormal conspiracy show in the middle of the night, right?

I've attached a quick clip of one of them while I dig out your requested episodes.

"Play the clip?" asked Zack, moving off his chair to the couch next to Osgood.

She nodded and hit the attachment, let it download. Out of her phone came the voice of the Guardian, low, affected. "Before the morning light bids us leave, my friends, we have eleven new rest stops this week. When it rains, it pours."

"There's electronic pitch modulation on his voice, making it lower than it actually is," said Zack.

"Shush," said Osgood, listening to the recitation of highways and exit numbers, in the echoey faraway voice of the Guardian. When he reached the end, he thanked the listeners for risking their own safety in discovering these sacred places and the secrets they brought.

"A complete listing can, as always, be found at…" the voice read a very long URL.

"Whoa, fucking Angelfire?"

Osgood cocked an eyebrow at him.

"It was an early 'I want my own website' service. No idea how he managed to be using that service into the middle of the aughts." Zack stared at his tablet, fingers moving. "Can you replay that last bit?"

Osgood slid the audio file back.

"Got it," said Zack.

"You got the list?" Osgood dropped her phone on the cushion next to her and leaned way over.

"Got the URL. Unfortunately, it's gone. Let me look in the archives."

She snickered as she saw him open a new site. "The Wayback Machine?"

"Hey, don't knock awesome people doing awesome things for free who like to name them in silly ways."

Osgood shook her head and waved her hands.

On the screen, Zack tapped backward through a calendar. He tapped on one link, and it brought up an empty white screen. Then another, the same. Another, the same. "Shit."

"No list?"

"Nothing. Even the archives are nothing. So, unless the website was literally a white screen with no HTML content on those dates, someone wiped the archives."

Zack jumped into a chat program, popping windows open and typing into them furiously, copying and pasting the URL over and over. She knew better to interrupt him in this zone. Without looking up, he asked, "What was one of the stops?"

She scanned back through the recording to the list and the Guardian's artificially enhanced, crackly voice intoned, "Minnesota, Polk County, Highway US2, Milepost 59."

"Got it," said Zack.

"What're you doing?"

He still didn't look up. "We have more data, so searches can be more— Yes!" His exclamation echoed off the ceiling of the living room and almost caused Osgood to leap off the couch. He turned his tablet to her, showing a website with the header **Backup List**.

"'If the Guardian becomes compromised, we need to be able to maintain the list of gates ourselves.'" Osgood read beneath the header. "'This is not meant to usurp the Guardian, only to serve as an off-site backup.'"

Midway down the page, a highlighted entry: **Minnesota, Polk County, Highway US2, Milepost 59.**

"Well, shit," said Osgood.

"Shit indeed," said Zack, scrolling down the page that showed hundreds of listings. "What do you want to do now?"

"Search for Illinois."

He swiped all the way up and then searched the page. "Just outside Metropolis."

"Jeez, that's…"

"Six, seven hours away?" He looked up. "Why?"

Osgood grinned at him.

"You know, with your purple hair, you look like the fucking Cheshire Cat."

"I know," she said. "Check Iowa, Indiana, and Wisconsin."

"You want to go to one?"

She nodded.

"Just like that."

"What're you doing tonight that's so important?" she asked.

"Well, I thought I'd go home and sleep at some point."

"Yeah, but until then?"

"I…" He frowned. "Hungry?"

"I hungry, too, Zack." She wrapped her arm around his neck and pulled him toward her. His head hit her shoulder and pain radiated, but the adrenaline of finding something, anything really, carried her through. Didn't even care that Zack's nose and mouth were digging into her right tit.

Zack pulled back and looked up at her with wide, perplexed eyes.

She could feel her heart beating, adrenaline rushing. *Why do you care so much, Pru? What is it?* She took two long and deep breaths and then smiled, hoping it was less manic than her earlier Cheshire grin. "I'm tired of having nothing to look for. Having nothing to investigate."

He nodded.

"It's been—"

"Months," said Zack.

"Months. And everything in the year and change before that went nowhere." She grabbed his hand and pulled him to her again. "Listen, I'm going. 'Cuz I've got nothing else to do. 'Cuz the rest of the plan is wait for more info. 'Cuz I have no intention of sleeping tonight—"

"Again, I'd like to—"

"And 'cuz it'll be good for us. You've wanted more field time, less Q time."

"Yes." He nodded to himself, trying to hide a glance at his watch. "Okay, but not more than two hours away."

Osgood shook her head. "Of course not. I'm not *crazy*."

9

Fingertips in the wind. The early autumn breezes. Osgood closed her eyes and felt the wind on her face. A touch of chill, but that was it. "Autumn is my favorite time of year," she said to Zack in the driver's seat.

"Hrm," mumbled Zack.

She looked at him, then back at her hand drifting through the driving wind as they headed north on I-90. She wondered if she should apologize again, but she'd already offered to pay for gas (hopefully he could add it to her tab) and drive to let him research. What more could she do? Her car had gotten towed. She gave him one more glance, then turned back toward the darkening sky. The whole world outside the Jeep had become blue-toned with the last vestiges of daylight after sunset. She hoped for a long autumn this year. The season had become dreadfully short in recent years, with summer heat bloating and crawling later and winter icing earlier. In her childhood, autumn had seemed to stretch on forever, though she thought that might as much to do with going back to school and the endless wait for Christmas.

"What was your favorite Halloween costume?" she asked him.

"I'm grumpy with you," he said, his eyes fixed on the road.

"I know," she said.

He pursed his lips and held the face for a good two minutes. She was just about to give up when he offered, "A Ninja Turtle."

She laughed. "Which one?"

"Donatello."

The techie, she thought. *Of course!* "I always loved Donatello."

"Me too." Zack tried to hide the slight smile on his face. "He was also the only turtle whose weapon my mother could fashion out of a piece of PVC pipe."

"Could make nunchucks with PVC," suggested Osgood.

"She'd have to craft a plastic chain." Zack shook his head as though the notion were preposterous. "And Michelangelo is irritating as hell."

"He's a party dude." She pressed her hand to her chest, hoping to charm the grumpy out of him. "I was April O'Neil."

He side-eyed her.

"I liked she had that badass yellow jumpsuit, instead of wearing garish lipstick and a skirt. And my mother told me that 'girls can't be Ghostbusters.'"

A laugh escaped Zack.

"I know, right?"

"Your mother was ahead of the curve. The whole troll internet thought that a few years ago."

"I showed her! I became a ghost*hunter!*" Osgood slapped her hand down on the armrest, but her triumph was short-lived. "She respected that even less, I think."

They were quiet again for a while.

"Am I your partner or your sidekick?" Zack asked.

Osgood turned her whole body toward him, leaning against the door of the Jeep Cherokee.

"I just wonder that."

"I..." She wasn't sure what to say. "You're Q."

"I go in the field sometimes," said Zack. "Like now."

"Yes."

"Q didn't."

"Well," she said, racking her brain to come up with a single instance of Q in the field. Coming up empty, she said, "You're essential."

He appeared to ponder that. "Essential."

"I can't do what you do." *Just call him a partner, Pru. Audrey won't give a shit.* Osgood scowled. Her mother would never use that language in real life. *No,* another desperate internal voice reassured her, *one day, Audrey Frost will return, and we can pick up where they left off. Partners. Friends. One day.*

"You okay?" asked Zack.

Osgood looked up, startled.

"You kinda just...deflated."

"I was thinking about Audrey."

"Aha," said Zack. He seemed resigned when he added, "*She* was your partner."

"Yeah." She watched the trees pass along the highway, gone beyond the blue-dark of twilight into the real dark. "Was."

"Essential is fine, Os," he said. "Just fine."

⚔ 10 ⚔

"We're gonna have to loop around at the next exit," Zack told Osgood from the passenger seat. "The rest stop is on the southbound side."

Osgood nodded and watched the rest stop pass by on the other side of the grassy valley of the median. Zack had surrendered the wheel just after Janesville, saying he was itching to get back to his searches. He'd turned on his phone's Wi-Fi beacon and tossed it on the dash, then gone face-down in his laptop, silent until this direction about turning around.

As Osgood drove, she felt her excitement begin to wane. Her energy level fell more as they turned around, and an ache began to consume her shoulder. Merging back onto the southbound side of the highway, she also felt *something* in her stomach. Hunger probably... Had she eaten since this morning? No, that wasn't what it was, though. She knew the feeling, didn't she? She'd felt it so many times in her life. Solemnly, she glanced at Zack, who had stopped typing and was staring out the windshield at the highway ahead. "I feel dread," she told him.

"I," he began but stopped.

"It's like this warmth in my stomach."

"The way I used to feel when I'd get sent to the principal's office."

"Yes!" She pushed her hand in, just below her diaphragm, hoping some pressure might relieve the feeling.

"Yeah," said Zack. "I certainly feel something. But mine might just be nerves 'cuz... rest stops are dangerous."

"Rest stops aren't dangerous," said Osgood dismissively. "Maybe years ago, when they weren't maintained by the states as well." She remembered a trip to Disney World with her parents when she was eight or nine-years-old, finding both a used condom and an empty syringe on the floor in one of their Georgia stops.

"Are you kidding? There's a whole network of long-haul trucker serial killers. Picking up sex workers at rest and truck stops and then dumping their bodies across state lines. Confuses the hell out of cops because of jurisdictional reasons, and makes the killers almost invisible." Zack nodded, then added as an apparent afterthought, "Also, cops are biased against sex workers."

"They are indeed," said Osgood, considering his network of serial killers. Some part of her wanted to deny it and say that surely that couldn't be true, surely there were other explanations, but the rest of her remembered her days of serial killer obsession, devouring the Green River Killer case facts. "Maybe that's what this is," she said finally. "An attempt to collate data that the cops were unwilling or unable to find."

"'The Rest Stop Papers,'" said Zack.

Osgood flipped on the right blinker and slowly pulled off the highway.

They pulled into the rest stop parking lot. Six spots down was parked an older model Dodge Caravan, side door open, packed to the roof. A woman was rummaging through a cooler, while a man in a baseball cap stood next to the hood of the van and stretched his back. The chattering of kids emanated from within.

She looked at Zack, the feeling in her stomach heavier. She could tell from his expression that he felt it too.

"I wonder if they feel the dread," he whispered to her, cocking his head toward the family.

"Last chance to pee," said Dad loudly, with a clap for emphasis.

"No!" and, "No, thank you!" came from the little ones inside.

"I doubt it," said Osgood.

"Then why do we?"

Osgood looked above the parking lot. "No high tension power lines."

"Do you smell anything?" asked Zack.

She took a long sniff. "Just grass. Must've cut it recently. You?"

He shook his head. "Should we…"

"Go in?" asked Osgood. "If we don't, I'd say we just made abysmal use of two hours."

As they climbed out of the Jeep, minivan Mom closed the Caravan's side door and got in the passenger seat. Dad patted the hood and got in the driver's side. Osgood and Zack watched them leave.

With a soundtrack of only the occasional *shuuush* of cars and trucks on the highway behind them, Osgood began looking for something, anything, out of the ordinary. In front of them stood a tan brick building that looked like every other rest stop in the country. Benches in front of it. A shelter off to the side with picnic tables. Past their parking area, a truck lot with a single semi in it. Not like hers, though. The elongated cab, not the flat front.

"Speaking of making abysmal use of two hours," said Zack, "it looks like a rest stop."

Osgood nodded. "Let's go," she said at last and strode toward the front doors.

Inside were fancier laminate picnic tables, a Coke machine, and various snack machines.

"Dad always bought me Starburst," she said quietly, more to herself than Zack.

"Easiest candy to shut a kid up," said Zack.

She looked at him, suddenly feeling the urge to defend her father. Zack was right, though. The reason her father had bought her Starburst on long trips was that she'd carefully unwrap each one and suck on it for as long as she possibly could, noting the mile markers they passed. He'd always told her how proud of her he was when she could make one last more than three miles. He'd encouraged her to break her record. He had indeed wanted to keep her quiet, hadn't he? Instead, she said, "My favorites were the pink ones."

"*Everybody's* favorite is pink."

She wondered if Zack's grumpiness had to do with the mundanity of this place or if he was still feeling that oppressive overlay of dread atop the rest. She certainly did, still holding her stomach, pressing it in until she could feel the pain of the pressure. "I'll check the ladies', you check the men's?"

He nodded and disappeared into the men's room. She watched the door slowly shut behind him and went into the ladies'. Four maroon stalls, three sinks with a mirror. A hand dryer with graffiti scratched into the chrome. She looked in the mirror, really seeing herself for the first time today. She lamented the heavy luggage under her eyes, the wildness of her hair. She'd even put her t-shirt on backward. *Not a great look, Pru.* Didn't matter so much; she'd been wearing her trench coat, so it just looked like black. Still, she pulled in her arms, exposed her pale belly to the mirror, and turned it around. She laughed, noticing that the shirt she'd randomly grabbed from her drawer. An iconic red circle and slash, a white ghost. Zack would be amused. Her mother would remind her that *girls can't be Ghostbusters.* She bent down slightly, not an easy feat as her pain reared up. No feet under any of the doors, so one by one she knocked them open with the toe of her All-Stars.

"Anything?" asked Zack when they returned to the vestibule. "Were you wearing that when you went in?"

She gave him an indignant, "I was!" and moved on. "Just some illegible graffiti scratched onto the mirror and hand dryer, and someone going old school by putting Jenny's number in one of the stalls." Osgood cocked her head. "Which is usually more of a *dude* thing."

Zack nodded. "I had some similar retro fun with one stall

trying to Rick-Roll me, another containing a sizable...bowel movement."

"Wonder if it was Dad?"

Zack laughed, and Osgood laughed with him. For the first time since they'd neared the rest stop, the dread felt less oppressive.

"The last one had 'out of order' tape on it."

"Boys are gross," said Osgood.

"They are indeed," said Zack. "One of the urinals also had a huge garbage bag over it and an 'out of order' sign. Plenty of pee collected in the bag, though." He pointed toward a display board on the wall with a large map of Wisconsin and a red arrow just below Lake Koshkonong telling them, *You are here.* "Let's check that." Beside the map were three heavily copied papers, each featuring an over-contrasted photo, one a 6-year-old boy, according to the words beneath it, last seen in March of this year. Another, a woman supposedly in her twenties who looked the worse side of forty. Disappeared the previous year. Zack tapped that photo. "Meth does that to your face."

"Let's not judge the missing, Zack."

"I'm just saying that twenty-two-year-olds don't look like that. It's the trucker network."

Osgood shook her head and conceded, "Maybe."

The final paper showed a fourteen-year-old girl. Awkward and gawky with braces. Disappeared in June of this year. Osgood stared at her – the hair that she hadn't quite figured out how to tame, the smile both trying to look happy and yet hide her mouth full of metal. Osgood knew this brand of awkward well. She pressed her fingertips to the glass for a moment and hoped that Fredrica Bimmel had or would make it home alright.

She straightened up and folded her arms, shoving her cuticle into her mouth.

"I have nail clippers."

Osgood flicked her eyes at him, and he immediately looked at his shoes. "Let's go out the back," she said after one last look around the interior yielded nothing. The building's rear doors led to a tiny park, just a single swing set with two big kid swings and one little, and one of those animals on a spring that bounce back and forth. "I thought they got rid of these because kids were crushing their hands."

"Probably haven't gotten to it as part of the refurb yet."

Osgood arched an eyebrow.

"Sign out front said refurb is going all this year into next."

She nodded. "You go right, I'll go left."

"Do you have any idea what I should be looking for?" asked Zack, his voice slightly higher pitched.

Is he whining?

"I don't, Zack. Look for literally anything."

They parted ways, and Osgood used her phone's flashlight to peer into the wooded brush beyond the manicured rest stop. Dense trees lay that way, the kind that kept you enclosed here. No kids wandering off on their own. No secure places to run off for a tryst or even a quick suck-and-go. "No," she said quietly. "If you're going to get your illicit fuck on, you're going to do it in a bathroom stall as God intended." She snickered at herself as she passed another shelter over three more picnic tables. The plastic bag insert of a drum garbage can fluttered in the night wind. The *shuuushing* of the highway traffic could barely be heard here.

Now that Osgood's sense of dread had lessened, she saw this place for what it was: merely a rest stop, a way station that you hit to go to the restroom, get a snack, maybe take a quick nap before you moved on. "No one's final destination," she told herself. "Even the sex workers probably got taken somewhere else before—"

Dark, Pru.

She nodded and shook the thought loose, rounding the corner back into the bright circle of white-orange light flooding the pathway up to the main building. Zack stood there as well, hands in his pants pockets.

When he saw her, he shrugged and shook his head. "Anything?"

"Nope." She said, giving the area another look. A new car

sat down at the end of the parking lot, rumbling in shadows. Even the semi had quit the rest stop. Time to ramble on.

"There's an A&W drive-in at the next exit," offered Zack.

Good, he's not too pissed at the excursion, thought Osgood. "Buy you a root beer?" she offered.

"Yeah," said Zack. "That sounds good."

11

As Osgood scarfed down a second burger, she ignored Zack's gaze. He always seemed so surprised that someone as slight as she was could put away so much food. And as his belly had begun to expand in earnest last year, she'd never thought it appropriate to talk about her difficulty gaining weight due to a whacked-out metabolism and very uneven desire to eat.

"I'm sorry I dragged you up here," she said after the waitress on honest-to-God roller skates took their trays away.

Zack shrugged. "I really didn't have anything to do. I'm remotely installing firewalls in four days. Until then..." He left it at that.

"Then I'm sorry it turned out to be nothing. I'll drive us home." Osgood wiped her hands and tossed the crumpled napkin from the window into a nearby trashcan. She slowly backed out of the spot and onto the street, tapping her fingers on the steering wheel at the stoplight between the A&W and the highway on-ramp. Zack already had his computer in his lap, logging in.

The light turned green, and she moved forward.

"I got a message from—"

She slammed on the brakes, her eyes fixed. It shouldn't be

here. She stared out her window, down the road. Zack's computer clattered to the floor.

"Jesus, Osgood, what the fuck?"

"Zack," she said, affecting calm.

"Yes?" he asked.

"An occasional side effect of my medication is hallucinations."

Zack paused for a long time before saying, "Okay. That's not…great."

"Is that an Amoco station?" She extended her finger out the window, pointing at a dark gas station a few blocks down the road in the opposite direction from the highway.

Zack bent down to pick up his laptop and examined it. Then he rested it on his lap and leaned toward the driver's side window. After a moment, he nodded. "Looks like." Behind them, a honk, then a flash of brights. Zack waved toward the back. "One minute!" he yelled, then added, "We're looking at an old gas station!"

"We have to go back," said Osgood, and she hit the gas toward the highway.

"Okay," said Zack. "I think maybe I should—"

"Amocos don't exist anymore," said Osgood.

"That one looked pretty closed," said Zack. "Do you think we could keep it below sixty before we get on—"

"Not since 2000, I think. BP bought them and switched all the Amocos over."

"All except—"

"No." Osgood shook her head. "They don't just leave a gas station derelict for almost twenty years."

"Okay," Zack repeated.

"I don't like the long ys on your 'okays,' by the way."

Zack nodded.

Osgood executed a tire-squealing turn onto the northbound ramp. "We have to go back because of my dream."

"Your dream," he repeated.

"In it, there was an Amoco station. No, not just *an* Amoco, *that* Amoco station."

Zack said nothing.

Osgood merged onto the highway, her speed climbing: sixty, seventy, eighty.

"How do you know it was *that* Amoco station?"

"Do you believe in premonitions?"

"No," said Zack.

"Neither do I," said Osgood. She could hear the blood pumping in her ears. "But I saw that Amoco station this afternoon in my dream."

Again, Zack said nothing.

"We're fucking ghosthunters, Zack."

"Yes," he agreed.

"Please, for a moment, can you just get on board some potentially paranormal phenomena?"

"Now you think 'the Rest Stop Papers' are paranormal?" he asked, skepticism wafting off the words.

"What I think is that I saw a gas station in my dream that hasn't really existed since the '90s and then saw the same one here, in reality."

"Why didn't we go to the gas—"

She shook her head. "Because we missed something at the rest stop. I'm sure of it."

"How can you—"

"The same way I can be sure of anything, Zack. Gut." She poked her stomach, noting that the dread had begun to creep back in. "Do you think we got food poisoning at Mary's this morning?"

"No, but—"

"Were we just starving at the rest stop?"

"Well, I was—"

"Or did we both feel real dread as we approached?"

Zack reluctantly nodded.

"Creeping dread. Dread that's creeping again, right now for me, as we get closer to the loop around."

"Me too," he admitted, almost a whisper.

"We'll just do one last look around, Zack," she told him, barreling off the exit after the rest stop and tapping out a staccato rhythm on the wheel as she waited for the light to turn green, so she could get back onto the highway headed south.

"And then we'll go home?"

"Then we'll go home."

When they pulled back into the rest stop, the dark car at the end remained. As Osgood passed it slowly, she could see a scruffy man inside leaned back in his seat, mouth wide open, eyes closed. "Do you have any of the big flashlights in the back?" she asked.

"Oh, leave him alone," said Zack.

She frowned at Zack and shook her head. "I'm not going to bother him." She pulled to a stop in front of the sign proclaiming *Wisconsin Department of Transportation – Rest Stop Refurbishment Program – Due for Completion in 2020.* "There," she said, pointing at it.

"Yeah?" asked Zack, irritation mixing with his confusion.

"That's a temporary sign on a permanent base." She pointed at the shingled roof over the sign, then at the wooden posts holding it up.

"Huh," said Zack. "Well, it's probably just covering the regular rest stop sign."

"Probably," said Osgood with a shrug. "Flashlight?"

Zack climbed out and opened the back hatch. He handed her an oversized yellow flashlight with a lens the size of a salad plate. "Don't look at it; that's like 1,600 candlepower LEDs there. Can *literally* blind you."

"Coming?"

"I'll stand here," he said, coming around to the side of the Jeep as she approached the sign.

She clicked the button on top of the flashlight and almost felt knocked back by the illumination. "Holy crap."

"Yeah," said Zack from behind her. "And God saw that it was good."

In the bottom corner of the sign, she saw brown and poked at it. "Cork," she called back. "This is a bulletin board. And the sign…" Sure enough, heavy-duty staples every few inches or so. "Have a knife?"

"What?"

"Do you have a knife, Zack." She turned back toward him, pointing the flashlight at his feet. Light radiated up even from the black asphalt.

"Yeah," he said, more exhaustion in his voice, more worry on his face. He reached into the back seat and pulled a small metal rectangle out of his messenger bag, then walked to her. "Your plan is to pull down a sign put up by WDOT?"

"Yes."

"I imagine that would fall under state police jurisdiction."

"Probably," reasoned Osgood. "The highways do."

He looked at her and stuck out his chin, then nodded. "Okay." Zack opened the multi-tool and pulled out a three-inch blade. He slid it behind the staple at the corner and popped it out. It *ping*ed down onto the concrete. He hit the next three along the bottom and three along the side quickly. *Ping ping ping ping ping ping.* He stepped back and waved her toward the sign with his hand.

Aiming the flashlight with her left hand, Osgood peeled back the corner of the heavy coated card-stock with her right. Beneath, stapled onto the corkboard, were what looked like sheaves of papers. Each one of them almost identical, the giant word *MISSING* up top, a box with a poorly photocopied picture, and some bold text beneath. "Missing people," she said.

"They've hungrily taken the most vulnerable people of our world."

"Yeah," said Osgood, recognizing the paraphrasing from that opening paragraph of 'The Rest Stop Papers,' a report by Clinton Mazarowski. A report the man had deemed so important that he'd used his real name, not the alias of the Guardian. Not hidden.

Zack moved toward the sign with the knife again, but Osgood closed her hand around the bottom corner and yanked. She heard a shower of staples hit the pavement, and the sign came halfway off. More papers beneath. More and more missing people. A quick glance showed the ages clustered together.

"What're you doing over there?" called a hoarse, sleepy voice.

Osgood swung the flashlight in its direction, and the man in the white tank-top standing in front of the car at the end held his arm up over his face.

"Looking for perverts," she shouted. "You a pervert?"

"No, I'm not a pervert," he grumbled back, turning away. He flumped down in his seat and slammed the door again.

She and Zack looked at each other, then back at the sign. She set the flashlight down on the curb behind them where it cast an impressive amount of light upward, leaving them use of both hands. They each grabbed the rest stop refurbishment sign. Osgood mouthed, *One, two, three,* and all it took was one great yank to send the sign sailing over their heads, one staple end dragging across Osgood's scalp before it fell behind them. She felt it but couldn't have cared less.

Before them was a ramshackle patchwork of lost and forgotten youth, sheets and sheets of paper. Multiple layers, with newer ones over older, some barely seen in back, yellowed and blurred with moisture, ink running. "Seventeen, seventeen, nineteen years old," said Osgood looking and looking, fourteen, sixteen, nineteen, eighteen. "There's no one over twenty-one on here. Only missing kids."

She turned to find Zack no longer standing beside her. The Jeep door slammed, and he rushed back to the board, a DSLR camera around his neck on a strap.

"Documentation," she said, pointing and snapping her fingers at him. "Yes, good! Brilliant!"

For the next several minutes, Zach took pictures of individual papers as Osgood examined others, their silence punctuated only by, "Switch," from Zack, and they'd switch sides.

"Almost all of these mark pre-2009 disappearances. Why are they still up? When people don't come back in a decade, they

(like Caroline)

probably aren't coming—" Osgood stopped. She hadn't thought of that name in quite some time.

"You okay?" asked Zack.

"Huh?"

"You're in my way."

Osgood stepped back all the way to the Jeep. She folded her arms in front of her and sat on the bumper. "Okay, so it's missing posters. A lot of missing posters," she said, loudly enough so Zack could hear.

"Uh huh," said Zack.

"Too many."

"Are you asking me?"

"I mean, I only ever really looked at the ones inside. I don't remember ever seeing—"

Zack held the camera for a moment, just looking around the expanse of pages. "My family took road trips during my entire childhood. We didn't fly once, but we visited LA; the Grand Canyon; Mount Rushmore; Walt Disney World; Branson, Missouri—"

"Yuck, Branson."

"Yeah, it sucked," Zack agreed, stepping back, also staring at the endless pages. "But I can tell you, without a doubt, I have never seen this many missing posters at a rest stop."

She reached out and took the camera from him, flipping through the pictures on the back screen. Zack had alternated between wide shots showing multiple pages and close-ups showing singles. "We should be able to piece together a full replication based on your—" She stopped dead.

"What?"

Osgood squinted and zoomed in on the image. "Shush."

Zack shushed.

"Where's this one?" she asked, tapping the back of the camera.

Zack took a close look at the image and flipped back and forth to the ones before and after. "Top right," he said without confidence, further undercut by, "I think."

Osgood stepped up to the board, standing in front of the top right. She put her hand on the pages and slid her fingers over them, feeling the different textures, crumple levels, waves of the paper, staples, thumbtacks. She stopped when the curled page hit the right side of her hand. She looked up to confirm that it was the one she'd seen on the camera's screen. "Writing."

"Writing?"

Osgood reached up and pulled the curl back. She pointed at it with her phone's flashlight. "Oh, fuck, a lot of writing."

The entire back side of the missing poster was a hand-written screed that seemed barely coherent. She tried to make out some of it without pulling down the page. "'Only now, after all the time passes that I can understand the truth and can embrace the glory that I see. In time, you shall...' Lots more, Zack."

"Pull it down," Zack said, stepping up and retrieving his camera from her left hand.

She looked at him. "But it's..."

"If they went missing a decade ago, they're not coming back because of some sign at a rest stop. Especially not one the state covered up." He reached up himself and yanked, pulling the page down and handing it to Osgood.

She turned it over, seeing that the rest was like what she'd read. Glory, light, exultation. Worthiness. Overall, nonsense. Osgood flipped the sheet over and saw that this missing person, fourteen, was named Ashley Sandborn. Flipping to the writing again, Osgood noted that several of the lowercase i's were dotted with circles.

"I don't know what this is," said Osgood after a long while.

"Well," said Zack. "We've got another one." He turned over another page, still stuck to the board by one corner. She walked over as Zack pulled it down and handed it to her. He pointed the flashlight at the pages.

"It's the same," said Osgood.

"Different handwriting."

"Yes, but the same text." She frowned and scanned through the messy, masculine writing on this new poster. The text was identical. Flipping it over, she found a photo of a missing boy, seventeen, named Lawrence.

She turned back to the board, suddenly sure that behind each one of the missing kids would be identical treatises about nothing, only varying in the penmanship. Without looking at Zack, Osgood told him, "We need to take them all."

Zack looked back at her, his face now ashen. He nodded, and they began.

⚔ 12 ⚔

Nearly empty highways stood between them and home, which was good, as Osgood drifted between lanes several times. She could make it back, of this she was sure. Think of how often she'd made that drive to and from DeKalb at night, so she could come home and see—

You didn't always make it, didja Pru?

"I lived," Osgood tartly told her mother's voice.

Zack slept in the passenger seat, having passed out after climbing aboard. On the seat behind them, the stack of posters were tucked safely beneath Zack's messenger bag. They'd lost count of how many somewhere past sixty. Osgood had the radio on low, set to one of those jukebox stations, pre-programmed with pre-recorded bumpers; no different from putting a mediocre mp3 collection on shuffle. But that was all Osgood needed tonight, just something to keep her eyes open.

A jolt of static brought her back to herself again, and she found that she'd drifted all the way into the far lane. She sat up straight, opening her eyes wide and blinking hard, hoping that would kick her back to fully awake. She shot a look at Zack, who still slept. "Alright," she told herself. "Might be time for an energy drink or two."

She pulled off the highway a few miles North of the

border to Illinois at a Love's truck stop. Before getting out, she saw the redness in her eyes in the rearview mirror, exhaustion, crusted mascara on her lashes. She sighed and went for her stimulant. As she exited the store with her energy drinks in a bag, she heard buzzing static emanating from the Jeep's radio through the window. She knew she'd left it on that jukebox station, but had she left the car running? And why was the static so loud? Osgood rushed back to the Jeep and saw that Zack, thankfully, had not stirred a bit. She tossed the energy drinks in the center console and reached to turn the radio off. An arc of static electricity leaped from the dial to her finger, startling her with its length and brightness. She leaned back in the driver's seat and stared at the console. Her fingers drifted again toward the knob to silence it when out of the static came the plaintive sound of '90s alt-rock – Smashing Pumpkins, maybe, not hard enough for Nirvana, like a ship emerging from a fogged-in bay.

"That'll do," she said to herself, then popped and chugged half of the purple drink. She pressed her fingers deep into her eye sockets, feeling the pressure on her optic nerves.

Awake now, Pru? Not gonna kill us?

She nodded and gave herself one last glance in the rearview, her eyes now weepy. "Alright," she said. She let out a long breath and pulled out of Love's and back onto the highway. The alt-rock song felt long and meandering, and she turned it up to better hear the lyrics over the rushing sounds of the highway. It wasn't Smashing Pumpkins, but she had heard it before. She couldn't recall when that had been, or the name of the—

"I would cross the hinterlands,
Because the valley's not that far…"

"The fuck?" Osgood looked up ahead and saw no one on the highway. No one in the rear-view mirror either. She grabbed her phone off the dash, swiping away from the map.

A notification popped up. **i hope I didn't do anything wrong**, said Nora.

"It's not you," said Osgood, brushing away the message.

Another notification. **Yann and I really want you to know that you were a valued member of our relationship, and—**

"Really valued. Jesus." She swiped again to make it stop.

"The drumbeats in the Hinterlands,
  Will lead me right to you…"

"The fucking drumbeats in the fucking Hinterlands!" exclaimed Osgood, swiping through her apps. The machine gun sound of her tires reaching the edge of the highway jolted her eyes back to the road in time to see a car trying merge in front of her. She heel-toed it and slid out of the lane, only to hear the blast of a semi horn. Her throbbing heart climbed into her throat as she flashed to her dreams, not the real *then*, but the version with two of her, one being crushed inside a Buick Skylark and one being flattened outside. Another bit of quick footwork and a hard yank on the wheel, and she found the far lane, with no one in front or behind. The semi passed her, and the driver looked down with wide-eyed apoplexy.

She changed lanes again, going right, right, and then riding the ridges until she passed entirely onto the shoulder. She slowed to a stop, making sure to stay far away from the drop into the drainage ravine beside the highway.

"is with me evermore…"

A quick musical phrase, a melody that Osgood had definitely heard years ago, and perhaps even more recently. Then the song was over. Again, the static fog rolled in before the station snapped into the middle of Pat Benatar asking to be hit. Osgood sat on the shoulder of the highway in stunned silence, considering the odds of hearing that song tonight of all nights. She glanced at her phone, the song recognition app finally open to tell her "Hit Me With Your Best Shot," by Pat Benatar was currently playing.

The app hadn't caught the song before to identify it. But Osgood didn't need that confirmation. She knew what that had been, didn't she? Knew it for multiple reasons. She searched for several of the lyrical phrases, just to confirm, and each returned the same result: "The End of What's Real" by In the Shallows. Released on the album *Ramparts Over the Hinterlands* in 1998. A banner year, that'd been. After all, in September of that year, she'd been dead for eight full minutes. Some kind of record.

A sign on the side of the road welcomed them back to the Land of Lincoln, and Osgood couldn't get it out of her head. The tune returned easily, a simple melody, slightly discordant here and there, the antidote to the pop rock of the late '90s.

"'The drumbeats in the Hinterlands,'" she sang quietly to herself. Where had she heard it before? According to her searches, it'd been a number one single in '98. "Hard to be in college and miss a number one." She nodded to herself. Yes, that was it. She'd heard it in college, or somewhere since. Or in one of those bizarre shows that felt the '90s were somehow already worthy of nostalgia. Certainly not where she thought she'd heard it. Certainly not when. Certainly not *then*.

As she swung onto I-94 past the ritzy northern suburbs, she again found herself alone on the highway, alone with her thoughts. Try as she did, she couldn't push the idea from her mind. "The last time I heard that song," she said, willing herself not to continue it, as though speaking the words would somehow make it real. "The last time I heard that song was just before a flat-fronted semi-truck blew through the amber caution beacon and t-boned my Skylark." Said aloud, she knew it to be true, the memory crawling back like paint spilling over her brain, getting into the nooks and crannies.

The dread returned to her belly. She didn't want this kind of mystery. Something felt off. Something deep. As she pulled off the highway on Peterson Avenue, she realized she was tapping her fingers to the rhythm of that song. "I was whistling it when the crash happened," she admitted to the Chicago morning. "Maybe even singing along." She shook her head and laughed. Couldn't believe it. The Osgood of two decades ago, when she'd still been Pru to her friends, had sung along to pop songs on the radio. She'd sung along as a semi crushed her car, as the top half of the cab came down on top of her. As the driver lost his head in the most literal and horrible way possible.

A mirthless laugh escaped her lips. *"The End of What's Real. No shit."*

13

"Should we reconvene in the morning?" Osgood asked Zack.

He looked out of the Jeep's window, up at her apartment, where Mary's neon sign was dark for the night. "What're you thinking?"

"Scanning the papers, looking at where investigations may have landed, that sort of thing." She smiled at him. The exhaustion had crept up on her a few times on their return drive from Wisconsin, but the jolt of the near accident had kept her wide-eyed. Couldn't sleep, not yet, not this lucid, not with all this in her head.

"I'm pretty awake now," said Zack.

"Are you sure? You don't have to be."

"I know I don't have to be," he said with a yawn. "But I'd as soon get some of the grunt work done."

Osgood laughed. "Why don't you head in and get the scanning going, I'll get us coffee."

"That's a plan."

Zack climbed out, taking his bag and the sheaf of missing posters from the back seat.

"Wait!" she called after him as he walked to the doors. "Keys!"

Zack turned back and smirked. "I'm banking on," he

grabbed the doorknob of the entrance between Mary's and the Swedish Bakery next door and opened it to the stairs up to her apartment, "Osgood being Osgood."

She frowned. If she had locked the upstairs door, which she was almost sure she had, then he could just stand on the landing until she got back. "Smug isn't a great look, Zack."

"Neither is strung out and sleep deprived, but I still love you."

She set her jaw with a tight grin and pulled the Jeep away toward the 24-hour coffee place down the road. On her return trip, she felt a shiver crawl first up and then back down her spine. Cold? The cold of fall? "Just fucking scared," Osgood said aloud. She climbed out of the Jeep. "I think it's an appropriate time to admit that to ourselves."

"Pages are scanning. Thank God we got the duplex feeder," said Zack as she came through the front door.

"Thank *God*," said Osgood, with the type of disdain for the sentiment that could only come from a decade and a half of Catholic school.

Zack either didn't notice or chose to ignore her tone as he held up another sheaf of papers. "These are a bit more damaged, and I don't think they'll go through the auto-feeder. We're going to have to do them by hand." He moved across the living room to the card table he'd set up near the front bay windows with his laptop and scanner atop, as well as two tablets of different sizes on stands.

"Alright," said Osgood, still standing near the door, holding the coffees, wearing her coat. Zack had energy she didn't, that's for sure.

"Oh, and, as you can see, since I am currently inside your apartment, your front door was unlocked. I'm getting you a Bluetooth deadbolt."

"I can't afford that."

Zack looked at her. "Like so many things, Osgood, let's leave its cost and origins a mystery."

She walked over to the table and set down the coffee. "You're in a good mood."

"We found something cool," he said, sipping the coffee and looking up at her with a grin.

"Cool, yeah," she said. She should probably tell him. Though what did it matter? She stared at the papers feeding themselves through the scanner, one page after another, each making a long *reee* sound. "Also creepy, and kinda sad with all the missing kids."

"Yes, creepy too." He stopped, set down the other pages he was holding, and folded his hands in front of his laptop. "Okay, what's going on with you? You're acting…off."

"Besides it just being really late?"

"Or really early, depending on how you want to look at it."

"That song about the Hinterlands," began Osgood.

"'The End of What's Real,'" said Zack.

"Yeah." She looked out the window, at the orange-pink-lit street below, devoid of the comforting movement and traffic that usually filled it, as empty as the nights in her dreams. She spoke carefully. "I think… I know where I've heard it before."

"Well, it was on the radio a ton at the end of the '90s. I remember it even though I was only five or six when it came out."

"Yeah," she said. "But that's not it. I heard it tonight."

"What do you mean?"

"After we left the rest stop, while you were asleep. It came on the radio."

"That's…" Zack began. "Odd. I haven't heard it in years."

"And it sorta brought back where I think I heard it before."

"Are you going to tell me?"

"I think it was playing when I was in my accident."

Zack stared at her, his face betraying surprise and something else, though staying as blank as usual. She could see skepticism, but also

(fear)

concern. He took a deep breath. "And that was in—"

"September of '98."

He nodded, "Song came out…" He picked up his phone.

Osgood didn't need to look it up again. "It hit the top of the charts in—"

"September of '98," he said. He stared at his phone a while longer.

She could see him processing, could almost imagine the flickering red light on the front of her computer as he did so. "I don't know what, if anything, it means. But I do know it's the first new bit of information I remember from the accident in…" She tried to remember how long it'd been, coming up with only, "a long time. And it's the first bit that hasn't constantly replayed itself when I go to sleep. At least, in the dreams that I remember."

"Okay. And you acknowledge that could mean—"

"That it's a false memory," she said. "Yes, fully."

"And if it's not," he continued. "It would hardly be surprising to find 'The End of What's Real' on most of the stations at that time."

"Yes," she said. "Right."

The room went silent. Zack turned back to the computer and tapped a few keys. "Running OCR on them so we can search the documents, and then I'll scrape the names off the front side. With the variances of the handwritten stuff on the back, though, I don't think we're going to get character recognition out of it. We'll have to manually compare those."

She moved over to the couch to examine several of the pages Zack had laid out on the coffee table.

"Those are the most readable," he said. "Legible, I mean. The text is culty nonsense."

Osgood picked up the first of the pages. The text was indeed legible, if hasty, scrawled as though the author had written it in a fury or panic. She looked at the other three on the table. "All of them write it the same."

"Hmm?"

"Their lines, they're the same, despite the size of their writing." Osgood picked up two pages, showing the written text dramatically different in size. She pointed to the last word on the first line, "we've," on one page, then the other. "Here, 'we've' is the end of the first line because it's at the edge of the page. But on this one," she held up the second page, "it's the end of the first line for no particular reason."

Zack nodded and lifted one off the stack in front of him. "Here, too."

Osgood looked at the others on the table. All the first lines ended in "we've." "Is it like a sonnet?"

"If it is," laughed Zack, "it's a bad one."

She held one of the pages in front of her face and affected a dramatic pose. "'He is the only one able to give the gifts that we've long sought. As pilgrims to the distant land, as children to the piper, we've found the way to cut through the noise as he offers out to us the glorious truth that our lives are above. I can't believe my eyes about what I've seen. Only now, after all the time passes that I can understand the truth and can embrace the glory that I see. In time, you shall see, too.'" Osgood nods. "Yeah, that would be a terrible sonnet."

"See?"

"The H in He is capitalized in these two," she told him, pointing at two of the other pages.

"The opening H?"

"No, the one in the middle. 'As He offers out to us the glorious truth…'"

Zack paged through several in front of him. "Some are capitalized, some aren't. Again, really culty. Do you think He is the *big* He?"

"Maybe," said Osgood. "*A* big He anyway."

Zack handed her his red-cased tablet. He pressed his thumb on the device to turn it on. "I've loaded all of the easy scans into this, so you can swipe through it. You can search by pressing the—"

"Magnifying glass?" she smiled at him.

"Yeah," he said. "Now I'm scanning the more difficult pages. Ones with rips or big wrinkles."

"How many more, do you think?" she asked.

"Maybe twenty?"

"How many are here?" She tapped the tablet.

"Fifty-seven."

"So almost eighty of these."

He nodded.

"At one rest stop. Potentially one rest stop of how many?"

"There's 142 on that list. But I don't know if that's all the ones mentioned on the show, and since that was being crowd-sourced, it's likely not all the ones in total."

"Would you mind typing out this text?" She pointed to the handwritten text on the first page on the table. "We could search that. There's no way we're the only ones to actually find these."

"No way at all," agreed Zack. "Though we may be the first ones to take them home."

Osgood's laugh sounded strained even to her own ears. "Like Herbert opening up Tut's tomb."

"Let's hope not." Zack didn't return her laugh.

14

irds began to chirp outside the front windows of
Osgood's apartment. She saw the first blues of dawn
coming from the east over Lake Michigan. Enormous
pendulous clouds hung on the horizon, creating the odd
effect that her science teacher had once called Chicago's
Mountains. Across the room, Zack was sleeping in a beat-up
La-Z-Boy recliner with his tablet face down on his chest.
Osgood took a breath, blinked her eyes to refocus, and
returned to her own tablet, stifling a yawn with the back of
her hand. A horn blasted outside the apartment, and Osgood
leaned out of the papasan chair to look toward the street,
where a liquor distributor was trying to get a rideshare driver
to move so he could deliver his wares to Mary's. Osgood
thought about how many of those wares she would be likely
to taste.

Not many, unless you do some work, Pru.

"This *is* work," she said, under her breath. But the voice of
her mother was correct. Unless she did some work that
produced income, she wouldn't have enough to pay rent this
month, let alone get her car back. "I will work today," she
assured the nagging voice. "I will work today, and everything
will be fine." She got paid by the word, so she wouldn't need
to produce much, and the death industry paid surprisingly

well. Why so many people didn't want to write or edit obituaries perplexed her.

She swiped through the scanned posters again to make sure she hadn't missed anything, zooming here and there on anomalies in the text. "There!" she said, finding another "59" hidden on the page. In all, she'd found nine numbers across numerous pages. Some were almost microscopic, some written then erased, some behind words, some on the fronts of the page, near the missing person's name or stats, but written in the same handwriting as the backs. She had no idea what they meant, but when she'd noticed the number "53" on two separate pages, she'd started looking closer.

That was how she'd powered through, after all. No visits to the crossroads last night. One had to be on their toes for this type of investigative work, and – short of downing a few shots of the Everclear she had under the sink in the kitchen – she couldn't reach blackout with expediency. Staying awake was the second-best plan. Though who knew how long it'd last. Maybe a few shots of NyQuil later today would put her down and out. She only needed three hours, maybe four. A couple decades of night terrors really do teach one to function with minimal sleep.

And a few decades of being a drunken addict teach you to function far better than people would expect, don't they, Pru?

She ignored her mother. To follow that thought down the tracks would cause her to question the thesis entirely. And that couldn't help but lead to the question of whether she *was* actually functioning? Osgood would flippantly tell people she was a functioning alcoholic. They didn't need to know about the Oxy. After all, she did deal with severe chronic pain, exacerbated by a body that had never completely healed due to terrible insurance coverage.

"But that's what bankruptcy is for," she said.

The liquor truck blasted its horn again, and Zack bolted up in the chair, shoving off the blanket Osgood had tossed onto him earlier. His tablet slid to the floor with a light thunk. "What?!"

"Morning," she said.

He blinked and smacked his lips, looking around the room wide-eyed.

Osgood recognized the disorientation. One of the side-effects of being a blackout drunk was often waking up in unexpected places. "Hey, Zack." She waved at him.

He turned to her, squinting in the growing morning light, and his face calmed. "Os," he said in raspy morning voice.

"Os," she confirmed.

"How long was I asleep?"

"About three hours. You're welcome to take the bed if you want to try for longer." She pointed down the hall with her pen. "It's dark in there. Blackout curtains."

He followed the point, then slowly turned back, seeming to notice as she set her pen on her notepad. "Find something?"

Osgood set the tablet in her lap and nodded. "I noticed numbers sorta hidden in the text in various ways. Erased, written over, scratched out. They're on maybe a third of these pages.

"Random?"

"Well, sorta. I don't know what they mean yet, but there's nine of them, some repeating."

"An actual pattern." Zach slowly stood and stretched.

"I don't know. But it's definitely a *thing*." She emphasized the word the way she did on the podcast. A *thing* was what they called it when they had no earthly idea what something was, but it seemed odd enough to get their attention. She lifted the notepad and read off the numbers. "12, 31, 38, 45, 53, 59, 66, 72, 83."

Zack laughed. "Wanna play the lottery?"

Osgood smiled. "You're buyin'. I'm unlucky."

"All two-digit numbers," he said, sitting on the end of the couch closest to her chair.

She nodded. "The most repeated numbers are 31, 53, and 83, with three times each. Only two numbers occurred once: 12 and 66."

"You included the new scans from—" Zack stifled a yawn, pointing his other hand at the scanner on the table.

"I did."

"Nine numbers?"

She nodded. "Eighteen digits."

"Social security numbers are nine digits long, could be two of them."

"Spread out over all these?"

He shrugged. "I'm just guessing. Phone number?"

"Ten digits. Eleven if you include the 1 at the beginning."

"Maybe twelve, if it's another country."

"True, but many countries have zeros in their country code," she said. "No zeros."

"Could be dates." He stood and looked at the pad over her shoulder. He reached his hand out for the pen, and she gave it to him. A quick slash turned 12 into January second, and 31 into March first."

She pondered that for a minute. "It'd be odd to just have one in January, two in March, one in April, two in May, one in June, July, and August. Then nothing."

He snapped his fingers and went to the card table, grabbing his own note pad.

"What?"

"What if it's like chapter and verse?"

"How so, there's only one paragraph."

"With eight lines, right?"

She nodded.

"Eight, three. Not 83."

"Oh!" said Osgood. Both of them took one of the handwritten sheets and started looking at the words. "I'll start from the back."

"Got it."

"Okay, from the back, I got 'see, glory, time, what, I,'" said Osgood.

Zack nodded. "I got 'is, long, land, to, and I.' But it's the same 'I' as yours."

"Land," Osgood suggested, with no idea. "Hinterlands?"

"Maybe." Zack sat back down on the couch, putting the notepad and page on the coffee table. He leaned his head back to stare at the ceiling, reciting the words, all of them, from memory. "Is long land to I what time glory see. See glory time what I to land long is."

Osgood was impressed.

He repeated them again, backward then forward, then started mixing up the words, growing quieter and quieter until Osgood could just see his lips moving.

He is essential, indeed, she thought, then looked back down at her notepad. She re-read the message, then opened a text document with the message typed out on the tablet, line breaks in the proper places.

"I've got nothing," said Zack. "The words don't match each other."

Osgood sighed and tossed down her notepad. "What else?" she asked nobody. "Oh, also, there are some symbols on a few of the pages. Could just be doodles, or even folded overprint. But I made a note of the page numbers and sent them to you."

Zack nodded toward the ceiling.

"'In time, you shall see, too,'" she read. "Promise?"

He laughed, sounding exhausted.

She'd been so excited about these numbers, so sure she'd found something, so looking forward to sharing them, only to reach this point of no pay-off. She rubbed her eyes. Ought to take these contacts out and go back to glasses. She read through the message again, chewing over each bit like a morsel of an exceptionally complex dish. When she reached the end, she moved her finger to turn off the tablet and saw. "Zack."

"What?"

"The message has eighty-four words."

He turned his head toward her.

"The numbers stop at 83, and the message is eighty-four long." She showed him the text-editing app. At the bottom of the page, a word count confirmed it. Eighty-four.

"So, it's not the—" He sat up rail straight. "Right!"

Both of them started counting words, making a note of the number.

"Quit counting out loud, Zack."

"Sorry."

When Osgood reached the end, having written the corresponding word for every number on the list, a chill ran through her. Unlike before, unlike their last cluster of words, unlike the Mazarowski email, this message was unambiguous.

"Holy shit," he said, staring at his own notepad.

She nodded at him and read the message aloud. "'We've cut out our eyes now we can see.' Jesus." She re-read the sentence twice to herself and felt the shudder again.

"Well, that's fucking dark," said Zack.

"Yeah."

"And not the kind of thing that could be random."

"Nope." She walked over to the card table, where the collection of rest stop papers was scattered. "It's also something you wouldn't get with just one of these. Only all of them."

"Like a puzzle that you can't tell is a puzzle until you step way back and look at the big picture." Zack joined her at the table and woke his laptop.

"Most repeated words: cut, eyes, and see."

Zack exhaled sharply.

She rested her hand on his shoulder, feeling the tension in him. She didn't know what to say, what might help, so she just offered, "If you want to take a break for a while, go home…" but he'd already begun to type like the wind on his laptop.

"No," he said flatly.

"Okay, just wanted to—"

"Three hits," said Zack.

"Three—"

"'We've cut out our eyes now we can see.'" Zack turned the laptop toward her, showing her search engine results. Three separate LiveJournal accounts, each containing exactly that phrase in a post, albeit with a comma after "eyes." He clicked through, opening all three in separate tabs.

Flipping between them seemed to not be flipping at all.

All three were defunct accounts, all three had only a single line, all three were punctuated the same.

"All three are from the same date," said Zack.

Osgood leaned forward to look, widening her eyes despite the contacts pain.

Zack saw her strain and read the date to her. "November 6, 1999."

Osgood felt the ground fall out beneath her.

15

"I need you to get me Audrey Frost's current cell number," Osgood said, regaining her focus.

Zack stared at her.

"Quickly, Zack."

"Audrey Frost," he repeated.

"Yes."

"Your old—"

"Quicker than that, Zack."

He held his dark eyes on her for another second, then turned to his computer. There was another pause, like a musical rest, and then he began to type slowly, ramping up to his average speed. Clicking clicking clicking. "Okay, it's 8-4-7—"

She shoved her face toward the computer and began to repeat the number under her breath. She typed it into her phone with shaking fingers.

"Any chance you're going to tell me what's going—"

Osgood loudly shushed Zack and waved him away. She put the phone to her ear and turned away from him, stalking down the hallway to the kitchen as it rang.

"Frost," came the voice, the voice from the past, from a different *then*, the voice of her friend that was.

Osgood froze.

"Hello?" asked Audrey Frost.

"Audrey, it's Prudence."

A long pause. Then a double beep. **Call Ended.**

"Fuck."

"Os," said Zack, from the door to the kitchen.

"This is fucked up, Zack."

"I know," he said.

"More than that, though." She turned to look at him, opening her call log and tapping the number again. She could feel her face grow hot. That date, November 6, 1999. It couldn't be a coincidence. "No fucking way it's a coincidence," she told him.

This time the other line only rang once. "This is Audrey Frost. Please leave a detailed message, and I will get back to you. If you are looking for me in a writing or editing capacity as Audrey Carolinas, please leave a detailed description, and consider no return call disinterest." *Beeep!*

"I *need* to talk to you," Osgood said into the phone, then hung it up and redialed.

"I wish you'd talk to *me*," said Zack.

"Caroline Frost," said Osgood. "Audrey's sister."

He looked at her blankly as the line rang once, twice, three times. Osgood hoped for an answer.

"Hello," in a strong male voice.

"Audrey, I—"

"The caller you have dialed is using a call screening service," the robotic voice continued. "They will get a copy of this conversation. Please tell us your name and why you are calling."

A pause. No beep. Osgood took a deep breath. "I know how you feel about me. This is not about me, or us. This is about Caroline." She paced frantically past Zack as she spoke, back down the hall, into then out of the office. "I'm pretty sure that she disappeared on November 6th, 1999. Confident, actually. And I need you to confirm that because I've stumbled across a weird collection of coincidences, people whose last messages were also November 6th, 1999. And I—"

"Stop."

Osgood stopped talking.

"Yes, Caroline did disappear on November 6th of '99." Audrey's voice was emotionless, firm, clipped.

"Okay, then, I think you need to see some of the stuff we've found."

"We?" asked Audrey.

"Me, and Zack, my—

(partner)

"assistant."

Zack scowled, and Osgood shook her head at him and waved. She could feel tears forming in her eyes. Just at the sound of Audrey's voice. It'd been ten years now? How long since the memorial? And her voice hadn't been so pleasant back—

"Tell me," said Audrey.

"Tell you what?" asked Osgood.

"Tell me what you've found that you think would convince me to see you." Now her voice contained an undercurrent of anger, boiling to the surface.

"Okay," said Osgood shakily, reminding herself not to blow this opportunity. "I'm going to put you on speaker phone."

"Fine."

Osgood set the phone on the kitchen table and pulled up a chair. Zack, still frowning, joined her.

"Okay," she said. "I'm here with Zack Nguyen."

"Hello…" He momentarily looked confused. "Miss Frost?"

"Audrey is fine."

"Audrey."

"Hello, Zack," said Audrey. "Tell me, is Osgood still a drunk?"

Zack looked at Osgood, who stared back at him. "Yes?" he said, his voice pitched much higher than usual.

"Are you?" asked Audrey.

"I don't drink," said Zack.

"How on *Earth* do you stand her, then?" asked Audrey

before immediately dismissing her own question. "Tell me what you have."

"We—" began Osgood.

"I'd like to hear it from Zack."

Zack asked for permission with his eyes. Osgood nodded.

"We got an— I mean— Long story short, we found a possible network of rest stops full of missing posters, and on the backs of those posters were handwritten…prose?"

"Almost like blank verse," said Osgood, wishing she could be the one to explain this. She'd be gentle. She'd be—

"And that blank verse occasionally hid numbers, which, when aligned with the words, held a hidden message. And when we searched that message, we got some LiveJournal accounts with that message. All three were the final posts of the accounts, and all three were posted on November 6, 1999." Zach drew a deep breath, his first of the explanation.

Audrey's voice shook. "And…what, uh, was the message?" At the end her voice went up, almost cheery. An *everything's fine* simulacrum.

Zack shook his head at Osgood.

"'We've cut out our eyes, now we can see,'" said Osgood.

Silence.

Both Zack and Osgood waited. After a while, Osgood thought she might have hung up, but the call duration counter still ticked away, and every so often they could hear breathing. Breathing that sounded like meditation, centering.

Osgood wanted to tell her it was okay, that they could continue this on their own. That she'd just needed to tell Audrey it had happened, this coincidence, and she was sure that was all it was. But she couldn't, because that'd be a lie. Coincidence? Do enough paranormal investigations that turn out not so easy to explain away, they're chock full of coincidence, symmetry, confluence.

"What—" Audrey began, then stopped again. After a moment, she drew a breath and continued. "What have you followed up on, beyond this?"

"As soon as we saw the LiveJournal dates, Osgood called

you." Zack nodded to Osgood, telling her with his eyes to take this conversation over again.

"And what got you onto this investigation of the rest stops?"

"*Across the Backroads*," said Zack.

Audrey snorted a genuine laugh. "The Guardian's show?"

"The path was labyrinth-y," explained Osgood. "But it started with an email."

"From?"

"No one," said Zack.

Another slight waver in Audrey's voice. "What'd it say?"

Osgood told her, the words etched into her memory. "'Mazarowskis idea. Rest stop plees. Drumbeats—'"

"'Find the Hinterlands,'" finished Audrey.

Zack leaned back in the chair, eyes wide, mouth agape.

Osgood's eyes narrowed. "Yes…"

"When did you get this email?"

"Two, uh—" Osgood looked at Zack, who confirmed. "Two nights ago."

"Late," said Audrey.

"Late," confirmed Osgood.

"I want to make myself crystal clear."

"Okay."

"You betrayed me, you betrayed us, you betrayed our audience, you betrayed what we stood for." Audrey's voice held incredibly firm.

Osgood could only nod at the phone. All of that was true.

"But as I received that same email two days ago and discarded it, I think it's clear that we should meet."

Osgood felt the redness in her cheeks, the embarrassment of knowing what she'd done the last time she'd worked with Audrey Frost, the weight of it all, and at once the joy that she'd get to attempt it again.

"I don't want you here," said Audrey.

"I get that," said Osgood.

"I hope so," said Audrey. "I will come to you. Just tell me where."

"How about Mary's, in Andersonville."

"On Clark?" asked Audrey after a moment.

"Yes. What time can—"

"I'll be there at eleven." Double beeps. **Call ended.**

"So…" said Zack, drawing out his O.

"You're going to get to meet Audrey. Please don't embarrass me."

"I was going to say the same to you," he said.

Osgood ignored the dig, whether Zack had intended it as a joke or not. "I need all of it on your tablet, easily searchable."

Zack nodded. "No problem."

"This is," began Osgood, considering the missing people, considering her long-estranged friend's missing sister. "This is big."

16

A ring on Osgood's left hand, a black band, given to her ages ago by someone who cared, someone she loved, clacked against the glossy Formica tabletop. After several clacks, Zack put his hand on top of hers.

"It's gonna be okay," he told her.

She looked at his earnest face. His youth, emphasized by baby cheeks and almost no wrinkles, essayed naivety. Though Osgood thought that might not be exactly fair. How many years did she have on him? Thirteen, right? Enough that she'd seen the man behind the curtain, the real face of the world. "Which part is going to be okay, Zack?"

He opened his mouth, then closed it again.

"Take away this new complication with Audrey, and it's still something…horrible."

When Inez came by for a drink order, she seemed surprised by Osgood's, "Coffee."

Zack mumbled, "Me too," as he stared out the window next to him. Clark Street bustled with activity. People walked dogs. Osgood took comfort in the glorious procession of couples of all stripes who intermingled with the straights one would find not so far south on the Magnificent Mile. Up here, at least, and in Boys' Town, a queer person could feel like they at least partially belonged.

Her tapping resumed.

When Audrey Frost appeared in the doorway, Osgood nearly didn't recognize her. Her old friend once had been what Osgood called Rubenesque (assuring Audrey when she had said it that she felt this to be an excellent thing) and Audrey's boyfriends had called curvy, what the world politely termed voluptuous. But this woman in the doorway looked night-and-day different.

Audrey's hair had been short, cut in a bob around her cheeks the last time Osgood had seen her, at a memorial service that Audrey had refused to attend once she noticed Osgood's presence. This Audrey Frost's hair fell past her shoulders, stringy, and dull blondish. Her skin was pale, as though she'd spent no time outdoors at all this past summer.

How much time did you *spend outdoors, Pru?*

Her cheekbones cut sharp swaths below her eyes, nearly casting shadows beneath. She was still quite beautiful, but severe weight loss had turned her from Rubenesque to almost gaunt and formless. Osgood tried not to focus on her body, so changed; her face, so different.

And what did Audrey think of her? Osgood had worn a dress to the memorial in '09. A full flowing black dress. One of the last dresses she'd ever worn, in fact. But this Prudence Osgood, today, hadn't slept since yesterday afternoon, was devoid of makeup save eyeliner and mascara, her hair a frizzy mess of purple curls on the right and number two buzz on the left. What did Audrey think of this vaguely androgynous queer?

Audrey remained in the entryway, looking at Osgood, expressionless. Osgood looked back, feeling the sadness on her own face.

"One?" asked Inez.

Audrey shook her head and pointed in Osgood and Zack's direction, the back corner, a booth.

Inez handed her a menu and waved her hand in their direction.

Osgood heard Audrey quietly order a bloody mary. Inez nodded and moved toward the kitchen before Audrey stopped her with a touch on the arm, holding up two fingers. Inez nodded and left.

Then Audrey stood mid-way across the restaurant from them, arms at her sides, hands clenching and unclenching. Finally, after a deep breath, she headed to the table. "Hello," she said, in that same clipped voice that had delivered the earlier rebuke to Osgood.

"Hi," said Osgood.

"I'm Zack."

Of course, you're Zack, thought Osgood.

Audrey shook his hand, then after weighing her options, sat next to him on the opposite side of the booth. Osgood nodded. Seemed about right.

Unsure how to begin, Osgood nudged the menu in front of her. "They have great brunch here."

She nearly flinched when Audrey looked directly at her. Her old friend's formerly piercing blue eyes seemed to have faded to a dull sky blue-gray. Had they always looked like that? Or had she just remembered them through the film of...

Love, Pru?

"I want to make something explicit," began Audrey. She turned to Zack. "And I trust you won't take offense, Zack, as this has nothing to do with you and everything to do with your...what, boss?"

"She said I'm essential," said Zack, then immediately seemed to regret speaking.

"Essential," repeated Audrey. "I do not intend to discuss anything with you other than things related to Caroline's disappearance. I've no interest in your life, or in rehashing what happened between us." Another aside to Zack, "Though if you intend to be essential to her for long, make sure she explains it all to you. It would be good for you to know."

Clearly intimidated, he nodded.

"Likewise, I will not be telling you about my life, my husband, or anything of the kind. I'm sure you've tracked down my writing, as keeping tabs on me is probably right in your wheelhouse—"

"Aud," said Osgood, using the nickname almost by default, pronouncing it the way she'd used to: Odd.

Audrey slammed her hand on the table. "No!"

Osgood jumped back, pressing herself into the cushioned back of the booth bench.

"Don't pretend we're friends."

Osgood nodded. She knew it, of course, objectively. They hadn't been friends in sixteen years. Not friends for longer than they had been friends in the first place. Every time, in those intervening sixteen years, that Osgood had yearned for that closeness, she'd remembered the look on Audrey's face when she'd realized she'd been lied to. Hell, scammed. By her friend. By her partner. By her producers. By everyone around her. Scammed in a way that couldn't be taken back. Actual proof of the paranormal? Nah, just your partner colluding with the producers to fake it. Just a hoax. A fraud. *Just like my great-grandparents,* thought Osgood. *The Osgoods are cheats and frauds, willing to ruin lives for a buck.* It hadn't mattered the reason for it. Lies were still lies. Betrayal was still betrayal. Osgood felt the hope of ever rekindling sliding further away.

The three of them sat in silence as Inez brought Audrey's bloody mary and refilled Zack and Osgood's coffee. "Would you like to order some food?"

A stare held between Osgood and Audrey. Zack cautiously said, "I think we're good for now."

Inez left.

"Miss— Audrey."

Audrey turned to Zack and waited.

"Would you mind telling me what happened to your sister?"

"Sure, Zack. I wasn't sure if Osgood had regaled you with this story."

"I haven't," said Osgood.

Half of Audrey's bloody mary disappeared up the straw before she took a deep breath and began. "Caroline is…was my twin sister. We looked identical for most of our lives. She had some difficulties in high school, mostly because I was spending so much time with this one," she poked her finger in Osgood's direction, "leaving precious little for her. She didn't have much of a social life, and I don't think she dated, but she worked hard, and when she left school it was with a full scholarship for a science degree at Iowa State.

"She told me that college would let her reinvent herself. Let her become someone new." Audrey laughed and looked down at the Formica. She ran a finger in a circle. "Told me she would shed her cocoon." The smile lingered for a moment, then disappeared. "It worked, for a while, but she withdrew again, got lonely. We didn't see much of each other that first year. I was at Columbia."

"University?"

"No, here, downtown."

Zack nodded.

"'99 was year three for her, and she'd stacked her schedule, determined to pick up as many majors and minors as possible. She also hadn't come home at all that fall. It wasn't just the class load; there was some friction with my parents. Not fighting or anything, just...they didn't get along great. But she told me she was looking forward to coming home for Thanksgiving, so I thought... I dunno... Maybe things were turning around for her? I was doing really well at school, too, and we were getting traction with our investigations—" Audrey again gestured toward Osgood, casually, but when their eyes met, she turned cold once more. "I'd just met a boy, In September of '99. Well, I mean, I met a man. He was a journalism grad student."

Zack nodded.

"And I'd been spending a lot of nights at his place. You know how it is with new love or passion or whatever. I don't think it was love, but we were so compatible otherwise that —" Audrey stopped herself with a shake of her head. "I'd been staying with him to be considerate of Pru...dence's own sex life."

"I didn't know you lived together," said Zack.

"We did," confirmed Audrey without elaboration. "Caroline had been trying to reach me all week. I had a cell phone then, but didn't have a lot of minutes and didn't always get my messages. It was also irritating because I'd keep telling her to text me, not call me." She looked mournfully at Zack. "Because I'd been so busy. So…distracted. I was selfish."

"I don't think so," said Zack.

"Well on the 6th, early in the morning, I was back at the apartment." She pointed between Osgood and herself. "Our apartment. And she called me. It was, like, three or four am, and I usually sleep like a rock. But the phone woke me, and…" Audrey gulped in air. She moved her mouth a few times as though unable to speak. "She was incoherent. The connection was terrible, and I kept hearing her say 'please,' and 'I can't,' but everything else was either garbled from a bad connection or didn't make any sense to me. Once, she seemed to be speaking Italian. I know she took that as for a language credit, but I didn't know why she'd—

"Anyway. I scrambled to get up and dressed, unsure what I was going to do, even what I could do. Her college was hours away." Audrey poked at her left shoulder. "My shoulder pops out of the socket with almost any pressure at all, and I fell in my room that night, in the dark, and it popped while I was trying to get up. I dropped the phone for a minute or two, but I could hear…something…on the other end. And Caroline crying.

"When I got to the phone, I asked her, I begged her to tell me what was wrong. What I could do. Anything!" Audrey's fingers tented on the table, then tapped once, twice, thrice. "And she said, 'My eyes.' And that was it. My sister was gone. The phone went dead. I woke up Prudence. We drove to Iowa and found nothing in her dorm room. Not even the barest indication that something had gone wrong. She didn't have a cell phone yet. Kept talking about how 'unnecessary' they were." Audrey tapped again, then covered her face with her hands.

"The guard at the front desk of the dorm said he hadn't seen her, in or out," added Osgood. "Seemed to know her."

Audrey nodded from behind her hands.

"The cops found nothing," said Osgood. "Her friends knew—"

"Friend," corrected Audrey, lowering her hands.

Osgood waited.

"She didn't have friend*s*." Audrey pronounced it friend-suh. "Her *friend* hadn't seen her in days. Lived in town. Said she hadn't been going to class either.

"The call on my phone that night was from her dorm line. And we were there maybe…" Seemingly exhausted, Audrey turned her eyes to Osgood.

"Four hours?" Osgood offered.

She nodded. "Four hours later. So the college put out a notice, searched the dorm. They wouldn't consider her legally missing yet, but they looked. Then when the police got involved, *they* looked. There was a lot of nonsense about her being troubled and reserved, and 'maybe she just went off somewhere, did she have a boyfriend?'" Bitterly, Audrey said, "She didn't have a boyfriend. She may not have had friends, but she had *me*.

"Having a twin is different," she told the table, then turned to Zack. "No matter what we fought about, or even when she was jealous of—" again she waved a hand toward Osgood. "We still could talk." Audrey sniffed, then composed herself, wiping her face with a napkin and crumpling it. "After a while, my parents insisted that she was dead. Pru and I kept looking."

Osgood nodded, remembering that time, how tough it'd been. She'd walked with a cane then, only about a year and a half since the accident. They'd interviewed nearly everybody on her floor at the dorm, everybody in her classes, her teachers. Osgood had even interviewed Audrey herself, to see if they'd missed anything.

They hadn't.

"I only agreed to a memorial in 2009." Audrey laughed without humor, taking on the distinct cadence of Julia Frost, her mother. "After all, 'When people have been gone as long as your sister has, they don't just *show up!* You spend your life waiting for the call that they've found a…'" She shook her head. "I wouldn't let them do it, for ten years, wouldn't let them call her dead. But now she's got a headstone out in

Galloway Cemetery. Nothing down below, but it's there. February 23, 1979, to November 6, 1999.

"I fought them so hard on that, too, that they would call that the day she died. My mother called it 'the day she left us.' At least they didn't put 'Died' on the headstone." Audrey fixed her eyes on Zack. "*I* think she's still alive." She poked her finger into her chest. "I think I would...*know* if she weren't."

Zack nodded. "Yeah."

"As soon as I saw those dates, Audrey," said Osgood.

Audrey looked at Osgood without fury, only exhaustion. "I almost called you, too. Really didn't want to, but...almost."

Wide-eyed, Osgood asked, "Why?"

Audrey pulled out her phone, unlocked it, and opened her email app. She scrolled a few times and then showed it to Zack.

"What the hell?" Zack turned to Osgood, shock on his face.

"What?" Osgood asked.

Audrey turned the phone to her. Open on it was an email. *The* email.

mazarowskis idea. rest stop plees. drumbeats .find the hinterlands

"Yeah, the email I got, but why would you—"

Audrey pointed, and Osgood understood. While her email had come from a nebulous @ symbol, Audrey's had come from **Prudence Osgood < .@. >**

Osgood let her mouth hang open. "What the fuck?"

"Indeed." Audrey nodded. "What the fuck, Prudence Osgood?"

🕷 17 🕷

"**I** didn't send that," Osgood told Zack, slamming her fist on her coffee table for emphasis. Down at Mary's she'd denied it as well, and it seemed as though Audrey believed her. Then the subject had turned to what they'd found – the posters, the variety, where they'd been, the likely hundreds more. Now, upstairs, with Audrey having excused herself to the restroom, Osgood felt the need to reassert it. "I did *not*."

"I know you didn't," said Zack, pointing to a command line page full of blocky white text. "It took the same route as your email. A whole lotta obfuscation to ultimately appear to come from…nowhere."

"Then why was my name attached to her sender: nobody at nowhere dot nothing?"

Zack shrugged.

"I'm also curious about that," said Audrey returning from down the hall. "But I'm more interested in the other disappearances."

"Yeah," said Osgood.

"If she wasn't the only…" Audrey flopped into the La-Z-Boy, letting the thought peter out.

For a moment Osgood could see her old friend in there. A different version; not better, not worse. Older. But still Audrey

Frost. Still the person she'd fallen in love with in that confusing junior high way, still the person she'd dated ever so briefly in high school, still the person she'd loved in a far different way from college on. The woman who'd cared for her when her parents wouldn't, the woman who'd investigated with her, written with her, laughed with her. The woman—

The woman you conned, Pru. And lied to and screwed over. The woman whose career you torpedoed because you don't fucking think things through.

She told her inner mother that was *enough*.

"While we were downstairs, I had a little crowdsourced investigating going on," said Zack. His voice took on the braggy timbre it often did when he was trying to convince Osgood how cool something was that she just didn't quite understand. "Looks like hundreds of people disappeared on or around that date. And that number really isn't so uncommon. People vanish all the time."

Audrey threw him a look.

He looked to Osgood for support. "Not...that...we... should be *blasé* about that... fifteen to twenty-year-olds make up the highest number of disappearances, most of which are ultimately deemed runaways. With that in mind, I sorted the list and pulled all names in the fourteen to twenty-one age range, since I noticed those ages on one poster each."

"Wait," asked Audrey, leaning forward to look at the sheaf of pages. "Did all these disappear on— Oh," she said, reading the one on top. "April 2001."

"The dates are all over," said Osgood.

"Details for a lot of these are still filling in, but it seems that most of them just...did not show back up at home, or for work, or for school. Boys, girls, different ages, different ethnicities, all over the country. Alaska and Hawaii included. No commonality."

Zack opened a folder on his desktop. "There are also three that are rather unusual, which I think you might find worth looking into further."

He clicked and opened an image of a blonde girl standing

on a red carpet. She couldn't be more than sixteen, but the dress she wore had a plunging neckline anyway.

Audrey leaned forward. "Is that—"

"Kayleigh Daniels," said Zack.

"Yes!" said Audrey, snapping her fingers.

Osgood had a vague recollection of the girl. "Mickey Mouse Club kid, wasn't she? Turned into a sorta pop-star?"

"If by 'sorta pop-star' you mean gold records at sixteen, then yes," said Zack with an extra dollop of snark. "This picture is 1997. The following year, Kayleigh went through the difficult adjustment to adulthood that a lot of young stars have. Drugs, booze, DUIs."

"At seventeen?"

"Role model, Pru?" asked Audrey.

Osgood scowled but didn't take the bait.

"Her parents had been doing sketchy shit with her money behind her back, and by eighteen most of the money had dried up, and she needed to duck some more aggressive male fans who were thrilled to find her, um, barely legal."

"Men are trash," said Osgood, still scowling.

"Yeah," said Zack. "In September of '99, she goes to this hotel in Paris that I can't pronounce. Blows all this money she really doesn't have on the room. Throws a lavish party, and in the middle of it—"

"She disappears," finished Audrey.

"Well, yes, but more interesting is what happened before she disappeared."

He clicked on another file, filling the screen with a grainy black and white video. In an opulent elevator was a young woman who sure looked like Kayleigh Daniels. Her hair was chopped to just above her ears, almost a boy's bowl cut. Mascara ran down her face. She looked terrified and shook as though sobbing. Kayleigh pressed a floor button, but nothing happened, the doors remained open. She pushed another, still nothing. Another, another, another, until all the floor buttons had been pressed, now lit up in the bottom corner of the video. She stopped and crept to the doors, peering out down the hall, first to her left, then right.

She flung herself back inside with renewed urgency, slamming her thumb against the close door button, over and over and over. She bent over in sobs, then slapped a hand to her face, covering her right eye, her mouth opened in a silent scream.

Suddenly she bolted to the other side of the elevator, flattening herself against the wall. Hiding. Several moments passed, the video appearing frozen until Kayleigh cautiously peered out the doors again. She exited the elevator slowly until all but one of her arms was out of the frame. Then, her arm moved… well, the only word Osgood could ascribe to it was *strangely*.

"What the…" began Osgood.

Audrey stood up from the chair and walked toward Zack and the laptop.

Kayleigh Daniels' arm seemed to be bending in the wrong directions at her wrist and elbow. Then the video froze.

No one in the room said anything as one minute passed, then two. A burst of static, and then Kayleigh was gone.

"What happened there?" asked Audrey.

"No one knows beyond typical speculation," said Zack. "Drug reaction, manic depression, etcetera. There's more though."

He played another video clip, this one of Kayleigh running down a long hotel hallway, mouth wide in a scream, mascara rivers on her cheeks, eyes squeezed shut. That clip ended, and Zack played one more. "Surveillance in the roof access corridor." In the clip, Kayleigh climbed awkwardly up a metal ladder until she left the frame.

"Did she jump?" asked Osgood.

Zack shook his head. "If she'd jumped, someone would've seen her body. She just disappeared. The family used the last of their, well, *her* money to hire a PI."

"Yeah, to get their golden goose back," said Audrey. "Vultures."

"He found nothing," said Zack. "No trace."

"Wow," said Osgood. "I hadn't thought at all about Kayleigh Daniels in so long. Had no idea she was dead."

Audrey snapped her head toward Osgood, and she quickly corrected herself. "Or missing."

"I've seen that video before," said Audrey. "The one in the elevator. During late night searches, it's amazing the rabbit holes you can fall down on the internet."

Zack gave her a vehement nod. "Oh, yes. And speaking of, this next one I'd heard about. It was actually the reason my parents used to tell me I couldn't go camping."

"What?" asked Osgood, surprised to hear herself laugh.

"Three couples, high schoolers from northern Cali, went up into the mountains for a weekend campout." Zack tapped and opened a new picture that showed the couples on what looked like a beautiful sunny day in the mountains. They wore sweaters, but no gloves. All three were grinning for the camera, set askew on a nearby table or rock.

"Shit," said Audrey. "I know this one! Wasn't there an avalanche?"

"Of what?" asked Osgood. "Look at how sunny—"

"They were camping at the base of—"

"A lot of people claimed it was an avalanche, but there's no actual record of that," said Zack, firmly enough to stop them both. "The record *does* show that a wild snowstorm hit the mountain. The next day, their families sent the rangers out after them, and their tent was found, torn open. Ragged. Blood on and in the tent. Blood on the snow. Tracks that just stopped. Rangers wrote it off as a bear attack. All of them gone. This was the last picture on their camera, apparently, found at the bottom of a ravine."

"Right," said Audrey. "I can't remember when I heard about it. Must've been far later, since I was so focused on Caroline. People said they ate each other."

Osgood nodded. "That's what I heard, too. But no one could explain why the last person vanished. He didn't eat himself."

"Well," said Zack, with a tinge of impatience in his voice. "And the last one I already have feelers out for more about. It's MandyCam."

"What is MandyCam?" asked Audrey.

"I know MandyCam," said Osgood. "She was a cute but like…normal-person-looking…woman who live-streamed her life via webcams. Not video, images."

"The software just wasn't there for live video updating back then," Zack explained. "Apparently, one still image update per minute was free on four of her cameras. But if you really wanted the full MandyCam experience, you could upgrade to all eight of her cameras and get updates every ten seconds."

"I did that for a month," said Osgood.

They looked at her.

"What do you want from me?" exclaimed Osgood. "I considered myself a lesbian then, and she masturbated on camera sometimes."

"Oh, Christ, Prudence."

Osgood snapped her fingers at Audrey. "That's enough of that tone. Yes, I fucked you over. I did. You know it, I know it, Zack knows it. A lot of the internet knows it, too. I've done everything I can to apologize to you. I've sent letters. I've called. Sent gifts. Everything. And you just ignore—"

"Betrayal isn't so easily forgiven."

"Fine," said Osgood. "But right now, we're talking about possible leads and connections to your hopefully *missing-instead-of-dead* sister. As a courtesy, we brought you here. You don't need to be nice, but you could try being fucking civil."

Audrey's face tightened.

Osgood held her stare. In her peripheral vision, she could see Zack ping-ponging his head between them. "I fucked up worse than I could've imagined. But right now, Audrey, I'm trying to help. Because I loved her, too."

"Yes," said Audrey, her face still angry, tears in her eyes. She brought her voice back to a pleasant tone. "Please continue, Zack."

"Okay," Zack began again, more cautious this time. "The MandyCam website had some trouble on November 5th. People in her forums (which were hosted by a different provider) started complaining about glitchiness and dark cameras. On November 6th, though, the entire site was gone.

Like, *gone* gone. When people who are curious about such things the way *I* am curious checked in, they found only an empty directory. Everything, every page had been cleared out.

"About a month later, someone posted a picture in her forums of a woman looking out on that hill over Machu Picchu, saying she was Mandy, and everything was fine, she'd gone on holiday, and decided that she needed more privacy. But that turned out to be a hoax, and the Machu Picchu woman wasn't Mandy. Despite the hoax, the idea that she'd shut down her site to return to a life with privacy took hold online and in articles about the site. But there are still many forums and posts theorizing what may have actually happened to her."

"And your feelers?" asked Audrey.

"Well, I know a collector," said Zack, seeming hesitant. "He goes around the internet scooping up shit. And I know he has other cam stuff that he just scraped from back then. So...maybe he'll have hers?"

"Where do you think that'll lead?"

Zack looked at Osgood. She'd always told him to never posit an ending, to follow the clues. After a moment, though, he turned to Audrey and answered. "Maybe she was online that night, and if she was, maybe we can see what happened in those last hours."

18

Eager to focus on something that didn't come with sideways looks from her former friend, Osgood volunteered to talk to the private investigator Kayleigh Daniels' family had hired after the disappearance. Zack's trademark digital witchcraft produced a current phone number, and Osgood retired to the office, closing the door behind her. When she dialed the number, the phone rang and rang. She was about to hang up when she heard the *click* of connection.

"Laughton," he said, his voice betraying decades of smoking. In the background, she heard driving sounds, wind whooshing through windows.

"Hi, yes, Mr. Laughton. My name is Osgood. I'm investigating some disappearances, and I was hoping I could have a few minutes of your time." Osgood's help request voice was well-practiced and effective. She played up feminine tones and delivery, lilted on words, even smiled as she spoke. People had called it disarming.

A long way from the real *you, isn't it, Pru?*

"I have about nineteen minutes before I arrive in Silver Lake. I can give you those."

"You worked for the Daniels family after Kayleigh disappeared."

"Yes," he said, his answer terse.

"I'm not looking for quotes or anything from you, Mr. Laughton," said Osgood, using the name repetition trick. "I'm sure you've had countless media vultures come looking for information on this case."

"I have," he said, still terse, and didn't offer more.

Now give a little to get a little. "The reason I'm calling is that we've found some other unusual disappearances that also occurred on that same date."

"Well," he began but didn't continue. The word had a different cadence than before. Osgood knew she'd, if not disarmed him, certainly surprised him with something he hadn't been told or asked about before. She waited a moment, to let him continue. When he didn't, she spoke again. "Mainly I wanted to know if you'd also encountered coincidences, abnormalities. Things that felt *off* to you, as an experienced private investigator."

Laughton again took his time, and Osgood found herself wondering about his drive to Silver Lake. "Listen," he said, finally. "The whole situation was fucked. I have an NDA from the family, so I really can't say…" He drew a deep breath. "I took the money, I looked for Kayleigh, but I never believed I'd find her."

"Why is that?"

Silence on his end, just the sound of a car driving on a highway.

"Mr. Laughton?"

"When you work for stars, or around stars, you're always part investigator, part fixer. Half of your job is maintaining the agreed-upon narrative."

"Alright."

"And when something doesn't fit that narrative, like a hypothetical star famous for her upbeat, bubbly personality going through a severe depression after her family hypothetically stole—" He stopped and cleared his throat. "That little girl deserved better than she got from folks who were supposedly invested in her best interests."

"Absolutely," said Osgood, unsure what else to say.

"Money, even the promise of money from a family that appeared— People give you things. They act against their own best interests. And when people freely hand you evidence that the police should— What the fuck am I doing?"

"I'm not sure," said Osgood, with a little laugh.

"People don't ask me about Kayleigh, anymore. People have, unfortunately, forgotten about her."

"We started our investigation because of someone that people, the police especially, forgot as well," Osgood said.

Laughton cleared his throat. "Okay, purely as an exercise, let's pretend that we're investigating a missing person and that there's a video of said person appearing to climb onto the roof of her hotel."

"Alright," said Osgood. The word "appearing" struck her as odd.

"And let's follow that up with actually visiting the site and noting that something has been done to the video. That it has been…adjusted."

Osgood held back comment.

"Something that can be seen when you look closer at the background instead of at that lovely girl. I have a daughter her age, you know? She was devastated when it all—" His voice shook. He cleared his throat again and was back to all-business. "That's all I can say. I'm sorry there isn't more I can share with you."

"I understand completely," said Osgood, in her most reassuring tone. "You have been quite helpful."

"Also," he said, a seeming afterthought. "Please don't—" He sighed. "If you find anything about Kayleigh, about what happened to her, would you tell me first? Tell me before you tell them."

"I will," said Osgood. "I promise."

"Thank you," he said, cleared his throat a final time, and hung up. Osgood set her phone on her desk and stared at the **Call Ended** screen for a while.

"Zack!" she called through the door.

"Yeah?" he called back.

"Please send me the Kayleigh Daniels hotel surveillance videos."

"On it."

Osgood turned from her phone and shook her mouse to wake up her monitor. She took a breath, combing through the conversation in her mind. He'd been at the same time forthcoming and not. He could have been leading her away from something, or to it. She always preferred to interview in-person, because unless you could sit across from someone and watch the faces they make as they talk, you could never really determine a motive or what side they were on. The one thing she could be pretty sure about from her call was that PI Laughton seemed to care a lot about Kayleigh Daniels. And he at least had given them something to follow up on.

"You should have them," called Zack from the other room.

Osgood opened her email. The Mazarowski email stood out, several spots down. The email that had come from nowhere. She clicked, instead, on the top one from Zack. In it were three links that started downloads when clicked. The first link was video inside the elevator, the second short clip showed Kayleigh in the hallway, the third showed the ladder and roof. She expanded that final video to fill her screen and clicked the repeat button.

She watched Kayleigh Daniels climb the ladder out of the view of the camera over and over. Just her head appearing in the bottom corner, then climbing the ladder. Appear and climb. Crying; appear and climb.

"Okay," she said to her office. "A young girl in clear distress runs onto the screen and climbs a ladder." Quieter, she repeated Laughton's suggestion, "Look closer at the background and not the girl."

Osgood leaned toward her monitor until she could see the individual pixels. From this vantage, she could study small portions of the screen without being distracted by the big picture. The room looked like a standard utility room, replete with ducts and pipes. Besides the duct and pipework, there wasn't a whole lot to the background on which she had been told to focus.

She frowned, then noticed, "No time and date on the video."

She clicked open the other two, which popped up in separate windows over the full screen. Each of them, in the bottom right corner, had the date 6/11/99 and a running time counter of hours, minutes, seconds. "Huh," she said.

Osgood found herself drawn to the elevator video in the smaller window. Kayleigh's terror, her desperate panic, really hit home. She had felt terror like that. Something coming. Someone. A boyfriend who didn't like that you fantasized about women, perhaps. Beyond threesomes, beyond him, you're not allowed to have your own sexuality.

She moved her mouse to close the window but stopped. Behind the two video windows showing the elevator and the hall, the ladder video continued to loop. She saw the point where Kayleigh's feet disappeared off the top of the screen. The video reset and moments later, Kayleigh climbed through the small gap between the elevator video and the top of her screen. She leaned forward and squinted. In the upper left corner of the video, she saw that what she'd thought was a pipe was, in fact, a broom or mop handle.

She minimized the other two videos and zoomed to two times, then to four. The video's pixels, huge and smudgy at this size, didn't give her a clear view, but when she sat back, what it was showing her became apparent, and what Laughton had told her without directly telling her became evident. In the second drop-down menu, Osgood clicked the rotate button once, and the video became a tall box bisecting her screen, then she clicked once more.

Now, without a doubt, in what had been the top left corner but was now the bottom right, a broom handle leaned against the wall just beneath a calendar with the word November showing above something that she couldn't quite distinguish but was likely a big-titted blonde.

She sat back and returned the video to its standard size. Now, what filled the screen felt accurate but also impossible.

Kayleigh Daniels appeared in the room on the ceiling and climbed headfirst down a ladder until she disappeared off the screen. Her short hair no longer just looked messy; it was hanging down. Climbing down instead of up left the crucial question: Where the hell had Kayleigh climbed down *to*?

19

A knock, then without time for a reply, the door to the living room opened. Osgood looked up from the video to see Audrey standing in the doorway. They eyed each other, each wondering who'd speak first.

"Find something?" asked Osgood. "Because I've—"

"I'm sorry," said Audrey. "You're right."

Osgood blinked back at her, unable to fathom about what she might have been right.

"This isn't about us. You contacted me because of Caroline."

"I did," said Osgood.

"Which is not something that you needed to do."

Osgood waited, thinking it better to say nothing just now.

"I want to be clear. I am not ready to have you as my friend again," said Audrey, stepping into the room and closing the door behind her. She walked to the window and looked out at the street below. "I'm not ready to think of our live episode as anything but a shocking betrayal of what we stood for."

"Of course," said Osgood. "I'm sorry."

"I know. You've said." She turned back around and sat in a small armchair near the window. "I read all your letters."

"I assumed you just threw them away," said Osgood, with a quiet nervous laugh.

"I did at first," admitted Audrey, "but always retrieved them."

"I sent letters 'cuz I figured it'd be far easier to just delete my emails."

"Good call." Audrey allowed a small smirk to cross her face. "I didn't read them until years later. But I *did* read them. You were my best friend, Pru."

"You were mine," said Osgood, a waver in her voice.

"But I couldn't recover from that wound. And it just kept coming back around, too. Whenever I'd get to a place where I thought I'd be respected as an investigator, as a journalist, whatever, someone would say, 'I heard a rumor that you and your partner faked the haunting on your old TV show.'"

Osgood was silent. She'd done everything she could to corral the rumors over the years. The ones that implied a far vaster conspiracy than the banal actuality of the producers of *Chicago Haunts*, their show, attempting to goose the ratings of their big live episode by faking a ballroom ghost. The rumors had hurt her, too, of course. Luckily one doesn't need the same credibility to host a podcast. But journalist... Again, all she could offer was, "I'm sorry."

"And Jesus, Osgood, I think we had footage of a real fucking ghost there, too."

Their video in room 721. The room with a rumored ghost that would nightly uncover guests. Their footage of the rolling back of covers. The footage that Osgood knew, without a doubt, had not been part of the planned hoax. "Yeah, that was real. They didn't think we'd get anything, which is why—"

Audrey waved away the excuse and Osgood went silent again. The general public didn't know the ballroom ghost had been fake, and the episode had been popular enough. But not popular enough to save the fledgling Spooknet channel that had paid for it, or to get it picked up elsewhere. And a couple years after, no less than three variations of the regular-folk-hunting-ghosts formula had popped up across various networks, including even the Discovery Channel. *Chicago Haunts* was just a footnote, and barely even that.

"I'm not sure what I'm saying here," said Audrey, abruptly rising again. "This is not forgiveness."

"I didn't expect it would be."

"But I'm willing to attempt a *détente*; however that might look."

Osgood gave a contrite nod, looking down at her hands.

"Now, you should come out here, 'cuz we've got some things," Audrey pointed at the door.

"Me too," said Osgood. After a beat, she stood and went. As she passed by Audrey, she smelled a scent that plunged her way back in memory. The smell of clean, maybe; of citrus, something. Something that Audrey seemed to produce naturally – she'd always smelled that way. Ever since they'd met. One of the first things that had drawn Osgood to her, in fact, was that scent, like those fruit-scented magic markers they loved as kids. That scent had been one of the first things to produce those confusing tingles.

Her lovely friend.

After years and years of silence, a *détente* didn't feel like merely a bridge. It felt like everything.

🗡 20 🗡

When Osgood returned to the living room, she saw dusk out the windows, and Zack had turned on the lights all around the room. She was struck by the speed with which one loses time when investigating.

"PI Laughton seems to have really cared about Kayleigh Daniels," she told them, "and he wants to know if we find anything. He did tell me to investigate the ladder video further."

"Okay," said Zack. He pulled it up on his screen.

"Flip it over," said Osgood.

"What?"

"The video. Rotate it 180 degrees."

Zack looked at her, confused, then flipped the video. He and Audrey watched it a few times on a loop, not seeing it. Then Osgood pressed her finger to the monitor above the calendar.

"Shit," said Audrey.

"Can't believe I missed that," said Zack, giving himself a smack on the side of the head.

"Can't believe the internet has, too," said Audrey.

Osgood sat on the couch. "That's mine, what've you two got?"

Zack and Audrey looked at each other, both seeming to defer to the other.

"Well," began Zack. "My stuff isn't all that impressive, yet. I talked to Ravager—"

"Ravager?" asked Osgood.

"Ravager," repeated Zack. "Oh, I don't know his real name."

"I figured that wasn't his Christian name," said Osgood.

"He's the collector I know."

"The collector," repeated Osgood.

"Yes."

"Of cam girl archives."

"Yes."

"Codename: Ravager."

Zack just stared at her, then looked to Audrey for…what? Guidance? "It's his—"

"Handle. Pseudonym. Avatar. Yes," said Osgood. "Please continue, Zack."

"Okay," said Zack, eyes narrowed at Osgood. She was sure he thought she was making fun of him. "Well, Ravager does have a data dump of MandyCam's site dated November 8th, 1999."

"Three days after it went dark," said Audrey.

"Yeah," said Zack. "But part of the dump is either corrupt or encrypted."

"He doesn't know?" asked Osgood.

"The translation was odd."

"Oh, Ravager doesn't speak English?"

Zack shook his head.

"He's going to work on it and then send it through tonight."

"It is tonight," said Osgood.

"Tonight…his time. Russia tonight."

"Russia tonight," confirmed Osgood.

"Russians like to hack," said Zack, without a trace of irony.

"This we know," said Audrey.

"But that's promising," said Zack, defensiveness in his voice.

"Absolutely," said Osgood, making sure her own voice was encouraging. "That *is* promising."

"Can't help it if my job wasn't as exciting as a creepy upside-down video…" grumbled Zack under his breath, turning back to his computer.

"Zack," said Osgood. She rose and put her hands on his shoulders.

"I'm exhausted, you know," he snapped.

"I know," she said. "Why don't you order us some Chinese food…"

He narrowed his eyes at her.

"On *my* credit card," she continued, handing him her wallet. She lowered her voice. "Just keep it under fifty bucks?" Then she brought her voice back up. "And then lie down in my nice dark room and nap until it gets here."

He looked between them, then back at Osgood. "Seriously, I've had like four hours of sleep in almost thirty-eight—"

"I know," she said. "Go on."

He stood, and looking back over his shoulder at them, disappeared down the hall.

"Where did you find him?" asked Audrey in a tone of amused dismay.

"When I started the podcast—"

Audrey waved her hands in circles, fingers bent, and affected a rather decent Vincent Price impersonation. "*The Spectral Inspector.*"

Osgood smiled, sheepishly. "Yes."

"That name makes it sound like *you* are a ghost."

"You know what?" snapped back Osgood, "People have said that, but an elevator operator isn't an operator who happens to be an anthropomorphic elevator!"

"Elevator operator?" laughed Audrey. "What century did you die in, Spectral Inspector?"

"Shaddup," said Osgood, poking Audrey's knee.

The gesture silenced both, the first time they'd touched

with affection in so long. The humor left Audrey's face almost immediately.

"My audio was terrible at first," Osgood said, clearing her throat. "Just using that weird microphone that Microsoft used to give out for free with new computers. The one that looks like…" She bent her finger. "A probe."

Audrey nodded.

"Zack was an early listener, and through my online forum, he offered to help me with equipment. His acquisitions seemed a bit shady, but he had the best stuff at good prices. And he kept coming around with more. And then he sorta… stuck around."

"Did you fuck him?" asked Audrey.

Osgood flinched. "No," she said with dismay.

"I don't know how you do things these days," said Audrey. "On that topic, you do know there are dildos in your drying rack, right?"

She'd forgotten the cardinal rule, hadn't she? Always make sure *all* the sex toys are put away before company arrives.

"I have not had any sort of relationship with Zack other than professional," insisted Osgood. She instantly felt bad about selling it short, though. "And friendship." Of *course*, friendship. "He's essential."

"He's good," she said. "He found a lot of connections quickly."

"Well," said Osgood. "We have found—"

"In *addition* to the things you found." Audrey lifted one of Zack's tablets off the table and handed it to her. On the screen was a database, a list of names, ages, and the date 11/6/99 over and over and over. "This is a list of all the people who were reported as having disappeared on the 6th. We're still working on the 5th and 7th, as sometimes people don't know for sure. And this is just the US, not internationally."

"This seems like a lot of people," said Osgood as she scrolled. She looked at Audrey. "Is it?"

"I did some research into statistical data, and it's sorta hard to track down. Seems like over a thousand people are reported missing in the US every day, some estimates are up to two thousand. But most are found. Or just come home and wonder what the fuss was about."

"Caroline's on here?"

Audrey nodded.

"How many names?"

"Eight hundred and ninety-one."

Osgood nodded and continued to scroll. "That's lower than the daily average."

"Oh, no," said Audrey. "That daily average includes children, which is a huge number, adults, the elderly. This is *only* people between fourteen and twenty-one. So it's a lot."

"Is there any way to see how many have been found?" asked Osgood.

"None on that list. Zack had them pulled out," said Audrey. "He had some of his minions or whatever cross-reference. The number was low, though."

"So, 891 teenagers went missing on a single day—"

"Yeah," said Audrey. "And we also excluded those whose bodies were found. These are without a trace."

"I'd guess that's—"

"A crazy statistical anomaly in the missing persons' database."

"Something wrong."

"Yeah."

Having reached the bottom, Osgood began to scroll back up. A name jumped out as she swiped past, and she had to swipe back down to confirm. "Joani Bergdoff."

"Hmm?"

"I remember seeing that name."

"Didn't we go to school with a Joani Bergdoff?" asked Audrey.

"Jessie Berghoff," said Osgood. "But I thought the same when I saw it."

"Where?"

Osgood pointed to the stack of posters. "In there."

"Were any of the people in that stack reported as missing since November 6th?"

"I don't think so," said Osgood. "I would've noticed."

Audrey grabbed the stack and handed half to Osgood. Both of them paged through in silence, and Osgood was reminded of the sound of the periodicals section at the library, almost oppressive quiet, broken only by turning pages.

"Got her," said Osgood. She pulled out the poster. On it was an overexposed picture of a young girl. "Joani Bergdoff," said Osgood, showing it to Audrey. "Disappeared on July 1st, 2001."

"Could be a different Joani Bergdoff," said Audrey. She lifted her phone off the coffee table, quickly thumbing at it. "Okay, a quick search reveals three people with that name, one is eighty-seven and just won $500 in the Orlando Lottery…two years ago. Good for her. One is four, according to a birth announcement, and one is a fourteen-year-old girl who vanished in Utah on November 6, 1999." Audrey turned her phone to Osgood to show a Utah Herald headline proclaiming: "No New Leads in Bergdoff Disappearance." Two concerned parents stood in front of a microphone in one image, the other was the same overexposed picture on the missing poster.

"That's the same girl."

Audrey nodded.

"That means…" she began but wasn't even sure where to go with it. "The date was changed? Wrong? Misinformed?"

"Obfuscated?"

Osgood looked at Audrey. "Pick a name."

"What?"

"From your stack of posters. Any name."

Audrey looked down for a moment, then shuffled through her pages and drew one at random. "'Lakisha Coleman, seventeen, missing since August of 1998, no exact date.'"

Osgood searched the database on Zack's tablet. Immediately, it highlighted "Lakisha Coleman, born May 17, 1981, missing since November 6, 1999."

"Seventeen," said Audrey.

"Another."

Audrey again pulled a page out of the stack. "Tristan Bryant, twenty, missing—"

Osgood didn't need her to go on. "Tristan Bryant, born January 28, 1979, missing since November 6, 1999. Twenty."

"Three could be a coincidence."

"Could it?" asked Osgood.

Audrey glanced at a new poster. "How old was Alana Masterson when she went missing?"

Osgood searched. "Alana Masterson was born April 1, 1984. She would've been fifteen in November of '99."

Audrey turned the sheet to Osgood, showing her Alana Masterson, fifteen, missing since December 20, 2002.

"We need Zack," said Osgood.

"You should let him sleep," said Audrey.

"But he can scrape the names from—"

"You ask too much of people, Pru."

"Do I?" Osgood asked with belligerence just below the surface. "Please don't call me Pru. My mother calls me Pru."

"You used to love being called Pru."

"I don't anymore."

"What would you prefer to be called?"

"Osgood. Some people call me Os."

"Friends?" asked Audrey.

"Some of them, yes."

"Alright," said Audrey. "You ask a lot of him, Osgood. Let him rest. Is it going to tell us anything different if we find two more matches or twenty? This isn't coincidence. This is connection."

Osgood nodded. "Yeah, it does."

"When did *you* sleep last?" asked Audrey.

Osgood just frowned at her.

"I know you."

"I don't sleep sober," said Osgood.

"Well, that's a novel explanation for alcoholism."

"The dreams are constant these days," said Osgood, firmly. "Almost every night."

"Which dreams."

Osgood just stared at her.

"You're still dreaming of the accident?"

"Of the accident, of his head coming off, of that fucking amber beacon. But now, Aud, now I get to stand in the middle of the intersection when it happens. I get to watch his head come off as the cab crumples, I get to see my head get smashed into the steering wheel and my left eye almost—"

"Okay, Os."

The nickname stopped Osgood.

"Do whatever you need," said Audrey.

"I need to work."

"Fine. You check these." Audrey handed half of the posters over to Osgood, then lifted the other half. "I'll do these." Audrey took her posters and one of the tablets and crossed the room to the papasan chair. She flopped into it and tucked her feet up underneath her. In the dim light of the living room, she looked just as she had decades ago, when Osgood had first fallen in love, when they were both young and Caroline was there and all these horrors, all of this life, were nothing more than phantom possibilities, years ahead of them.

How she wished she could roll back the years and try again. Just one more go. She was confident she could do better.

21

Osgood bestrides two worlds, both the living room of her apartment on Clark Street and the crossroads of nowhere. She sees both at once and knows that this convergence is happening because she's descending into sleep. Across the gulf, drifting further away, Audrey Frost sits on a papasan chair in the small nook created by Osgood's apartment's front windows. But the windows are dematerializing, as well as the walls around them. Yet still, Audrey sits, taking page after page off the stack, licking her finger and sliding each page, which scrapes across the one below it in an almost deafening cacophony that causes Osgood to fall to her knees.

Below the beacon.

There's a glow on the horizon to the right, but it's artificial, a factory or mall or sports stadium. Osgood is surprised by it, as she doesn't remember this detail from past visits.

The horrible sound of Audrey shuffling papers draws her attention back to the left, where the windows and walls of her apartment have vanished. The papasan chair containing this lovely woman she used to love, still loves, an end table, and a tall lamp with a beat up lampshade, stand in the middle of a street that stretches into emptiness behind them.

"Apparently this world only has one direction," says Osgood with a laugh.

Audrey looks up. "Hmm?"

Osgood turns to her. "What?"

"Did you say something?" asks Audrey.

"I—" Osgood starts, then stops, looking down at herself. Always exposed here. She covers her nude body. Can Audrey see that? See her? If she can, why hasn't she commented on it? "No."

Audrey looks at her for a moment longer, then returns to her pages, scraping one off and dropping it to her side. The end table has vanished as well, and the page drifts lazily to the ground, where it is consumed by darkness.

Osgood takes a deep breath. "I don't want to be here," she tells the void and notices that the Amoco station has emerged from the emptiness behind her. This time, both her old Skylark and the semi are parked side-by-side.

"If they're both coming from the same direction, they can't crash," she demands to the crossroads itself, to the amber beacon above her. "They can't—" The beacon's *cha-click* is loud and grows louder, flipping from north-south to east-west, then back, forth, back, forth. *Cha-click cha-click cha-click cha-click.*

Audrey peels off another page.

"Audrey." Osgood feels a swell of yearning. She's not sure whether she yearns for when they'd dated, as short as that time had been, for when they'd lived together, for when they'd been partners, or just when talking with each other had been part of their daily routine. Not a day had gone by, back then, where they hadn't spent at least twenty minutes on the phone talking through—

The semi pulls out of the gas station.

Osgood watches it slowly rumble up to the intersection and wait. Holding. Waiting for what?

Can he see me? she asks herself and is surprised to find that she can hear her thoughts externally, not only in her head. Osgood supposes it'd be hard to miss the curly haired wraith, paler than pale, with uneven tits and an overgrown bush that she doesn't bother with because, well, her one-nighters never complain. Surely a truck driver would notice, would look her over, if only to determine whether she was worth the time to catcall.

She walks toward the semi, standing between the headlights, looking up into the cab. She shivers when she finally sees the driver, with that same horrified look that she remembers from so long ago frozen on his face. His eyes aren't focused on her, they're concentrated on the distance, on his crash. He's not here, is he? None of it is.

Audrey peels off another page. The lamp has vanished.

Osgood sees illumination from another set of headlights and turns. A sob escapes her. Now comes her Skylark. The two vehicles have diverged from the Amoco and now come at the crossroads from south and east. That's not correct, though, not how it happened, not how it once was. Hadn't they both just been over—

The Amoco Station is gone as well, of course, replaced by a tent cut to bloody ribbons, on a strange mound of melting snow sending rivers of runoff onto the side of the street.

Both the Skylark and the semi rumble at the stop.

Osgood looks through the Skylark windshield into her own much-younger eyes. The young girl, without a care, behind the wheel. eighteen-year-old Prudence with her newly-purchased Buick Skylark that's only two years her junior, heading back to school much later than she should've been, after a long dinner and hang with her best friend, Aud.

Osgood hears the bassline. Quiet at first, but growing. Then the discordant melody.

"I would cross the hinterlands,
Because the valley's not that far…
The drumbeats in the hinterlands,
Will lead me right to you…"

Prudence reaches forward to her dash to turn it up and the song, *that* song playing on the radio, blasts from the aftermarket speakers of the Skylark. Young Prudence knows the song, too, it seems. She taps her fingers on the wheel waiting, waiting—

Waiting for what? They both are, aren't they? The semi and the Skylark. They're waiting for—

Osgood turns back to Audrey, seeing now only the woman on the papasan chair atop the yellow dashes leading west, the rest of her apartment, her tether to the real world, has receded. When she lets go of another page, it pops out of existence.

"When the memories of our lives fade,
  We return to the valley in dreams,
  Spend our nights in the hinterlands,
  And never have to be alone…"

Osgood frowns. Are those really the lyrics? Or is it just for her? Is this all for her? "Audrey," she whispers, then repeats it, louder. "Audrey!"

Her friend ignores her, or doesn't hear her, just flips page after page; the cataclysmic sounds have faded to a murmur.

"He'll marry us in the hinterlands,
  And we'll never have to return.
  Let the world around us crumble.
  Let the world around us burn."

"Surely those aren't really the lyrics." Osgood laughs nervously. "It was a fucking hit single!"

Audrey has grown thin, nearly translucent, and Osgood can see the connection between them stretched to the breaking point. She calls her friend's name, then screams it over and over, but Audrey pays no mind. Then her friend is gone in the blackness beyond the amber light of the beacon, beyond the harsh headlights of the semi and the Skylark.

Osgood falls to her knees, feeling the pitted rocks and bits of asphalt rip into her naked legs. "Just let it happen," she begs the crossroads. At least when it does, she'll wake up. At least when she dies, this horrible dream ends.

She flings her head back to scream. The beacon above her is gone, and what has replaced it causes her to choke on the scream.

Whereas in the past, the sky above the crossroads has been full dark, no stars, tonight…tonight she can't fully take in the vastness of the star field. Endless and crowded, burning in the heavens, bleeding into one another. Unfamiliar constellations, obscuring or obliterating her comfortable standbys. No bears, no hunters, no sisters.

Beyond, though impossibly close, a quasar pulses and swirls. The spiraling stars and gasses of this galaxy are packed so densely they appear as a single solid, swirling and writhing. From the center of the disc blasts a new beacon of light, still amber, but almost living, crawling, erupting forth from the quasar, aimed downward, directly at her. The pulsing center of a galactic nucleus. She can feel the electro-magnetic radiation vibrating through her body. Again, she wishes, yearns, for the crash, to be crushed between the semi and Skylark, if only to stop the pulsing within her, stop the beam, stop the unfathomable swirling of the quasar above her as it seems to expand. With her neck bent all the way back, she watches the quasar's galactic swirl gathering other stars into its orbit, obliterating many entirely until it has consumed the entire sky in its pulsing, spinning, living horror.

"Come on already!" Osgood screams into its center as it blurs, and she loses focus. Her eyes run down her cheeks, burned out by the radiation belching forth from the galactic monstrosity. "Kill me!" she begs the semi and Skylark. If they'd just hit the gas, just speed through the intersection, this could all be over.

Somehow, she still sees the quasar, even with her neck bent backward beyond ninety degrees, her spine broken, her eyes melted, she still feels it pulsing. The crossroads are gone, as is the possibility of her horrible deliverance via the semi and Skylark. She floats in the Stygian black emptiness beyond the horrible light above. A hole of pure nothingness opens in the center of the quasar's swirling disk, like a great eye, pupil focusing. Osgood again pleads for the end, any end, for release, for relief from perdition.

She falls upward toward the hungry quasar, now sure that what has opened isn't an eye, but a mouth. A hole in space-time. A terrible maw, ready to consume. She can feel the walls of her cells breaking down, nuclei falling through, organs liquefying, decaying, combining. The gravity of the black hole at the center of the quasar tears apart her very molecules. As she falls toward the growing blackness, the event horizon, she slows, the pain growing and expanding beyond her ability to comprehend. She falls slower and slower, screaming louder and louder until her vocal cords snap.

Now she has only soundless screams into the darkness. Osgood yearns for the sweet release of the semi and the Skylark. The momentary searing pain, the crush. The end.

Beautiful friend.

Audrey.

22

"What is it?" Audrey shook her. "Osgood, what?"

"What's going on?" asked Zack in a panic.

Finding her voice at last, Osgood screamed.

"Jesus!" exclaimed Audrey.

"Os," said Zack, rushing to her side. "You're awake. It's over."

Slowly, Osgood found focus and looked between the two at her side, Audrey and Zack, both ashen and worried. She felt her heartbeat return to something resembling a normal rhythm. Each gasped breath burned. Each blink felt like sandpaper across her corneas.

"What do you need?" asked Zack.

"Wuh. Water."

"Got it," said Audrey.

Her eyes hurt so much. She closed them to mitigate. "Glasses."

"Your desk?" confirmed Zack.

"Probably."

Osgood reached up and, with trembling hands, flicked the contacts out of her eyes, sending her into a world of hazy fog, but fog with less pain. She sat up on the couch and oriented herself by the sounds of the cars on Clark outside her apartment, the fan on her computer tower in the office behind her, the music of Mary's night entertainment through that wall.

Home.

Audrey pressed a chilled glass into her hand, and Osgood poured the water down her burning throat, spilling a healthy portion down her chest. She felt it soak into her shirt, icy, bracing.

"Found 'em," shouted Zack from the office. His hazy black and tan form made its way to her side. Rather than putting them in her hand, he slid the glasses onto Osgood's face, and like a camera finding its focal point, everything snapped back to sharp.

Osgood blinked at them. "And that, my friends, is why I aim for blackout drunk rather than sleeping sober." A shot of pain knifed into her lower back, at once icy and burning. She stumbled to her feet. "I'll be back."

"Do you need help?" asked Zack.

"Got this," she said, slamming into the wall beside her hallway. The pain in her shoulder ping-ponged back and forth through her torso, ultimately appending itself to her lower back. She held up her right hand over her shoulder, her left holding onto the wall, and offered a thumbs-up without turning back to them.

First door, closet. Second door, bedroom. Third door she shoved, and it swung open to the white tile of her bathroom. She pushed her way past the sink to turn on the water in the tub. She kicked the door closed, then leaned forward to pull the plunger, and the shower sprayed into the claw-footed bathtub, icy, then beginning to grow warm. She lurched back to the sink and the medicine cabinet above. She swung it open. Pill bottles, pill bottles, pill bottles galore, but no brown bottle with an O on it. The pills were nice, sure, could get her almost there, but without the tincture, without the liquid—

"Zack?!" she shrieked, then tried to steady her voice. "Pain meds."

"Right," she heard him say.

She yanked her shirt over her head with one hand, feeling shooting pain in her shoulder again, this time zig-zagging back and forth between them, crawling right up her neck. Thankful she'd not put on a bra or panties today, making it easy to shuffle out of her jeans and climbed into the tub. She yanked the curtain closed, up to her shoulder, just in time for a knock at the door.

"Bring it," she said.

"Are you sure?" he asked.

"Yes!"

He came in, eyes averted, tincture bottle held before him like a talisman to ward off the vampiric pain.

"Jesus Christ, Zack," snapped Osgood. "Look at me so you can give it to me."

Zack slowly lifted his eyes to her. Upon seeing the protective barrier of the shower curtain, he nodded, placed the bottle in her outstretched hand, and left.

"Thank you!" called Osgood after him. She shakily opened the bottle, squeezed the bulb on the dropper, and deposited drops under her tongue. She knew, almost instinctively, that the first ebbs of pain were likely psychosomatic, but what did she care about the placebo effect if it worked? "Would you pick up bourbon from JJ's, Zack?" she shouted, hoping that it sounded remotely friendly.

"Yeah, yeah," she heard him say. A few moments later, her front door opened and closed.

She leaned her head against the back of the tub and breathed slowly and deliberately, making sure to take the air all the way in and then let it all the way back out. She closed her eyes. In the blackness behind her eyelids, she saw the quasar and snapped her eyes back open.

She noticed movement in her peripheral and swiveled her head in that direction, immediately regretting the action as pain consumed her neck. Audrey stood in the doorway, her face a puzzle, at once judgy and empathetic and something else that Osgood could not place.

"Why not come on in and revel in my pain, Aud?" asked Osgood.

"Why would I want to revel in your pain, Prudence?" asked Audrey, walking into the bathroom with arms folded.

She seemed to catch a glimpse of herself in the bathroom mirror, then she turned her eyes back to Osgood's.

"Because I'm the cunt that ruined your life." Osgood couldn't help but sneer. She'd managed to stay apologetic all day, but the pain seemed to have unleashed bitterness. "Isn't that what you told your mother. Why you couldn't go to Caroline's memorial? 'Cuz you wouldn't be anywhere with the cunt that ruined your life."

Audrey pursed her lips and sat on the closed toilet seat.

They sat in silence, only the sound of the shower running. Osgood knocked the plug into the drain, and the water began to pool beneath her. The warmth didn't always help, but it seemed to move the Oxy through her body quicker. Imagination and perceived effect were potent things. They sat in silence long enough that the tub filled a few inches before Audrey stood back up. She turned away from Osgood, putting one hand on her hip, one on her face.

You've done it now, Pru, said her mother. *I guess* détente *isn't good enough for you.*

This inner chastisement caused her to scowl. "I mean, look at me, Aud. Is this enough for you? Enough punishment?"

"I wasn't punishing you," said Audrey, without turning back.

"Some days I can barely move."

"What happened, Pru?" Audrey turned back around. "You were doing fine. You were healthy. You were on *This American Life.*"

"Turns out repercussions of major car accidents can linger long after the accident themselves," Osgood spat at her, "and sometimes surgeries have unexpected consequences that your insurance doesn't really want to pay for."

"Why the hell are you angry with me?" asked Audrey. She stormed closer to the tub until she stood almost directly over Osgood's face. "You have so much rage in you. And *I'm* the one who got fucked."

"We *both* got fucked, Aud. Turns out when your producer tells you that you're going to help them fake something, whether you actually do or not, you probably aren't going to come out of it well. And when rumors of that hoax resurface periodically, Ira Glass and NPR don't want to take your calls anymore."

Audrey stared at her, waiting.

Osgood stared back with intensity for as long as she could manage. Then, as always eventually happened, the pain pushed through, and she closed her eyes, leaning her head back against the side of the tub. How many drops of the tincture had she taken? Three? Four? Well, then, she could do at least one more. She dropped another under her tongue and screwed the top back on.

Audrey snatched the tiny brown bottle without a label from her hand and studied it. "And this is—?"

"An exit strategy?" laughed Osgood. Seeing the deep frown on Audrey's face, she poked further, "In case of emergency, 'Drink me.'"

Audrey set the bottle on the sink and folded her arms again.

"What? Not funny? Like <u>Alice</u>— Never mind. It's Oxycodone."

"Looks nice and prescribed."

"I'm right out of health insurance at the moment. Also, money." Osgood shook her head. "Don't fucking stand here in my bathroom while I'm trying to manage *severe* pain throughout my body and judge me for how I cope. I also smoke pot and drink. Have problems with that too?"

"Actually," said Audrey, "The pot would be preferable to Oxycodone, as far as I'm concerned."

"It's more a yes, and?" Osgood shrugged, a gesture that made her cringe from the pain but felt worth it. "And I didn't ask."

Audrey's jaw clenched. She held it for a moment, then sat, cross-legged, next to the tub. "I don't know what to do, Os." She covered her face in her hands.

The sound of her chosen name felt like a blow to the gut. Osgood could feel tears in her eyes and was thankful for the splash-up from the shower across her chest.

"I don't know if you noticed," said Audrey without looking at her, "but I'm not so healthy either."

"You've lost weight."

"Yeah," said Audrey with a laugh. "Weight, hair, muscle. At one point I weighed ninety-seven pounds. Can you believe that?"

Osgood couldn't, but said nothing.

"I work from home now. Conduct all my interviews over the phone. Apparently, I was making people uncomfortable. They'd call my boss to ask if they could recommend a good oncologist."

"And were you sick? *Are* you?" asked Osgood, regretting how confrontational it sounded.

"I take eight pills a day for mental health," said Audrey.

"Five," said Osgood. At Audrey's eyebrow raise, she added, "A local clinic will see you for free if you don't have insurance."

"That's good," said Audrey. "Well, it has taken me the better part of six years to get anywhere near balanced."

"And are you balanced now?" asked Osgood.

"Is that a crack?" asked Audrey.

"Honestly, no," said Osgood. "It isn't."

Audrey evaluated Osgood's assurance, then held up her hand and tilted it side to side. "Better than before the medication, for sure. Do you know what I did instead of going to Caroline's memorial?"

Osgood shook her head.

"First, I went to Harold Laudermilk's place."

"Eew," said Osgood, "Why?"

"Because I knew he'd fuck me."

"I know a *lot* of people who would fuck you that are—"

Audrey plowed through. "*Then* I went to my mother's and dug out Caroline's boxes from storage in the basement. I scoured through them. I thought maybe something, anything…"

"Was there?"

"What?"

"Anything?"

"Nothing helpful. But there was plenty in there that scared the hell out of me. Stuff I hadn't seen before. Put this pit…" She pressed her fingers against her diaphragm.

"Dread."

"Yeah," said Audrey. "Dread. And that's what I'm feeling now, with all this stuff. I could easily dismiss it as coincidence or irrational, but—"

"Easily?"

"Okay," conceded Audrey. "Maybe not *easily*. But I feel it. Right here. Dread. That shit with the campers, and that girl climbing upside-down on the video."

"Dread," repeated Osgood.

Audrey nodded.

"Maybe we can," Osgood slowly suggested, "*not* jab at each other."

"That'd be good." Audrey put her hand on Osgood's arm. "I will do my best."

"I'll do mine."

"Do you want me to leave you to soak? Or would you like to continue to investigate?"

"*Would* I?" asked Osgood, phony joy in her voice and an enormous fake smile on her face.

"Shall we?"

She nodded.

"I can help you," said Audrey. "Not like I haven't seen you naked before."

Osgood frowned and looked down her body, at the raised white road map of old scars on her stomach and thighs. Audrey would surely notice those, would judge, would say something, and they'd be right back where—

"C'mon," said Audrey, standing and reaching out her hands. "Let the broken help the broken."

Osgood reluctantly took those hands and shakily stood. She felt the pain still, radiating up and down from her lower spine, but the whole sensation had become muted, nearly manageable. For now, at least.

Sure enough, Audrey's eyes paused as she gave Osgood's body an unconscious once-over. "Things are rarely easy," she said, wrapping Osgood in a towel that'd been hanging over the radiator. So warm.

"I couldn't agree more," said Osgood.

Audrey dried her off, wrapping her arms around Osgood in the process. For a moment, Osgood could believe that this was a real embrace, the love of a friend. For a moment, she felt Audrey pause and hold, and thought her old friend might feel the same way.

☄ 23 ☄

"Have you notated the symbols anywhere?"

When both Osgood and Zack turned to look at Audrey, she held up one of the pages and pointed. On the edge, in blue roller-ball pen, was a small arc and a dot, cut off by the end of the paper.

Osgood opened her mouth and closed it again. She'd noticed them, yes, but not— "Honestly I'd forgotten about what I saw. I assumed they were bits of the numbering thing that got cut off. That could be a three or—"

"Two."

Thank you, Zack, thought Osgood.

"There aren't many," said Audrey. "But I've seen them on a few edges. Including what's…" she flipped through pages at her feet until she found one and showed them. "…possibly a star?"

"Are they all on the edges?" asked Zack.

"No," she said. "Some just sort of stop in the middle of the page, like this one." She held up one, with some sort of geometric pattern beginning just above the image of a young boy, and tapped it. "There's like a shadow along here."

"Where another page covered it."

Audrey nodded.

153

"Zack," said Osgood, "Did you assemble the big photos of the board?"

"With all of them?" he asked. "Yeah."

"Can you put it on the projector?" asked Osgood.

Zack nodded and futzed with some cables, connecting his laptop to his video projector on the shelf.

Osgood reached up and snapped the lights off, plunging the room into twilight darkness, still lit in reds and oranges from the streetlights and Mary's neon outside. She heard Audrey mumble something under her breath, and then the brilliant white light of Audrey's phone flashlight pierced the dimness.

The projector began to cast a faint blue rectangle on the wall as it warmed up. The box became brighter and richer.

"We're looking for Melanie Kurtzleben," said Audrey, standing with the paper. She walked into the beam of light as Zack's computer monitor appeared, and he dragged the image window over. Audrey stopped abruptly. "Jesus," she said.

"What?" asked Zack.

"It's…"

"Overwhelming," suggested Osgood.

"Yeah." She moved closer to the image. "Can you focus it a bit more, Zack?"

He adjusted, first the wrong way, taking it so far out of focus Osgood had to close her eyes, then back, showing the image in sharp enough relief to see the edges of pixels.

Audrey leaned in, turning to look across the plane of the image, so as not to block the projection. "I see one!"

"Melanie?" asked Osgood.

"No, something else." She put her finger up to the wall, where a small symbol appeared. Suddenly, everything tripled in size.

"Whoa, Zack!" called Osgood.

Audrey pulled her finger back as though she'd been bitten by the image.

"Sorry," said Zack. "Zooming in."

The rectangle on the wall now showed only a handful of

the posters, and the symbol appeared much larger. He drew a red circle around it.

"Can you screen-shot that, Zack?" asked Osgood.

"I'll compile them, sure," he replied. "Zooming out!"

The women braced themselves as he clicked, and the rectangle showed the full breadth of the posters once again.

"Two down, three from the left, Zack," said Audrey.

A small red circle appeared on what looked like no more than a smudge to Osgood. She rose and stood opposite Audrey, with the projector's beam cast between them. Now she could see the symbol, circular, like a nearly complete crescent with a diamond on it. "How'd we miss that?"

"It's on the corners of three separate pages," said Zack. "These were not meant to be found."

"Got one!" Osgood exclaimed and crouched.

"Where?" asked Audrey.

"Six over, one up," said Osgood.

Audrey leaned in to see it closer. Papers fell from her hands. "God," she said.

"What?" asked Osgood.

Audrey reeled back from the screen.

"What is it?" asked Zack.

She rushed to her messenger bag and pulled out her own tablet. Her voice shook as she requested, "Zoom please, Zack. Closer than before."

Zack tapped on the track-pad, and again the image lurched forward. Osgood wished she'd closed her eyes this time. Now only part of three different posters appeared on the screen, another symbol spread across all of them, perhaps no larger than a centimeter in real life.

"That's it," said Audrey. Her tablet cast its own blue glow on her face.

She brought it up and held it next to the deliberately drawn symbol spanning multiple papers. Sure enough, that symbol matched the one on Audrey's tablet. The one on the tablet appeared slightly washed-out, rough, painted broadly, with paint splattered around it.

"It matches," said Audrey. She took several rapid breaths and moved away from the screen, collapsing onto the couch.

"Audrey," said Osgood, going to her. "Aud."

The lights snapped back on. Zack stood by the switch, looking at them with worry.

"It's one thing to think that this might be related and another thing entirely to have evidence." Audrey's words came out stilted and shaky. She brought her knees up to her chest and rested her cheek on her right knee. "Something happened, something bad."

"We think so too, but—"

"To Caroline," Audrey snapped at Osgood, then returned her cheek to her knee.

Osgood looked down to the floor where Audrey's tablet lay. She lifted it cautiously, looking at the painting of the symbol, a sigil with arcs and crescents offset, lines emanating from the interior, some pointed.

Osgood felt her stomach lurch as she realized how much it looked like the quasar of her nightmare. She swiped it away. The next image showed a fuller view of the painted sigil. Nearly floor to ceiling, on a wall of white-painted concrete bricks, the sigil bled black drips. On the floor in front of it were the tools of the painting: a bucket of black house paint and a broad brush lying on the linoleum floor, a pool of black spreading from it.

"Caroline painted that on the laundry room wall in her dorm building," said Audrey. "I mean, they never directly identified her as the vandal, but after they found the other paintings, there couldn't really be much doubt."

Osgood swiped backward through the images, finding various versions of the sigil, rougher, less cohesive, as though each time she drew or painted it, she got closer. Each one became more refined. As Osgood swiped backward through the process, the sigil lost its structure and form. It moved through various mediums, from white canvas to paper in watercolors, even ink on corrugated cardboard.

"The university found her art when they began to remodel the art department and had them all sent them to my parents. They got stashed in the basement with Caroline's other belongings. All her belongings, actually. Packed up her entire room, as though she'd never been there." Audrey gasped in air, still shaky. "The student who found the paintings remembered the vandalism in the laundry room and included a picture of that as well."

Osgood nodded, swiping back further. In one image, various tiny versions of the sigil appeared haphazardly everywhere on a sheet of college-ruled notebook paper. No two attempts were identical, but all were similar enough to be recognizable as part of a whole. She swiped back a few more pages, and the sketches became less and less alike, more and more like the doodles she used to make in her notes margins while zoning out in class.

Three more swipes confirmed what she had in front of her. "These are notes from one of her classes."

Audrey nodded sideways, twisting her cheek against her knee. "Anthropology 201."

Among the notes, growing less shaky and scattered as Osgood moved backward in time, were small proto-sketches of the sigil here and there, in margins, at the top of the page.

"I'd never looked before because it's all normal in the front. I mean, real anthropology notes. But the last page." Audrey didn't look up.

Osgood swiped through the legit notes until reaching the last one with text. In the middle of a paragraph about language emergence among undiscovered tribes were the words "The Records Lie." Each word capitalized, the entire thing underlined. Then the paragraph continued as though nothing was amiss.

"What records?" asked Osgood.

"What?" asked Audrey.

"'The Records Lie.'"

"I don't know. I thought it might be related to the class, but a few pages earlier, in all caps, she wrote 'TRUST THE RECORDS.' In her diary, she mentioned looking through school history, so maybe that?" suggested Audrey, finally picking up her head.

"There's nothing like this in her diary? The symbols, etcetera?"

"No," said Audrey. She reached out her hand for the tablet, and Osgood handed it to her. "Just this," she continued and opened another image, handing it back to Osgood.

"'I have to,'" read Osgood. She noted the date at the top of the page. "November 6th."

"There's one other collection of notes that descend similarly," said Audrey. "Look at the History of War notes."

Osgood tapped to open a different gallery.

"All the way at the end," said Audrey.

Osgood swiped through copious pages of tight and neat notes that loosened as she went. Again proto-sigils began to appear in the margins. Another reference to lying records. The final swipe, though, was what caused her to drop the tablet.

"You two really need to take better care of—" Zack began.

Osgood stared at the scribbled blocky text. Clearly written in a hurry, but intended to fill the page, was a warning. "'Beware the Lord of the Hinterlands,'" read Osgood. Below the word Lord, a tight and carefully-drawn variant of the sigil.

"I assumed it was because of the song," said Audrey. "I'd completely forgotten. That's in the email, right?"

"In the email," said Osgood, "yes."

"What song?" asked Zack.

Audrey, fortified by being asked to talk about something

other than her sister, waved her fingers as she thought. "It's called…"

"'The End of What's Real?'" asked Osgood.

"No," said Audrey.

Osgood felt her chest loosen a bit.

"From the album before that one."

"But the same band though?"

"Yeah," Audrey narrowed her eyes at Osgood. "What aren't you telling me?"

"The song 'The End of What's Real,'" said Osgood.

"Yeah, by In the Shallows," confirmed Audrey. "That's from their last album, I don't remember the name."

Zack, at his computer, offered over his shoulder, "*Ramparts Over the Hinterlands.*" He pointed to the screen. "I have their discography up here."

"The album before that," said Audrey.

"*Tether,*" said Zack.

"There's a song about the lord of—"

"'The Wise Lord of Hinterland,'" said Zack.

"Land," repeated Osgood. "Not lands?"

"Land."

"That's it," said Audrey.

"I've been hearing 'The End of What's Real.' It played in the car on the way back from the rest stop. It's played in my dreams. And I'm pretty fucking sure it was on the radio when I had my accident."

Audrey seemed less impressed than unsure what to say. "They were a popular band. I think that album had come out earlier that summer. The summer before—"

"*Ramparts Over the Hinterlands,*" said Osgood.

"Yeah," Audrey said. "I think the symbol is far more—"

"Guys," said Zack, pointing at the now much dimmer rectangle on the screen.

"I'm not a guy," said Osgood, more reflexively than intentionally. She looked at the screen and saw an image of medieval-looking fortifications over a darkened forest expanse. Above the trees, emerging from darkness, the album title appeared as *Ramparts Over the Hinterlands.*

Zack lurched them all forward with a zoom to show the edge of the band's name, In the Shallows. Behind it, almost obscured, flew a midnight blue flag, and on that flag, they saw:

"The sigil of The Lord of Hinterland," said Osgood.

24

"First, I wanna say that this doesn't make *any* sense," said Zack.

"Nice preface," said Osgood.

"It would appear that none of the songs or albums by this band, under the name Rhapsody in the Shallows or In the Shallows, are online."

"What about the streaming music services?" asked Audrey.

"Nothing."

Osgood laughed. "How about the piracy sites. Like the newsgroup thing you wanted me to join?"

"Tried to *help* you join so you could get—" Zack shook his head. "Listen to me. In the Shallows, in both of their incarnations, are not online at all."

They stared at him.

"How is that possible?" asked Audrey.

"Well, it seems partly because the band never allowed their work to be officially released on anything but vinyl..." said Zack, bringing the band's info page back up.

"Why would anyone let them be so esoteric?" asked Osgood.

"Partly because the publisher..." Zack drew the "r" out while he tracked down the name on the page, "Gloria Mundi

Records, also seems to be shockingly litigious when it comes to keeping their music off streaming, tube sites, and bit torrents."

"But still, though."

"I know," agreed Zack. "Remember when I prefaced with, 'this doesn't make *any* sense?'"

"Can you get a high-resolution version of the cover of that album?" asked Audrey. "The *Hinterlands* one. I want to see if there are any other symbol connections."

"In every single image search, there's only this one, and it's 500 pixels square." Zack tapped his monitor showing a grid of squares showcasing *Ramparts Over the Hinterlands'* cover art. "I think we got lucky recognizing the sigil. If we want to scrutinize further, we'll probably need to get the album itself."

"Is that the best research direction?" asked Audrey.

Osgood turned to her. "I'm all ears for a better one."

Audrey frowned. "No, I just— I can't see what a pop band from the '80s and '90s could possibly have to do with—"

"We're following leads from an email from nowhere, Aud, full of nonsensical phrases, that led Zack and me to a rest stop in Wisconsin and then to the date your—"

"Okay," said Audrey, holding up her hands. "I get it. It doesn't make sense—"

"None," confirmed Zack.

"But I get it," finished Audrey. She looked at her phone. "Listen, it's after ten. I think we could all use sleep, probably a shower, and some downtime."

Zack nodded, his head bobbing so quickly it looked like it might fall off.

"Shall we rendezvous back here in the morning?" asked Audrey.

"I'll certainly be here," said Osgood. "Are you sure you don't want to keep working the—"

"Os," said Audrey, putting her hand on Osgood's shoulder. "Exhaustion won't help. What *will* help is me coming back in the morning with donuts and coffee. I will also stop at my mother's to see if Caroline had that album."

Audrey held her hand there a moment longer, looking sadly into Osgood's face.

Should I say something? wondered Osgood. *Is she waiting?*

If she had been, she waited no longer. "Nice to meet you, Zack. Big first day."

Zack agreed. "See you tomorrow."

Audrey left, with Zack following her to the door. He juggled his shoulder bag and tablet. "The bourbon is on the kitchen counter. I put your tincture bottle back into the medicine cabinet. You should know that it's low. I don't know how or where you get it, but you probably should get more."

He looked at her the way Audrey had.

"What? Is everybody pitying me tonight?"

Zack looked at his shoes. "I haven't seen you so bad, like yesterday, like today."

"Oh, c'mon," said Osgood. "I wasn't that much worse than—"

"You were." He took a deep breath. "I've got your back, Os. But you have to share what you need with me."

Osgood nodded but looked away.

"I have a TENS unit," he offered. "You could try it if you wanted."

"Why do you have a TENS unit?" asked Osgood.

"My mother used it. She had chronic pain."

"What stopped hers?" asked Osgood.

"Dying," said Zack. He nodded at the floor, then left, leaving Osgood with her mouth agape. *Catching flies, Pru?* How had she not known that Zack's mother was dead? Did they really not talk about their lives that much? Should they—

Osgood could feel the march of exhaustion up her spine, along with the endless returning ache. "Death *would* stop it," she said, allowing a morbid laugh that she'd never have loosed if Zack were still there.

Considering him, though, she turned the deadbolt on the door and slid the chain into the latch. The only real dangers, after all, were already inside with her.

⚔ 25 ⚔

The front door buzzer was ungodly loud. Osgood opened her left eye just a smidge while squeezing her right shut hard. Living room. Daylight. She'd made it the whole fucking night! Slept straight through. Sure, it'd taken three doses of NyQuil PM, but it had worked! *Can't do this every night, Pru. You're busy enough damaging your liver through other means...*

"No hangover, neither," she said aloud, ignoring the voice in her head.

The front door buzzed again.

"Yeah," she said, smacking her dry lips. "Yeah."

On shaky legs, she rose from the La-Z-Boy and immediately crashed into the side table, knocking it and a glass of water to the ground.

"Fuck me," she grumbled as another buzz sounded. "I'm fucking coming!"

She tried to step over the growing puddle of water, but her equilibrium failed her, and she put her left foot into its center. Her sock sopped up enough of the liquid to squish as she walked to the door. She pressed the buzzer, undid the lock and the chain, and staggered her way down the hall to the kitchen, ricocheting off the walls as she went. Only one framed photo crashed down. One of her and Yann and Carla

165

at the Botanical Garden, when they'd just started dating. She looked at it, a trace of melancholy hitting her, then continued down the hall.

"No hangover," she told herself in the kitchen. "Just a loss of bodily control. No big."

She snatched a large dishrag off the counter, noting the dildos still in the drying rack, and focused on returning down the hall without hitting another wall. She hugged the wall opposite the shattered photo, knowing it was impossible to tell when tiny shards of glass were afoot. "Until they're in your foot," she said with a pallid laugh. Then she flung open the front door.

"How did you sleep?" asked Audrey as she stepped inside.

Osgood blinked at her, seeing a woman far different from the day before. Color had returned to her face, whether via nature or makeup Osgood couldn't be sure. Her hair shone. Her clothing looked more put together, less *I'm going to visit the woman who fucked me over, so I don't give a fuck* lazy.

"What?"

"You look," began Osgood, growing immediately self-conscious about the thought. She wondered how it'd be received. *Already halfway there, Pru. May as well say something nice.* "Good. You look...really good."

"Thank you," Audrey replied. Her smile seemed genuine, if still cautious. "You look like you didn't get much sleep. Or are hung-over."

"No to both!" said Osgood, shooting her wavering finger into the air. "Lots of NyQuil produced dreamless sleep. Or at least, blackout. And who cares, one or the other."

Audrey nodded. "*Might* want to find some alternative methods to cope with your dreams."

"Your concern is noted," said Osgood, echoing Audrey's tenseness. "Remember our agreement."

"I do." She held up an oversized shopping bag. "I have things."

"I'm hoping for the promised donuts and coffee."

"Those are two of the things," replied Audrey. She lifted a box of donuts and a boxed coffee dispenser out of her bag.

Osgood reached to take them from her, but Audrey moved away. "How about you let me set them down."

"That's fair."

Audrey walked around the couch and set the donuts and coffee on the coffee table. "You know your floor is wet," she said, lifting one of the rest stop papers out of the puddle.

"Shit," said Osgood, noticing the dishrag still hanging over her shoulder. She grabbed it and tossed it into the puddle.

"No, no," said Audrey, "allow me."

Osgood swallowed a snide retort and went to the kitchen for mugs. She impressed herself by making it all the way there without crashing into or breaking anything. As she took mugs out of the cabinet, she heard the buzzer again.

"Can you—"

"I've got it," called Audrey.

By the time she returned to the living room, Zack crouched just inside the door removing his shoes. "How did you sleep?"

"Fine. It was fine. I'm fine." Osgood gave them both a tight smile, feeling the tension headache beginning. Some caffeine should do the trick. She handed them each a mug, then walked around to where the coffee sat and poured herself a cup, leaving it black as a moonless night, the way someone she'd adored used to order it. "There's glass in the hallway," she told them and leaned herself back in the La-Z-Boy, wishing she'd brought her tincture with her. She could always send Zack. *You might* ask *Zack, instead of sending him, Pru.* Yes, she would ask him.

"Why is there glass in the hallway, Os?" asked Zack.

"Picture broke."

"How did the picture break?"

She didn't like his tone, that of a man with his hands up trying to slowly guide a jumper off their ledge in a way that won't make a mess. "Pictures break. The world is an imperfect place."

Zack's expression remained tense as he set up his laptop on the table. He put both of his tablets down and then sat, facing the room. Audrey took a seat in the middle of the couch, gathering the rest stop papers together into a neat stack, leaving the one that'd been in the puddle to dry.

"So," said Osgood, clapping her hands. "You both insisted I needed sleep, and I slept. Therefore, I am no further along in this investigation than when you left here last night. I'm hoping the case is different with the two of you. Who wants to go first?"

Audrey and Zack looked at each other.

"Do you have anything?" Audrey asked Zack.

"Yeah," said Zack, a certain reluctance in his voice. Audrey ceded the floor to him. "The Ravager managed to restore some of MandyCam's photo collection and site posts from those last two days."

"That's good. Anything of value?"

Zack silently lifted his tablet off the table, tapped the screen, and turned it toward them.

On a loop, four photos played through a grim animation. The images were grainy, black and white, with the telltale gradation of night-vision. On it, a woman stood, nude, facing away from the camera. Her hand at first hung at her side, but in the following frames, she swung her hand up toward her unseen face. The animation repeated. Again, and again.

"Wuh—" said Osgood, not sure what to ask.

"These are the last four images from MandyCam's broadcast," explained Zack. "This is the last camera she appeared on. It's an image every second. I think she has scissors in her hand."

Osgood leaned closer and watched as Mandy's hand jerked up to her face. The flash of brightness in the arc did indeed look like a pair of scissors as much as it looked like anything. What concerned Osgood most, though, is that when the scissors returned to her side in the final frame, the blades were black.

"Did she just stab herself in the face?" asked Audrey, her voice anxious.

"Her...*eyes?*" intoned Zack, with oozing emphasis on the word.

"'We've cut out our eyes, now we can see,'" said Osgood.

Audrey leaned back, sinking into the couch. Her hand went to her cheek.

"That's not all," said Zack. "Mandy spent a lot of time outside the range of the cameras in the twelve-ish hours after she woke up on the 6th. Ravager said she'd built in safe zones, where she could get away." He returned to his gallery and pulled up another camera. "This is three hours earlier."

Mandy stood fully clothed and lit in what looked like a den or living room. The view was still of her back, jeans and a t-shirt with an enlarged neckline that hung off one shoulder. She stood uncomfortably close to the woofer of a large wood-trimmed speaker, staring into it. Minute movements of her shoulders were all they could see between frames. Next to the speaker sat a turntable with a record on it.

"Listening to music?" asked Audrey.

"In the really bad-for-your-ears way?" offered Osgood.

Zack nodded. "The record is spinning. I can only tell that by the logo's location around the spindle. But the point is, she stood here for literally ninety minutes or so."

"That's not just a few frames cycled?" asked Osgood.

"No," said Zack.

"Creepy," said Osgood, as matter-of-factly as she could.

"Then she takes the record." Zack swiped, and they saw the stuttery animation of her taking the record and walking out of the room. "And disappears for another hour or so. Before showing up naked in the bedroom."

He swiped the screen again, showing a desk with an old iMac on it, but no Mandy. "I *think* she's on the phone here." He pointed at a phone cradle without the handset on it. "This is timestamped to just before the bedroom."

"Any idea what she was doing between the two?" asked Audrey.

Zack shook his head.

Osgood leaned forward. "What about the day before?"

"The 5th looks like a normal day on MandyCam. She had

breakfast, worked on her computer, had a quickie with her boyfriend at lunch, worked on her computer again, masturbated, and went to sleep."

Audrey rolled her eyes. "Some of that had to be performative."

"By this point, she was taking home thousands per month off subscriptions to the one-image-per-second feeds."

"Man," said Osgood. "Maybe I should put up cams and charge people to watch me have night terrors."

"It was unique then," said Zack, dismissively. "Not so much anymore."

"I was also—"

"But what I wanted to show you," said Zack. "Before the record player, there are about thirty minutes where Ravager wasn't able to recover the images. Something corrupted them, or his drive got corrupted, he gave me multiple explanations. But this is the last one we have before that gap."

The empty living room, the turntable, the speakers.

"What are we looking for, Zack?"

Zack reached down and pinched on the screen to zoom in. A familiar looking image of battlements and a forest sat on the turntable's plastic cover.

"Yeah," said Audrey. She leaned forward and lifted a large square of cardboard out of her bag. The image on it matched the one on Zack's tablet.

"*Ramparts Over the Hinterlands,*" said Osgood without a bit of surprise, reading the text on the album cover in Audrey's hands.

"From Caroline's things," said Audrey. She reached into the cardboard sleeve and removed the black vinyl disk. "And we aren't going to be playing this one." She tilted it back and forth a few times, enough to reveal that gouged across its surface on both sides were the sigil, words, and various other symbols.

"Okay," said Osgood, feeling a shiver crawl down her spine. "Looks like we're going record shopping today."

"Before we do," said Audrey. She looked at the vinyl

album in her hand and then flipped and rotated it. "Here," she said, tapping a spot near the label.

"Hel…" said Zack, squinting at it.

"Help?" asked Osgood.

"Yeah," said Audrey. "When I found this, I thought that too. Also thought she just didn't like the record. I never liked it, after all."

"But you don't think so now?" asked Zack.

"Now I've seen this." Audrey reached up and slid her nail under the center label at the center proclaiming *Ramparts Over the Hinterlands* – A Gloria Mundi Record.

Osgood watched as Audrey peeled back the label and felt the dread return. Why this was particularly surprising, she didn't know; at this point everything seemed rather dark, but the dread still grew further as Audrey confirmed:

"It says 'hell,' not 'help.'"

🜨 26 🜨

Their first stop was Records Circle, only a mile up Clark from Osgood's apartment. The smell of old cardboard and paper filled the air as Audrey and Osgood stepped through the door. They both breathed it in.

"The undercurrent of pot is especially welcoming," said Audrey.

"Be nice. Stoners are helpful, they just take longer to get there." Osgood pushed her Wayfarers to the top of her head, shoving the purple curls back with it. She approached the thin young man staffing the desk, made to look much older by his wizard beard and the shock of blonde dreadlocks off the back of his head.

Osgood had dressed for this excursion, too, wearing her *Dark Side of the Moon* shirt that was a size too small. She'd even put on lipstick. Audrey had asked if they were going to a costume party.

"Hi there," said Osgood to the dreadlocked man.

"Help you?" he asked in return, without looking up from an album he was intensely studying.

"Yeah," she said, putting her elbows on the counter, leading with her tits. "I'm looking for the records by In the Shallows..."

"We have *Race to the Island*. It's in classic rock. Not under I, under R." The dreadlocked man scraped an old price tag off the upper corner of the album with a distressingly long thumbnail.

Osgood turned to Audrey, who shrugged before stepping up to the desk for her turn. "Do you have either of the later albums?"

"They're quite rare," he said.

"We know," said Osgood.

"Then you'll understand that when I said we have *Race to the Island,* my statement wasn't intended to suggest I would eventually reveal that we also happen to have copies of *Tether* and *Ramparts Over the Hinterlands.*" The thumbnail stopped scraping, the orange tag still only half off. He didn't look up. "Do you plan to buy *Race to the Island*?"

Osgood looked to Audrey for suggestions and shrugged again. Osgood cocked her head in the direction of the classic rock sign, noting some identifiable album covers facing out on the rack. *Oh,* Sgt. Pepper, *how I loved you,* thought Osgood.

Audrey nodded and headed over there.

"Um, what's your name?" asked Osgood.

The man scratched his cheek through his long beard. "Anton."

"Anton," said Osgood, turning on her smooth voice, putting a smile back on her face.

"Yes," he said. He finally got the old tag off the album and flicked it into the trash, then slid the whole thing into a sleeve. Osgood raised an eyebrow at the title, *Freddy's Greatest Hits,* with the burned visage of everybody's favorite dream monster on the cover.

"I didn't realize they gave Freddy an album," said Osgood.

Anton stopped, and his eyes finally met hers. She smiled at him. He returned only annoyance. "They gave him everything else, why not a shitty album?"

"Cool," said Osgood. She threw a glance over her shoulder at Audrey flipping through albums in classic rock.

"Under R, not I," Anton said to her, harsh and loud. "They were *Rhapsody* in the Shallows then."

"Right," said Audrey, moving down the rack.

"So, Anton," Osgood twirled one of her purple curls around a finger.

"Look, just tell me what you want." He finally looked up at her with a theatrical sigh. "But you can knock this shit off." He waved at her tits dismissively. "I'm gay."

"Oh," said Osgood, dropping her hands to the counter, standing up straight.

"So your blatant manipulation tactics won't—"

"I really wasn't—"

Anton put both hands on the counter top. He had tattoos on his knuckles, but Osgood couldn't read them. "What do you want?"

"Do you know of any record stores who might have—"

"The In the Shallows albums?"

"Yes."

"I don't." He tossed the red Freddy album, now in its new slip-sleeve, behind him, then ducked almost entirely behind the counter.

Osgood looked back over to Audrey, still flipping. Finally, her friend lifted an album off the rack and held it aloft triumphantly.

"We'll buy *Race to the Island* if you help—"

"I don't give a shit if you buy anything," said Anton.

"Here I was worried about toxic masculinity in record stores, but I forgot that sometimes men are just assholes."

Anton shrugged and folded his arms. "Tell you what, you buy that," he pointed at Audrey, coming forward with the album, "*and* you buy this piece of shit so that I don't have to actually work at a record store that stocks it." He lifted the Freddy album back up to the counter. "Ten dollars."

"For both, or—"

"For *both*?" Anton snorted derisively. "Ten dollars for Freddy. *Race to the Island* is twenty-five."

"Seems steep," said Osgood under her breath.

"Oh, does it?" snapped Anton, ringing up the records on the register. "Why don't you head over to Planet Vinyl and die of sticker shock?"

"And why would we go there?" asked Osgood.

Anton scowled. "If anyone in Chicago's going to have *Ramparts* and *Tether*, Planet Vinyl is the place. Forty-four."

"I think your math is wrong there," said Audrey.

"Unfortunately, the information about Planet Vinyl came with a five-dollar surcharge on *Island*." Anton dropped both albums into a thin square bag with RC on the side.

"Yunno," said Osgood, "I'd ask to talk to your manager, but I don't really want to spend any more time in here."

"I'll be sure to pass on your comments."

Audrey looked at Osgood, who looked back at her. Osgood indicated the register with her head. Audrey rolled her eyes and took out her wallet. She handed Anton a fifty, and he returned six ones and the bag.

"Records Circle appreciates your patronage," he said, turning and walking away from the register toward the back of the store.

27

Back in the sun, Osgood put down her Ray-Bans and reached her hand out for the bag. She ignored Audrey's lingering look.

"We're splitting the cost of this research, right?" asked Audrey quietly as they walked toward her car. "We've got no one to bill."

"Yeah," said Osgood. "Just haven't been paid in a bit, so I need to move some money around."

In the passenger seat, Osgood pulled the albums from the bag and tossed *Freddy's Greatest Hits* over her shoulder into the back seat. She beheld *Race to the Island* by Rhapsody in the Shallows.

"That's their second album," said Audrey, typing Planet Vinyl into her phone's GPS.

The cover of the album was a product of its time. Late '80s, with a border of pale green and yellow triangles and zig-zags surrounding a thinly-inked sketch of a small island with a limited color palette, full of trees, an enormous radio transmitter poking out from them. "Looks like a Nagel," said Osgood.

Audrey glanced over. "I don't think that's Nagel," she said. "Maybe a knockoff."

"This band was popular, though, right?"

"In fourth through sixth grade, they were huge," said Audrey.

"Really?" Osgood asked, flipping the album over. "It seems real...poppy...compared to the stuff we were finding last night, and compared to what I can remember of 'The End of What's Real.'"

"Oh, yeah. Very poppy," said Audrey. "I mean, it was the '80s."

"Wonder what changed."

"Their lead singer died," Audrey said, glancing over at a photo of the band on the back cover. "This guy." She tapped the image.

The foursome on the back looked happy, holding their instruments, sitting around outside in a posed-to-look-relaxed way. The guitarist Audrey had pointed to leaned against two amps stacked on top of each other. Below the image was tiny text: *(from left: Len Antrell, Will Knox, Hank Fordham, Pete Briggs.)*

"Thank you for driving," said Osgood.

Audrey looked over, then back out the windshield. "My car was out front, seemed like the easiest plan," she said. "Where do you park, anyway? Is there a back lot?"

"I usually park where you did, but my car is in impound."

"I won't get towed if I park there overnight, will I?" asked Audrey.

"Not unless you owe the city like $300 in unpaid parking tickets."

"Jesus, Pru— Osgood."

"Money isn't exactly flowing right now," she said. "I have a hard time focusing on the things that pay."

"What else is new?" asked Audrey with a mirthless laugh. She threw a sidelong glance at Osgood, who scowled. "Sorry. Force of habit."

Osgood looked out the side window. "No need to be sorry," she said, tasting the bitterness. "I'm a fuck-up, always have been."

"You're not going to get me to disagree out of pity."

"Good," snapped Osgood. "I don't want your fucking

pity."

They sat in silence for a while, until Osgood couldn't take it any longer. "How far is Planet—"

"You have tremendous potential, Prudence."

"Thanks, Mom."

"But your ego gets in the way."

"*My* ego?" Osgood snorted. "Are you serious?"

"Is your emphasis on the word 'my' meant to imply that it's actually—"

"My upcoming emphasis on the word bitch will be meant to imply—"

"Okay, stop!" said Audrey, slamming her hands on the steering wheel. "I'm sorry I said anything."

Osgood nodded, looking out the window again, and mumbled, "I'm sorry I did, too."

"You're not a fuck up," offered Audrey, after more silence had gone by. "You were the driving force behind our show. You set up meetings. You planned the investigations, you—"

"Colluded with the producers to defraud the public and hid it from you until it became clear that they didn't particularly care if the ruse killed us on live TV?"

Audrey pinched her lips together until they turned white. "You keep bringing up what you did."

"Yeah."

"I'm just pointing out," said Audrey, "that *you* are bringing it up, not me."

"Regret's a bitch."

"A bitch like me?" asked Audrey.

Osgood laughed. "Nicely done."

"Thank you." Audrey unleashed a dramatic sigh, one that would've been at home in a shoe-box theater, loud enough for the back row to hear. "I know it wasn't your idea. They came to me the following season."

"And?"

"They wanted to see if we could get back together, do a cross-country series."

"*Chicago Haunts, Across the Country,*" said Osgood.

"I think they were planning to call it *American Haunts,*"

said Audrey. "But yeah. They asked. I said no."

"The thought of working with me again was that unbearable…"

Audrey let the comment percolate for a moment. "At that point? Yes. Even if the hoax wasn't your idea, you helped. You led me to it. You put me under the chandelier that—"

"They didn't tell me that part of the plan," insisted Osgood, recalling when the shards of the chandelier, rigged only to shake, had begun to fall on them. One had sliced her shoulder, leaving a scar she could still see.

"And that part I didn't blame you for, but the rest—" Audrey sniffed, and Osgood noticed the tears. "Do you remember why we started investigating?"

"I do," said Osgood. "Proof."

"Proof," agreed Audrey. "The value of proof of afterlife. Because proof shows that there is more after this. Proof offers comfort." She wiped at her eyes with the back of her hand. "Where everybody else wanted to find monsters and darkness, we wanted to show them the light. The beauty of knowing that death isn't the end."

"I know," said Osgood. She looked down at her hands and scraped the last of the midnight blue polish off a fingernail.

"Because if death isn't the end, then even if Caroline—" Audrey stopped herself. "Anyway."

"I really—"

"Please don't apologize anymore."

"Okay."

"You brought me here," said Audrey. "After all these years, at the barest hope of finding my sister, you called."

"I never stopped looking for her," said Osgood.

"I know."

Ray Parker, Jr. blared, asking them what they might do if something odd was going on in their general vicinity.

"Seriously?" asked Osgood, laughing at Audrey's ringtone.

"I'm a goddamned ghosthunter," said Audrey. "I don't fancy it up, Miss Spectral Inspector."

"That's Zack's number," said Osgood, looking at the

phone.

Audrey tapped a button on her steering wheel. "Zack."

"Yeah, you got Os there?"

"She has not thrown me from the passenger seat yet, Zack."

"Okay?" said Zack. "Good."

"We got *Race to the Island*," said Audrey.

"And *Freddy's Greatest Hits*," said Osgood.

"I don't know that—" began Zack, sounding nervous that he'd missed something.

"Of 'One-two-he's-coming-for-you' fame."

"Why would you buy that?"

"Because the hipster yeti at Records Circle made us."

"Oh, why did you go there?" asked Zack.

"Did you just call to second guess our decisions, Zack?" asked Osgood.

"No!" said Zack. "I called to tell you that Planet Vinyl has both of the In the Shallows albums, but they're sealed and *expensive.*"

"Figures," said Audrey.

"They probably also have *Rhapsody in the Shallows*," he said.

"Isn't that the band?" asked Osgood.

"Eponymous first album," said Audrey.

"Actually," began Zack.

"Oh, how I love a man starting a sentence with that word," said Audrey.

"Oh, right," stammered Zack. "Um. I just—"

"It's fine, Zack, she's smiling."

"Oh. I really didn't mean—"

"Zack," said Audrey.

"I'm really not mansplaining—"

"Zack!" laughed Osgood.

"The band actually named themselves after the album, was all I was going to say. They had such a hard time getting a deal for it that they were broken up before everything came together. Hadn't even thought of a name." He waited for a response, then added, "Thus, not eponymous."

"Huh," said Osgood, hoping it would encourage him to continue.

Audrey wasn't as patient. "Do you have anything other than pedantic trivia to share?"

"Well, yeah," he said, "it's kinda weird. The first album was from a small company that had just formed, and they couldn't keep up with the wild success. I'm talking multiple-number-one-singles-at-once success. That small company grew into Gloria Mundi Records for their second album."

Osgood examined the record company's logo on the upper left corner of the jacket, a globe with an old fashioned furled banner reading 'Gloria Mundi.' "Gloria—"

"It means Glory of the World," said Audrey.

"Yeah," said Zack. "So, *Race to the Island* is even bigger than *Rhapsody*. The band, still living in their home town in Minnesota, experiences the transformative power of fame. They start touring. They play arenas. Even played Wrigley!"

"Wow," said Osgood.

Zack took a deep breath. "Then lead singer Len Antrell is diagnosed with…something."

"Something?" asked Audrey.

"There's a lot of debate over what he had. The internet seems to think it was AIDS, but there's never been a confirmation or denial. This was 1991, so it would've been hard to keep AIDS a secret. Anyway, some sort of autoimmune disease. They stop touring and return to the studio to work on their next album. He goes downhill fast and dies in '92."

"Jeez," said Osgood.

"Yeah," said Zack. "And the band goes silent. No touring, no interviews. Nothing. Gloria Mundi issues press releases that insist the band is still working on their next album, and that Len Antrell had written most of the songs and recorded his vocals. The delay is suspicious, and the press clamors for info. But they don't expect what happens next."

"It's like you're narrating an episode of *Behind the Music* here, Zack," said Osgood. "Can you de-gild this lily a bit?"

Audrey snorted a laugh.

"Fine," said Zack, sounding distinctly disappointed. "The

remaining band members – Knox, Fordham, and Briggs – hold a press conference in January of 1995. It's a surprise even to Gloria Mundi. The three of them announce that their next album is finished and about seventy-five percent of it is material co-written and co-sung by Len Antrell, but, since he's died, they no longer feel like they're Rhapsody in the Shallows. They announce they're ceasing touring, and henceforth will be known as In the Shallows. 'Because Len held our Rhapsody.'"

Audrey squinted, puzzled. "That seems—"

"Extreme?" suggested Osgood. "Foolish? Like when Prince became…symbol man."

"Yes to both," said Zack. "One of the most popular bands in the world not only stops touring but changes their name, making it harder to find their work. Then they go back into the studio and never give another interview."

"Never?"

"That's it, that press conference. No promotion, no profiles, nothing. Lots of speculation pieces, mostly opining on the idea that Will Knox, the co-founder and de facto new leader, just couldn't cope with losing Antrell, who'd been his partner for so long."

"That'll fuck with you," said Osgood, throwing a sidelong glance at Audrey.

"But despite stacking all odds against them, *Tether* is a huge hit, arguably bigger than *Race to the Island*, even without touring. More singles shoot to the top of the charts, including 'The Wise Lord of Hinterland.'"

"Zack, we're almost to Planet Vinyl," said Audrey.

"Right, okay, so there's some weirdness that I'm looking into a bit more surrounding the album releases, but I thought the *Hinterlands* one was especially interesting."

"Good, since we're going to be paying a ton for it," said Osgood.

"There are only four tracks on *Ramparts Over the Hinterlands*, three of which are long experimental pieces. Sound effects, weird repeated music, backmasking—"

"Back—" began Audrey.

"When they record something that can only be heard when the album is played backward."

"Aha," said Audrey. "Paul is dead."

Osgood nodded. "Turn me on, dead man."

"Can I finish?"

"Please," said Osgood. "Continue, Zack."

"But despite only releasing four tracks, they'd apparently recorded a bunch of new songs with a trove of tracks that Antrell's daughter had discovered in his things. Demos, other recordings. It would've been an album with all four of them again. A huge deal, a whole decade after his death. Instead, the band, who had signed a final approval deal, yanked all but one of the Antrell songs, 'The End of What's Real,' and replaced them with their own versions of 'Revolution No. 9.' Only, if you can believe it, even longer and more incomprehensible."

"And the album flopped?" asked Osgood.

"It was the biggest hit of their careers," said Zack.

"None of this makes sense," said Osgood.

"Especially considering both *Tether* and *Ramparts* were *only* released on vinyl, and this is before the hipster vinyl renaissance. In '95 and '98, people just weren't buying vinyl. Other than these two albums."

As Audrey pulled into the parking lot, Osgood looked out the window and saw a large planet logo with a retro pinup girl, complete with blaster and a fishbowl helmet, sitting atop it. "I like that," she said.

"We're at Planet Vinyl, Zack."

"Okay," he said. "Based on the other stuff I'm looking at, we need to buy those albums. The only way to—"

"Do you want to share any of that before we go in?" asked Audrey.

"I want to verify before I share."

"Fair enough."

"Text me when you're headed back," said Zack.

They agreed, then climbed out of the car.

28

Osgood's phone buzzed as she walked into Planet Vinyl. She thumbed it open, expecting Zack, definitely not expecting the woman she'd forgotten about.

thinking about u + thought id msg.

"Shit, Nora," said Osgood.

"What?" asked Audrey.

Osgood shook her head, putting her phone back in her pocket, and followed Audrey toward the desk.

Planet Vinyl was about as far from the dingy stacks and racks of Records Circle as one could get and still manage to have a distinct hipster vibe. Its proximity to downtown was its secret, perhaps. The ceilings were high, the racks well lit, and framed cover art lined the walls.

"Maybe this one will be friendlier," said Audrey, gesturing to the young woman behind the register.

Osgood didn't know if she'd be friendlier, but said, "She's certainly cuter than Beardy McBeardface."

"Welcome to Planet Vinyl," said the young woman.

Osgood didn't even hear the welcome; she just stared. The young woman – April, according to her name-tag – had hair shorn almost to her scalp on either side, with a shock of blue in the middle pulled back into a ponytail that looked like feathers at the back of her head. Had it been moussed up, it would've made a hell of a mohawk. Her nose was pierced on the right side and her lower lip in the center.

Thankfully for their mission, Audrey seemed immune to the woman's charms. "My associate called ahead about a pair of albums by In the Shallows."

"Oh, yes!" April bounced to it, moving quickly down the length of the counter and around a corner. "I pulled it for you," she called from the back.

"That bounce," whispered Osgood to Audrey.

"Keep it in your pants, Osgood," Audrey whispered back.

Osgood snickered and caught a smile on Audrey's face out of the corner of her eye.

When April returned, she held two albums covered in several layers of shrink-wrap. "I know it's expensive, but that's just 'cuz my manager decided to lump the two of them together."

"Oh?" asked Audrey.

April set the albums on the counter, and Osgood saw the now eerily-familiar cover art of *Ramparts Over the Hinterlands*, hazy under the layers of translucent plastic.

"We seldom get this one," said April, tapping *Ramparts*. "And when we do, it's usually in a lot, and we have to throw it out."

"Why?" asked Osgood. "And also, 'lot?'"

"When people give us big collections of records, they're called lots. Those donating often don't know exactly what's in them. Like, it came from their parents' basement or something. And the 'why' is because *Ramparts* is usually really damaged."

Osgood's eyes narrowed, the words distracting her from watching April's lower lip as she snapped her gum in between sentences.

"People mess it up for some reason. I can show you, we got one in last week."

"Yes," insisted Audrey. "Please!"

"Gimme a sec, I have to go in back."

"Take your time," said Osgood, smiling at April. Her

phone vibrated in her pocket again. She pulled it out quickly and looked at it.

if you really don't want to see me again, just tell me. U seemed so excited about the [ghost emoji]!

Ghost? Osgood asked herself. *What ghost?* She shook her head. Too much going on just now, so the phone went back into her pocket.

"Something wrong?"

"Ducking a girl— Woman."

"Aha," said Audrey.

Osgood waited for the dressing down, but Audrey turned back to the counter and lifted the two-album pack, flipping it over. The cover art for *Tether* depicted a multi-colored set of sound-waves narrowing to a woven rope in the middle of the album and unwinding again on the other side. The word *"Tether"* was tiny below it, and, even smaller, "In the Shallows."

She handed it to Osgood, who peered at it, then noticed the $400 price tag on the upper right and let out an involuntary "Wheeeew…" under her breath.

"This was on the throw-out pile," said April, returning. "Not even good enough for the dollar bin." She held up a tattered cardboard sleeve. In places, it was so worn the album itself was visible through it. "You're lucky I hadn't gotten to that yet today." She grinned and handed it over to Audrey, going back around the counter.

Audrey examined the front and back of the album, then pulled the vinyl record itself out. She froze, dropping the album sleeve to the floor.

Osgood set the expensive albums back on the table and bent to grab the sleeve.

"Everything okay?" asked April

As Osgood came back up, she saw the reason for Audrey's reaction. Carved on this side, all over, were small sigils, including the one from Caroline's album. The sigil of the Lord of the Hinterlands. Audrey met her eyes and flipped the record over, showing that, just like her sister's, this side had been carved with a giant sigil.

"Everything's fine," said Audrey, her eyes not leaving Osgood's. "I assume you take credit card."

"Absolutely," said April, ringing the purchase through. "You can have that one if you want it. I mean, it's not playable in the least. We get two or three a year like that."

"*Just* like this?" asked Osgood.

"What do you mean?"

"Like, same symbols, same cut marks?"

April shrugged and nodded. "Haven't looked that close, but it's the symbol on the flag, see." She flipped the wrapped albums and pointed to the midnight blue flag flying over the ramparts.

"It is," said Audrey.

"I guess," April shrugged again. "Superfans? But couldn't be big enough fans, 'cuz they destroyed their record, right?"

"Right."

"Want a bag?"

"No," said Osgood, reaching her hand out for the albums. April handed them over.

Audrey slid the scratched copy of *Ramparts Over the Hinterlands* back into its tattered sleeve.

"Well," said April, "I hope you listen to them and don't just keep them in the sleeves. Vinyl is meant to be played."

"We plan to," said Osgood with a grin, distracted again from the implications of the scratched album. She reached into her pocket and produced a beat-up business card. "If you ever want someone to buy you a drink and listen to you with a smile on their face, gimme a call." She held out the card.

With a light dusting of blush appearing on her cheeks, April took it. "Maybe I will."

"I hope you do."

"Prudence?" called Audrey, holding her hand out toward the door.

"Coming, dear," said Osgood, throwing one more smile at April. Her pocket buzzed again.

"Popular," said Audrey, as they emerged into the sunlight.

"I really need to tell her that I'm busy," said Osgood, pulling out her phone.

"Or, if you're not interested, you could just tell her that," said Audrey, cocking her head. "Yunno, the truth."

Osgood rolled her eyes and shook her head. The notification wasn't from Nora, though, but an **Unknown Sender**.

She clicked it and felt the ground become shaky below her.

I'm watching. Be careful, said the message. Below it, a photo of the two of them climbing out of Audrey's car in the parking lot, this parking lot, with Planet Vinyl in the background.

She turned the phone toward Audrey, whose eyebrows went up. "And this is *not* from your new friend?"

"No," said Osgood.

"We should get back to the apartment," said Audrey. She extended her arm and clicked her key fob. The car beeped twice and unlocked.

As they climbed in, Osgood threw a glance over her shoulder looking for someone, anyone, who could've or would've sent this, but saw no one of note.

🪐 29 🪐

Osgood's demand, **tell me who you are,** went without response, and she clutched the purchased albums to her chest for the entire drive back to her apartment. Audrey threw her sidelong glances when she wasn't staring determinedly out the windshield. When they reached the apartment, they bolted up the stairs inside and slammed the door behind them. Zack looked up at them from his laptop, warily.

"Did you get—"

Osgood tossed her phone to him. "I need you to track the last text."

"Okay," he said.

She moved to the front windows and looked down at the street below. A man stood on the corner, not crossing the street. Two men smoked in the doorway of JJ's Liquors.

"Are you both okay?" asked Zack.

Audrey went to the table next to him. "Someone sent a threatening—"

"'I'm watching. Be careful,'" Zack read.

"Yeah," said Audrey, "and the picture."

"You were followed," he said.

"Seems like."

Satisfied that no one was watching them from the street,

Osgood moved back. She pulled strings on each window's slat blinds to bring them down, one after another. Finally, she turned to Zack and Audrey, setting the albums down on the table.

"And it's not from your new—"

"No, Zack," said Osgood. She took the phone and opened a separate text chain.

was this fucking you? She pasted a screen-shot of the text and photo below that.

what??? no! Then, following the initial response, **Are you okay? Do u need anything?**

leave me alone! said Osgood, then tossed her phone back to Zack.

"Well, that's one way to get her to stop texting." Zack nodded. "Did you lock the door?"

"I locked downstairs," said Audrey.

Osgood went to the apartment door and slid the chain across.

"The number's unregistered. Also looks like it's coming from one of the burner phone number companies, like Text-Forward or ObfusText."

"That's a pretty good name," said Audrey, sitting on the couch.

Osgood went down the hall to the kitchen, returning with three glasses and the bottle of bourbon Zack had picked up the night before. As she walked, she poured and drank two fingers of the bourbon. "Drink?" she asked them all when she reached the living room.

"Not for me," said Zack.

Audrey looked from Zack to Osgood. "I think it's a bit early to—"

Osgood widened her eyes at Audrey.

Her friend tugged at her lower lip with her teeth, then said, "Yeah, hit me."

Osgood poured her nearly six ounces of brown, despite Audrey's protests.

"That's *way* too much," she said.

"Fine," said Osgood, moving the glass to the side table

next to the La-Z-Boy. She poured a neat two fingers into the other glass and slid it to Audrey.

"Thank you," said Audrey, eying Osgood as she gulped half of hers. "I just want to make it known that I'm uncomfort—"

"We got the albums, Zack," said Osgood, pointing to the table.

Zack nodded. "While you were out, I ran down to the Brown Elephant and got a turntable and some speakers." He pointed behind Osgood.

She leaned out of the chair, feeling the sweet sway of the bourbon, and saw that a beat-up pair of speakers sat on either side of a turntable on her sidebar.

"Well," said Osgood. "I, for one, am interested in hearing the actual lyrics of 'The End of What's Real,' 'cuz I don't think the ones I remember are right."

Zack looked between them, then lifted the record stack. "$400," he said and whistled. "Where'd you get that kind of mon—"

"I paid for it," said Audrey.

"That makes more sense," said Zack.

He snapped open his multi-tool and slit the plastic wrap, separating the two albums and removing all but the original cellophane. "It's almost a shame to open this. MIB and all."

"Men in black?" asked Osgood.

"Mint in box," said Zack with dismay. "Seriously, men in black?"

"Fucking Big Willie Style," said Osgood, knocking back the last of her bourbon. She leaned forward to pour another.

Audrey slid the bourbon away to the other end of the coffee table. They locked eyes for a moment. Audrey's unwavering and piercing blue eyes held her frozen, and ultimately Osgood sat back.

Zack pulled the pristine black circle of vinyl from its protective sleeve. He looked at both sides. "I'm also worried about using an old and beat up needle on it."

"We're not preserving it for future generations, Zack,"

snapped Osgood, grumpy about the standoff. "We'd just like to hear it."

"Okay," said Zack. "I've also run the aux out to my digital recorder here." He held up a small recorder with two crossed microphones atop it, a wire running behind the turntable. "I think it's time In the Shallows met The Pirate Bay."

"I thought that got shut down," said Audrey.

"It always gets shut down."

"Don't you mean sunk?" asked Osgood.

Audrey rolled her eyes.

"And it rises like a phoenix," said Zack. He carefully put the record on the platter. There was a crackle and pop in the speakers. He lifted the tonearm and gingerly set it on the intro groove of side A of *Ramparts Over the Hinterlands*. Crackling, then the quiet, smooth cycling sound of fresh vinyl.

The tune began, one Osgood knew instantly. Not just from her dreams, or from the car the other night, but from years ago. From the radio. From everywhere. This chord progression, this run of major and minor notes, sounding both pleasant and discordant at once.

"I know this one," said Audrey.

"Yeah," said Osgood. "Yeah."

The music built, moving from piano to include guitar, bass, and drums.

> *"You and I, we can go,*
> *to the end of what's real,*
> *Take my hand, we'll lie down,*
> *watch the turn of the wheel…"*

"Huh," said Osgood.

"What?" asked Audrey.

"I remember the music so vividly, but not the lyrics."

"Me too," agreed Audrey.

"You?" Osgood asked Zack.

He looked up from the record, over to them. "Oh, no, I haven't heard this before."

The song continued, moving through its refrain to the first

verse, full of romantic notions of love and "evermore," back to the chorus. When the second verse began, though, Osgood felt the strangest *déjà vu*, as though she were listening to a variation on a tune long since lost in her head.

"When the memory of our love fades,
I go to the valley in my dreams…"

Osgood shook her head, whispering the lyrics she'd heard, the ones she remembered. "When the memories of our lives fade, we return to the valley in our dreams."

"What?"

"Shh!" Osgood put her finger up.

"My world without you's darkness,
And always my heart yearns."

"Angsty," said Audrey.

The third verse appeared to be an imagined scenario about a wedding between what seemed to be kingdoms in medieval Europe, which finally gave them the line:

"The drumbeats in the hinterlands,
Will lead me right to you…"

And then it was back to the refrain.

"We'll marry in the hinterlands,
And be together evermore,
And the outside world around us,
Erupts into applause."

"That is *not* the song I heard in my dream," said Osgood, feeling herself emphasizing the point with an odd forcefulness.

"Often when we dream, we conflate things that we saw or heard recently into other things that we heard, or that our mind is improvising," offered Zack.

"Thank you," said Osgood. "But the one from my dream is the one I remember from years ago."

"Osgood," said Audrey, putting her hand on top of Osgood's on the La-Z-Boy arm.

Osgood yanked her hand back, narrowing her eyes at them as the melody that had opened the song slowed and minimized, losing its drums, then its base and guitar, until only the piano remained. She heard it echo off the ceiling and the walls, as though it was obscured, somehow. The way she'd used to listen to her mother play that theme from Swan Lake, while she, little Pru, was supposed to be putting her jammies on and brushing her teeth. Hearing the piano echo with a song, sweet and sinister at once.

Silence.

"Okay, now we're onto 'Revelation,' which clocks in at a frankly astonishing-for-a-pop-band seventeen minutes." Audrey read through more text on the back of the album.

Zack added, "That's two seconds longer than 'In-A-Gadda-Da-Vida.'"

As they talked and listened, this time to inharmony and discordance with unusual sounds, sound effects, and cycling music played with little rhyme or reason, Osgood couldn't get that other music out of her head, or the image of herself sitting halfway down the staircase. She stood, walking away from them, ignoring their calls. She knew, *knew for a fact*, that she'd heard that other version, with the lyrics from her dreams. "'Spend our nights in the hinterlands,' and never have to be alone...'" she whispered as she moved into the bathroom and locked the door behind her.

Osgood felt the sway of the bourbon, but the happiness it brought had turned on her. She stared at herself in the mirror and could see that one of her eyes looked almost black. Her pupils dilated separately sometimes, after the accident, and the occurrence usually foretold a migraine. If one was coming, she should probably knock herself right out before it stabbed into her brain.

She turned on the shower, stripped, and sat down on the floor of the tub.

"Os?" Audrey asked, with a knock at the door. "You okay?"

"I'm fine," said Osgood. Maybe the migraine would pass her by, perhaps the pupil dilation wasn't a portent. *What if it's a harbinger of something worse,* she thought and shivered.

She turned up the heat and the water went from warm to hot. The rising steam opened her sinuses. She closed her eyes and concentrated on the water hitting her head and shoulders, rolling down her back and breasts. She opened her eyes for a moment, already feeling the blinding white of the tub stabbing into her brain. Keep them closed just now, keeping them closed would be fine. As she took her slow breaths and concentrated on the sensation of the water cascading down her body, she found herself whispering the last two lyrics she remembered, "'Let the world around us crumble, let the world around us burn.'" She could almost still hear the music and wondered if they were playing it again in the other room. She opened her right eye, the one that still dilated properly – leaving the left scrunched closed – and looked toward the door. The music wasn't coming from out there, it was coming from inside her, like that time she'd been at the library and been certain she heard that one pop song. Which one had it been? Endlessly, for the entire afternoon, just that looping inane refrain. "The fucking 'Right Stuff,'" she realized with a laugh. She'd looked everywhere and found nothing.

"It's called an ear-worm," her teacher had told her. Junior High Prudence had scoffed at that.

But this, she could hear it, couldn't she? The music was here. She was about to call out to them, to ask them if they heard it too, but with the way they'd looked at her when she said she remembered a different version of the song – from her dream, no less – she was confident they wouldn't enjoy the whole "can you still hear the music?" question.

Audrey had already started looking at her that way. The way so many did. The "maybe you've had enough" way. The "I think you're paranoid" way. The "do we need to look for some sort of program?" way. Osgood shook her head and took a deep breath.

The music had begun to fade, and soon, all that remained were the sounds of the running shower. She sighed, feeling the dread ache replaced with relief. She caught a quick glimpse of her medicine cabinet, open still. Had she gotten out the tincture before getting in the shower? She probably should've. "Standing up out of here is going to hurt like a mother—"

Osgood stopped. In the mirror, slightly out of focus, she could see that something was in the corner behind the tub. Like a shadow, but not formless. Her view of that something was blocked from her position by the shower curtain. It... crouched? She blinked hard, trying to focus, willing her uncooperative pupil to pull itself back to functionality. "What the hell is—"

The mirror snapped shut, taking the angle of visibility with it. Osgood yelped.

What had it been? What had she seen? The dark and crouching form of

(the screaming thing)

something that shouldn't be there.

She turned, sliding her butt in a 180 on the tub base. Now, only the frosted vinyl curtain hung between her, and whatever it was. A clicking sound came from behind the curtain.

It could be anything, but it's probably nothing, she tried to assure herself. But she had a weird certainty that whatever she'd seen in the mirror had just clicked from deep in its throat, from beyond its yawning mouth. Slowly, she reached out her hand, wrapping her fingers one after another around the edge of the curtain. She took a deep breath and held it, then yanked the curtain aside.

Revealing nothing.

Nothing at all.

$$\cancel{X} \ 3 \ 0 \ \cancel{X}$$

"Do you feel better?" asked Audrey.

"I do," said Osgood. She had swapped her contacts for glasses and threw on a battered Peter Capaldi Doctor Who shirt and tartan pajama pants. "Do me a favor, though, look at my eyes and tell me if they're back to being dilated the same."

Audrey looked unnerved by the request but did so. "Your eyes look fine to me."

"I apologize if I got...weird, earlier," said Osgood. "I've been on edge because I haven't gotten much sleep, and that song was... anyway."

"Well," said Zack. "You didn't miss much. The other songs on the record—"

"I wouldn't even charitably call them songs," said Audrey. "I think I stopped listening to the band when they were still Rhapsody in the Shallows. This incarnation is...weird."

"Yeah, noise symphonies," laughed Zack.

"Any luck on the text messager?"

"Nothing to report, unfortunately," sighed Zack. "I *did* set up a reply bomb, though. If he sends you another message, it'll automatically send him a file. He has to click on it, but almost everybody does, and it's a zip file that unzips a hundred zip files that unzip a thousand zip files. It's zip files all the way down. His phone'll be toast!"

As he seemed quite proud of himself, Osgood commended Zack and patted his shoulder. She sat in the La-Z-Boy, reached down, and yanked the bar to stick the footrest out.

The printer ejected a piece of paper onto the table and Zack snatched it up along with a roll of scotch tape. He walked past Osgood. She looked around the side of the La-Z-Boy to where he was headed and what she saw startled her. On the wall were dozens of pieces of paper, making up a full-color mural reproduction of the cover of *Ramparts Over the Hinterlands*, pieced together. "Wow."

"Oh, yeah." Zack gave a nervous laugh as he taped up the last page in the bottom right corner. "Hope you don't mind."

"I told him it'd be fine," said Audrey.

"And why do we have this massive piece of 'art' on my wall now?" She looked it over, noting that the font used for the title and the band's name was similar, but not the same, and there were slight inconsistencies in the typeface for the album title itself. Blown up to this size, though, you couldn't miss the sigil on the flag in the background.

"There's stuff hidden all over it," said Zack. "Front and back."

"Where is the back?"

"We, uh, thought the hallway has the room," he grinned, but the grin looked nervous.

Osgood waited for more information but received none, so she repeated his words: "Stuff hidden?" She stood and walked around her chair to the massive cover art collage.

"Well, hidden might be a misnomer, it's more details," said Audrey. "Like this guy." She pointed with a Sharpie to a small animal of some sort, peering out from behind the trees, its body hairy, its face eerily human. "I don't know that it means anything, but these details are all over it." She pointed to two more odd bits of wildlife in the forest below the ramparts.

"How Bosch," said Osgood, taking it in.

The final one, a crouching black and brown beast which faced into the forest instead of out, sent shivers down Osgood's spine as her mind flashed back to the thing in the mirror, the thing behind the shower curtain, the thing that had *click*ed. Osgood backed up, the enormity of the cover overwhelming her. As though if she weren't careful, the dark forest of the Hinterlands would swallow her whole. She was jolted away from the image by the sound of the printer, beginning to spit out the other side of the album.

Zack went back to the computer to check on it.

"Are you really okay?" asked Audrey, quietly.

"Yeah."

"You're doing your thing."

Osgood turned to her. "Am I?"

"The one-word fine-but-not thing," Audrey said, poking a finger at Osgood's shoulder. "What else do you dream about, Prudence?"

Osgood stared at her, frowning, looking into the reflecting pools of her eyes. "You remember that artist colony in Minnesota?"

"I..." Audrey began, eyes wandering up and to the left. "No."

"You remember our trip to California. On our way home, we went north to avoid snow-closed passes in the Rockies."

"I remember that."

"And after that long stretch of nothing, after we passed into Minnesota, we started seeing—"

Audrey's eyes widened. "Goblins! With spears!"

"Yes!"

"What?" asked Zack over his shoulder.

"Off of a highway, I don't remember which, way up north-west of Minneapolis, there's an artist colony. As you get close to it, you see these plaster goblins or something, with spears," Audrey told him. She held her hand about three feet above the floor. "This high, maybe? And you know you're almost there when the..."

"When the screaming thing rises in the east," said Osgood.

"Shit," said Audrey. "Yeah. How the fuck did I forget that thing."

"Then you do remember the enormous screaming idol that terrified me?" asked Osgood.

"I do," said Audrey.

"What the *fuck?*" said Zack, furious.

They turned to him as he threw his headphones onto the table.

"What?" asked Osgood.

"I have no *fucking* idea." Zack didn't swear often, so Osgood felt that the fact he had worth noting.

He unplugged his headphones from the computer. They heard the tink tink tink of the volume being raised. He hit the space bar. "Now listen as I set the tonearm on the record." The distinct sound of it being set down and beginning to whir, the rising and falling cyclical sound of an uneven platter.

"Okay..." said Osgood, dragging out the "y."

"Notice anything not happening?"

They waited. And waited.

"Where's the—"

"Yes!" exclaimed Zack, turning back to his computer. "Where's the *fucking* music?" He clicked around on a timeline that displayed a low baseline wave-form, but nothing else. No peaks, no music. "Nothing. Oh, and here's where the record ends, and I lift the tonearm back up." He moved the cursor. Sure enough, a click and pop and silence.

"Are you sure you—" Audrey began, but Osgood grabbed her arm, stopping her. Osgood knew that Zack had almost always done things right, but when very occasionally he didn't, it was better to let him be the one who recognized it.

"I was going to play you the obvious bit of backmasking," he grumbled, lurching back to his feet toward the turntable. "I wanted to do it digitally so we wouldn't risk damaging, since it's pristine." He flipped the switch, and the platter began to spin up to speed. He lifted the tonearm and dropped it right before the end of the track.

A whirring, uneven scales. The sounds of wind and water

running. In the background, a muttering, something she couldn't understand, but without question speech. A crackling, like fire, began, and the muttering grew to a more reasonable volume, but it sounded odd.

"Backward?" asked Osgood.

Zack nodded.

"Have you spun it the other way?"

"Not yet."

The talking stopped, and a progression of six notes played, again, again, again. Osgood could feel the notes lulling her, like staring into the spinning blades of a ceiling fan or watching the dashed yellow highway line in your headlights. Though she knew, of course, how important it was to pay close attention to the road and not get lost in those dashes.

"How long does this go on?" Osgood asked, beginning to feel overwhelmed by it.

"Forever," said Audrey.

Osgood again felt the incongruence, something was wrong, and that something was deepening. She shook her head to clear it, as well as to display her confusion.

Zack beckoned with his finger. "C'mere."

She walked to the turntable. He pointed to the end of the groove. As she watched, the tonearm moved toward the center sticker and then away, toward and away, toward and away.

"They've made a loop, it just feeds itself back into the sequence at the end."

"It's unsettling," said Osgood. She put her hand on the wall next to the turntable to steady herself.

"Yeah," said Zack. He grabbed the speed adjustment arm and stopped the platter from spinning. He lifted the tone arm and set it back down just before the grooved loop. Then he pressed his index finger onto the album's label and looked at them. "You really shouldn't do this," he said.

"Well Zack," laughed Osgood. "If it's..." She waved her arms around, "...*Magic music* that can't be recorded, this is our only option, innit?"

"Glad you're having fun," he said, then began to spin the record backward.

Osgood felt disorientation hearing the sequence of notes run backward, the strangeness that always accompanied piano being played in reverse, the slow reverb build to the moment of strike, then silence.

"You're closer than you think," a deep voice said, full-throated though distorted.

Osgood was unsure if the distortion was in the recording or due to the inconsistency of the human motor spinning the record. "That's—"

With the same crackling sound, the voice continued, "From the hinterlands, we come, and to the hinterlands, we shall return. We rest below the ramparts. You're closer than you think."

Osgood felt her humor vanish. The idea of magic music felt no longer fun, only dangerous.

The voice dropped to a mutter. "Don't trust him. Don't trust the Lord. Don't trust him. Don't trust the Lord. Don't trust him. Don't trust the Lord." Water running, but backward, wind, but backward. Then the uneven scales, which Osgood recognized were now being played forward, reversed in the normal direction of the record.

"Those scales," she said. "They're the opening notes of 'The End of What's Real.'"

Zack stopped spinning the record. "There's more," he said. "But we'll have to find it again."

"I've heard enough for now," said Osgood. She rubbed at her right hip, then the left. "The ache is back."

"Why don't you sit down," suggested Audrey. "Don't need three of us looking at this at once." She gestured toward the printout on the wall.

Osgood nodded and allowed herself to fall back into the La-Z-Boy, turning it toward them and the art. Zack moved back toward his computer, but Osgood caught his wrist. She pulled him down, and he leaned in close. "Don't let me fall asleep."

"I'll do my best," he said. "Sometimes you just go."

Sometimes she did just go, shuffle off, quit reality and light out for the territories. Or was it the hinterlands? She shuddered. Osgood lifted her phone off the table and grimaced as she looked at her last text exchange with Nora. She stared at it for a moment, at her final request: **leave me alone**. Nora had, hadn't she?

I'm sorry, Osgood typed. **I'm bad at...people-ing.**

Three dots appeared, then disappeared. Nora was waiting.

It has been a rough few days, Osgood added.

i kno how that is, said Nora.

Osgood suspected the young woman had no idea how it was, but she remembered how she'd felt when she was young and knew everything. And how young was Nora?

i just had fun is all, continued Nora in a separate text bubble. **and I didnt want you to think I didnt. If you want me to give you space, that's totally cool. I've got papers to do. People to see. LOL.**

Osgood smiled. She couldn't remember the last time she'd seen **LOL** in a text. Of course, who but Zack, Yann, and Carla had she texted recently? Yann and Carla certainly didn't **LOL**, and Zack loathed text-speak. She tapped out her response after a sigh. **For now, that's probably best. I can assure you that it has nothing to do with you.**

thank you for that, said Nora. **Why don't you text me if you want someone to listen. Or to eat you out. ;)**

Jeez, thought Osgood. As sloppy as she'd been that night, this girl had gone down on her and still wanted seconds? **I will.**

She put the phone on her lap and closed her eyes, feeling a bit better about that situation. It buzzed again, and she lifted it, sure it'd be a **<3** or **:)**. She swiped to unlock the phone and clicked the notification to find a photo of her apartment windows. She could see Zack through the far one, sitting in front of his laptop.

"Fuck," she said under her breath. She looked up at the number, different from before. No text bomb had been sent.

We should talk, it said. Ellipses, ellipses. **How're the burgers below you?**

Osgood shook her head, the pit in her stomach growing. But Mary's would be familiar ground, home turf, wouldn't it?

She gave him a single word. **Good.**

The menu posted outside showed impressive variety. Let's have lunch tomorrow.

She scowled. **I'm not in the habit of being stalked into lunch.** "Hey, uh, guys?" she said to Zack and Audrey.

I'm not in the habit of risking exposure. Ellipses, ellipses. **Unless you're planning to kill the Lord of the Hinterlands yourself. And I don't think the three of you have the sand for that.**

Osgood showed Audrey and Zack the phone.

"Shit," said Zack. "Didn't plan on him using another number."

"S'okay, Zack," said Osgood.

"Kill the Lord of the Hinterlands?" asked Audrey. "That's quite an escalation from what we're doing here." She pointed at the wall.

"I'm in for lunch if we all go," said Osgood, looking between them.

"Should be pretty safe, mid-day," said Zack.

"Unless he's looking to get even with a fucking queer," said Osgood.

Zack's face fell.

"I have mace," said Audrey.

Why don't you tell us something we don't know first, suggested Osgood to the anonymous texter.

The ellipses came and went for a more extended period this time. **I imagine you know that my father died.**

They looked at each other.

But you probably don't know that after the cops roundly ignored his Rest Stop Papers report, he went down the track you're on: the symbols, the records. Then he blew his brains out. Ellipses. **Noon?**

"It's Mazarowski's fucking son," said Osgood. **Noon,** she replied.

🖈 31 🖈

"Y ou two'll be okay here, alone?" Zack asked, looking toward the front windows.

Osgood cocked her head at him. "I live alone all the time, you know."

"Well, not usually with a stalker outside."

"I'm a visibly queer woman, Zack," said Osgood. "The world is my stalker."

"Okay then. I will be back here by eleven," he said. He looked down at his shoes for a moment then threw his arms around Osgood. She sighed and wrapped hers around him. She realized with surprise that in all their time together they hadn't hugged before. No more than a touch on the arm or an encouraging punch on the shoulder. She wondered if maybe she held people a little too far from her. Essential people.

Zack let go and turned to Audrey, uncertainty on his face.

"Bring it in, Zack," said Audrey, opening her arms.

He slammed a hug on her as well. When he stepped back into the doorway, he pulled his bag over his shoulder, pointing to the three separate locks on her door. "Lock all three," he said.

"All three," repeated Osgood.

"And you should really follow me down and lock the deadbolt downstairs."

"I'll do it," said Audrey.

"Okay," said Zack. "Eleven tomorrow."

"Eleven," said Osgood.

Zack headed down the stairs, and Audrey followed.

Osgood looked around her living room, at the table full of gear, printers, and the projector. Papers stacked on the coffee table and end table. The record player and speakers. And, of course, the gigantic mosaic of *Ramparts Over the Hinterlands*. While that last item still unnerved her, as she continued to find small monstrous animals that looked like they'd wandered directly out of *The Garden of Earthly Delights*, the rest felt so good. A real investigation. A team. Prudence and Audrey, Pru and Odd, Frost and Osgood, solving mysteries. *Also Zack,* she thought.

She stepped right up to the mosaic, and the individual pages ruffled from the breeze of her movement. The apartment felt too silent. She knew that she could flip the record player back on to fill the silence but thought perhaps hearing more In the Shallows was the last thing she needed now. This close to the art, at this size, she realized she could see the individual brush-strokes in the battlements. Fortifications in grays and brick reds, medieval style. She noticed a small point poking out from behind one, and realized it was the tip of a spear. Something climbing the wall?

Audrey closed the apartment door behind her, and, as requested, locked all three locks.

"The detail is pretty stunning for an album cover," said Osgood, without looking away.

"We couldn't find any record of who painted it. And there's no credit in the liner notes."

"That's odd," said Osgood. "Isn't it?"

"Yes," confirmed Audrey, stepping up next to her. "Did you see the numbers?"

"No," said Osgood, scanning the painting for a number.

Audrey reached up into one of the treetops and traced the number six with her finger. "And there's another..." she trailed off, looking, looking, then found the number three in another treetop.

"We should mark those," said Osgood.

"Zack's going to bring silver pens tomorrow. They'll mark better on top of this color." Audrey smiled at her. "He's got an excellent head on his shoulders."

Osgood smiled back. "Not as good as yours."

Audrey's smile faltered. "I'm not competing with him."

"No," said Osgood. "But like it or not, everybody's competing with you."

"Please, don't," said Audrey, sitting on the couch. After a moment, she poured herself three fingers of the bourbon and took a long sip.

"I'm sorry." Osgood looked at her hands and gave voice to a nagging itch. "Sometimes I wonder if I just like belong alone. Can't say shit right. Can't do shit right."

"Are we looking for sympathy now?" asked Audrey.

"No," said Osgood. "Just thinking aloud. I say what I think. It gets me in trouble."

"Indeed," said Audrey.

"I just got out of a three-year relationship with a couple, and the cracks appeared because I started…saying shit."

"I'm not sure I even understand how you could be in a relationship with a couple."

Osgood felt herself clench. "Don't judge my relationships."

"I'm not," said Audrey, emphatically. "I don't understand the objective organizational dynamics of dating a couple."

"Oh," said Osgood, feeling some of her tension ebb. "Well, when it worked, it was amazing. I had two people who loved me, together and separately. Two people who were there. People who encouraged my walkabouts and dalliances. People who had their own extended clusters."

"And then?"

"I thought I'd been valuable, wanted, needed. But turns out, couples are still couples at the end of the day. And when your presence points to issues between them, sometimes they close the gates, and it's no longer we three, but them and you." Osgood took a deep breath. "And then you say more shit. And then *they* say shit. And in the end, you're single again because some things can't be unsaid." The two of them sat in silence until Osgood couldn't take it. "And behold, I say shit, and the conversation dies."

"That's not it," said Audrey.

"Oh?"

"It's hard to be here," Audrey said, after another endless stretch of silence.

"I'm glad you are."

"It's hard to look at you and not think about—"

"I know," said Osgood. "What a fraud I am."

"No," said Audrey, smacking her hand on the cushion next to her. She stared into her bourbon with a cocked jaw, then downed the rest. "You were my first love, Prudence."

Osgood blinked in surprise. She had expected a dressing down, another berating. Not that.

"I can't put you aside, you know?" Audrey wiped her nose with the back of her hand. "It doesn't matter that I'm not gay."

"I sorta identify as bi or pan," offered Osgood. "Queer, mostly."

Audrey's eyes snapped to her. "I don't see how that helps."

"Sorry."

"What I'm saying is that, when a lot of partnerships break up, or bands, or whatever, they can all go their separate ways and leave the past in the past." Audrey leaned back on the couch, her face tilted toward the ceiling. "I can't. I wish we'd never been friends. I wish we'd never been girlfriends."

Osgood felt punched in the gut. "I don't," she whispered.

"If we hadn't, if we'd just been co-hosts of that stupid show, I could've let it go after what you did. Chalked it up as a bad experience, taken the hush money, run. Cashed in. All of that." Audrey sighed. "But instead, Pru, you're a part of me. Forever. Slipped in early, at the dawn of sexuality, and set up shop."

"You'll always be a part of me," said Osgood, pressing her hand to her chest.

"I wish that wasn't the case."

"But why?" Osgood held onto her tears. "Why not wish away just the shitty part, instead? Wish we'd not done that show. Or wish we were never partners? Why wish away the good?" She choked back a sob.

"Because without the love, it would've hurt less." Audrey looked at her. "Do you have any idea how much I've missed you? How many times I've wanted to call you, to reach out. How often I look up your social media profiles and *almost* click the friend button? How often I listen to the introduction of your podcast before turning it off when you go live? Nice music, by the way."

"Zack wrote it," said Osgood, processing her comments. "I do that with you all the time. I left a message when I was going to be on *This American Life*, to ask you to be a part of it. But I had to leave it at your parents' number, 'cuz I couldn't find a current one for you."

"My mother told me the week after it aired. She said that she didn't see why I couldn't just forgive you." Audrey took another drink. "I told her she didn't understand."

Osgood looked at the side of Audrey's face, at the stress-induced thinness, at the shadows under her cheekbones. She asked the question and wasn't sure if she could survive the answer. "Do you think you ever could forgive me?"

"Yes," said Audrey, without hesitation.

"How?" asked Osgood in surprise. "What would it take?"

"The amount you care about Caroline, about this. The fact that you never abandoned the hunt like everybody else. Even me." Audrey finally turned to look at her. "Well, that's a start."

"I loved her, too," said Osgood.

"I know you did," said Audrey. "She loved you."

"I still think about that morning, you know. That drive to Iowa." Osgood remembered Audrey waking her up, banging on her bedroom door. They'd lived together then. "You said 'I need to go—'"

"And you got dressed and said you'd take me, didn't even ask where." Audrey refilled her glass, then poured a healthy amount into Osgood's empty.

"You sure you want to drink like—"

"You sure you want to lecture me about drinking?" asked Audrey.

Osgood didn't. She sat on the couch next to her and lifted the glass. "To Caroline."

"To Caroline," said Audrey, clinking her glass against Osgood's. "Sometimes in my dreams, she was there, in her dorm room."

"And everything was fine?"

"No," said Audrey. "Sometimes when we're leaving, we remember that we saw her glasses on the floor, poking out from under her bed, and go back."

"We did go back," said Osgood, wondering if she remembered accurately.

"I know, but in the dream, when we get the glasses, we find her. Stuffed under her bed, mutilated beyond... Missing her eyes." Audrey pressed her hand over her own. "I see her all the time like that, under there, eyeless. In closets. In the dark. When I close my eyes."

Osgood nodded, not knowing what to say. She put her hand on Audrey's knee. "We'll find her," she said, knowing that it was likely not the truth, but knowing they could both use a little fictional encouragement right now.

"Not alive, we won't," said Audrey.

Osgood nodded. "Now the investigation is about—"

"Now I just want to know what happened. I haven't *really* thought she was still alive for a while. I just need closure." She leaned forward and tapped the sheaf of posters from the rest stop, topped with a Spectral Inspector mug holding them in place. "And I'm sure these kids' families need closure, too." She knocked back the last of her drink. "I waited, I looked, longer than anyone else. Longer than my parents, longer than the police. But it's twenty years now. Twenty years of wondering, for me, for them." Audrey waved her hand at the album art. "And this..." She opened and closed her mouth a few times, unable to finish. "Whatever the fuck this is, it's connected."

"Yeah," agreed Osgood. "I think so, too."

"Do you want to know what would help me to forgive you? What you can do?"

"I really do."

"See this through with me. To the bitter end. No matter how horrible that end might be." Audrey's eyes emphasized the plea.

"I'm here." Osgood took her hand. "To the end, to beyond."

✗ 32 ✗

"**F**uck."

Osgood looks around and repeats it. "Fuck."

At least the sky above the crossroads has returned to full dark with nary a quasar in sight. She wishes, though, that she could see a few stars. Just enough to ground her. Orion, the Big Dipper, the Pleiades. The constellations she saw with her father, long ago, when she was his princess, and he'd take her on Saturday mornings to the planetarium, to see the sky show, to look at the planetary dioramas.

No comfort from above here, though, just a beacon. *Cha-click*, north-south; *cha-click*, east-west.

She decides to try something new and begins to walk toward the ancient Amoco station that has no business still existing in 2019. The gas prices are laughable at less than a buck. She only remembers that happening once in her life. Just after she got her first car. It seems so long ago.

Her Skylark sits in the station's parking lot, the engine running in that stuttery way that old engines do. She folds her arms across her breasts and wonders why she must always be naked here.

"Well, this is my omnibus anxiety dream, isn't it?" she suggests to herself. "It replaced naked in class. It replaced the test I'd forgotten. It's the sum of all dreams. The tower at the center." She laughs and hears that laugh echo around the desolate gas station. "And I even die at the end!"

She wonders what would happen if she went inside the service center. Would it have an interior at all? Would it fill in as she explored? Is this world complete in her mind, or is it building itself as she goes?

She's reached the parking lot and stands next to the passenger side of the Skylark. She takes a deep breath, ready to look deeper into her past. Then she reaches down and pulls on the latch. The door swings open. She bends down and looks inside at the other her. The her from 1998, maybe still *in* 1998, behind the wheel. That Prudence turns her head to look, blankly, at Osgood, the nude woman who has just opened her passenger door.

Osgood climbs into the passenger seat of the Skylark, uncertain why on earth she is doing such a thing as she closes the door behind her. She turns to her younger self. "What now?"

After a moment, the blank expression on young Prudence's face is replaced with a smile, starting friendly, warm, her natural smile from those days where there was more to smile about. Of course, like those days, that smile doesn't last. It tightens to the look of rictus setting in, lockjaw, the horrid disfigured grin of Conrad Veidt in *The Man Who Laughs*. Then, horribly, it continues to expand, and Prudence's face is bisected by the smile, filled with far too many teeth.

When Prudence speaks, it's the voice of the damned, the voice of the man on the record, "You're getting closer, but you mustn't trust." Then her teeth clamp shut, severing the tip of her tongue, which flops down her shirt. Prudence, the thing that was Prudence, laughs from within her clenched jaws, and black pitch-like tears pour down her face.

The voice is different when it continues, multitudes layered atop each other including her own, not her voice from decades passed, but now. "You like to look, don't you girl." Her words don't match the movements of her mouth.

"Don't call me girl," whispers Osgood.

"But you are," says Prudence, "nothing but a frightened little girl. Terrified to sleep. Terrified to come back here."

Osgood watches the skin below Prudence's right ear split as the smile widens further. The muscles snap, and the jaw hangs, yawning open, still smiling.

Having had enough, Osgood reaches for the handle to get back out. She needs to get out, but the handle is gone, not so much as a hole where it had been.

"You know where you are," says Prudence, leaning over her shoulder, pouring foul breath into her face, tainted with an even more horrible layer of decaying sweetness beneath. "It's not where you've convinced yourself that you are."

Osgood bangs on the window. There's a lurch, and the Buick moves forward. She feels the terror, confident that now she's about to experience an entirely new version of the crash, being driven by the thing in her eighteen-year-old body. The thing destroying her pretty young face with its mouth. She hazards a glance at it and sees that the outer edges of Prudence's grin have begun to curl around behind its ears, and the jaw hangs

(you let your face grow long)

even lower. She's sure at this moment that this version of her, Prudence at the wheel, and the screaming thing are—

"Oh, yes," Prudence confirms. "One and the same. You let us inside when we met."

The Buick pulls up to the intersection and idles. The driver's gaping mouth has almost crawled all the way behind its

(hers, my)

neck to connect in the back.

Osgood wonders what'll happen then. Will the lower jaw just slump down, the entire bottom half of her face coming loose? She finds herself woozy at the prospect.

"I'm afraid this is where you get out," says Prudence, in the voice of millions. Children and adults, screaming, crying, laughing.

The passenger door unlocks. "What if I don't?" she asks unable to mask her desperation. This is enough, isn't it? This horror, this abomination driving her old car? She doesn't really have to go through the crushing accident from her position below the beacon, does she? Not tonight. Not *tonight!*

"Oh?" asks Prudence, cackling.

"Not tonight," says Osgood, firm.

"Very well," laughs Prudence. "You have work to do. The world is thin."

Prudence reaches out, putting her hand over Osgood's face. With a shove, Osgood passes through the passenger door of the Buick Skylark and into—

Her La-Z-Boy.

The lights in the apartment are out, and the sign for Mary's casts a sickening red light over everything. "Audrey?" Osgood asks in a voice that can barely whisper, diaphragm still compressed from tension.

Behind her comes music, that sickening progression of backward piano notes, on a cycle that'll play until the last star dies if she lets it continue. She pulls the chair lever, folding down the footrest, restoring the seat to upright position.

For once, for fucking once, she's managed to get out of the crossroads without being crushed. Without experiencing the accident. Without—

Audrey stands before the turntable, head down, listening to the music. On the wall beyond her, the ramparts are massive. The forest, in the dim red neon light, looks hungry and monstrous.

"Aud," says Osgood. "You okay?"

Audrey doesn't reply, but her body sways ever so slightly with the music, as though moving in an unfelt breeze.

"Maybe we can turn this off?" suggests Osgood. She smiles, tightly, and then immediately closes her lips, the splitting face of Prudence in the car swimming before her eyes.

"I have to listen," says Audrey. "How else will I hear."

"That's...true," says Osgood. *Maybe she's sleepwalking,* she thinks.

"And if I don't look," continues Audrey, "How else will I see?"

Osgood laughs a nervous laugh. "Again, can't argue with your airtight logic."

Audrey slowly turns to face Osgood, and the horror knocks her back against the La-Z-Boy. Gouts of blood pour from a golf-ball sized hole where Audrey's left eye used to be, covering half of her face in slick, shiny red. Her other eye has rolled back, showing only the tiny bottom crescent of her iris.

"No! Jesus, Aud!" Osgood reaches her hand out, unsure what to do. Apply pressure? Where? *Hospital, Pru.* Hospital, yes, of course.

"I have to see," says Audrey, in a trembling voice. In a flash, she pulls the scissors in her right hand to her face. The impossibly long blades slide through her skin, above and below her right eye. It pops and oozes, then Audrey squeezes the scissors shut, tearing out her other eye, sending a new cascade of blood down her face and spurting onto Osgood.

"You can see too, Os," says Audrey. "We can see together." The scissors make a horrible slurp as Audrey yanks them from her skull. She twirls them on her index finger like a gunfighter, sending a cascade of blood droplets toward Osgood. Then she lifts the dual blades and aims them at Osgood's face.

"Please, Aud," says Osgood.

"It's beautiful," insists eyeless Audrey, wet sockets illuminated by the blinking of the Mary's neon. "In the center of an impossibly steep valley, you'll find the tower. In the tower, dwells The Lord. I've cut out my eyes, now I can see."

She swings the scissors up and Osgood feels the blades connect.

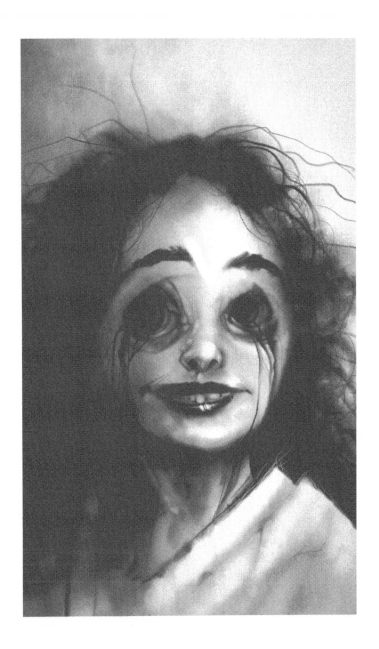

🪐 33 🪐

Osgood screamed. She couldn't see. All reddish black. All hidden away. Hands held her face still. Suddenly piercing light. The ceiling of her apartment. Audrey's face, concerned but complete with eyes.

"I'm sorry, I didn't want to disturb you with the lights," said Audrey, holding up the face mask that had darkened Osgood's vision moments before. "I couldn't sleep because I kept thinking about—"

"Jesus Christ," said Osgood, holding her hand to her chest. Her heart felt as though it could shove its way right through her sternum. "Fuck."

"I'm really sorry," said Audrey.

"No," gasped Osgood. "It's— Not you."

"Okay." Audrey nodded. "The same nightmare, then?"

"Something new. A rare fresh hell," said Osgood, feeling her heartbeat and breathing slowly return to normal. "And you..." she said, pointing at Audrey. But she didn't want to say. Audrey didn't need that idea in her head. "You were there, too."

Audrey gave her a crooked half-smile. "Hope I wasn't the bad guy."

"You weren't," said Osgood, adding, "I think I was," under her breath. She concentrated on taking longer breaths, calming herself, feeling her heartbeat stabilize. She wanted more than anything to lean forward and have another drink, but she could already see the disapproval on Audrey's face in her head. "What time is it?"

"Almost five," said Audrey.

Osgood nodded. "Have a while."

"Do you want to go and sleep in your bedroom, so I'm not bothering you?"

Osgood looked over her shoulder. The record player's plastic protective top was closed, and the album wasn't on the turntable. Above it, though, Osgood saw an alarming sight. On the enormous *Ramparts Over the Hinterlands* cover were massive black circles and outlines, some the sigil of the Lord, others a wholly different but repeated sigil, one they'd seen before on the rest stop papers. "Audrey?"

"Yeah, I, uh—"

"Tell me you're not just randomly doodling this stuff?"

"What?" Audrey looked at the mural on the wall. "No. This is all there!" She rushed over to it. "There's the six and the three we found earlier. A two; a seven, which I'll admit might be an arrow, considering what it's pointing to; a zero, one of the nil ones with the slash through it. The sigil, it's… well, it's everywhere." She pointed with her thick black marker at five different spots where the sigil appeared. "And this doesn't even get into the stuff on the other side."

Osgood stood slowly, feeling the shakiness in her thighs and lower back. She held onto the back of the chair offering only wobbly support. "How many numbers?"

"Ten," said Audrey, looking back at the mural. "If we count that seven as an arrow, which I'm inclined to."

"You've made coffee, I take it?" asked Osgood, noticing her manic movements.

"I brought my own…supplements," Audrey answered with slight hesitation.

Osgood smirked at her. "Why, Miss Frost, are you on speed?"

"Supplements!" Audrey repeated, pointedly. "Miss Oxy 2019."

"I imagine Miss Oxy would get as much as she wanted," said Osgood. "I'm forced to scrounge." She moved toward the mural. "Ten. Like a—"

"Phone number, I think," said Audrey. "It's out of service, though." She handed Osgood a small notebook with the ten numbers written out on it.

"320 area code?"

"Minnesota. That's if we go in order, from top to bottom."

Osgood nodded. "Well, I'll be damned if that doesn't feel like it fits."

"Not just that," said Audrey. "But the exchange is the same as the original phone number for Gloria Mundi records. In Minnesota."

"Intentional."

"How could it not be?"

"Well," said Osgood, "at this point in the investigation, maybe we can just follow the coincidences that seem to be cropping up at an insane pace. What'd you find on the back? More numbers?"

"Flip the page."

Osgood did. "Yeah," she said, seeing another set of numbers. "That seems right." 1-1-0-6-1-9-9-9, 11/06/1999. Osgood sighed.

Audrey shoved the album cover of *Ramparts Over the Hinterlands* into Osgood's free hand so quickly that she almost dropped it. "So you don't have to walk all the way down the hall."

"Well, I have to pee anyway," said Osgood.

"Then come and see the big one," said Audrey, leading the way to where the mural featuring the back cover of *Ramparts Over the Hinterlands* was taped. "I initially just thought it was a devil connection. Yunno, 666," she said and pointed to a cluster of sixes at the upper left corner of the mural. She traced an angle from it, down and to the right, to a one, a nine, zero, one, and one.

"Upside down," said Osgood.

"It's too coincidental to *not* be the date at this point," said Audrey.

"Okay. Give me a minute so I don't pee myself while you talk." Osgood walked toward the bathroom and her knee buckled. Audrey was there to catch her before she fell. The pain throbbed up her leg like a good morning alarm clock to her usual aches and pains, putting them all on full alert.

"Let me help you."

"You don't need to help me pee."

"Oh?" asked Audrey. "I should just let go, then?"

Osgood scowled. "No. Fine. I just—"

"Dial back the pride, Os. This is what friends do."

"Are we friends?"

"We were friends in high school, weren't we?" asked Audrey with a laugh. "Wouldn't be the first time I've seen you pee."

"We're a long way from high school," said Osgood, feeling gratitude that the gulf seemed to be narrowing. She didn't want to say more and ruin it. Friends.

Audrey even turned her back as she went.

"Here," said Audrey, handing Osgood the tincture bottle from the medicine cabinet. "Though I'd really recommend trying to switch over to pot."

"Doesn't work as well."

"And what sort of dose are you on here?" She pointed to the bottle as Osgood placed several drops beneath her tongue.

"Less than OD levels," said Osgood, sliding the dropper back into the bottle and shoving it in her pocket. "I've got this."

"You don't seem…"

"In control?" asked Osgood.

"Yeah."

"I'm trying to be," said Osgood.

"I'm trying, too," said Audrey. "But I know when I need help."

Osgood looked at Audrey, wearing pajama pants and a spaghetti-strap tank top, one hand held out in an offer of help. She took Audrey's hand.

As they drifted back down the hallway, Osgood's pain ebbing as they went, she asked, "What else did you find?"

"The sigils are everywhere, in constellations in the sky, carved into the trees..." They stopped in front of the second mural.

Osgood took it in: broken and crumbling bricks formed the background, with the album credits on the right and the minimal track listing on the left. Here, as in the front room, the sigils were traced in cracks in the brick and around words. Most disturbing to Osgood was a new sigil that popped up many times, a pointed oval with a circle inside, bisected by a bulging vertical line.

"That's an eye, isn't it?" Osgood suggested, putting her finger on it.

"I wouldn't be surprised," said Audrey. "I've image searched some of these, and only the one on the flag comes up, and only because it's on that flag. It is, interestingly, called the Sign of the Lord."

"The one we're not supposed to trust," said Osgood. "The one Mazarowski's son wants to kill."

"The Lord of the Hinterlands."

They returned to the living room, and Osgood curled up in the papasan chair. Outside her front windows, dawn had just begun to break.

🐦 34 🐦

Osgood noticed when a skinny man with the slightly lopsided face walked through the door of Mary's Diner. His eyes never left them. A waitress walked up to ask what she could get him, and he held up a hand, jerking away from her as she neared. His eyes connected with Osgoods, then Audrey's and Zack's and he sat, not in the chair they'd left, but at the next table, across the table.

Osgood sat directly opposite him, with Zack on her left and Audrey on her right. Their table for four was separated from his by several feet. Inez came by, and he jumped, startled, then said, "Water," and shooed her away. "In a bottle!" he called after.

The three of them stared, waiting for Mazarowski's son's opening salvo.

His hair was close-cropped against his head and uneven, that of a man determined to cut his own with scissors rather than electric clippers. His face had five or six days of patchy salt-and-pepper beard growth. One of his eyes was dark and the other pale blue. The side of his head, above the icy eye, bulged outward. Osgood realized she was staring and averted her eyes. Before she looked away entirely, though, she saw him smirk at her discomfort.

Zack looked from Osgood to Audrey and back, expectant, nervous.

"You're Mazarowski," said Audrey.

He banged on the table with both hands, fury on his face, then he became serene and held an index finger to his lips. "Privileged information."

"Your father was Clinton—"

"Again, privileged. Please, don't make me leave."

"You're also Guardian," said Osgood, turning her eyes back to his, only to find him staring deep into her.

"This I am," he said. "*The* Guardian, though, please."

"Well," said Osgood, pursing her lips. "I'm not going to call you that. So you either give us your first name, or I'm going to make one up for you. You look like..." she leaned forward toward him. "...a Todd."

He seemed to recoil, the grin leaving his face, and he flinched multiple times as he drummed his fingers on the table top.

"I am—" he began, lower than a whisper, so low they could barely hear it.

"We cannot hear you," said Osgood, voice raised. Other patrons at Mary's looked over curiously.

"Keep your voice down!" he demanded in a desperate stage whisper.

"No!" said Osgood. She pointed at the chair across the table from her. "Sit there." She kicked the chair and it screeched backward, banging into the one opposite it at his table. "If we're going to speak, we're going to speak together, and if you want quiet, you'll have to sit with us, and if you want respect, you will have to fucking start showing some."

The man, son of Mazarowski, the Guardian, tilted his head like a dog, first one way, then the other, sizing her up. He stood and crossed to their table. As he came closer, she could see that his black jeans were worn pale, and his black t-shirt had run holes in the neck.

"So?" she asked as he sat. "What is your name?"

"Robert."

"Robert," Audrey repeated.

"Robert Mazarowski?" asked Zack.

"Yes, though I mostly use my mother's name," he furtively glanced around and dropped his voice again. "Cahill. Security, you see. My father spent much of his life as a fugitive of one form or another, from everyone including governmental entities, police and sheriff departments, agencies of espionage, to...other."

"Other?" asked Osgood, knowing precisely what he was trying to imply but not willing to let this awkward weirdo who'd taken pictures of them off the hook.

"Forces beyond. Surely you know that," he lowered his voice to a bassy rumble, "Spectral Inspector."

"You know me."

"I know all of you."

"You don't know me," said Zack, sneering at him.

"Zack Nguyen."

"And? It's a common name."

"It may be, but you are not," Mazarowski said. "You live in your father's garage. Your mother died when you were—"

"Fine," snapped Zack.

"You, Miss Frost, I empathize with so much," said Mazarowski. "First you lose your beautiful sister and then are torched by this one," he flicked a dismissive finger toward Osgood, "and now, dragged back in, they're going to walk you into the snake pit with nary a concern for your safety and security."

Audrey's eyes rolled a minute amount, but she steadied. "You're so perceptive," she told him.

"I am," he said with a smile. Osgood saw, as his smile widened, that his molars were missing. "But I assure you that I'm not here to fight with you."

"Oh?" asked Osgood. "Any reason why you were threatening us and taking pictures?"

"I did not threaten you."

Osgood scrolled up, then read the message. "'I'm watching. Be careful.'"

"As I just told your friend here, I'm concerned for your safety."

"All of ours, or just hers?"

"Everyone's." He folded his hands on the edge of the table. "You—" he cut himself off, then took a noisy breath through his nose. "You have no idea what you're digging into here. You're on a mountain in the fog and are moving slowly, but not slowly enough, and if you move your feet just a bit to the right, you'll plunge into an abyss."

"So," said Audrey, shaking her head. "Tell us."

Mazarowski took another noisy breath, the sound of a severely-deviated septum, and leaned down below the table.

All three of them shoved their chairs back as he did.

"What're you doing?" asked Zack, reaching into his pocket.

"I'm only getting my bag," said Mazarowski, lifting a skinny messenger bag onto the table. "You all are so jumpy. I imagine he's shown himself to you already, then?"

"Who?" asked Osgood.

"He will," said Mazarowski. "Patience, Prudence Osgood, you'll have no need to fake it this time. He's going to rock. Your. World."

Osgood didn't know how to respond to that and allowed her mouth to hang open for a moment.

"Hey!" said Zack firmly.

Mazarowski waved him away with a smile, as though brushing off lint – inconsequential. The smile vanished when Zack grabbed his wrist. His eyes went wide, showing how different the brown and the blue one really were. He turned his head toward Zack. "You shouldn't touch me."

"I'm not interested in your philosophy, or in you saying shitty things to them. I'm interested in whatever real, concrete information you might have to give us. And if you don't have that, I'm interested in kicking your ass out of here."

The two men stared at each other, each trying to out-masculine the other. Osgood just shrugged at Audrey.

"Fair," Mazarowski said, finally. He folded his hands on the edge of the table again but recoiled when Inez set a glass of water in front of him. "Bottled, I said! Bottled."

"Only thing we have in a bottle is beer, bucko. If you want

bottled water, I can show you where you *can* find it." Inez stood, hands on her hips, staring down at him intensely. He didn't look up to meet her eyes.

"Fine." He slid the water away from him an extra inch and refolded his hands. "What have you found?"

Zack began. "We—"

"'The Rest Stop Papers?'" interrupted Mazarowski.

"Yes," said Osgood.

"And they led you to…"

"The date," said Zack.

"Which turned into…"

"The date my sister vanished," said Audrey.

"A victim of The Garnering," said Mazarowski. He reached toward her, then put his hand down again. "I truly am so sorry."

"You're saying she's dead," snapped Audrey, raising her voice. "They're all dead?"

"You know that she's dead, already. You've known it in yourself for quite some time." He held her eyes until she looked away. "And you are withholding," he turned his face back to Osgood and ran his pale pink tongue over his thin lips.

"What?" snapped Osgood.

"Well, I know you found the band, or you would not have gone to Planet Vinyl."

"We did," Osgood confirmed.

"Have you found the phone number yet?" asked Mazarowski with a grin.

"Yes," said Audrey, sliding her notebook toward him. "It's out of service."

"Only until it's ready," he snapped. "I'm talking about the *other* one. You need that one, yes," he tapped the notepaper. "But the other one opens the gate. So naive and full of yourselves."

"Alright, twitchy," said Osgood. "Where's this other number?"

"On the Brutal Cover," he said and waited.

"You're going to have to continue that statement."

"Then you really don't know anything," he said.

Audrey shook her head. "Listen, asshole."

Mazarowski stood, quickly, and all three of them flinched backward, unsure what he'd do. "I don't have to be here. I could just let you walk right into the trap. He'd devour you three, and I wouldn't bat an eye."

"He," repeated Osgood. "The Lord of the Hinterlands."

"I wouldn't speak too loudly," said Mazarowski. "They're listening everywhere. Not all the people," he waved his hand around to indicate the other diners, then leaned forward to whisper, "are real."

"Okay," said Audrey. "I've had enough of your *Beautiful Mind*ing."

He turned to her, his smile fading.

"Here's what's going to happen. You're going to leave here, and," she leaned close to him, and he pulled himself away from the table, "I want to be 100 percent clear on this part: You're never going to text message or email or call or otherwise contact—"

Mazarowski coughed into his hand, the cough of a fifty-year smoker in the body of someone under forty.

"Jesus," said Audrey, as he continued to cough.

"You, of all people, should want my help," he told Audrey.

"Why is that?"

Mazarowski looked around furtively, then looked around once more. His voice dropped to just above a whisper again, and they all leaned in to hear.

"When I first noticed you pinging," he pointed to Zack, "I didn't think much of it. People ping, people search. But then this one," his finger went to Osgood, "started talking out loud, and that's dangerous." He wagged his finger in a *tsk*ing gesture that infuriated Osgood. "She asked some friends for information, and they also happen to be my friends, so I recharted my course toward The Windy City." The volume of his voice had begun to increase. "And if you search Prudence Osgood, what do you find first? I'm sure she wishes it were the illustrious *Spectral Inspector Podcast*, and congratulations, by the way, ten years is an awfully long time for a podcast. I count myself as a," he smirked, "Specterino.

"But no, sadly, the most common search is about that episode the two of you did. *Chicago Haunts*, live from the shuttered-but-soon-to-reopen Waverly Hotel. The episode where you played your audience for fools and created your own ghost hoax."

"Shut up," said Osgood. "And she had nothing to do with that."

"Well, from there, it was easy to learn that your partner Audrey Frost had written countless pleas to the public and to law enforcement to continue the investigation into her missing sister, Caroline Frost." He turned to Audrey. "And you do, you look just like her. Though I do believe you could use some sun and perhaps a bit more protein in your diet."

He smirked. "How do we feel?" asked Mazarowski, turning back to the table. "Trust that I know what I'm talking about, now?"

Osgood didn't know what to say and, from the look on her compatriot's faces, they didn't either.

"The phone number," said Mazarowski.

"The out of service one," Osgood reiterated.

Mazarowski began to laugh, a horrid gasping sound that toed the line between choking and coughing. Had his lips not pulled back from his teeth in a smile that reminded Osgood of a long dead and decaying body, she would've thought him about to die. "Oh yes, it's out of service for you. Pity."

Osgood felt an audible growl escape her.

Mazarowski eyed her, cautiously. "How about I just tell you where that number leads." He tapped the paper.

"Please do," said Audrey, entirely over the encounter with this man.

"It rings a rest stop along I-94 in western Minnesota." Mazarowski smiled. "And by the looks on your faces, I'd say that fact means something to you already, which means my visit here wasn't a fool's errand, after all."

"And the other number?" asked Audrey, openly refusing to give him the satisfaction of her gratitude.

"On the fabled Brutal Cover." He put his finger in front of his lips again, this time with a bit of impish glee on his face. "But we don't talk about that one. It's dangerous."

"That rest stop, Miss Frost, should be of special note to you," he told her, reaching into his bag and removing a small envelope which he set before Audrey. "It is, after all, where I found this."

Audrey lifted the envelope gingerly.

Mazarowski stood, quickly enough to knock over the chair where he'd been sitting. "I don't stay anywhere longer than necessary. And you've convinced me that you're worth helping and are possibly the warriors I need."

"Wait," said Osgood. "What are you—"

"I will be happy to answer more questions in a less public setting. For now, you need to make a choice. In two days, I'm going to Minnesota to pass through the gate. And you need to decide if you're coming, too. I can do it without you easily, of course, but you may prove useful."

Audrey opened the envelope and pulled a piece of paper out of it, folded in fourths.

"Until then, ask yourself, how does a band from nowhere become an overnight sensation, especially after they lose their lead singer and go out of their way to make themselves as noncommercial as possible." He slung his bag over his shoulder. "I'll be in touch, but for now, I must go. I'm a steady-rollin' man, after all, with a hellhound on my trail."

He gave the three of them a wink and shoved his way back out of the restaurant, hands up so as not to touch anybody.

"What the *fuck?*" asked Osgood, looking after him. She turned to Zack, whose expression of perplexity mirrored hers.

Then she turned to Audrey, who was staring at the paper in front of her with tears in her eyes. The creased paper was covered with handwriting on one side and dark black photocopy print on the other. She looked from front to back to front to back, until she broke down. As she flipped the page, Osgood saw the picture on the front. It could very well have been a picture of the woman in tears next to her. Years and mileage had changed her, but the face remained the same.

"It's her writing," said Audrey with a choked sob.

Despite the similarity, of course, the text below the photo confirmed the truth in stark black text: *Caroline Frost. Missing since—* The fold in the paper obscured the rest.

35

Osgood stood at the front windows of her apartment and watched people walk up and down Clark below. She wondered if they felt the same unsettling dread as she did, if it was somehow emanating from her apartment, from the record player, from the mural on her wall. But no, of course not. They were blissfully unaware, as she'd once been. She remembered graduating high school and feeling like an adult for the first time: Like she'd arrived. She and Audrey had taken a road trip to California that summer, spending hours talking about their futures and what adulthood might yield. On the way home, they met the screaming thing. And then she got into her accident. And then Caroline disappeared. And they'd grown up for real, really fucking fast, hadn't they? If she'd grown up for real twenty years ago, what was she now, teetering on the edge of forty? Standing in her apartment window, Osgood wondered if she was finally a grownup? And beyond that, if she had any interest in being one.

"I'm a steady-rollin' man," she said to the street outside, unable to shake Mazarowski's parting words. "With a hellhound on my trail."

"All that build-up, and he's just playing with us," fumed Zack, slamming his bag onto the floor next to the table. He flopped down in front of his laptop and woke it up with a smack of the space bar. "I don't know if you got anything of value from that, but I— Osgood?"

Osgood turned. "That wasn't just a goodbye," she told him. "That was a clue."

"I thought it might be, too," said Zack.

"Where's Audrey?"

"Kitchen, I think," he said. "What did he say?"

She could see Robert Mazarowski, with that douchey expression on his face, standing before them to deliver his farewell. Osgood repeated it to Zack, "I'm a steady-rollin' man, after all, with a hellhound on my trail."

He typed it into the laptop and slapped his enter key harder than usual.

"He upset you," said Osgood.

"He's a smug asshole who talked down to all of us," said Zack. "And I don't trust him in the least."

"Good," said Osgood. "I don't either."

"Okay. Well, both 'I'm a Steady Rollin' Man' and 'Hellhound on My Trail' are songs."

"By Rhapsody in the Shallows?"

"No," said Zack. "By a blues musician in the '30s. Robert Johnson."

"Robert Johnson." Osgood walked over to the table. "Why do I know that name?"

"It's pretty generic." Zack continued to read the article about him. "Died when he was only twenty-seven. Considered to be one of the most important blues singers who ever lived."

"The devil," said Osgood, snapping her fingers.

"No," said Zack, slowly. "Blues musician."

"Yes, thank you, Zack," Osgood said, rolling her eyes. "Look up Robert Johnson and the devil."

He typed. After a moment, he read: "'Johnson's wild success and early death gave rise to many rumors around him, including the legend that, while living on a plantation in Mississippi and yearning to be the greatest blues musician of all time, he was told to bring his guitar to a crossroad.'"

"Where he met the devil," said Osgood.

"Yeah, looks like a variant on the Faust myth. Guitar skill for his soul." Zack leaned back down to skim through the rest of the text. "Many also suggest that 'the devil' was actually a representation of an African trickster deity named Legba." Zack leaned back from his computer. "Sounds to me like white people refusing to acknowledge natural talent in a black man and suggesting he *must* have made a deal with the devil for it."

"Probably," said Osgood. From the center of the cross-roads in her mind, Prudence, the *other* Prudence, with the mouth that went around her entire head, grinned at her. She shuddered.

"Mazarowski wasn't just using that line as a sign-off," said Zack. "He gave us a lead."

"Yeah," agreed Osgood. "To think about how a band from nowhere becomes so famous and continues to sell, despite doing seemingly everything in their power to halt their success. Maybe Rhapsody in the Shallows made a deal with the devil as well, and whatever happened to these kids was the penance for reneging."

"That's a stretch," said Zack.

"Is *any* of this not a stretch, Zack?"

He frowned.

"Didn't think so." Osgood took one last look out the window. "Do me a favor and dig into, what was his other name?"

"Cahill."

Osgood nodded. "That, yes. Also, that thing he called the Brutal Cover."

"We should've asked for elaboration on some of this."

"I think I spent all the time I care to with Robert Cahill-Mazarowski, personally."

Zack shrugged. "Me too." He slammed his hand down on the table.

"You okay?"

"I thought I could trust these people. I've been talking to them for so long."

"Your…" Osgood searched for the right word. "Sources?"

"To know they just fed our information and our requests to someone else. It's…" He slammed his hand down again. "I'm sorry."

"It's not your fault," said Osgood.

"I led him to us."

"No," said Osgood. "Do not take that on yourself."

Zack stared at his laptop. After a while, he looked at her, his eyes intense. "I've got some wireless security systems in the Jeep. I'm going to get them installed before nightfall."

"Do what you think is best, Zack. I trust *you*."

His intensity mellowed, and he smiled. "Thank you, Os."

"I'm going to go check on Audrey," she told Zack, and then to herself, repeated, "'I'm a steady-rollin' man.'"

Osgood found the kitchen empty, then peaked into her bedroom, also empty. She knocked on the bathroom door and heard a loud sniff and shuffle.

"Yeah?" asked Audrey from inside, her voice wavering.

"Aud."

"Yes."

"Would you like to talk?"

Silence. Osgood waited. A click, the door unlocked, then more shuffling in the bathroom.

"I'm going to come in, okay?" asked Osgood.

"S'why I unlocked the door," said Audrey, a note of indignance in her voice.

Osgood slowly opened the door to find Audrey sitting on the fluffy bath-mat with her legs crossed, a box of tissues by her side and a pile of crumpled tissues opposite her.

"This is stupid," said Audrey, sniffing hard.

"What is stupid?" asked Osgood. She sat slowly, cross-legged, in front of Audrey, then wondered if she should've chosen another position, as the aches began almost immediately. *No,* she reminded herself, *Mirror her body language.*

"This," she held up the paper, the rest stop paper with Caroline's face on it. With Audrey's face. "That she wrote this. That she's really connected to all this. Not just maybe. But really."

"One of the rest stop children."

"It's like that 'Wise Lord' song on *Tether*," said Audrey.

"I don't know it," said Osgood.

"I'd forgotten a lot of it but re-listened last night. It's weird. It kind of sounds like a praise song. 'Children come unto me,' and stuff like that. The Lord of Hinterland was wise like Solomon. He could solve your problems, set you on the path."

"Praise song, indeed," said Osgood.

"I'm sure she's dead. But I need to know what happened to her."

"I get it," said Osgood. "I want to know, too. And if this is someone, or some*thing*, taking people, I want to fucking stop it if it is within our power."

Audrey looked at her and smiled. "You look so different now."

"That's an abrupt conversational shift," said Osgood. "You look quite different yourself."

"Sick," said Audrey. "I look sick."

"No."

"I do. I look like I've been starved for weeks. I just can't keep food down." She sighed and put her hand on Osgood's knee. "I don't try to throw up, really; I just do."

Osgood nodded. "Is Tony helping?"

"Tony left," she said and held a tissue to her mouth to stifle a weak laugh. "A year ago, now. Well, a year next month."

"I'm sorry," said Osgood.

"He said I wasn't taking care of myself. Physically or mentally. And he couldn't be around me. Just waiting for the divorce papers to make this thing official!" She pointed at Osgood. "You'da liked him. He's a drunk, too."

"Ouch," said Osgood.

"Sorry." Audrey looked down at her feet. "I don't mean to do that."

"I deserve it," said Osgood, also looking down.

"What you deserved, Osgood," said Audrey with intensity, "was for me to deal with my emotional bullshit and work through it with you. I knew it wasn't your plan. I knew you didn't want to do it."

"I just wanted—"

Audrey held up her hands. "We've talked through that moment enough, I think. We both mishandled it."

"Agreed," said Osgood. "And I am a drunk," she added after a while. "Though drunks don't always prefer the company of other drunks. Most of the time we enjoy the solitude."

"Or pick people up?"

"Well, I *do* do that," said Osgood with a laugh. "With Tony being gone so long, when was the last time you were good and fucked?"

Audrey laughed. "Honestly, I don't know if I was ever good and fucked by Tony."

"Eh," said Osgood. "Not many people are that good at it."

"Women better?"

Osgood shrugged. "Different. Not better, not worse." After hesitating, Osgood added, "You were good."

"Oh, whatever, Os," said Audrey, waving away the compliment.

They sat in silence for a long while.

"What would you do, to see this through to the end?" asked Osgood.

"Anything. Everything," said Audrey. "I would trade myself for her."

"I'd rather you not do that."

"I would've, back then."

"I know," said Osgood. She put her hand over Audrey's, on her knee. "But I mean now. I'd rather you didn't do anything and everything to see this through now." Looking into Audrey's eyes, Osgood thought she understood.

"How about you?" asked Audrey, breaking the eye contact.

"Well," said Osgood, "I want to meet the Lord of the Hinterlands so I can tell him to go fuck himself."

Audrey laughed, then Osgood joined her. The two of them

sat, laughing on the floor of the bathroom until Zack knocked on the door.

"You two are being weird in there!"

"Be right out," said Audrey. She leaned forward and kissed Osgood's cheek.

For a moment, Osgood felt all was right with the world. Pity, moments like that can't last.

Entropy kicks in; the center does not hold.

36

"This is Robert Mazarowski," said Zack, showing them a picture on his tablet. The photo looked like a work ID photo of a much healthier-looking man against a blue background. Healthier then, but still the man they'd met downstairs. "That's 2005. He was working at a tech company back then. Based in, wait for it, Minneapolis. After 2006, he seems to fall off the radar. I have his mother, Eileen Cahill, but nothing further back than that. My guess is he ghosted himself. Since we share friends, shouldn't have been too hard for him."

"I'm surprised he told the truth," said Audrey.

Osgood nodded.

"I still don't trust him," said Zack.

"Me neither."

"Only one hit for Robert Cahill in the deep corners of the web, so it's clear he doesn't use that name online much. But it's an interesting one and leads me to believe he wanted me to find it," Zack handed them each a tablet with an open PDF.

Osgood read the title aloud. "'The Hinterland Messages.'"

"He goes full 'Paul is Dead' conspiracy here, on messages to be found on Rhapsody in the Shallows and In the Shallows' records, cover art, interviews, and songs."

Audrey swiped through and stopped. "'If you pause the

track at exactly halfway through, which is one minute and fifty-seven seconds, then reverse the turntable, you'll find it sliding into a different groove and playing a different song.'"

"Ramparts?" asked Osgood.

"No, *Race to the Island*," said Audrey.

"They were putting stuff in that early?"

"Honestly," said Zack, holding his hands up, "I think most of this shit is blowing stuff out of proportion or outright invention. For instance..." He searched through the pdf on his laptop to a sentence he'd highlighted. "'You'll find two sets of four-digit numbers, 3827 and 5849, now you'll notice if you add up each of those digits, they add up to 46, 4 and 6 is 10. If you add 3827 to 5849, you get 9676, adding those digits comes to 28, 2 and 8 is 10.'"

"Does he have a point?" asked Osgood.

Zack shrugged and shook his head. "Ten seems to be a lynchpin for him." He reached over to the stack of albums. "If we want to take him at face value and believe he's onto something..." He held up *Tether*, flipping to the track listing on the back side. "The tenth song is 'The Wise Lord of Hinterland.'"

"Of course," said Osgood. "Have you looked for references to the Lord of Hinterland or Hinterlands beyond this band?"

"One of the first things I did after he texted about it yesterday. There's nothing. Literally nothing. Which is interesting, considering this essay exists online, so it should be coming up in searches." Zack scowled. "I—" He stopped. "I don't know how to help." He looked up at them, forlorn.

"You *are* helping, Zack," said Audrey. "I promise."

"Okay, look," said Osgood. "There's every likelihood that much of this is coincidence."

"Is there?" asked Audrey.

"I need you to be Frost the Skeptic right now, Aud," said Osgood. "Not Caroline's sister."

Audrey blinked for a moment, then nodded. "Alright."

"And that the disappearances are also coincidences."

"Wait," said Zack. "No."

"I'm trying to talk something—"

"No!" Zack said, firmer.

Osgood stopped and waited.

"Those names, those people that disappeared. All on the same day. All showing up in that stack," he pointed to the sheaf of pages on the table, then to Audrey. "And Caroline! No way it's a coincidence. No fucking way. There certainly could be non-supernatural explanations, and all this shit with In the Shallows, *that* might be coincidence, but the rest—"

"I'm trying really hard to be objective," said Osgood.

"I think we might have officially passed that," said Audrey. She held up her tablet again to read. "'The Brutal Cover may be the key to all of this. While *Tether* was a huge hit, selling over thirty million copies, *Ramparts Over the Hinterlands* defied all logic, managing forty-two million, putting it among the top-selling records of all time, despite being released *only on vinyl* in 1998, long past the prime of vinyl.'"

"How did they manage to release only on vinyl in '98?" asked Osgood, incredulously.

Audrey held up a finger and continued. "'Of those forty-two million, though, less than a thousand were part of the initial run with the 'Brutal Cover' as it's come to be known. No pictures seem to exist of this cover, and descriptions vary wildly. But the Brutal Cover takes its name from an interview with Knox just after release. 'We made a mistake with that brutal cover, so the studio just pasted the new art over the top. Didn't think it'd sell anyway.'"

"I've got nothing more about that cover, unfortunately," said Zack. "He mentions later that the phone number that opens the gate is on that cover."

Osgood picked up *Ramparts Over the Hinterlands* and inspected the front cover. "All one piece of cardboard. Nothing pasted over."

"What're the odds you'd get one of the thousand?" asked Zack.

Audrey looked at him. "One in forty thousand?"

"Well…" Zack said huffily. "Yes."

Osgood lifted the gifted and beat-up copy of *Ramparts* they'd received from Planet Vinyl. "This one isn't either."

"Wait," said Audrey. "Less than a thousand."

"Yeah," said Osgood.

"And that cover—"

"Opens the gate," finished Osgood. "Zack!"

"What?"

"Bring up that photo from MandyCam, where we see the album."

"Please would be—"

"Sorry, Zack," Osgood said and waved her hands. "I appreciate you, and you're essential and wonderful. Now, pretty please—"

"Yeah, yeah," he said. He opened a folder, then double clicked an image and made it full screen. The grainy black and white night vision seemed to have a more ominous and eerie quality than before.

"Can you zoom in on the cover?" asked Osgood.

Zack drew a box around it with the magnifying glass, and it filled the screen, pixelated, but clearly *Ramparts Over the Hinterlands*.

"Look," said Osgood, poking at the screen. The upper left corner of *Ramparts* had rolled, like a label coming off. They couldn't see what was below it.

"The ones who disappeared had that version," said Audrey.

"Where's Caroline's copy?" asked Osgood.

"In the office with my stuff," said Audrey, already on her way there. She returned with a third copy of *Ramparts Over the Hinterlands*, holding it up to inspect. "Holy shit."

"Is it—"

"Do you have a razor blade?"

"Does your suicidal friend Osgood have razor blades?" asked Osgood, laughing. "Sorry, adrenaline is high, and most of my humor is gallows." She frowned, then went to the bathroom and brought back a box of razor blades. "I really didn't mean to sour—"

"Os, stoppit," said Audrey, reaching for a blade. She slid it carefully along the side, then she set the album on the coffee table and knelt before it. She worked diligently, her hands steady, up and back, only once slicing through the main cover. After five minutes of silence, she looked up at them. "This is it." She sped up, and her focus intensified. She slid the razor back and forth, little *shish* noises rising, as she peeled back the battlements and the forest, finally with some paste still in place and a few stuck-on pieces of the paste-over, revealing the Brutal Cover.

"What the fuck?" said Zack.

"I can see why this wasn't the way to go," said Osgood.

Audrey nodded.

The Brutal Cover featured four men against a seamless white backdrop. Three were turned toward the camera, one facing away. The smiles on the men facing the camera looked, not forced, really, but empty. Their eyes had a long-distance focus that wasn't on the camera. The man facing away looked down. Osgood followed his look down his arm, to a hand covered in crimson. Following his hand to the floor, she found a puddle of liquid crimson, with a splash frozen in time in the center.

"Well, this is in poor taste," said Zack.

"Agreed," said Audrey.

"I mean, yeah," said Osgood poking her finger at the blood pool. "But why, specifically?"

"Right," said Audrey. "You didn't know the band." She put her finger on each of the faces from left to right, skipping the man facing away. "This is Will Knox, co-founder, co-writer, the new lead singer once Antrell died. Hank Fordham, bassist. Pete Briggs, drums."

"And the one facing away..."

"Is probably meant to represent their fallen lead singer, Len Antrell."

"That's a 2," said Zack, poking at a fold in Pete Briggs' pant leg.

Sure enough, when Osgood looked closely, she could see that the natural-looking folds of cloth formed a 2, lightly highlighted with some airbrushing. The kind of thing you wouldn't see unless you were studying, obsessed, or under some sort of external influence.

"4," said Audrey.

"A 3 and a 0," said Osgood, poking out her own two numbers in the sleeves of a shirt.

Within a matter of minutes, they had six more digits in alignment from top to bottom.

"Another 320 area code," Zack said.

"Minnesota," said Osgood.

Zack set his phone on the table and turned on speakerphone, the dial tone cutting through the silence. He dialed the number slowly and deliberately, referencing the paper he'd written it down on for almost every digit.

The three of them sat, waiting. Silence for a while, three clicks just as Zack was about to hang up, then silence again.

They listened.

They waited.

Nothing more.

✗ 37 ✗

"**W**e need to go with him, don't we?" asked Audrey
"I think so," said Osgood.

The two of them stood in the window alcove as the sky darkened. Zack stood in front of the record player consulting a tablet while snippets of music periodically started and stopped.

"I have guns," he called over, then amended after a pause. "Not that I think we should use guns."

They both looked over at him in time to catch a random blast of musical crescendo.

"What are you doing over there?" asked Osgood.

"There's supposedly an alternate version of this song on here."

"Which song?" asked Audrey.

"'The Wise Lord of Hinterland.'" He set the needle down again, generating another blast of music.

"How can there be an alternate version?" Osgood walked over to Zack, hands in her pockets, one eyebrow cocked.

"Okay, according to this," he said waving his tablet showing Mazarowski's conspiracy missive, "if you play the album straight through, you'll always hear the same version, but!" He lifted the screen to his face. "'Dropping the needle at precisely the right location after the standard version has already begun will lead to an alternate version. This version reveals the Wise Lord to be a trickster deity that has led the protagonist astray.'"

"Huh," said Osgood.

"So," Zack said. "I'm trying to drop the needle in the right spot."

"Concentric grooves?"

"Yeah," he said. "But not at the start of the song where it'd be easy to notice."

"I've got an idea," said Osgood, nodding quickly to herself. She rushed into the office.

"What is it?" called Zack.

"Gimme a second!" she called back. She pulled open the bottom cabinet of her bookshelf and removed a black bag. Inside it was her Nikon DSLR camera and several lenses. She dug around for a moment, found the one she wanted, and brought the DSLR with her back into the living room. "Zack, tripod in the coat closet?" She followed it with a smile that said please.

Zack nodded. "Oh! You want me to get it." He went to the closet and returned with her black metal tripod. When he saw the lens in her hand, he understood. "Macro."

"Macro," repeated Osgood, attaching the lens to the camera and the camera to the tripod.

"We're going to take pictures of it?" asked Audrey.

"No, a macro lens works like a magnifying glass," said Zack.

"I know that," said Audrey.

"Point your camera flashlight at the album," said Osgood to Audrey.

Uncertain, she turned on her light and pointed it at the album from above.

"Try across it," said Zack, pointing to the side. "Should show the grooves better."

"Yes!" said Osgood. She locked down the tripod and positioned it right next to the turntable, the lens close to the tonearm. She pressed a button on the back, and the rear LCD turned on, showing an extreme close-up of the record. "Am I in the right place?"

Zack looked at the tonearm, then at the LCD, then at the tonearm again. "If it's there, we'll see it," said Zack.

"This is good?" asked Audrey.

Zack touched Audrey's hands ever-so-gently to reposition her light source.

"Perfect," said Osgood, giving her a smile.

Audrey smiled back.

"Okay..." Zack put his finger on the center of the record and lifted the tonearm. "Tell me if you see it." He slowly began to turn the record, running it a full 360 degrees. "Anything?"

"No," said Osgood with a frown.

Zack looked back at the screen. "Can you zoom further with this one?"

"Digitally, yeah," said Osgood, pressing the magnifying glass twice. The image got grainier, but it jumped forward, the needle looking massive in the frame.

"Let's try again." He began to turn the record, slower and slower than before, slowing as he went.

"Wait," said Osgood. She leaned close to the screen. "Go back a bit."

Zack did, and there it was, a small new groove appearing between two others.

"I see it!"

"No shit," said Zack. He leaned back to look at the LCD. "Okay," he said, trying to line up the needle while leaning that way. "I can't do both. Be my eyes, Os."

"On it," said Osgood.

Audrey shuffled, asking, "Just stay—"

"You're fabulous," said Zack.

"Forward," said Osgood. "No, toward you."

Zack moved the needle, and it jumped out of frame.

"Much smaller movements," Osgood said, shaking her head. "Away, away, slower..."

The needle reappeared on the screen, blowing past the groove.

"Stop! Back toward you. More. More." She saw alignment. "There! Lower it. Up, back, lower." Osgood clapped her hand above the camera. "And step back."

Zack jumped in to look at the LCD. "Well, that's right on there."

"Do you still need the light?" asked Audrey.

"No," said Osgood. "Come look at this."

Audrey looked at the LCD, and Zack pointed with his pinkie. "See where the fresh groove starts?" He reached out and pressed on the center of the album, giving it a slow turn. "It just winds in between the other grooves."

"I've never seen that before," said Audrey.

"Neither have I," said Zack. "Heard about it. But mostly as a way to encode messages during wars."

"During wars?" asked Osgood.

"Say you're the Allied forces, and you want to get a message to troops quickly but don't have access to code machines. If you can hide a message inside that new 45 single of the jitterbug..."

"I think you've conflated a number of things there, Zack," said Audrey. "Are we going to play this or what?"

"Yes, right!" Zack leaned back to look at the LCD and wound the record back until the needle was just inside the beginning of the groove. "I listened to the song a few times earlier," he said. "The original lyrics of 'The Wise Lord of Hinterland' are somewhat whimsical, like a cross between 'Jesus Loves Me' and old folk songs. You know the song about Atlantis by Donovan?"

Osgood shook her head while Audrey nodded.

"Fables, stories, not just a song. 'Puff the Magic Dragon,' and all that. So there's no refrain, it's more like a poem. A man meets a woman he wants to marry, but she's nobility, and he's a commoner. So, he goes out into Hinterland, the forest beyond the kingdom, to seek out the Lord of Hinterland for counsel. The Lord teaches him enough to impress the nobles and suggest he has a much higher birth, and he gets the girl."

Zack flipped the switch, and the music began. The song

started much as Zack had described, with the commoner, young Lawrence, and the highborn girl, Cordelia. Sure enough, the wise Lord of Hinterland taught him how to make his way in polite society, and there was a wedding.

"It's the same song," said Zack with disappointment. "Looks like—" he stopped as another verse began.

"Once our wedding night was through,
and I ascended to her kind,
the Lord of Hinterland came to us,
collection on his mind."

"Huh," said Zack. He leaned down to look at the record. "This groove cuts into the next song!"

"This wasn't there originally?"

"Not in the one I've heard," said Audrey.

"And not when I listened to it earlier," said Zack. "Right now, it should be playing 'Unbroken,' the next song on the album."

As they listened, this version revealed that young Lawrence has been deceived. In a fate worthy of the brothers Grimm, he loses his wife, status, and, ultimately, life for daring to try to renege on his deal with the Lord of Hinterland.

"And as I lie on grass of green
in death as we'd in life,
I see no stars above me weep
in tenderness for my strife.

They all just now have gone away
and left me to my fate.
The Lord extends his glove-ed
hand and brings me to the gate."

"That's..." said Zack.

"Bleak," finished Audrey.

"Gate," said Osgood to herself. "Both Mazarowskis called

them gates." She snapped her fingers before her conscious mind caught up to her subconscious. "'The End of What's Real!'"

"What about it?" asked Audrey.

"An alternate version, maybe," said Osgood. She lifted the *Ramparts* album from the side of the table and held it in front of the macro lens. "Audrey, light?"

Audrey turned her flashlight back on. "Yes. Two grooves. One here," she pointed with her pinkie. "Another here." She pointed again. "We need to play this, now. I need to hear it."

"Okay," said Zack, intimidated by her intensity. He moved the tonearm out of the way, removed *Tether*, and took the album from Osgood. Gingerly, he settled it on the platter as Osgood realigned the camera.

She directed him forward and back and forward again until they found the second groove, roughly half a spin inside the first. "That would never be played directly."

"No, the outside groove would take you," agreed Zack. "You'd need to drop it in exactly the right place."

The three of them stood in silence as In the Shallows' final single, 'The End of What's Real,' began.

Osgood felt tears in her eyes as she heard the song change and become every bit the one she'd heard in the car the other day, in her dreams, just before her accident. She spoke the final lines with the album, salty tears streaming down her cheeks.

> *"He'll marry us in the hinterlands,*
> *And we'll never have to return.*
> *Let the world around us crumble.*
> *Let the world around us burn."*

"It's real," she said.

"We never doubted you," said Audrey.

"I doubted me," admitted Osgood. "I did."

From the record, quiet murmurs played, then more backward speech. The sounds repeated twice, then once more before fading away.

38

We will go, said Osgood via text.

Without even a beat, Mazarowski responded, **Excellent. I've hoped so.**

What is the address? asked Osgood.

Ellipses. Ellipses.

"I don't want to go with him," said Zack. "He's creepy and clearly has his own agenda."

"Agreed," said Osgood. "That's why I'm asking for the address."

It's near the old recording studio. He sent an address.

How near? asked Osgood, showing Zack.

Zack quickly brought up a map, followed by the street-view. "Well, if it *was* their recording studio, it's a Jiffy Lube now."

Near.

"How do we play this?" Osgood asked Audrey.

"Maybe…" Audrey nibbled on her lower lip. "Tell him we'll meet him at the recording—"

"Jiffy Lube," interrupted Zack.

"At the Jiffy Lube," Audrey finished.

Osgood frowned. **Near the Jiffy Lube?**

I'm not confident you trust me, said Mazarowski.

Osgood let that one hang for a moment before responding directly, **We don't.**

Reasonable, he said. **Like the *X-Files:* Trust No One.**

Then why should we trust you to take us where we need to go?

Because, replied Mazarowski, **you really don't have any other options.**

"Fuck that," said Zack, sitting at his laptop. He switched back to the map view and zoomed out. "Here's I-94," he said, pointing at the thick yellow line. "And here's the Jiffy Lube. The two nearest rest stops are here," he pointed way up along the line, "and here. Neither are close enough to make meeting at the Jiffy Lube make sense."

You're not helping me trust you more, said Osgood to Mazarowski.

Sorry 'bout that, said Mazarowski to Osgood.

"I just need to say," said Zack, "that, well, we never officially all decided to go."

Osgood looked at him. His face looked firm, resolute, but beneath that, scared. "I'm not making you do anything, Zack. Ever."

"You don't have a car, Os."

Osgood blew air through her lips. *Pssht!*

"I do," said Audrey. Then she turned to Osgood. "Where's your car?"

"Impounded, I think," said Osgood. "I really ought to look into that."

"Don't they assess a daily fine?" asked Audrey.

Zack nodded. "They do."

"At a certain point it'll make more sense for me to let them keep it," said Osgood.

"I think you still have to pay the fine," said Zack. "But you haven't distracted me from the fact that we haven't discussed it." He stood in front of the two of them, seated on the couch. "Have we considered what we're even going there for? The first number is out of order, the second just gives us clicks. We're driving to Minnesota to find a rest stop and, according to, I'm pretty sure a crazy person, kill the Lord of the Hinterlands, who is quite likely a fictional character created by a pop band." He waited for a response.

Osgood looked from him to Audrey, then back to him.

"Okay," he said, incredulously. "You're just going to go along with that, huh? I mean in ten years, Osgood, you and I haven't ever even seen a ghost."

"We've seen—" began Osgood.

"Orbs, shimmers, glows, shadows."

"Well, Zack," said Audrey. "That's really what ghost hunting is."

Zack's intensity waned a bit at Audrey's interjection.

"We're not looking for the ghost, we're looking for what it means," continued Audrey. "The phantom doesn't matter; the reality of the phantom's existence does."

"Okay," agreed Zack. "But what we're doing here is saying that some sort of entity possibly made a deal with a band in the '80s to make them famous in exchange for hiding his hypnotic shit in their music so he could make a whole lot of teenagers gouge their eyes out and disappear."

"Pretty much," said Osgood. "Look, Zack." She stood up and went to him, putting her hands on his shoulders. "I would never make you go anywhere you're afraid to—"

"I'm not afraid," sulked Zack. "I'd just like to have a plan. And acknowledgement of the wackiness of this theory."

"That is quite reasonable," said Osgood. She turned to Audrey and smiled. "And this is quite wacky."

"In every investigation that I've ever done, Zack," said Audrey, "there's the preparatory stage and then the field-work. We were lucky in that most of our fieldwork could be done online. Now, though, we're out of leads beyond the possibility that *something* is at whatever this rest stop is or was, and we need to figure—"

"Was," said Zack, turning away.

"Was?" asked Audrey.

"What if the rest stop is no longer in service? It wouldn't be on a current map." Zack's enthusiasm overwhelmed his hesitance, and he turned back to his computer. He clicked the back button on the browser a few times, and the Jiffy Lube filled the screen.

He zoomed out, then again, and again, until the big yellow line of I-94 swept southeast through the frame. "Now we go to the satellite," he said. "I've can access the really high-resolution one if we find anything."

"The government one?" asked Audrey.

Zack nonchalantly whistled a tune.

"I try not to ask questions like that," said Osgood.

Zack moved the screen up and to the left. He followed I-94 down further and further and further until he got to the clearly-defined parking lot and building of a rest stop.

"Is that—"

"No, that's the far one," he said. He clicked back and re-centered his map on the Jiffy Lube. "Now we go north." He started to swipe, again and again and again, speeding up as he went.

"Wait!" exclaimed Audrey.

He turned and looked at her.

"Go back, like…two swipes."

He did, and they saw a small patch of broken asphalt on the south side of the highway.

"There!" she exclaimed, reaching forward and tapping the screen.

Zack zoomed out a bit, then moved his image further down and to the left. Sure enough, the broken asphalt led to a parking lot that had been almost entirely consumed by grass, a tree even grew in the center of it. Beyond the lot, some chunks of light color delineated a path to a dilapidated building.

"Okay," said Zack. He copied the latitude and longitude coordinates to what looked like a digital sticky note and opened a new browser. On a stripped-down website, he typed in a username and password, which led to a page with two unmarked buttons on it; he clicked the left, and when prompted, entered another username and password. This led to a page that was blank, save for a long empty box. Zack clicked into the box and tapped out an astonishingly long string of numbers. When finished, he hit the enter key with a satisfied tap.

A new site, with a satellite image background, prompted him for Lat and Long. He copied and pasted each into the window and hit enter. The map zoomed back and out quickly, and soon they saw most of the earth, then it drilled back down. North America. the Great Lakes, then Lakes Michigan and Superior, then pockets of cities, until finally, they saw, minuscule, the outline of the ruins they'd seen on the other map.

The image zoomed more and more and more until the ruins showed clearly: a broken parking lot, broken walkway, and the roof of a small building so damaged, the roof had given way in the upper left corner.

"If I had to put money on it," said Zack, "and, as I assume I'll be driving and paying for gas, I will be…"

"I'll pay for gas," said Audrey quietly. She hadn't taken her eyes off the building.

"Thank you, Audrey." Zack nodded, turning back to the screen. "I'd say that's where Mazarowski intends to take us. Whether it's to murder us and wear our skin for hats or to take us to see the Lord of the Hinterlands, I've no idea, but that's the place." He tapped the screen once more, letting his finger linger over the wrecked building, a small and satisfied smile on his face.

"I agree," said Osgood.

Zack's phone pinged. He frowned and lifted it, then began to furiously type.

"He's right, though," whispered Audrey to Osgood. "We don't have a plan."

"I don't know how to plan for this, Aud," said Osgood. "Mazarowski either wants to kill us or show us something. And if he wants to kill us, well, Zack has guns."

"That's *not* a plan," said Audrey.

"It's nearly a plan," said Osgood. "Do you know how to shoot?"

"No, I don't," said Audrey. "Do you?"

"I've been to a range," said Osgood. "Honestly, with as

weird and panicky as he was, I think if we pulled a gun on Mazarowski, he'd piss himself and run away."

"Maybe," said Audrey.

"And if he actually has something to show us," said Osgood, "it'll either be fake, in which case we can spend a lovely night in Minneapolis and then come home, or it'll be real and there is, in fact, some sort of music deity that likes to convince teenagers to cut out their eyes. If that's the case, then who the fuck knows how to plan for that?"

Audrey frowned, then nodded to herself. "Fuck you, Os."

Osgood snickered.

"Okay, so, guys?" said Zack.

"Still not a guy," said Osgood.

"Noted," said Zack. "I'm surer than ever that this is the place."

"Why?" asked Audrey.

"Well, I've sorta been voice mail bombing that first number we found."

"And let's pretend I know what that means," said Osgood, "but you want to tell us anyway, to impress us with your brilliance."

"It's a program that just calls a number continuously. It's designed to overload a voice mail system. But this number was out of service, so it just kept calling. Until a couple minutes ago when we found that rest stop." He pointed to the laptop screen. "And then it went through."

He held up his phone and played a recording. Crackly and distant, they heard the cycling notes from the end of *Ramparts Over the Hinterlands*, and then a voice, low, harsh, and wispy, said, "Getting closer."

39

"I can feel it," said Osgood, pressing her fingers to her sternum. "Fucking dread. Real and palpable."

"We just crossed into Minnesota," said Zack from the driver's seat.

Osgood leaned back against the rear seat of the Jeep and held her chest, feeling the sensation radiating. The taste of bile crawled up her throat onto the back of her tongue. Zack's eyes in the rearview mirror alternated between the road and her, back and forth.

"Just let me know if you need to stop," he said.

"I'm okay," assured Osgood.

Audrey suddenly gasped in the front passenger seat, lurching out of sleep, pulling at the seatbelt holding her down, thrashing. "Fuck, fuck, no!" She took a moment, her gasping breaths slowing and slowing as she looked from Zack to Osgood to the dark road out the windshield, red tail lights in the distance.

Osgood leaned forward, pushing through the dreadful discomfort, and put her hand on Audrey's shoulder. A moment later, Audrey rested her own atop it and squeezed.

"Nightmares," Audrey said.

"S'why I don't sleep if I can help it," said Osgood with a wry chuckle. "Or just put myself *down*."

"The exhaustion is real," said Audrey, her voice still shaky.

"It is," agreed Zack.

"If you need either of us to drive—"

"I'm good," he said, then nodded as if to confirm it to himself. "I'll let you know."

"How far out are we?" asked Audrey.

Zack pointed to the GPS app on his phone. "Five-ish hours. For whatever reason, the GPS has elected to take us around Minneapolis rather than straight through."

"Did you try recalculating the route?" asked Audrey.

Zack nodded. "Even tried other apps."

"Something compels us in that direction," said Osgood. "Do you feel the dread?"

"Yeah," said Audrey, pointing directly below her breasts. "In the nightmare, I was being crushed."

"By what?" asked Osgood.

"Caroline," said Audrey, then turned her face toward the window.

Osgood knew better than to ask for more information. Instead, she tugged at the thread she'd been feeling for the last few hours. "Aud?"

"Yeah." Audrey didn't turn from the window.

"Whatever happens, you're coming back, right?"

She didn't reply, but in the hazy reflection, Osgood could see her cheeks were wet with tears.

"Look at the lights," Audrey said finally, pointing out the windshield toward the horizon. Red dots, in strange patterns, hovered over the landscape ahead.

"It's a wind farm," said Zack. "Lights on each turbine."

They said no more as they drove. The lights on the horizon blinked lazily, and seemed to remain fixed in place, despite the miles rolling by. It took them nearly half an hour to reach the wind farm, and Osgood watched as the hulking structures passed over the Jeep's expansive sunroof.

"They're enormous," said Osgood.

"Quixote would've certainly assumed them giants,"

added Audrey, her voice a bit hoarse, but less shaky than earlier.

This place, with the massive ghostly blades turning their patient turns, felt like another world entirely. The sky beyond the turbines was dotted with stars, the faintest smudge of the Milky Way above them. The hour was late, and they no longer saw headlights behind or taillights ahead.

They were alone in the field of the giants.

"I'm coming back," said Audrey, nearly an hour after Osgood had asked the question. "Unless we die there. Unless something cataclysmic happens. If left to my own devices, I plan to return from this journey."

"Good," said Osgood.

"And you?" Audrey turned in her seat, hand on the back, fixing her eyes in the darkness on Osgood.

Osgood looked from her to Zack's eyes in the mirror. "Do you think I have a death wish?"

"I *know* you do," retorted Audrey. "Do you think I do?"

"I think," Osgood began, reminding herself to tread lightly, "that you have, in the past, forgotten yourself when it comes to Caroline."

Audrey's eyebrows flicked, and her lips tightened.

"I'm worried about losing you," said Osgood quickly, hoping to mitigate the potential damage from her comment.

Way to go, Pru, said her mother's voice inside her, breaking its surprisingly long silence.

Audrey's face softened, but she remained tense.

"I feel like I just got you back," Osgood continued. She realized that her statement implied a lot of water had passed under the bridge. Perhaps she was assuming too much.

"I'm worried about you, too," said Audrey. "For many reasons."

Fair, thought Osgood. She nodded.

"I, uh," stuttered Zack. "I, too, plan to come back from this."

"You're a rockstar, Zack," said Osgood. "I never doubted your resilience." *Nice save,* she told herself before chastising: *Way to forget to be concerned for an entire member of your team.*

But she wasn't worried about him, no more than she was worried they'd all suffer some massive calamity. Audrey's desire to see (but hopefully not experience) what Caroline had gone through, and Osgood's general tendency toward self-destructive behavior – both came on this journey with their own individual potential for a terrible end.

Osgood looked at Zack in the mirror, but his eyes were back on the road. She reached forward and put her hand on his arm. "I mean it."

"Yeah," he said quietly. After a long while, he added, "And, uh, while we're talking about this, I just want to say I'm happy that you trust me. Have trusted me."

She gave his arm another squeeze and flashed him a smile. His earnestness made her nervous, made her realize what they were doing: Like soldiers waiting for landfall, they were preparing for war with an unknown opponent. The three of them were driving north without even a decent concept of what the thing was that they were going to encounter. Osgood broke another long silence, admitting what they were all feeling. "I'm afraid."

"Me too," said Audrey.

Zack nodded.

Osgood hadn't felt fear like this in the real world in so long. The Oxy and alcohol numbed almost everything, didn't it? She'd fed herself such a steady diet of buffers, where could real fear find a way in? But true fear ran deep. It was a vein of shimmering ore within her psyche that exploded outward when REM state kicked in, and the movie theater in her mind began to show the same film that'd been playing for over a thousand weeks straight. Boffo box office. Step up to see the show of shows, as the weak and pathetic Prudence Osgood is crushed to death by two hunks of speeding metal.

"I also feel guilty," said Audrey. "I wondered what happened to Caroline for so long. Was obsessed, is probably more accurate than wondered. After she disappeared, when you and I were investigating. Through all those days and weeks and months that passed with no information. Then, one morning a few years ago, I woke up without the obsession. One day, I just didn't think about Caroline at all. I forgot."

"That's good, isn't it?" asked Zack. "That's how mourning works."

"I wasn't mourning, I was obsessing—"

"No, I know," he said. "But while you were obsessing, I'm sure you mourned, too."

She fixed him with a look.

"Look, Audrey," he said, his words sounding like a retreat. "I'm just saying that—"

"No, you're right," she said. "I did mourn, but I never accepted her death. So, forgetting was—"

"Understandable," said Osgood.

"Unforgivable," said Audrey.

"Aud," Osgood leaned forward. "As someone who has done her fair share of unforgivable things, even to some people in this car, I assure you—"

Audrey laughed hollowly, and then immediately covered her mouth until the smile passed. Her face sank and her eyes lost their sparkle. "My cousin Bernadette died when she was sixteen, killed by a drunk driver. She was my aunt and uncle's only child. I was so young when it happened, so I missed most of their mourning. But after a while, they were happy again. The same as they'd been before. I used to wonder how you come back from that. How you can possibly experience happiness again, after losing someone so important? I wondered that, and then Caroline was gone. And years later, I forgot. And I met Tony. And got married. And years of worry and angst, and getting older, made it so I didn't look like her anymore. So, when I looked in the mirror, I didn't see her. And when I saw mom or dad, they didn't see her in me, either. We moved on."

Osgood waited, wanting to jump in with reassurances, with condolences, with something, anything. But sometimes, silence was best. Sometimes people don't need your fucking opinions. She saw Zack's eyes darting between the road and Audrey, road, Audrey.

"Thank you for reminding me," Audrey said, finally. "It

may seem like cruelty, but I assure you it's not. For the first time, since our earliest leads, I feel like closure may lie ahead. And then, after that, I can be okay with occasionally forgetting. Because the obligation of memory will be lifted."

"And you can forgive yourself," said Osgood.

"Yeah," said Audrey, quietly. She turned her head toward the window and repeated the word. "Yeah."

The trio fell silent as the miles rolled by and the hours fell away. Their destination grew ever closer.

⚔ 40 ⚔

"I swear," said Zack. "If I didn't know better, I'd say whatever's doing all this has attempted to make these places difficult to get to." He flicked on his turn signal and turned off the highway onto an exit ramp.

"*Do* you know better?" asked Osgood.

"I suppose I don't."

As he had days earlier, a lifetime ago, Zack swung around, making a pair of left turns, and merging back onto the highway in the opposite direction.

"How many miles, now?" asked Audrey.

"It took us thirty miles past the rest stop to hit this exit. Would've been closer, but construction closed the last two."

"Jeez," said Osgood. "Well, I'm not in much of a rush."

"Me neither," said Audrey.

Zack only nodded.

"Thirty miles ago?" confirmed Osgood. "I could feel it then, as we passed. I thought it was indigestion."

"I couldn't see it as we went by," said Zack. "But the divided highway and lack of lights made that possibility unlikely."

Osgood wasn't anxious to get to the rest stop and walk into a situation she didn't even remotely understand, but the monotony of quiet exhaustion in the Jeep made her yearn for a conclusion to the journey. If only that journey wasn't leading into what the dread in her stomach said was a trap.

"Os!" exclaimed Audrey.

Osgood jolted, leaning forward.

"Look!" Audrey pointed out the windshield toward the shoulder of the road, and whatever she pointed to passed by the side of the Jeep.

"Should I slow down?" asked Zack.

"What is it?" asked Osgood. "I missed it."

"I know where we are!" Audrey said. "There!" She pointed out the windshield once again, and Zack slowed the Jeep to a stop.

"What is that?" he asked.

Osgood wondered the same, peering at a small, misshapen form, lit by the Jeep's LED headlights.

Audrey tugged at her seatbelt once, twice, finally unlatching it, and hopped from the Jeep.

Zack turned around and looked at Osgood, questioningly. She shook her head and shrugged, then got out as well.

Audrey stood about ten feet ahead, crouched in front of whatever the thing was. Osgood could see the blue-white light of her cell phone's flashlight moving around.

Only when Osgood came right up on top of the thing did she understand. "The goblins."

"The goblins," repeated Audrey. She held up a long staff of what looked like rusted rebar covered in rotted *papier-mâché* painted a dingy brown. "I saw the first one maybe a mile back, and they're showing up more frequently. This one is pretty wrecked."

Osgood crouched next to the three-foot vaguely humanoid form with an oversized head that had crumbled and slumped over. Its metal skeleton poked out in several places. It, too, seemed to be covered with once-glossy *papier-mâché* over foam and chicken wire.

"I still don't understand," said Zack, behind them.

"The artist colony," said Osgood, turning to look at him. He appeared as a silhouette, back-lit by the bright LED headlamps.

"With the statue?" asked Zack.

"Yeah," said Audrey.

"About two miles down," said Osgood. "All this land was theirs back then. If it still is, they've certainly stopped maintaining it." She looked southwest down the highway, knowing that, at least twenty years ago or so, if it were daylight, they'd be able to see the round head of that massive screaming figure rising above the horizon. "Happy I can't see it," she said with a shudder.

"Oh, I don't like that these are here," said Audrey, snapping a picture of the fallen goblin.

"It just makes it feel even more...right," said Osgood. She stood out of her crouch, aching from too much time in the car, a dull and growing throb in her lower back. She hoped she could make it through this without collapse.

When they returned to the Jeep, Osgood stood at the door for a moment, stretching her legs and back as much as she could without doubling over in pain. She should take the Oxy soon, she knew, but wanted to remain as lucid as possible, right up until the moment she couldn't handle the pain.

"Pop the back, Zack?" asked Audrey.

Zack pointed his remote toward the back hatch, which beeped and slowly opened. He climbed into the driver's seat.

When they were all inside, he asked: "What'd you need in the back?"

"A place to put something," said Audrey, embarrassment on her face in the dim interior lighting.

"What?"

"I took the spear," she said.

"Okay," said Zack.

"Why?" asked Osgood.

"I don't know." Audrey looked at her hands for a long while, then brushed off flakes of rust. "I thought I should."

Osgood looked at the side of her friend's face, trying to parse something from it, anything. All she could see was dread. "Trust your gut."

Audrey laughed to herself, the sound of someone laughing so they don't cry, laughing so they don't scream. She nodded at the words she'd always said to Osgood when a hunch was involved. Back when they were investigators together, once upon a time.

Despite being the only ones on the road, seemingly the only ones in the world, Zack flicked on his turn signal, then slowly returned to the highway from the shoulder. Osgood knew why he'd done that, and why his acceleration was so gradual. Procedural delay. Following order to avoid chaos.

After all, how far away could chaos possibly be?

According to the GPS on Zack's phone above the dash… about six minutes.

She took a deep breath and didn't want to let it back out. The dread in her stomach suggesting she might have a limited number of breaths remaining.

"**N**o offramp," Zack said, startling Osgood.

She realized that she'd been clenched, waiting for the screaming giant to materialize from the darkness, but it never came. She supposed that if someone had bought the property, they'd be far more likely to tear down that monstrosity than to wander down the highway for miles ripping out goblins. She wondered what had become of the screaming thing. Perhaps it was still there, invisible in the black of night, beyond the trees. Waiting for someone to come, to visit, to foolishly crawl near enough to fall into its gaping maw.

She unclenched as Zack rolled to a stop.

"You two buckled?" he asked.

They both affirmed.

"Hold on," he said, turning the Jeep in a hard right, straight off the highway. They went down and down and down into the drainage ditch, then the Jeep began to climb again. She felt the underside being scraped. "Shit."

"Do we need to walk?" offered Audrey.

"No," said Zack. "Just wish I'd come at it a bit more diagonally. I was worried we'd roll."

"Top over teakettle," her mother said in her mind, and out

of her mouth. When they both turned to look at her, she shrugged. "I don't know what that means."

The scraping continued, the sounds of brush and sticks, and then the Jeep had switched its plane from full decline to incline. The land leveled out, and Osgood could feel the growing dread tension in her chest and stomach. It gnawed at her like her period cramps. Her muscles ached. Everything began to hurt. "I think we're going in the right direction," she said.

Zack leaned in to look closely at his GPS, which he'd set to satellite mode. "We should see it just past the trees." The app on his phone kept spinning, trying to redirect this poor lost car back to the highway. He ignored it and continued. The Jeep moved up to the tree barrier. They shouldn't be this tall if they'd only been planted in the last twenty years. He leaned forward, looking back and forth, and finally pointing. "I think I can get through there."

"Don't do it if you doubt it," said Audrey.

"I can do it." He rolled his window down and grabbed his side mirror, turning it in so that it rested almost flat against his door. He turned to Audrey, who nodded and flipped her mirror in as well.

As the Jeep slid between the trees, with no more than inches to spare on either side, Osgood knew they were crossing a threshold, squeezing through a doorway that many others might have gone through in the past, but none in a long, long while.

The Jeep shook over bumpy terrain, it then mellowed. "We're on pavement," Zack said.

The trees remained far too close, seeming to tilt over the Jeep. She could no longer see the sky above them for the branches. Having pavement below them was better than driving on the uneven ground, but not by much. Finally, they reached a sort of clearing.

Osgood climbed out first, and she could feel the tug from the building at the center of the clearing. "This is it. No question," she told the others.

As with every other rest stop she'd been to, there was an

angular parking lot, this one broken and upended in many places. An entire sapling had torn its way through a handicapped parking space. A small path, also torn asunder, leading to a slant-roofed cinderblock building. Most of the shingles had long since abandoned the roof, and the cinderblock walls were pocked with a lifetime's worth of cavities and disrepair. The night around them had become absolutely still, nary a breeze or bird to be found, but Osgood could feel that tug from within her toward the building. She began to approach it, shuffling her feet as though being dragged.

"Os," said Zack, and she snapped to look at him.

She stood at least ten feet from the Jeep, where Zack and Audrey stood with concern in their eyes. She threw a look at the building, then back at them, and walked to the Jeep.

"Flashlight," said Zack, putting a heavy metal Mag-Lite into her hand. "Stun gun," he said, holding a small device out to her.

Osgood took it.

"I wish we'd brought cameras," he said.

She waved her phone at him. "Besides, how many hands do you have?"

"Are you *sure* you don't want a gun?"

"I—"

"I'm not judging," he said. "Just confirming."

"I don't think it will be effective against what we're going to find in there," Osgood said, clicking the flashlight on and pointing it at the building. "Therefore, I—"

"No problem," he said and walked to Audrey, who also seemed transfixed. He made the same offers to her, and she made the same choices, adding only her rebar spear to her personal arsenal.

"That could do some damage," said Osgood, as Audrey sidled up next to her at the edge of the former parking lot.

"Counting on it," said Audrey.

The sound of ringing, a phone, an old phone.

"What the fuck?" Osgood threw a look back at Zack, who held his phone to his ear.

"The number from the cover," he said, then pointed toward the building.

As the three of them approached, the ringing continued, not from within, but from behind.

Zack, gun in one hand, flashlight in another, looking every bit the private dick, waved them left. "You go that way, I'll go this way."

"When did you take charge?" asked Osgood.

"Do you have a better plan?" he asked.

"No," she said, "I like it. Happy to follow your lead."

The ringing stopped, and Zack tucked his flashlight under his chin to redial the number as the two groups diverged.

As Osgood and Audrey rounded the corner to the side of the building, the ringing began again, closer now. Their path grew more and more narrow as the trees reached out for them, scraping against their arms and legs.

"Jesus," said Osgood, momentarily caught by a branch in her hair.

"Hold still," said Audrey. "I've got you." She untangled Osgood's hair, and the two women stood before each other for a moment.

"I'm sorry," said Osgood, wondering what Audrey would say to that. Would she have to explain precisely what she was sorry for, at this point? Could she, if she wanted to?

"Me too," said Audrey, then leaned forward and kissed Osgood on the lips. Her hand moved from Osgood's hair to her cheek. "I love you, Prudence Osgood."

"Now you're *really* making me worry you're going to do something stupid," said Osgood with a nervous laugh.

"Don't ruin it," said Audrey. She sniffed and kissed Osgood again, this time lightly, on the corner of her mouth. "Onward."

"Onward," repeated Osgood.

They turned the last corner, and the ringing payphone came into view, enclosed in a rounded brushed aluminum box on a square metal pedestal jutting from the ground, a circle of stones surrounding it in an at once haphazard and deliberate way.

Osgood jumped and threw her flashlight beam toward movement in the trees, but only found Zack emerging from the other side, holding his hand up before his eyes. Osgood directed the light back at the payphone.

Zack hung up, and the payphone stopped ringing. He put his phone back in his pocket.

As if on cue, the moon passed from behind a cloud, illuminating the circle and what was beyond. Past the payphone, in its own arc, was a carved brick and stone battlement, and beyond and below that, a valley of treetops.

"Ramparts over the Hinterlands," said Osgood. She blinked again, sure that it would vanish if she looked away long enough. "This spot, those battlements, they look just like the album cover."

"Yeah," said Zack, unashamedly letting his mouth hang open.

Osgood looked out over the valley for a moment longer to steel herself for what came next. She took a deep breath, turned, and strode up to the payphone. "Okay, we doing this?"

"Yeah," said Audrey.

"It can't be as easy as simply dialing a number, right?" asked Zack.

Osgood shrugged at him, the action sending pain radiating down her spine and up her neck. "Fuck," she said.

"Pain?" asked Audrey, rushing to her.

She nodded.

"Do you have your—"

"Yeah," said Osgood. Her hand shaking, she reached into her pocket and pulled out the small brown bottle with the O on it. "The dropper came out," she said. "I don't know where it is at home. I just put tape over it."

"How do you know how much—"

"I got it," said Osgood. She held the tincture bottle up in front of her flashlight and saw how little remained. Just enough to roll around the bottom. "That should do it."

"Os, I don't like—"

"Drink me," said Osgood with a pained laugh, pouring the remaining liquid into her mouth.

"Os!" yelled Zack, rushing to them. "What if that was—"

"It's done," said Osgood.

"Such reckless—" began Audrey, but she stopped when Osgood grabbed the phone receiver.

Lifting the receiver to her ear, Osgood heard nothing. She tapped the disconnect switch a few times. "It's dead."

"Let's dial the number from the Brutal Cover," said Zack.

Audrey pointed her phone at them. Osgood looked over to her. "Documentation," she said. Osgood nodded.

Zack swiped twice on his phone, then read the Brutal Cover's number to her, slowly and deliberately.

Osgood pressed the keys one at a time, matching Zack's deliberate speed, making sure to press them down all the way. Without tones, it was hard to know if a connection was—

Piano chords. Loud.

They turned toward the rest stop building and noted a single bullhorn style speaker on the back. From it came the cycling piano music that ended the *Ramparts Over the Hinterlands* album. Endless repetition of the same notes.

Osgood could feel her head moving with the cycle, as though someone held it in their hands, lulling her to sleep. Her eyes widened. *Oh god,* she thought, *did I just OD?* She looked at Audrey and Zack, who both also stared into the speaker as the music grew louder. Audrey held her phone aloft, recording video, but seemingly with no specific aim. The music continued, cyclical, but then began to change. Background orchestra joined, then other pianos, a calliope. Osgood felt herself swaying, first just a little, then a sudden surge forward caused her to drop her flashlight and the phone receiver. She grabbed Zack and Audrey's shoulders for support. The tug inside her, connecting to precisely the place where she'd felt the dread, pulled as though reeling her in from somewhere inside the building. But no, not inside the building. On the back wall. From a spot. Right there. In the center. Had that spot always been there? A spot like a hole, a black circle of nothing, in the center of the cinderblocks making up the back—

"Hey, guys!" called a friendly voice. Osgood turned her head in that direction, overcome by dizziness, trails in her vision.

"Is...Mazarows—" began Osgood, but she couldn't get more out. She heard a pop and wondered if someone had dropped something.

Zack fell from beneath her left hand, and she swayed more.

"Trying to screw me over?" The voice had lost its friendliness.

Osgood opened her mouth to explain herself. She also wanted to ask if anyone else was feeling disoriented or if she'd seriously just OD'ed.

Zack lay on the ground, clutching his side. Redness. What was—

The spot on the side of the building had grown into a gaping black hole that covered the entire wall and seemed to be pulling harder.

But what's going on with Zack? Had she asked that out loud or just thought it? Her eyes felt itchy, and she reached up to rub them. As she pressed her fists into her eyes, she felt the world shift, like gravity had given up the ghost out of nowhere and the ground beneath her could no longer be counted on to remain in place.

The hole grew beyond the wall, and now Osgood knew that it was a hole in the world. It began to crawl outward in strands of perfect black. Crawling, grabbing, consuming.

True darkness.

And Osgood tumbled into its cavernous void.

⚔ 42 ⚔

Osgood crashed and tumbled over grass and rocks both smooth and sharp. The incline was steep, and she continued to roll, seeing the sky and grass switching position over and over. The world swirled and tumbled. She squeezed her eyes shut to push away the spinning world and the blinding daylight illuminating everything. It felt so wrong, so incongruent. The rocks tore at her clothing and flesh, aches and pains throughout her body flaring up. She willed herself to open her eyes. She tried desperately to find something, anything, to focus on, but couldn't. Instead, she felt her eyes begin to roll back into her head. Her tumble ended abruptly, and she landed in large greenish-purple blades of sharp cutting grass.

She curled into a fetal position, hoping that something would stop the world from spinning, even though she was no longer rolling. Laying there, the image of that gaping hole in reality at the rest stop, beginning to turn, swallowing her, remained etched in her mind. She felt a cool breeze slide over her, sending a shudder of chills down her spine. She rolled onto her back and lay flat, moving her right hand when it banged against the smooth wet side of a large rock.

In the darkness behind her closed eyes, she took a mental

inventory. *I am Prudence Osgood. I am thirty-nine. I'm here with Audrey Frost and Zack— oh fuck! Zack!*

What had happened? Zack? The pop. A gunshot? Mazarowski?

Osgood opened her eyes and became immediately dizzy. She felt the spins starting back up and clutched at the grass, which cut into her hands like razors. Slowly, she steadied herself and took in the world. The sky had the green-blue tint of an oncoming storm, but without clouds. She wished for clouds, almost sobbed a desperate request for clouds. The barest of cloud cover would hide that *thing* in the sky! A natural-looking sun held point near the noon position, but just past the zenith hovered a second one, a red monstrosity, six or seven times larger than the other sun. The rays it emitted reminded her of an infrared sauna she'd tried once and felt as though she were cooking herself. She felt that again here, lying in the grass beneath the yellow sun and the monstrous red one sharing space in the sky, fighting for dominance.

She turned her head to the right, needing to escape from the sky, and looked back up the slope she'd crashed down. How was it possible that it stretched so far? Three hundred feet up, maybe? Was that even— More importantly, she realized, was how on earth had she managed to survive her tumble down that rocky incline. She tilted her head until she saw the top, and the monster star again intruded into her vision. She closed her eyes and turned away from the incline. In the darkness she heard Audrey's voice from her dream. "In the center of an impossibly steep valley, you'll find the tower."

"I guess we made it," Osgood said. Her mouth tasted of batteries, but she felt no cuts within it. Every inhalation brought the scent of putrefaction, way in the back of her throat. The smell of death, decay...wrongness. Opening her eyes again, she realized that she was less than fifteen feet from the base of a structure made of massive decorative stone blocks. She tilted her head up and up and up to take in the entire tower, ancient and crumbling, yet still tall, still standing. Her neck strained as she viewed the squared battlements at the top.

And in that tower dwells the Lord, Osgood told herself. *Time to sit up.*

She leaned once, twice, thrice, and finally managed to lurch painfully to a sitting position. Her back screamed, her shoulder throbbed, and the base of her skull added its own stabbing cluster headache into the mix. She moved her arms, first the left, then the right. Fingers opened and closed. Somehow, she was intact.

"You stay the fuck away from him!" came Audrey's voice from just out of sight, just around the corner of the tower.

Osgood bolted to a standing position, but her knees buckled and took her back to the ground. *Slowly now,* she reminded herself. *Let's not kill ourselves and deprive the Lord of the Hinterlands that privilege.* She got to her feet once again, at a more reasonable speed. She held her hands above her kneecaps until she was confident she could support herself.

"Get back!" Audrey shouted, somewhere out of sight.

Osgood staggered forward, lumbering, her head leading the way. As she went, she realized she was no longer holding the flashlight. She managed to pull the stun gun out of her pocket and hold it up in front of her face. A click showed her what she needed to see: a blue electric arc, it could still zap. When she rounded the corner of the tower fortress, she stopped and blinked, trying to adjust once again.

The steep valley created a circle around the tower, just a quarter of it open and giving way to a vast field beyond. All she could focus on, though, was Audrey, brandishing her rebar spear in both hands, and Zack on the ground fifteen feet or so from her, bleeding harsh reds onto the pale blues of his shirt. She saw blood glistening on the purple-green grass like morning dew.

The incongruity of Audrey poised like a cave-person going up against a mammoth, and Zack, lying on the ground severely hurt, almost managed to eclipse the third figure entirely. But there stood Robert Mazarowski, looking even more sickly and unsettled than a few days before. His gun was at his side, and Osgood realized that he had shot Zack before they'd entered the portal. He'd come around the corner all friendly-like and got a shot off before they could even register what was happening. Now he raised the gun at Audrey, who met its unseeing gaze with fury on her face.

"Stay back," said Mazarowski, calmer than seemed possible. He waved her further back with his gun.

Osgood wondered if she could get the drop on him. He was closer than Zack and Audrey, and his back was mostly to her. If he turned his head even a bit to the right, though, he'd see her immediately.

"He is my offering," he said, almost a plea. As if on instinct, he turned his head and his eyes met Osgood's. He adjusted his pose so he could watch them both, then re-aimed the gun from Audrey to Osgood. "I don't have other options, here," he said. "I can't just wait until this tumor kills me and I'm here on my own." He tapped his forehead with his gun, then pointed it back at Osgood.

"I don't give a fuck about your only option!" she told him.

He shook his head, desperation on his face, then tilted his head back and bellowed, "Receive my offering!" He bent his arms back as though he could thrust his voice louder and further. "I lay my sacrifice on the altar of the Lord of the Hinterlands! I pray that he finds it worthy."

Audrey's mouth hung open, and her eyes darted between the three of them.

Feeling a shadow, Osgood looked up to see the red sun passing behind one of the parapets atop the tower. She again felt dizzy at having allowed that star into her sight and dragged her eyes back down to focus on Mazarowski before her. His bellowing distracted him. She could rush him now. All she'd have to—

"Behold!" laughed Mazarowski. He turned and pointed at Osgood, a gesture of resentment and triumph. *I gotcha!* His eyes were so wide that she could see the whites on both the top and bottom of his irises. He looked wild. Feral. Crazy.

"Behold what?" asked Osgood, knowing as soon as the

words left her lips that she really didn't want an answer to that question.

"The Wise Lord of the Hinterlands!" screamed Mazarowski, coughing on his own words.

A tattered robe of linen and sackcloth billowed and flowed out of a stone arch that Osgood was confident hadn't been in that wall of the tower moments before. The linen expanded, pieces of it hanging in tatters. The thing inside the robe wouldn't solidify in her vision. She could both see through it and not. The being, the thing, the Lord of the Hinterlands, flickered and moved like a candle flame. The tattered robe flowed around the creature as he expanded out of the doorway in the tower. The robes were substantial in places, but undulated outward in others, flowing like

(tentacles)

long hair under water.

The Lord passed before her, seeming not to notice her, but she couldn't be sure because she couldn't make sense of this thing's head, or if it even had one. As he moved toward Mazarowski, she saw long, sharp fingers poking out of the arms of his robe. They twitched and pointed, wiggling as though waving.

You have come of your own volition, said the Lord of the Hinterlands to Mazarowski. The voice came not from the robed figure, but from everywhere. It sounded at once like a single voice and a multitude.

For a horrifying moment, Osgood thought it might be coming from the offensive star above her. She wondered why she found that idea so much more horrible than the thing right in front of her.

"I have a proposition," Mazarowski begged, trying to pretend confidence. "A trade."

Your family's debt is long overdue.

"I know, but I brought..." Mazarowski gestured toward Zack on the ground.

For a moment, the Lord of the Hinterlands paused, his flowing robes settling, the flickering of his body slowing and solidifying into something far more horrible. He turned what appeared to be his head to look at Zack, then waved a black-ened hand at him. *You brought this?*

Mazarowski, nodding like a madman, knelt beside Zack, ready to plead his case. "You can take him."

You do not offer me anything I do not already possess. The Lord of the Hinterlands waved his right arm, and his tatters billowed and shook, then the ground joined in. Bits of concrete and stone crumbled off the tower, rocks tumbled down the valley sides. Zack, lying on the ground, shudder-ing, lifted his head to see what monstrous thing hovered before him. For a moment, his eyes met Osgood's.

"Os—" he began but snapped down to a singularity, a pinpoint, like an old tube TV being turned off. Then Zack Nguyen was gone.

"No!" screamed Audrey.

Again, the Lord appeared to pause and turn his head, perhaps noticing Audrey for the first time. Mazarowski seized on the distraction and dove toward the side of the valley, then began to scramble up the embankment.

Stop, child, said the Lord of the Hinterlands.

Mazarowski stopped.

Osgood saw blood on his forehead, probably from a bounce off one of the jagged rocks on the incline. *Good,* she thought. She felt her chest tighten as felt the gravity that Zack was gone. Gone from here. Gone from everywhere? Had the Lord of the Hinterlands taken him? Was that it? After all their time together. Was that—

Do not be foolish, said the Lord.

She looked back at him. He faced her head on now, fingers steepled against each other like a monk. For just a moment she could see something that looked vaguely like a face: an egg cracked open to show a mouth yawning open in the center. But his eyes, black holes, were fixed on her. Was he telling *her* not to be foolish? About what? About Zack? About any of the various plans to deal with this problem that were running through her mind without any sense or order?

How can one approach order from within chaos?

Without giving her further indication, the Lord turned

back to Mazarowski, who had chosen a foolish plan of his own and now stood awkwardly on the incline, pointing the gun at the shimmery face.

Do you not tire of running? the Lord asked him, moving closer and closer, seeming to expand until his flowing body, his swirling robes, filled the entire distance between the tower and the edge of the valley. He appeared to be emanating from beyond the doorway, like smoke from a chimney.

"Yes," said Mazarowski, tears streaming down his cheeks.

Do you not tire of hiding?

"Yes," Mazarowski said again, dropping his hand with the gun to his side. After a moment, he lost the weapon entirely, and it tumbled down the valley slope.

Then assume the debt of your father.

"It's not fair," said Mazarowski.

If you were not ready to give of yourself, you should not have come. Now is the time. You shall be a voice in my choir, one of my joyous flock. The billowing robes began to flap at Mazarowski's arms and legs, tentacles in a breeze.

The Lord of the Hinterlands raised both arms, his stick-like fingers lengthening. He moved them with the precision of an orchestra conductor, and Osgood heard the music begin, first so quietly it might have been within her head, but growing to a full symphony. Those horrific notes from *Ramparts Over the Hinterlands*, the notes that had opened the gate. She could feel them within her and without as they built, tugging at her neurons, at her heart, at her stomach, at her sex.

Give of yourself, Mazarowski. Surrender and settle the debt. Join the choir on high.

Mazarowski's jaw slackened, dropping to his neck. He reached into his pocket, removed a straight razor, and clicked it open. With almost inhumanly fast motion, Robert Mazarowski carved out his eyes.

Osgood felt the bile rise in her throat as she watched one of Mazarowski's eyeballs stick on the breast of his shirt, then roll a red snail trail down his chest and belly before plopping onto the ground.

Audrey whimpered, drawing Osgood's attention away from these horrors. Her friend had made it almost all the way around the Lord and now crouched mere yards from her. She tapped furiously at her phone. "Dammit!" She mouthed, "Phone died."

Osgood waved her over. "I think I dropped my phone in Kansas."

The razor fell from Mazarowski's hand, and the now eyeless man walked down the incline. He turned his face up to the Lord's enormous presence and smiled. "Now I can see."

Your incorporation is at hand. The Lord extended one blackened hand and Mazarowski followed it like an automaton toward the valley beyond. The spectral Lord moved behind him.

Osgood grabbed Audrey's hand, squeezing it hard. "Are you okay?" she asked.

"Zack," said Audrey.

"I know," said Osgood. She opened her mouth but couldn't say anything more about him without choking on her own tears. "C'mon," she said finally, tugging Audrey to a standing position.

The two of them followed Mazarowski's processional. Osgood heard a sickening titter from the Lord of the Hinterlands as he hovered behind shining, shaking, and laughing.

As they left the shadow of the tower, Osgood saw the valley beyond and gasped. She could barely take it in, nearly couldn't even comprehend the hundreds, perhaps thousands of people; children, teenagers, young adults, all with crimson-crusted and scabbed-over eyes. They stood in the field with their mouths open, singing along with the music in an unfamiliar language. An apocalyptic chorus, all singing for the favor of the Lord of the Hinterlands.

Robert Mazarowski stepped into the crowd and wound his way between singer after singer, eyeless face after eyeless face, until Osgood could no longer see him.

"It's now or never," whispered Audrey.

"What?" asked Osgood, panicking.

Audrey stepped forward.

"No! It's never!" Osgood shouted after her. "Never do what you're about to—"

"I seek an audience with the Lord of the Hinterlands," said Audrey, standing defiantly just behind the shimmering, flowing figure with her fists clenched. For a moment the chorus ceased, and the world went silent. All heads turned toward Audrey, seeing her and not.

The Lord also turned, his face phasing and flickering. He cycled through forms, from solid to invisible to nothing but twinkling light.

"My sister," said Audrey, firmly.

The Lord appeared to cock his head, which struck Osgood as absurdly funny. As though Audrey were asking an enormous and terrifying golden retriever for a favor.

Caroline, said the Lord in their heads. *So sad, before, so lonely. Now she sings the songs of the living gods and the dead in my congregation. She sings praise to them all, worshiping at my altar, and is rewarded with the glory of everlasting life.*

The Lord glanced at the legions of eyeless, his flock, and the chorus began again. With each nonsensical word they sang, Osgood could feel their song banging around inside her head. The Lord slowly raised a hand with a single finger extended toward the center of the flock. A figure was raised up from the crowd and floated out over their heads, toward Osgood and Audrey. The rest of the chorus turned to follow with their song as the figure passed overhead. As it neared, Osgood saw the face of her friend, almost that of her beloved Audrey twenty years younger, chubby-cheeked and freckled. But this figure was not Audrey.

The Lord presented Caroline who settled in front of Audrey. Audrey hugged her sister, sobbing into her shoulder. Caroline's eyeless face seemed to take no notice, continuing to sing her horrible foreign chorus.

Osgood collapsed to her knees. Osgood felt both horror and relief at once. After all this time, to see Caroline, to see that this was where she'd gone, where she'd been damned for her eternity. To know was better than not knowing, wasn't it? "No," she said. "Sometimes knowing isn't better."

Now you, said the Lord of the Hinterlands, turning toward her. His robes billowed like an octopus about to strike, but he paradoxically began to shrink to the size of a man. His form neared her, and the flickering solidified and brightened.

She narrowed her eyes at the brightness emanating from the face of the Lord.

Osgood returned to her feet. "Let her go."

I do not hold her, said the Lord.

"Let us go."

I do not keep you.

Osgood clenched her fists. "Let. Us. Go."

You came to my *door. You sought* my *hospitality. Besides, we know each other, don't we?* The face of the Lord of the Hinterlands solidified long enough for Osgood to again see that broken hole of a mouth. His face cracked, and the mouth grew.

Osgood opened her own mouth to deny him, to refute him, but found she could say nothing as the Lord of the Hinterlands shoved his blackened skeletal hand forward, pressing it, like hot pokers through butter, into her head. She felt him poke around in her brain, a sensation that reminded her of when her wisdom teeth had been removed, and she'd come down with dry socket.

She had a hole, after all; a hole

(where the rain gets in)

in her mind, and this being, this god, this *thing* was sliding around within it. At first, she could only feel the darkness and cold, and the Hinterlands themselves became similarly dark and cold. She looked up and saw that the horrid red sun had gone, and the sky had turned a bruised blackish-purple.

In that sky full of endless unfamiliar constellations, hung the monstrous quasar from her dreams. She didn't know if the Lord of the Hinterlands had drawn this image from her to fill his sky, or if, *dear God,* he somehow *was* the quasar.

She looked upon its impossible expanse, and in the darkness where she could no longer see the valley, or Audrey and

Caroline, or even the Lord of the Hinterlands, she felt more than the dread that had pulled at her heart like a tether. She felt pure and honest despair. A depth of hopelessness she'd never experienced.

The energy beam that the quasar emitted

(like a su-papa-troo-papa)

trained on her like the tractor beam from a space ship. Osgood wondered if she'd be beamed up. If she'd leave the ground and tumble toward its event horizon once again, to be torn apart in a way that would make Einstein both giddy and horrified.

What did the Lord want with her? She tried to ask the question, to use her tongue and her lips and her teeth to ask it aloud, but the attempt was of no use or consequence. She'd frozen in the spot, and the world had left her behind. Now, in full darkness, there was just Prudence Osgood in the black halls of the Lord of the Hinterlands, being sandblasted by a quasar.

She felt her eyes rolling in her head again, but it hardly mattered. She couldn't see, could only feel, and even that sense was fading. She knew the quasar had her, would rend her clothing, her flesh, would rend her mind. She felt her very sense of self ripping as the Lord dug around within her. He moved through her neurons and synapses like a gluttonous serpent, stopping here and there to nibble and taste.

For a glorious, horrible moment, Osgood realized that she could no longer feel the pain, the day-to-day agony she'd lived with for twenty years. No longer did her spine scream, no longer did her shoulders and hips and thighs throb with shuddering pain.

She simply felt...nothing.

And then Osgood was no one.

43

woman floats in liminal space. Nothingness, a void. She, too, is nothingness, and the void dwells within her. The woman cannot see or feel or hear. Even the most basic essential elements – the knowledge of human, of woman, of conscious – have faded. Deep in her psyche, though, beyond scar tissue and damaged cells, beyond a brain abused by alcohol and drugs, something reawakens. She is only vaguely aware that *anything* is, much less herself. But the reawakening taps at her, like a trapped miner trapped sending a Morse code SOS, tapping and rapping on anything connected to the outside world.

She is of two parts now, the mind and the body, only barely connected to one another via a frail and decaying tether clutched in the grip of something other.

Something greater.

Something beyond.

She thinks she knows what that higher being might be. But the discordance makes her question what *being* even is. Surely once she was, had been. Or has she always danced here in the darkness amid the belching elements of cosmic creation? In the embrace of the godbeam, tugging and pushing

(all things serve the Beam)

at once, spinning a crown of stars being birthed and dying, forming their own families of solar systems, then exploding into supernovae. How is it possible to feel alone, when one isn't?

We are one, something within her assures her, then adds, *for now.*

She would respond if she knew what it meant, or if she could convince herself that what said it *is.* But she cannot. Will not. The tapping deep within her continues, and she feels...something. Not a human emotion, for she has ascended beyond those. Or did she ever have them? After all, what is human? Instead, she merely feels in the darkness. Spinning in endless night. The taps grow louder, seeming to echo, waking a migraine that first perplexes, then delights her. Pain has risen to the surface. And pain means form. Pain means life. But what does life mean?

The woman is uncertain but surprises herself by being thrilled to death by the pain. Thrilled to death. Such an odd idea. She fancies it. She smiles? Tapping again, harder, more rapid. As though pounding on the inside of the skull that she is now certain she has. A head and a skull and a brain and, connected to that, a body. *Her* body. She again feels movement beyond herself, as though she is rocketing through space with incredible momentum. The tapping deepens, hollow and echoing, the sound of something ancient. *Boom-baboom-boom-baboom.*

Words solidify, not without but within. Initially, the woman cannot understand. She squints with her mind to see, to feel the words, to feel at least—

drumbeats

Yes, that is the sound, and that is the word. The sound and the word are one, and the rest swims, not into focus, but into cohesion, into a self-explanation.

.find the hinterlands

The Hinterlands. She has just left there, has she not? Isn't that where she belongs? Or... The woman is uncertain. The idea seems incorrect. But if it is false, where does she belong? Is it here, in the darkness, in the void? The cosmic dance?

More words come, faster, as the drums beat harder.

rest

stop

She cannot capture the last one; it floats away from understanding and becomes formless again. She concentrates, feeling the migraine and the tension. She pushes her mind, shoving back the grasping fingers and tendrils within it, and sees, vaguely, the final word.

plees.

She knows, though she is unsure how, that her pleading will not take her back

(must've been a door)

to that rest stop in

(where I came in)

Minnesota to see if—

A word. A feeling. A person. A friend.

Zack is there. At the rest stop. *Please send me back to the rest stop.*

The woman gasps at her first coherent thought, a thought that makes her think she is not just an entity destined to drift through the cosmos for time eternal. Zack is at the rest stop.

Zack disappeared from the Hinterlands and

(drumbeats)

has returned to the rest stop but

(plees)

is still hurt. Still bleeds. Hurts, like she can, now. Bleeds, like she would if she sliced a long thin line of crimson into her inner thigh.

From where did that thought come?

The woman is uncertain and frightened. She senses that time, which once felt limitless, has begun to contract. The concept of the finite returns.

She feels something else, as well.

Frustration. She isn't sure what it means, or why she feels it, but she is confident that it isn't her own. That emotion belongs to something else. Something trying to control, or

(puppet)

take advantage. Something within her that isn't her.

The distraction. A distraction from what she needs to think about. She mustn't let it distract her. Must not allow its

(the Lord's)

diversion.

It is good that *he* is frustrated, isn't it? Something feels right about that. Essential. Let him grow frustrated. Let him become angry.

Zack needs help. Help at the rest stop. Because it had all been—

mazarowskis idea

The words knock her back, both her mind and body, her head snapping back on her neck, sending waves of pain down her back.

It was Mazarowski's idea. To come. Not to come here, no. He didn't make it here. What had happened?

She sees, in vague, impressionistic strokes within her mind: One figure standing before another, a wand of death in the figure's hand. The other turning sickeningly red. Mazarowski's idea to come here. Both Mazarowskis', in fact. The phrase *sins of the father* swims into her mind, a fully formed thought with no bearing or meaning to her.

What can she do? Here? Nothing.

Audrey.

She feels the kiss. "I love you, Prudence Osgood."

Prudence Osgood, thinks the woman. "Audrey," says the woman.

She needs to tell Audrey. Needs to tell her about Zack. To help. To do— Well, she's unsure what, but she focuses her mind, picturing the light-waves and particle blasts beaming from the center of the quasar as she sends the words, so that Audrey, somewhere, somehow, can realize the same thing she has.

mazarowskis idea. rest stop plees. drumbeats .find the hinterlands

The blast she emits is powerful enough to throw her entire

body, floating in nothing, into spasmic contortions. She feels exquisite pain. Once more, she sends a burst of energy, sending the warning, this time, not to Audrey, but to Prudence Osgood, the other—

Wait.

The woman floats in silence.

Prudence Osgood.

Words drift through the void: *The Osgoods were grifters, way back.* Not out loud, exactly, but she feels it, senses it. *The Osgoods were grifters, but Lilian was*—

"I don't want to be a fraud," she says aloud, the first words she has spoken in what feels like eons. The first proof of working vocal cords. If those work, what else works?

Slowly, Prudence Osgood opens her eyes. Before her and surrounding her is not blackness at all, just tattered robes and rags, sackcloth and burlap and linens so old they've come apart, dirtied with centuries of sweat and bile and blood and tears. They flow around her, enclosing her, throbbing and undulating. They all flow forth from him with his arm extended, his hand in her brain. The Lord of the Hinterlands. She concentrates on his searching, his exploration, and feels her memories of self flow back. She feels the hand of the Lord trying to lead her somewhere, somewhere else, but she diverts, cataloging and combing through memories of her past and future. She sees Audrey kissing her outside the rest stop. Zack's excitement when she first asked him to join her. Moments with friends and family. With her Yann and Carla. With Nora.

When it surfaces in her mind, she feels his hand grasp at it. She knows it's the place, the moment that he's been looking for, and she tries to push it away, to shove it back down deep. Let it go once more. *There's not enough Oxy or alcohol or pot here, though, Pru.*

"Please," she whispers, a beg. "No."

She feels him draw up in triumph, and the face of the Lord of the Hinterlands cracks open. Osgood can see within it where they are going, where he is taking her. She knows it in an instant. Knows it better than any place she's been in her entire life.

A single alternating amber light blinks caution at her as the Lord of the Hinterlands swallows Osgood back to the crossroads.

⚔ 44 ⚔

Cha-click, cha-click, cha-click, cha-click.

She stands alone beneath the beacon. For a moment, Osgood is sure that she's been dreaming this entire time. She fell asleep on the ride north and has concocted this bizarre and awful fantasy out of the ether. *And if not that*, she worries, *what if I did OD?* What if she overdosed, and this is her coma dream? This is her now and forever.

She puts a shaky hand to her chest and feels her heart throb. The fabric beneath her fingers surprises her. Has she ever had the crossroads dream clothed? She looks down and finds herself in the clothes she wore to the rest stop – her trench coat, dark jeans. Something is different. And if not, she calls to the starless sky above her, "At least I won't be naked when I die." The silence of the crossroads swallows her voice and returns no echo.

She hears the beat up and uneven idle of her Skylark. She turns and sees the blue car in the Amoco parking lot. Curiously, though, Zack's Jeep is parked next to it. She frowns. "You shouldn't be here," she says to the Jeep.

"Are we upset by change?"

Osgood turns, and backlit by the glowing horizon is herself, young Prudence, walking down the center line, swinging her hips and bouncing her hair, flaunting the feminine wiles of youth.

Can I blame her? Osgood thinks. *She's pretty hot.*

"Not upset by change at all," Osgood tells her younger self. "Though I must admit, this whole thing is feeling rather rote by now." She checks her nails, wearing apathy on her face. "Don't we have more important things to do?"

Prudence laughs. "I find this pretty important."

"I assume that's why you've chosen not to make me cut my own eyes out." Osgood fixes Prudence with a glare and sees a flicker in the other's eyes.

Prudence tilts her head and smiles.

"I know that you're not me," says Osgood.

"And circle gets the square," says Prudence with a wink, pressing her left index finger to her nose, and throwing her right in Osgood's direction.

Osgood narrows her eyes at the simulacrum. "But you're not exactly him, either, are you?"

"I am us. You, as I found you. Me, as you found me." Prudence saunters forward and cocks her head.

He's observing me, thinks Osgood.

"I am," says Prudence. "Why do you think I allowed you to draw yourself here?"

"To the crossroads?" Osgood scoffs. "I was coming here anyway."

"To the Hinterlands," says Prudence. "Within the Hinterlands, we find ourselves here, now." She points to the ground in the center of the crossroads, directly below the beacon. "Because this is where I found you. And you saw my face. Before I was ready to rise, you saw."

Osgood blinks and frowns. She has no idea what that means, but the sentence tugs at something within her mind, like an itch she can't scratch without reaching for a scalpel and a hacksaw. "Where is Audrey?"

"With me," says Prudence.

"And where are you?"

"I am in The Hinterlands. Both here and there. In the margins, as you've called it. The liminal space between life and death, between world and outer-world, between something and nothing."

"Now you're just vamping," says Osgood.

Prudence scowls, the edges of her frown drooping right off her chin.

Osgood shudders. "Is Audrey alive?"

"Of course," Prudence replies, her frown vanishing and her jovial demeanor returning. "She is of no consequence to me."

"And Zack?"

Prudence waves the thought away, as though turning down an offer to pay for dinner. "I sent him back. A stuck pig is no meal for a god."

"Is that what you are?"

"I am many things."

"A god?"

Prudence smiles, showing too many teeth.

"I want to see them," insists Osgood.

"We are not with them," Prudence says, gesturing in a full arc around the crossroads. "We are here."

"Why?"

"Because here we can see each other as we are."

"You are annoying." Osgood shook her head. "And, um, how *am* I?"

"Different," says Prudence, tenting her fingers before her lips.

"Different how?"

She laughs, and the laugh draws the jawline downward, mouth opening far too broadly.

Osgood pushes away a shudder. "I'm bored," she says, and points toward the Skylark. "So, I'm going to get in that car and run you right the fuck over."

The smile vanishes from Prudence's face, leaving a tight-lipped grimace in its place. "I thought that we could be friendly, that you would be as curious about me as I am about you." The grimace melts into a frown. "Such a pity." Prudence raises her right hand and snaps her fingers.

Incomprehensibly fast, before Osgood can even register

what has happened, the Skylark and semi crash, between her and her younger self. Of all the times Osgood has experienced this crash, she's never once seen it from this horrifying vantage point.

Prudence moves around the wreckage, smiling again. She takes Osgood's arm with fingers the burning cold of dry ice. Osgood lets herself be dragged forward.

"The driver, I'm afraid, is a lost cause." Prudence points into the smashed cab of the semi, at the now-headless driver. "And you…" She extends her right hand to point at her them, in the driver's seat of the Skylark. She lets Osgood's arm go, and the burning sweet relief of warmth floods the patches of skin where her fingers had been. Prudence waves her other hand across the sky, and the world is filled with the sound of a heartbeat slowing. The beeping of a monitor, shooting stars crossing the heavens with the telltale blip in the center. Once, twice, weaker, weaker.

Beeeeeeeeep…

"I'm sorry to inform you that you've died."

Osgood feels tears on her face, and one lonely meteor blazes a straight path across the heavens. "But I lived," she whispers.

"Are you so sure?" Prudence asks. "At this moment you have not…lived." The wraith, this earlier version of Osgood, slides closer to the wreckage, reaching directly through the door of the Skylark and hurling a pale figure out, sending it across the road and into the weedy corner of the intersection. "I am here, and you are here, and we are here together. At the crossroads. At the end of things and at the dawn of your perception."

Osgood can't look away from the weeds, where she's positive her body lies. A younger her, a *real* her.

Prudence nods as if to confirm and waves her over.

Pale and dying, young Prudence Osgood lies in the weeds, blood caked in her eyes, arms bent at horrific angles. She begs, pleads. "Let me be alright. Let me go back."

"I pity you, because you interest me," says the thing wearing Prudence as a costume.

"Why do I interest you?"

"You are able to sidestep between worlds," Prudence tells her with a smile, "as I can."

Osgood shakes her head. Her fury grows as she looks between her own mangled body lying in the weeds, where it never had been, never should be, begging for her life, while this creature pretends to be

(me)

her.

"This isn't another world," Osgood snarls. "This is an intersection outside of DeKalb, Illinois. And this place isn't special or magic. It's just a place where I was in an accident once upon a time."

"No. This is a way station," Prudence tells her in a stern voice. "As I built my kingdom, so have you built yours."

Osgood shakes her head. "I built this?" The notion is absurd.

Prudence smiles. The look on her borrowed face might be admiration. "Over time, yes. You've spent eons here. Stars have been born and died. Whole galaxies have emerged, and others have been consumed."

Osgood frowns. "And how, *exactly*, did I do that?"

"You built your kingdom because you have potential. I see tremendous capability in you." Prudence pokes a blackening finger toward the body in the weeds. "So, I show you my true face."

The impostor Prudence opens her mouth well beyond the boundaries of her face, extending downward and downward until her lower jaw hits the floor.

Osgood staggers back, falling to the ground, shoving herself butt first across the asphalt to get away from the screaming thing. "How are you...that?"

"The artist came a little too close to my tether to the world. I'm afraid he couldn't handle what he found and spent his remaining years trying and sadly failing to show the world." With the words, the last of Prudence sloughs down to the pavement like a costume, and what has emerged is incomprehensible. A rip in space, a shimmering hole filled with glittery light that shines in all directions. It has no features, no face, no limbs. It doesn't walk; instead, it slides through space to Prudence, the *real* Prudence lying in the weeds.

You have died, the being tells Prudence. *I weep for you.*

"Over?" her dying younger self croaks.

You can go back, it says. *If you choose to.*

"Ye—" says Prudence. "Please."

Is it worth anything to you? This life?

"Worth. Every. Thing."

The voice is louder inside Osgood's head, and she knows that it is now speaking directly to her. *We see each other, and you live.*

The shimmering thing raises the pale body of young Prudence Osgood into the air, sliding it gently back into the wreckage. *An ambulance nears. I have willed it.* A gesture, like smoke and fire, points Osgood's attention to the horizon, where she can indeed see an ambulance.

"You're not in charge of who lives or dies," Osgood says, firmly. She's uncertain if that's true, of course, but it seems crucial to demand.

You are right, of course. I am merely a bystander. A witness of a new birth, preparing to pass out of liminal space.

"I asked to live, so I lived?" Osgood asks it with disbelief.

You choose to live, so you live, it tells her. *I just facilitate the rebirth, midwife to your reemergence.*

Osgood watches the ambulance near, then looks at herself from over twenty years before, head trapped between the crumpled roof of the car and steering wheel. She's not sure how to process any of this, but she feels rage still within her. "I was dead then. For eight minutes, they said."

They merely cannot comprehend what you are.

"They couldn't then?" Osgood asks, begs, for more information. "This happened then?"

This happens. Is happening. Does happen. You live.

As though the world suddenly fast-forwards, Prudence is loaded into an ambulance, which then speeds away. Police lift a head out of the semi's wheel well. Osgood watches, and the itch in her memory returns.

"I remember seeing you," she tells it.

You say you would give anything to live. I take what will hurt least. Not your beloved, but her sister. I show pity, love. I see you. How can you not appreciate my kindness?

"Kindness?" Osgood spits out the word, squeezing bitter tears from her eyes. "Not even my almost-death was mine. Why are we here?"

This is where you end, Prudence Osgood.

"Ah," she replies. "Now you're going to take me?"

No, it says, and she thinks she there is meant to be a calming tone in its voice in her head. *You don't understand. You will be here. You are here. You were here. Here is where you are in the beginning, here is where you are in the end.* Its tone changes to confusion. *Why do you try so hard to stay away? Is it not a comfort to know where you finish? You can become—*

"Like you?"

I once lived.

"And now you're—"

You may consider me a god.

"Oh, *may* I?" Osgood asks. "Then this is my world?"

Your kingdom, your margin, your space between.

"My own private Idaho," murmurs Osgood.

It makes a noise that causes Osgood to wonder if it is laughing at her joke. The noise ceases though, and it continues. *A pocket universe of endless wonder.* It moves close enough to her that she can feel a pulse radiating from its light.

Osgood turns her back on the shimmering thing and faces the wreckage. She closes her eyes, and in the darkness of her own head, she makes a move. When she opens her eyes again, the intersection is clear, and the semi and Skylark are back at the Amoco next to the Jeep.

You take to it like a suckling to a teat.

"It seems that I do," says Osgood, walking toward the service station. She looks over her shoulder at the shimmering being. "I'd like to share something with you. To show my gratitude."

I have no need of such considerations.

Osgood grins and waves it over. She walks around the

Jeep and opens the back hatch. She's impressed to see that, just as she pictured it, the speakers and turntable are set up in the back with *Ramparts Over the Hinterlands* on the platter. "In the Shallows tried to stop you, didn't they? Len Antrell died in his attempt."

They are weak and full of hubris, it tells her, *with no stomach for the reality of our agreement. No matter, though, their attempts are ineffectual and catastrophic for them and those they love.*

"Maybe they just didn't reach the right people," says Osgood, snapping the turntable on, but spinning the record backward with her finger.

As she'd hoped, as she'd envisioned, the needle is in precisely the right place, and the voice of the resistance blasts forth. "Don't trust him. Don't trust the Lord. Don't trust him. Don't trust the Lord. Don't trust him. Don't trust the Lord."

"I'm *not* like you," she tells the being of light, finally turning on it as she continues to spin *Ramparts Over the Hinterlands* in reverse.

The brilliant whites of its shimmer pulse. Sickly colors cycle. Its edges shake and zigzag, not holding the pattern. With a shriek into Osgood's head, the thing strikes out, an appendage of light plunging into her chest, seeming to freeze her body outward around it, activating all the chronic pain she's ever experienced. It takes every bit of her fortitude to reach out, and, with a quick swipe of the knob, turn the volume all the way up.

"DON'T TRUST HIM. DON'T TRUST THE LORD. DON'T TRUST HIM. DON'T TRUST THE LORD. DON'T TRUST HIM. DON'T TRUST THE LORD."

The voice and music echo over the crossroads and the shimmering thing begins to tear itself asunder. It yanks its appendage out of her chest, causing her to gasp in a hot breath, the air burning into her lungs. It starts to tumble, turning itself inside-out over and over, faster and faster.

The entire world, every element, begins to vibrate and bend. The beacon's wire snaps, and it crashes down into the center of the street, darkening everything. She hears the words cycle over and over, feeling the scratchy tug of noncorporeal screams in her brain.

Osgood looks up just in time to see the sky above her explode into brilliant white light as her world, her kingdom, comes tumbling down.

🏹 45 🗡

Osgood threw her arm across her face, blinded by sunlight from the two suns above her. They seemed impossibly close now, and the crimson inferno boiled still closer. She retched, overcome by the taste of copper, of blood, and somehow knew that what she tasted was the blood of the horrible sun above her. She looked around, seeing nothing at first but the green-blue sky and the dreadful red sun. Then she noticed the battlements. She stood up and looked over the side, finding that she stood atop the Lord of the Hinterlands' tower on the ramparts. She saw that, as improbable as it seemed, the turntable and speakers had crossed between worlds with her. Her finger still rested on the label of the album, and she took it for a counter-clockwise spin. When the voice began again, it came not from the speakers, but from everywhere.

"DON'T TRUST HIM. DON'T TRUST THE LORD. DON'T TRUST HIM. DON'T TRUST THE LORD. DON'T TRUST HIM. DON'T TRUST THE LORD."

She peered over the battlements at the vast valley of chorus members, no longer singing, with their mouths agape in silent screams.

When the verse ran out, Osgood moved the needle back and played the loop again, and again, screaming the words along with the man on the record, the man she'd become certain was Len Antrell. Perhaps this had been his final contribution, his final stand before the Lord. "Don't trust him. Don't trust the Lord. Don't trust him. Don't trust the Lord. Don't trust him. Don't trust the Lord."

An earthquake shook the valley, and she heard rocks break off and tumble down the sides of the tower. She braced herself for another quake which did not come. She was about to give the record another spin when she heard voices in the distance speaking in unison. "Don't trust him. Don't trust the Lord. Don't trust him. Don't trust the Lord. Don't trust him. Don't trust the Lord." When she did play it again, the voices grew louder with it. She felt the tower crumbling beneath her and let go of the album, rushing to a small staircase that lead into the tower. She followed the stairs around and around and around along the outer edge of the structure, feeling every step and every shake of the tower as it crumbled. Behind her and above her, massive stones began to fall. The stair directly before her cracked right up the middle, but she leaped over before it could take her down the shaft with it. She glanced over the side when she dared, seeing the ground rushing up toward her. As it grew closer, she hazarded a nervous glance above and saw that the tower intended to come down directly on top of her.

She skidded to a stop when she reached the grass outside, finding the Lord of the Hinterlands waiting for her, no longer the shimmering being of light from the crossroads, his tattered robes smoldering, his face shaky. The chorus of the crowd grew deafening, and the monster in front of her, that horrible Lord, began to fall apart.

Osgood stepped toward him, shouting, "Don't trust him! Don't trust the Lord! Don't trust him! Don't trust the lord!"

She felt a hand take hers and Audrey was there next to her, with Caroline beside her. The three of them stood tall and rejected the Lord of the Hinterlands, shouting in unison with the chorus of his flock.

The Lord began to expand, his tendrils shooting in every direction, grabbing and grasping. His form grew larger and larger until he nearly blotted out the horrid red sun and its calmer partner. *Have you no mercy, child?*

"None," said Osgood, before resuming the chant.

The sound of thunder crashed and echoed through the valley. It knocked the three of them back against the crumbling rubble of the tower.

Osgood saw the sound's origin out of the corner of her eye and turned to gape in stunned silence. The valley beyond was flooded by light from the distance. Warm, inviting brilliance. She saw members of the flock beginning to turn and walk toward the brilliance, chanting all the way. "Don't trust him. Don't trust the Lord. Don't trust him. Don't trust the lord."

Osgood looked back at the Lord of the Hinterlands, whose expansion had failed, his efforts fallen short. His form deflated and collapsed in on itself, shrinking down until he was no more than the size of a man.

"No!" screamed Audrey. Osgood turned to see Caroline walking toward the flock, Audrey rushing after, grabbing at her sister's hand and missing, grabbing again and catching.

"I can't leave without you!" sobbed Audrey. "I can't... be...without you! Let me come!"

Caroline stopped. Slowly she turned back toward her sister. When she spoke, it was a whisper, but one Osgood could hear despite the distance. "I feel no pain." She lifted Audrey's hand to her mouth and kissed it. "Life is for the living."

The twins held hands for a moment longer, then Audrey let Caroline go, to walk into the field, toward the brilliant light.

Audrey fell to her knees, sobbing.

Osgood looked back at the Lord of the Hinterlands, a mass of writhing cloth no bigger now than a child, his form seeming to bleed at the margins like ink.

This is not my end, he insisted. *Just as you know yours, I know mine.* His face began to reassemble, to show a horrid smile cracked into its surface.

Suddenly the smile was pierced. Osgood staggered backward and fell to the ground. Before her, standing over the diminished Lord of the Hinterlands, stood Audrey, both hands on the rebar spear jutting from the Lord's face. She let go of the bar, which she'd stabbed so hard that it stuck through the face of the Lord into the grass and mud.

"Fuck your end," said Audrey.

The once Lord of the Hinterlands on the ground spasmed a few times, then the tattered ends of his robes turned to embers and ash, swirling up and away. Soon nothing remained but a *papier-mâché* covered length of rebar.

The same cataclysmic crash came again, and in the distance, they saw the brilliant light flicker and begin to dim. The rumbles from the ground beneath them grew more and more frequent. Behind them, the remains of the tower collapsed, creating and then descending into a seemingly bottomless abyss. The ground broke toward them, falling into the chasm.

Osgood pulled Audrey back from the precipice, and they both collapsed onto the valley's steep incline.

"We're stuck here, now, aren't we?" asked Audrey.

"No," said Osgood, with a confidence she was sure she hadn't earned. "This is not our end."

The Hinterlands tore apart, falling down upon them. Osgood embraced her friend, her beloved, shielding Audrey with her body as the world fell away. The sky ripped open and fell to the ground, like curtains onto a stage, then the ground beneath them fell away, leaving them in darkness and quiet.

In peace.

☿ 46 ☿

Osgood supposed that there were worse ways to die. Being inside a pocket world in an unknown dimension hadn't been on her list, of course, but there in the darkness, she felt that anywhere other than the crossroads marked an excellent departure from the final destination that had seemed preordained since that night in September 1998. When she and a semi met in blood at the crossroads.

When, near death, she'd met the Lord.

But here, with Audrey, this wasn't so bad.

In the darkness, she heard crickets playing their woeful and desperate songs. Confusion washed over her, then she began to notice sensations to go along with the sounds of the crickets. First, the feeling of grass under her right hand. Then, beneath her crouched body, she felt someone, breathing, moving. She kept her eyes closed, confident that if she opened them, she'd just let in some fresh horror that had spawned within the abyss. Or, worse, the Lord of the Hinterlands demonstrating that he was right, he had *not* ended there. As the person below her began to move, though, Osgood took the risk and opened her eyes. The world swam before slowly coming into focus. Here was darkness, only flickering reds and blues to interrupt it. But her eyes began to adjust, and she saw, beneath her, her beloved friend.

"Os," Audrey whispered. Her face was a mask of confusion, pain, and heartbreak. Tear streaks marked her cheeks. "Are we okay?"

"Well, I think we lived," said Osgood, feeling her own tears. "So, that's good news."

Audrey laughed and then sorrow returned to her face. "Caroline is gone."

Osgood nodded. "I'm so sorry." She knew that was just the platitude that people said, the more colloquial incarnation of *my sympathies*, but it never felt adequate. Then again, what did? Mostly, Osgood was inclined to say nothing when told about death or illness. *Sorry* never felt appropriate, never felt like enough. Here, though the words were definitely not enough, they were entirely appropriate. "I brought you there. I made you confront—"

"No, Os," said Audrey. "You gave me what I needed. You gave me closure."

"I'm so sorry," Osgood said again and wrapped her arms around Audrey. Audrey enclosed Osgood as well, and the two squeezed each other tightly. The comfort, the familiarity of the embrace felt glorious, but it was short-lived, as other sensations began to creep back in, the chronic pain crawling up Osgood's spine and down her legs. Still, she squeezed her friend. She wouldn't let Audrey go, not again, not ever.

"Really," said Audrey, firmly. "Thank you. Closure was the best I could've hoped for. She was never coming back."

Slowly the two of them helped each other to sitting positions, opposite each other, on the grass outside the rest stop.

"My friends! They need help!"

They turned to see the flashing lights of ambulances and fire trucks. How on earth they'd managed to get through the trees, Osgood had no idea. But lying on a gurney, head turned to look at them, was Zack Nguyen. Wonderful Zack. He pointed and exclaimed, "Them!"

A bloc of three EMTs in reflective jackets rushed to them and immediately began asking questions too quickly to answer. "Are you alright?" "Were you inside when it collapsed?" "Have either of you been shot?"

"We're okay," said Audrey. "I think."

"I wouldn't mind a once-over," said Osgood feeling pain beginning to echo through her body. "What collapsed?" she asked, recalling the catastrophic destruction of the tower in the Hinterlands, and the gaping chasm in the

(not Earth)

ground that swallowed it up.

The EMT crouched next to Osgood pointed toward the rest stop building. Or rather, where the rest stop building had been. Now, looking, she could see only rubble. The building had fallen, and beyond, the ramparts had too.

"No more ramparts over the Hinterlands," said Osgood to Audrey.

"Like the record?" the EMT asked.

Osgood looked at her. So young and earnest. "Like the record," Osgood said. "We just barely made it out before it collapsed."

"Looks like you got nailed by something as it happened," the EMT said, pointing to her chest. "We're bringing over a gurney, don't move."

Osgood looked down and realized that she was exposed. Her left breast hung free, though the right was somehow still tucked in what remained of her bra. More concerning than the breasts themselves was the purple-black welt between them. The spot where she'd been stabbed by the Lord of the Hinterlands.

"Shit, Os," said Audrey as she noticed it. An EMT helped her to a standing position. Audrey wobbled for a moment, but then stood strong. "Is Zack alright?" she asked her own EMT.

"He's a trooper," the EMT said. "And the wound looked through and through...also somehow cauterized."

"Can we go together?" asked Osgood. She wanted to thank Zack for his bravery. For everything. To promise never to take him for granted again. To treat him the way she always should have.

"We're sending him along now," said the EMT, "but you two can go together."

The gurney arrived, and Osgood's EMT moved to her shoulders to help lift her aching body onto the padded dolly. As they wheeled her toward the ambulance, Osgood looked up at the sky and felt such relief. The stars above made sense. The constellations were hers.

"A smile," said her EMT. "That's good."

The smile, the overwhelming ache in her chest, these two things should've been at odds with each other, but Osgood took solace in the ache. The pain meant life, one she had no desire to snuff out. "Perhaps once you experience something like that, it's harder to have suicidal ideation."

"You know, you say things like that in the presence of a mandated reporter..."

"Oh, no," assured Osgood. "It's good stuff."

The lovely woman nodded.

In the ambulance, the EMT leaned down over her, and Osgood felt the stirrings of lust. *What did they call that?* she asked herself. "Florence Nightingale Effect."

"Really, Os?" asked Audrey, taking a small seat next to her.

"Did I say that out loud?" asked Osgood.

"You did."

"Are you in pain?" asked the EMT, hiding a partial smile.

"I'm always in pain," said Osgood.

"Let's try one through ten."

"Holding steady at an eight."

"What are you usually?" the EMT asked.

Osgood shrugged, then winced. "Six-ish?"

The EMT laughed and went about starting an IV. "We're going to go ahead with some morphine."

"Oh," said Osgood, flashing her eyelashes at the EMT. "Oh yes, pretty please."

Audrey took Osgood's other hand. "Looks like only about ten minutes passed," she whispered. "From when we went in until we came out."

"Really?" Osgood whispered back as the warmth of the IV's contents flowed into her.

"Zack must've called for the medics immediately after he fell...out?"

Osgood nodded, feeling hazy. "Hey," she said.

"What?"

"Come closer."

Audrey leaned down until their noses nearly touched.

"I love you, Audrey. Pure and true love. All encompassing. Always."

Audrey laughed, but a tear dropped from her cheek onto Osgood's. "I love you too, Osgood."

"Promise," said Osgood, holding out her pinky.

"Promise," repeated Audrey, wrapping her pinky around Osgood's and shaking it.

"No," Osgood said, pulling back her pinky and shaking her head, a movement that left trails in her vision. "No, promise you'll... Promise you won't leave."

"Why would I leave?"

"Just," said Osgood. "I'm drifting. When I wake up, I—"

"I'll be here," said Audrey. "I promise."

Osgood nodded and gave herself over to the exhaustion and morphine. She drifted off into sleep, a warm and dreamless expanse, with no sign of the crossroads.

✖ 47 ✖

"I'm so happy you messaged me."

Osgood smiled. She was also happy she'd called, laying on her bed thoroughly satisfied to the point of exhaustion.

"I was starting to think you didn't like me."

"Sorry about that," said Osgood, turning to Nora next to her. She ran her fingers through Nora's auburn curls, sliding her thumb along a freckled cheek. The woman was young, yes, but twenty was definitely an adult. "You should know something," said Osgood after a deep breath.

Nora looked into her eyes.

"My life is complicated," said Osgood. "I'm complicated, at least. And I'm inconsistent. And I'm a runner. You should know that, too. I get distracted and run."

"Thank you for the heads up," said Nora with a smile. "I'm happy to take each day as it comes."

Osgood kissed her, her lips inviting, her tongue soft.

"You do still want to talk about my ghost at some point, right?" asked Nora, after they lay quiet for a while.

"Yes," said Osgood. A ghost investigation. A standard paranormal rodeo. Boy, wouldn't that be a lovely change of pace from the weirdness? "But not yet, not yet." She kissed

Nora, their tongues intertwining, then another kiss, this one more chaste, before she climbed out of bed.

"Going somewhere?"

"Feel compelled to do something."

"I'm surprised you have any energy left," laughed Nora. "That's a good look, by the way."

Osgood, pulling a shirt over her head, looked down at the leather straps and silicone dildo. "Why thank you," she said, shaking her hips and bouncing the rainbow phallus back and forth against her thighs. "Though I might go sans-cock for this." She slid her harness off and pulled on sweatpants.

"You'll come back?" asked Nora.

"I'll come back," said Osgood. She moved into the hall and felt the effects of the sustained thrusting. "Boys do *that* all the time," she said to herself. Before she continued down the hall, she deposited her accouterments in the bathroom sink and washed her hands. She looked in the mirror, feeling mild horror at the darkness of the bruise on her sternum radiating up over the collar of her shirt.

Nora had expressed concern, which Osgood had waved away with "If it were terrible, it would've broken some ribs, right? They also wouldn't have let me leave the hospital."

Nora had supposed that was true.

Osgood still wondered what the doctors at the ER thought had happened. Something that could make such a severe bruise without doing internal damage? She shook her head and shrugged it off, flicking on the light in her office to counteract the oranges from the street-lamps and the red glow of Mary's sign.

She sat behind her desk and pulled the microphone close. She pressed the button that sent out the spectral bird heralds to the subscribed fans and across various social networks to announce that *The Spectral Inspector* was going live. She waited, waited, waited.

On Air, popped up on the screen.

"A late good evening, Specterinos," she said, smiling at the microphone. "Osgood here, your Spectral Inspector, and have I a story for you. I will caveat that I have had a few drinks and been good and fucked, so forgive any haziness. There will be more to this story, perhaps weeks' worth, but tonight, I want to tell you about a band called Rhapsody in the Shallows.

"I know, weird, right? I'm sure many of you know them, or knew them when you were young. Or, I suppose, since I'm older than a lot of you, knew them from your older siblings or parents. But our story is not just about them, but about the desperation that comes when the thing you feel you are meant to do doesn't take care of you. When you do your best, and your best isn't good enough. Sometimes desperation leads to bad ideas, and sometimes it leads to pitch dark places.

"Not sure why I'm being so vague here. Perhaps it's because I'm not sure exactly what happened, only have ideas and notions based on a week of research and a truly bizarre experience. But tonight, our story is about a band that made a deal with an entity they didn't truly understand, and when their bill came due, and they realized the horrors it entailed, they tried everything to get out of it. Unfortunately, as happens to too many, once you walk down the road to darkness, it's so much harder to walk back. So hard, in fact, that we usually don't.

"This is a story about kids and teenagers and young adults, people who only wanted a place to fit in. This band, and their ethereal patron, gave them that place, only to take their youth and lives."

Osgood leaned back, pouring herself a finger of bourbon. She only needed the one tonight. In three days, she had not gone back to the crossroads. No reason to expect tonight would be any different.

"But before we dive deep, I want to start with why I'm involved. The sister of a woman I love vanished on November 6th, 1999, along with hundreds of others. Those kids, teenagers, and young adults I mentioned all left this world on that date. Some in horrific ways. All to a horrendous purgatory. All in service of Rhapsody in the Shallows' patron, the Lord of the Hinterlands, who was not wise, like the song on *Tether* suggests, but manipulative and cruel.

"Now the Lord is gone, or has at least receded. What cult leader doesn't crumble when you take away his faithful?"

Osgood smiled as a ping on her screen drew her attention to the fact that she currently had seventy live listeners. Another ping, and a private message notification bounced. She clicked on it.

Speaking of (Rhapsody) In the Shallows, there's a new album coming out! There was a link below the message.

Osgood's smile vanished as she clicked the link and read the press release from Gloria Mundi Records.

We are so pleased to announce that, now that we have wrapped up all the rights issues, and the terms of the vinyl-exclusive contract have expired, we can not only bring all four of the Rhapsody in the Shallows and In the Shallows albums to modern formats (including CD, digital, and streaming) but we can finally open the vault!

While producing *Ramparts Over the Hinterlands*, their most experimental album to date, In the Shallows rejected over twenty finished tracks, replacing them with what appeared on the final album.

Now those tracks have been remastered under the guidance of Abigail Antrell, daughter of the late lead singer / songwriter Len Antrell and fantastic musician in her own right.

Watch for the brand-new album by one of the most celebrated bands of the 80s and '90s, *The Shore to the Deep* – In the Shallows' best album yet!"

Osgood's mouth hung open, and her fingers drifted absently to her bruised sternum, the pain jolting her back.

This could be dealt with later, after all. Just because a new album was coming didn't mean…

"Sorry, Specterinos, where was I?"

48

"I've slid between worlds," said Osgood, through the media player on Audrey's computer. Audrey wondered what had made her voice so shaky suddenly.

Back at home, Audrey had laid out all her notes and files on her bed. She surveyed the breadth of the investigation into Caroline's disappearance and took a moment with each file folder, each notepad, before putting them in storage boxes. After all, the investigation was now closed.

She sat on the bed, amid the files, and set a framed photo on her nightstand. It'd been packed away for so long, she'd nearly wept when she discovered it with the files. In the photograph were three girls, so happy, so hopeful. Two looked almost identical, the third was tall and gawky. Audrey smiled at the picture, the three of them, Caroline, her, and Prudence, arms around each other, futures ahead for two of them. She put her fingers over her sister's face.

Audrey sighed. "Goodbye, Caroline."

"And what I've seen has confirmed a lot of my ideas," continued Osgood's livestream. "I know that may sound egotistical, but I assure you, that's not what I'm doing. Though, as constant listeners, you must know that my ego could never be considered small.

"I saw people pass on, pass from the margins to the place

beyond." Osgood stopped, sounding choked up. "It was beautiful, hopeful.

"I've never had more confidence in an actual afterlife, a real next place, than I have right now. And that kind of faith is a fantastic thing. To know that we'll all go somewhere new, somewhere different. Perhaps somewhere better. Where our differences, our colors, our sexualities, our broken bits won't matter at all.

"Won't that be wonderful? Won't... Oof." Osgood took a long pause. "Sorry, some discomfort. Though I suppose if you got stabbed in the chest by a spectral being, you might experience some discomfort, too.

"What I can tell you, beyond the rest of this scattered micro-cast, is that my team survived. We all came back. Each of us a bit worse for the wear, sure, but Zack's recovering and should be going home tomorrow, and Audrey's felt the catharsis I think she's always been searching for. And me. Well, I'm still me, still Osgood, your— Jesus that stings. Still your Spectral Inspector. Looking forward to what the future — Fucking hell!"

Audrey turned toward her computer. Nothing but silence. She leaned down and saw that the **Listen Live** button was still clicked, and the skeuomorphic spools of the cassette tape graphic still turned. The spinning spools, coupled with the silence, worried her. She grabbed for her phone and dialed Osgood's number. It rang, again, again, again... She froze when she heard the vibration of Osgood's phone over the live feed. "No, Os, answer!"

What to do? Rush over, like the cavalry?

"I have a date tonight," Osgood had told her over lunch, with a slightly embarrassed smile on her face.

"Oh yeah? Finally call that girl back?" Audrey had asked.

"Woman," Osgood had corrected. "And yes. Thought it wouldn't be a bad idea to...attempt..." She slashed air quotes through the space between them. "Normalcy."

"Prudence Osgood and normalcy don't usually go together."

"Shaddup."

"It's good," Audrey had assured her. "Normalcy is good."

Osgood had nodded and put her hand on Audrey's, across the table at Mary's. "You're not going to run away, now that this investigation is over, right?"

Audrey had shaken her head. "I'm not going anywhere."

"Thank the gods," Osgood had said. "'Cuz I'm rather fond of you."

Audrey had taken a deep breath. "I'm rather fond of you as well, Osgood."

In her bedroom, Audrey redialed Osgood's number and again heard the phone ringing over the streaming audio feed. Listeners in the chat room were starting to become concerned.

"Coming back, sexy?" asked a voice in the distance. "Osgood?" The buzzing ceased. "Hello? Um, Osgood's phone."

"Hi," Audrey said. "This is Nora, isn't it?"

"Yes."

Audrey closed her laptop to stop the echo of the voice coming from both the phone and the live podcast. "This is Audrey Frost. Do you know where Osgood is?"

"I'm actually wondering the same thing."

"She's not in the apartment?" Audrey felt the panic rise.

"I. I, uh—"

"Nora," said Audrey, calmly.

"What?"

"Please look on Osgood's computer and see if you can turn off the live broadcast."

She heard some shuffling, then Nora came back to the phone. "We were being broadcast live?"

"Osgood was podcasting."

"Oh," said Nora. "And then she—"

"Stopped."

"Her bourbon is sitting on her desk."

The panic continued to rise. Osgood leaving without her phone, without her drink? No, something far worse—

"Osgood!" shouted Nora, muffled, hand over the phone. Again, she shouted Osgood's name. "Where'd you go?" Some shuffling, then Nora was back. "She's not here. I don't know what to do. I—"

"I'm on my way," said Audrey.

Audrey heard Nora choke back a nervous cry. She understood, of course. She felt it herself. That ominous feeling growing into certainty that something terrible had happened. As Audrey grabbed her coat, she could no longer deny the terrifying fact she knew to be true.

Osgood, like her sister years before, was gone.

Dying to know what happens next?

There are as many stories in The Spectral Inspector 'verse as there are things that go bump in the night.

Sign up at the address below and **Be a Specterino!** Then you won't miss a single thing, including exclusive shorts, early access to novels in progress, artwork reveals, conversations with the author, and more!

SpectralInspector.com/news

In the indie publishing world, reviews are more important than anything! If you enjoyed Osgood as Gone and are looking forward to future Osgood adventures, please post a review where you bought the book and on Goodreads! It's free and it helps a lot!

Prudence Osgood Will Return in

Osgood Riddance

Coming back won't be the first thing she's done wrong...

AUTHOR'S REFLECTION

(OR, WHENCE I CAME...)

When I first began creating stories in Junior High, everything I created were horror stories. It has long been my favorite genre because a horror story can encompass so much more than horror. Love, sex, humor, drama, can all exist in horror, while horror cannot just randomly show up in a comedy or drama. (You try to have a monster storm out of a closet and eat your protagonist's boyfriend in your teen drama...)

The last decade-or-so of my life has turned my creative outlet toward sexuality, erotica, and non-monogamy fiction. I've thoroughly enjoyed creating stories in that realm as well, and it gave me the opportunity to really embrace my own quirks of sexuality (namely, my queerness) in a safe genre for exploration.

But over the last few years, I've felt the dark siren call to return to my first love, and to a story that has been rattling around in my head for decades.

Love it or hate it, *The Blair Witch Project* was a seminal moment in horror media. It took something simple and basic an elevated it to terrifying. (I'm sure you can guess which side of the love/hate spectrum I fall on.) What it, and the superior and sadly less known fakeumentary *The Last Broadcast*, did was show me a new way to tell a scary story.

In high school I'd been obsessed with The Beatles (because

they're amazing, duh) and the bizarre offshoot "Paul is Dead" hoax: The idea that Paul McCartney, while driving home after a date one night, got into a car accident and died, leaving the Beatles to scramble to replace him with a lookalike, while still putting clues into their albums to let their fans know of the ruse. (Which side The Beatles were supposed to be on in this story, I'll never know.) Tales were told of hidden phone numbers, John shouting "I buried Paul!," a mysterious Pepperland, the creepy idea that Paul was fixing a hole in his head, and so much more.

At the same time, I'd followed the urban legends rabbit hole way down, and I began to percolate a story about a band that made a deal with a demon to become famous, and in exchange, the demon got a whole lot of kids.

Over the last two decades, I've started versions of this story as a fake documentary about the disappearances, a tv series, three different novels, two different screenplays, and none of them worked for me.

In my vanilla days, I'd created a male ghost hunter, modeled off the cocky rogue archetype that informs Han Solo, Indiana Jones, and Fletch (not Chevy Chase's version). He was front and center in multiple attempts.

When I reflected on this story again, I realized that I no longer wanted to tell stories about a cocky womanizing walking example of toxic masculinity. That moment was a paradigm shift, and I set out to figure out who I did want to tell stories about.

In every piece of fiction I write my characters are broken in some way, usually pulling traits I dislike about myself to inform their brokenness. I the darkness, I met Prudence Osgood, a decidedly very broken pansexual non-monoga-mous ghosthunter.

Even then, the story didn't reveal itself to me right away. About 50 pages of another Osgood story exist, as well as the 25-page "prequel" A Haunting at The Waverly Hotel.

Everything crashed home to me, though, while watching a documentary about the Toynbee Tiles called *Resurrect Dead*.

My story was a mystery, not straight horror; an investigation, not a haunted house tale.

That clinched it, and I wrote straight through.

Osgood As Gone gave me an opportunity to tell a story about a queer character in a world where her queerness wasn't THE STORY, to show a broken individual just trying to scramble through life. Not gonna lie, I fell in love with Osgood, problems, neuroses, and all.

I can't wait to see what happens to her next.

Cooper S. Beckett
March 23, 2019

ABOUT THE AUTHOR

As a queer non-monogamous writer, Cooper S. Beckett endeavors to create characters that reflect the diverse lifestyles of his friends, his partners, and himself. If he can pit those characters against monsters and cosmic horrors he's all the happier. From a young age, his obsession with horror movies and books seriously concerned his mother. It probably still does. Given a choice, he would rather winter at the Overlook than the Waldorf. Like Lydia Deetz, he has always thought of himself strange and unusual, and is thrilled to be putting that foot forward in his first horror novel.

He lives in Chicago with his wife, constant, and binary star, Ophilia Tesla, and their black cats Xander and Willow. He misses his dog Giles daily.

Want short stories, updates, and discounts in your email? Sign up today at CooperSBeckett.com/news

CooperSBeckett.com

PRAISE FOR OSGOOD AS GONE

"Prudence Osgood is a true heroine for our times – gritty, complex and sharp-witted, vulnerable but never broken. A darkly captivating mystery infused with the warmth of well-loved characters and an undercurrent of creeping dread."
  - Claire C. Holland, I Am Not Your Final Girl

"Cooper S. Beckett has created a wonderfully disturbing world in this ominous mystery brimming with fractured friendships and nightmarish scenes."
  - Lisa Diaz Meyer, All Roads Shattered

"Touches on many of my favorite things: cults, weird conspiracy theories, sex, vinyl backmasking, 90s pop star breakdowns, ghosthunters, inter-dimensional beings... all wrapped up with crackling dialogue & relatable characters."
  - David Sodergren, The Forgotten Island

"A phenomenal book! It's CreepyPasta by way of Stephen King and sticks the landing on LGBT+ characters. Creepy, funny, clever, and captivating. You'll love this!"
  - Tyler Hayes, The Imaginary Corpse

"A bourbon soaked supernatural mystery leading to a heart pounding climax. Prudence Osgood is a force to be reckoned with in any dimension. The ethereal ending was filled with beautiful imagery. A truly great read!"
  - Joe Tassone, *FearScale*

"Beckett lends his unique voice to the horror genre, weaving a tangled mystery filled with dark turns into even darker places."
  - Summer Johnson, *The ABCs of Death*

"Sometimes delightful. More oftentimes, deliciously dark. But always anchored by a small group of compelling, misfit characters that you will never stop rooting for, especially our unlikely heroine, Osgood."

- Julieann Stipidis, *Horrormonal*

"A masterfully vulnerable and relatable 21st Century horror story. Combines classic and contemporary horror elements with a moving exploration of the vulnerability of maintaining and rebuilding relationships after personal trauma."

- Flynn Bailey, *Adult Salad*

"Queer heroine Prudence Osgood is intriguingly flawed, yet one can't help but root for her success. The story is captivating, twisted, and sure to keep you awake at night!"

- Angela Elmore, *By the Bi*

56136918R00212

Made in the USA
Columbia, SC
21 April 2019